# A JADE OF DESTINY

### By Jeffery Farnol

THE BROAD HIGHWAY

THE AMATEUR GENTLEMAN

THE HONORABLE MR. TAWNISH

BELTANE THE SMITH

THE DEFINITE OBJECT

GREAT BRITAIN AT WAR

OUR ADMIRABLE BETTY

THE GESTE OF DUKE JOCELYN

BLACK BARTLEMY'S TREASURE

MARTIN CONISBY'S VENGEANCE

PEREGRINE'S PROGRESS

SIR JOHN DERING

THE LORING MYSTERY

THE HIGH ADVENTURE

THE QUEST OF YOUTH

FAMOUS PRIZE FIGHTS

GUYFFORD OF WEARE

THE SHADOW AND OTHER STORIES

ANOTHER DAY

OVER THE HILLS

A JADE OF DESTINY

# A JADE OF DESTINY

BY

JEFFERY FARNOL

BOSTON

LITTLE, BROWN, AND COMPANY

1931

c.14

To

## BLANCHE

MY LOYAL COMPANION
I DEDICATE THIS BOOK

*Sunnyside, August, 1931*

# CONTENTS

# CONTENTS

# Contents

# Contents

# A JADE OF DESTINY

# CHAPTER I

## Telleth How the Captain Took Service

THE Captain gave his battered hat the true swashbuckling cock, cast his ragged cloak about him with superb, braggadocio flourish, clashed his rusty spurs and bowed. And his nose seemed arrogant, his mouth grim, his chin aggressive, but his eyes — these wide-set, long-lashed, wistful gray eyes — gave to all the lie direct, or so it seemed to her who, seated in great elbow-chair, surveyed him with much interest and no little disdain.

And as she viewed him thus beneath pucker of slim brows, he, viewing her, mentally classified her as a glooming Juno.

"You are Captain Jocelyn Dinwiddie?" said she at last, her dark eyes still intent.

"That same, madam," he answered, in voice to match his look, "and late of the English company of gentlemen volunteers in Flanders."

"But later sir, in the Fleet Prison, I believe."

The Captain's sallow cheek flushed, his moustachio quivered, but his gray eyes were serenely steady as he answered:

"Admitted, madam, and shame it is that such right body and high-vaulting soul should ha' been so pent for base gold. But the most of my good comrades are heroically dead, the old company is disbanded and my steel lacks employ. Thus am I, that was of late the compeer of demigods, become poor squire of Alsatia. Here is eclipse methinks might shake the very firmament!"

"In fine, sir, you are a mere bravo open to hire."

"Madam, your mistake, if allowable, is infinite. I am Dinwiddie! Poor gentleman and soldier o' fortune I, yet verily of fortune none. Howbeit, such as I seem to you, that will I be to your supremest content."

"One that will fight, sir, and kill a man for sufficient pay?"

"With all my heart, gentle lady, — if I judge that man worthy death so honourable."

"Here shall be no ' ifs ', sir."

"Ha, 'sdeath and zounds, madam, in any small, ordinary matter o' blood, your ladyship shall find me apt, instant and of charges reasonable.　Thus can I blind you husband that seeth too much, maim you indifferent lover that seeth too little, for consideration paltry and fee trifling, — then, if needs must and may, I shall slay you a man cheaply as any of the cutting, swashing fraternity."

"Enough!" said she imperiously.　"Be serious."

"As owl, lady, as moping owl."

"Captain Dinwiddie, you were recommended to me as desperate fellow, very resolute and hardy."

Captain Jocelyn bowed and folded his arms.

"Lady," said he with his most superb air, "think now of the victorious Achilles, the valiant Hector, of Ulysses that Jove's thunderbolts defied, — then look on me!　I say no more."

"O' my conscience," she cried, "you say overmuch, you babble, you clack, — you chatter and prate me deaf and dumb!"

"Then, lady, here's chance for word more and of my hardiness, rest assured, madam, for I am one holdeth life twixt thumb and finger-tip, let snatch who may.　And so, what would ye be with such fellow adamantine?"

"Deeds, man, deeds."

"They shall achieve.　But what is your precise need?"

"An impossibility."

"Name it, prithee."

"I seek a paladin, sir, a knight chivalrous, a man of wit, of gentle birth, bold as lion, cunning as fox, guileful as serpent, a gentleman honourable but of such desperate fortune shall risk his life willingly and often."

"Madam," said the Captain, bowing, "madam, he salutes you!　'T is evident you begin to discern me somewhat.　So then I await your ladyship's instructions as to——" But here she clapped her white hands, laughing so youthfully that Captain Jocelyn thought no more of glooming Juno but of blithe nymphs and joyous, white-throated dryads that mocked secure amid sun-kissed leaves. But, even as he watched, the lovely face clouded again and she sighed distressfully.

"Captain," said she after a moment's silence, "you are acquaint with Monsieur de Bergerac, the French *maître d'armes?*"

"Madam, I have discovered to him a volte and pass or so new in his curriculum."

"You make an idle brag, sir, for Monsieur de Bergerac is esteemed the greatest swordsman in London; nay——in all England."

"But then your ladyship must remember I have been in England scarce a month."

"Faith, sir," said she, faintly scornful, "yourself is vastly sure and mightily pleased with yourself!"

"Reasonably so, madam, since I have known myself achieve some notable exploits ere now and——"

"And yet," cried she, curling red lip at him, "must lie in debtor's prison!"

"Yet in despite of which I remain myself, madam, serene o' soul and steadfast, heeding Fortune's dastard ploys and buffets no whit."

"And would you, sir, you that I gather from yourself is manhood's very perfection, nay, indeed, Dame Nature's crowning achievement, stoop to my poor service——for payment sufficient?"

"I await your kind ladyship's behest."

"Then be seated, sir!" Captain Jocelyn bowed, and sinking upon the nearest chair, sat wholly at his ease, looking through the open window at the pleasant prospect of blooming flowers, shaven lawns, trim-clipped hedges and the noble park beyond, while my lady regarded him frowningly,——his lean face that, despite prison pallor, showed so strangely at odds with his poverty of dress. And when she had viewed him thus and the Captain had gazed serenely out of the window for some while, she sighed and spoke:

"Captain Dinwiddie, I am troubled for my only brother, Lord Aldrington, and I grieve because I love him. Sir, he is very young and headstrong and is in London to the peril of his health and — honourable name." Here she paused to sigh again and the Captain, his gaze still averted, ventured a word of comfort:

"Youth is Folly's season, madam. My lord shall doubtless amend with time, so have patience and — "

"Patience?" she cried, starting up from her chair. "Oh, 't is counsel of fools!" And now, watching as she paced tempestuous to and fro, the Captain bethought him of a baffled Pallas Athena. "Patience, forsooth!" she repeated. "And even as I stand here my poor Richard is sinking deeper to his destruction! A boy scarce nineteen turned! And left to my care! And I, dear heaven, so helpless!"

"Yet content you, lady, be largely comforted, since at thy service is Jocelyn Dinwiddie!"

"You!" she cried, bitterly scornful, and turning on him, was dumb. He had risen also and thus, as she met his level gaze, the contemptuous words upon her lip died unuttered; for here was no mere bravo, no empty, swaggering braggart, but man of action, somewhat grim, very assured and infinitely capable, yet whose sad eyes held a sympathy very comforting. So she sat down again, motioning him to do the like.

"You know my name, I think?"

"Ione," he answered, "Lady Fane."

"And you are willing to serve me in this matter, Captain Jocelyn?"

"With all my heart."

"Risking your blood — wounds; perchance — death?"

"Joyfully."

"Then, sir, you shall bear me letter to my brother in London. You shall — prevail on him to come back to me

— and his neglected tenantry, — you shall persuade him to this, whether he will or no."

"He shall come, madam."

"Richard, as I say, is but a boy," she sighed, "all too young for such vast inheritance, yet 't was my dear father's will . . . our mother died — too long ago, alas! So Richard's curse is overmuch money, his danger is evil companionship and — himself. Of his wicked friends the most evil and dangerous are Colonel Malone, Sir Walter Fearn and Lord Riderwood. It is of these three in especial I would have you deliver him . . . by force an' it prove needful, sir!"

"Madam, 't is good as done!"

"Heaven's light!" she cried, frowning on him; "such assurance is merest folly; these men are perilous all."

"Neither am I a dove, lady."

"These be notorious for deadly duellists, all three, and you are but one."

"Yet this same one is — Dinwiddie, madam! And so, having rid your ladyship's brother of these three and hither conveyed him, what — "

"Ah, think you this shall prove matter so simple?"

"I make no doubt on 't, madam."

"Sir, these windy vaunts and boasts do but shake my so small faith in you."

"Howbeit, madam, you may count the business good as determined and successfully accompt. And what then?"

Her ladyship sneered daintily:

"Why, then, most infallible sir, you shall be duly feed and rewarded." The Captain bowed.

"Your ladyship will admit that the labourer, even the humblest, is worthy his hire and thus I — "

"Ha, buzz not your pragmatisms at me, sir!" she cried. "But, and perpend, sir, an' you be such can indeed save my brother from these so deadly, wicked men, you may perchance do yet greater thing and save him — from himself?"

"On two conditions, madam. First that I am given

time sufficient thereto, and second — that I am nowise
hampered therein."

"Hampered, sir? As how?"

"By the pampering of doting sister."

"Indeed," cried she, "and do I seem such fool?"

"Lady, I said 'sister.' These conditions agreed, I
pledge myself to the venture."

"And will doubtless need money?"

Here again the Captain flushed while she watched him
with a malicious joy.

"Alas, madam," he sighed, "I cannot deny it."

"Nay," she mocked, "what need, since the labourer is
worthy his hire, a bird i' the hand worth two in a bush,
a stitch in time — and the like ineptitudes?"

Rising with whisper of silks, she crossed to a tall press
and took thence a bag that jingled pleasantly. "Here,
sir, is your earnest money; there shall be as much again
when you bring me my Richard."

Captain Jocelyn took the money somewhat hastily, hid
it upon his shabby person and bowed.

"Will you not count it, sir?"

"Not I, madam."

"You will set out for London to-day?"

"This hour."

"You have a horse?"

"'T is so its mistaken owner describeth it."

"Well, my stables be at your service."

"I thank your ladyship, but the Bucephalus that hither
bore me hath legs, indifferent, four, yet sufficient to my
need. And now, if your ladyship hath the letter to your
brother—"

"It is here, sir, and unsealed for your perusal. Nay,
you shall hear it," and unfolding the letter, she read this:

"'Dearest Richard, the bearer of this is the redoubtable Captain Jocelyn Dinwiddie, a veteran officer of the Spanish Wars, and
gentleman of very many notable achievements. He is also one
very well able to speak for himself. I yearn for sight of thee, dear

Richard. Also, my lord, there be many of your people do look to see you home for the harvest, next month. Our dear father, as you'll mind, ever made this a season of gladness and rejoicing to his tenantry, the rich and poor. Indeed, our father was a great and noble gentleman. God send we, each of us, prove worthy of him and the unblemished name he left to you, my lord.

"My dear love to thee, Richard. I pray thee come home soon. So I rest, thy ever-loving sister Ione.

"Post Scriptus. I learn, with a qualm, that Captain Dinwiddie is gentleman something bloodily minded, a rapier and dagger gallant very instant in quarrel. Therefore, beseech thee, dear Richard, be warned for thine own sake and mine.'"

"Well, sir?" she demanded, for the Captain was staring out of the window again; "you frown, I think?"

"Faith, now," he questioned, sombre gaze still averted, "seem I indeed so bloodily disposed, lady?"

"Beyond expression!" she answered, folding the letter.

"But you know me not!"

"But I know my brother, sir, and for such wild, young hothead he'll be for clashing steel with you to prove my words."

"Zounds!" murmured the Captain. "And, o' your grace, what must I do?"

"As his sister's envoy, sir, you ha' one of three courses. You may suffer him to wound you and earn his instant pity, for he is of tender heart. You may permit him to disarm you and earn golden sop, for he is madly generous. Third, you may outfence him, winning his instant hate, for, alas, he is sadly passionate. Of these three courses I permit you the choice, sir."

"Your ladyship overwhelms me!" he murmured.

"And lo, here the letter, sir!" Captain Jocelyn took it, frowned at it, shook his head at it, thrust it into the bosom of his faded doublet and bowed; quoth he:

"So much for your Letter Number Two, madam. Now for Number One." My lady widened haughty eyes on him.

"Truth, sir," she retorted, "your meaning passeth my

poor wit; prithee stoop to my sluggish intelligence, be plain."

"Your letter, madam, if sufficiently well expressed, yet goeth wide o' the mark; 't is so many words to no purpose ——"

"And now, Sir Captain, I think you become impertinent."

"Impossible, madam, I am Dinwiddie! I dare suggest, and with all submission, 't is yourself is poor in strategy and ——"

"Ha!" she exclaimed angrily. "And am I so indeed?"

"Madam, beyond expression!" he murmured, with gracious inclination of dark head. Whereat my lady eyed him askance, biting a finger quite viciously.

"Oh, peerless gentleman," said she scornfully, yet cherishing her ill-used finger against soft cheek, "I cry you grace and — a mercy's name, show me, good Sir Wisdom, wherein I err."

"With joy, madam! Thus — you err in every word that pertaineth to my humble self. 'Stead o' roaring lion you must show me for meekest of mild lambs. 'Stead of painting me in my true colours as heroic gentleman of fame redoubtable, wise in humanity and worldly chicane, I must seem a gentle innocent, agape on life and all agog for ventures dubious."

Her ladyship frowned, pouted, pinched tenderly at dimpled chin and laughed.

"But couldst twist that grim visage to look of meek innocence, indeed?"

"Indeed, madam, for I am ——"

"Oh, verily, sir, you are Dinwiddie. I become aware o' this."

"Captain, lady. Jocelyn, madame! Humbly at your ladyship's command."

"For payment sufficient!" she jibed.

The Captain winced, scowled down at his worn and dusty boots, felt for his moustachio, twisted it and spoke:

"Admitted, lady. Creature for hire I, by reason o' base

Fortune's shrewish dealings, for — remark this, madam, despite noble pride and a lofty soul, e'en the Dinwiddie must eat now and then, detestable yet true, alas!" Here her ladyship made to bite her finger again but remembering in time, kissed it instead and spake in voice so sweetly kind that he in turn viewed her askance.

"Then, sir, of your wiles and strategies I would have you instruct poor me how I must write your letter Number One."

"Briefly, your ladyship, something on this wise —"

"Nay, wait!" cried she, and seating herself gracefully mid billowing silks, took up her quill and to his dictation wrote this:

"'Dear my Richard and lordly brother, I implore your patronage on a worthy, country gentleman new to town, one Master Jocelyn Dinwiddie. He cometh to thee by my good will, seeking instruction how to carry himself towards gentlemen, thy friends, in the great world of London. Induct him, prithee, into all such gentle sophisms and arts punctilious that unto gentlehood pertaineth —'"

"Oh, nay!" cried she, with bubble of laughter. "Here speaketh Master Euphues, 't is none o' me . . . 'Induct him', forsooth! Thus shall it go!

"'Learn him, dear Richard, by thine own noble carriage, how to bear himself 'mong gentlemen less noble than thy dear self.'"

"'T will serve!" murmured the Captain.

"Oh, sir," she mocked, "your so kind commendation touches me sensibly! Must I write more, sir?" The Captain bowed and dictated thus:

"'Cherish him, my Richard, and love him right heartily for thy dear sister's sake.'"

"Oh?" quoth she, quill arrested. "But wherefore, sir, for his sister's sake?"

"For that I must seem his sister's very dear and well-loved friend, madam."

"'T is lie outrageous, sir!"

"But 't is lie diplomatic, madam!" So, my lady, having frowned at him, wrote it down with loud, protesting squeak of rapid and indignant pen; whereafter the Captain continued his dictation, thus:

"'Show him the modeful diversions of the town but, oh, dear brother, look he be not lured from thine own so virtuous rectitude, guide his untutored steps that he may o'erleap the thousand pitfalls, sloughs and quags of soul-seducing, sin-smirched Babylon —'"

"Oh, Heaven aid me!" cried Ione and leaned back in her chair the better to laugh, and thus meeting his look of grave surprise, laughed the more. "Oh, Captain Jocelyn — sir! Here's wordy exaltation beyond poor Dick and me; needs must we modify, as thus:

"'Shield him by thine own good sense and worldly knowledge that he commit no follies, or few, as be humanly possible. So God keep thee, dear brother, and come soon home again to thy loving sister, Ione.'"

"There!" sighed she, sanding the letter. "Here is your letter Number One, sir."

"It should suffice," he answered dubiously, "though i' faith, ' soul-seducing, sin-smirched Babylon ' is sounding phrase and likes me well."

"Alack, Sir Captain," she laughed, folding the missive, "thou art, in very sooth, so Dinwiddie-ish, the poor, mere world shall never attain unto thee."

Captain Jocelyn accepted the letter, saluted her with the stately arrogance of a grand seigneur and turned to the door; but there she stayed him.

"Tell me," she demanded, "how shall you go about winning brother Richard back to me?"

"This lieth i' the lap o' Chance, madam."

Swift and light-footed she was beside him, slim hand on his frayed sleeve, her dark eyes uplifted and widening to his.

"You will not harm him!" she commanded in quick anxiety. "Not so much as a scratch, I charge you."

"My lady," he answered, gently removing that arresting hand, "I do not harm or scratch children." So saying, he stepped from the room and across a wide hall, splendid with rich arras and burnished armour; yet, when he reached the terrace, he found her still beside him.

"Captain Dinwiddie," said she, her imperiousness tempered now with something of humility, "'t is very like I am sending you to death."

"Why, 't is no stranger, lady."

"You may have to fight — there be many shall be fierce to hinder your winning Richard from London town."

"Well, madam, your labourer shall prove worthy his hire and —"

"Ah, fleer not, sir. There be men, as well I know, alas, do kill wantonly and laugh to do it, — Lord Riderwood killed a poor young gentleman scarce a month since and — smiled as he stabbed!"

"I shall be the happier to meet my Lord Riderwood."

"Sir, this gentleman he slew was well beknown to me and so — I do confess — 't is not alone on Richard's account I send you."

"Loved you this unfortunate gentleman, madam?"

"Nay, indeed I love no man save Richard and do begin to think I never shall, — but this same gentleman was my childhood's friend and — young."

"I shall take pains to meet my Lord Riderwood."

Now at this she clasped her hands and looked from the speaker's grim visage to the peaceful countryside and back again, and thus seeing how his sinewy hand was dropped instinctive to the hilt of his long rapier, she recoiled and shook her head.

"Ah, no!" she murmured, "I would be no man's death, — not even his!"

"Then I shall permit him to survive, madam."

"But you'll bring Richard away from them all, safe back to me?"

"Your ladyship may rest assured on 't."

"Then I pray God speed thee, Captain Jocelyn." He eyed her askance, smiling a little bitterly.

"For my lord, your brother's sake?" he questioned.

"And for your own!" she answered and meeting his quizzical gaze, flushed hotly, frowned darkly, yet returned his look with eyes unwavering. "And for you!"

"I' faith," said he, with gentle laugh, "now might the choiring cherubim twang their harps, the seraphim puff their clarions for very wonder, since thine are the first woman's lips ha' blessed me so with prayer since I donned sword. Sweet heaven bless your ladyship; so, till we meet again, your devoted, humble servant giveth you farewell." Then, clapping on his shabby hat, Captain Jocelyn Dinwiddie went his way and she standing there very thoughtful long after he was out of sight.

# CHAPTER II

## Wherein Is Description of Two Philosophers of the Sword

In leafy byway where two bony nags cropped ravenous at tender grass and birds piped jubilant, a man whistled very melodiously, a slim, comely fellow quick with youth who, sprawled beneath the hedge, stared up at soaring lark.

Hither presently jingled the Captain, at sight of whom the man leapt nimbly afoot and, snatching off his hat, bowed with a supple grace but with such fervour of look that Captain Jocelyn shook his head, smiling in his crooked, wistful fashion.

"How now, Florian," quoth he, "was't not agreed to be done with thy bowing subservience?"

"Verily, my Captain. But, sir, old habits stick, and to thee I bow as I breathe, since for me thou art the only man of all men."

"Though mighty poor one, alack."

"And yet," nodded young Florian, "I mind a day in the leaguer at Sluys, when Parma himself, with proffers of gold and titles, would ha' bribed you to smite for Spain. And laughed you did, sir, but fought and starved on with the harassed Dutchmen."

"I was never overly wise," mourned the Captain, "for in the end Sluys fell and — to-day here we stand, thou and I, with nought to show for it all but scars and tatters! In such matters I was ever the fool. And yet, so too was bold Roger Williams and Frankie Vere. Here's some comfort to our own present sorry state. But, zounds, with all my long years of hardship and fighting, marches, battles and leaguers, I do something marvel to find myself thus destitute."

"Why, here's no marvel, sir," cried Florian, his eyes very bright, his shapely hands eloquent, "for you have ever chosen to fight o' the losing side, the weak 'gainst the strong — so long as I have known you, ay, since yon distant hour when you snatched from shameful death the beaten, starving wretch that was me. Cock's body, sir, there is some folly better than wisdom, methinks. Howbeit, I had liefer be servant to such valiant fool than peer to the noblest — " But here the Captain pished and scowled and jingled his spurs, muttering oaths French, Spanish, Dutch and English, a very farrago, and becoming coherent at last, bade Florian put on his hat.

"For," said he, tugging at moustachio, "thou and I ha' marched and fought and starved so long together we must needs be friends — comrades well-proven we. So mind it, lad, mind it and bear yourself accordingly. Is't understood, ha?"

"It is!" murmured Florian, his smooth cheeks flushed, his great eyes radiant. "Aha, to-day I live, I breathe; thanks to thee, I am a man."

"Why, then," growled the Captain, "come and eat!" So they rode one behind the other and no word until they reached a shady highway where, backing upon the green of aged trees, rose the chimneys and thatched roof of a cosy tavern with sign over door that proclaimed it:

Ye Peck o' Malt.
Jno. Bly.

And all very pleasant to sight on such hot morning. Here they halted and having tethered their bony steeds, they jingled up a step and down a step into cool, dim chamber redolent of wood smoke, and herbs, and something gently a-simmering in large, black pot over the fire. A wide chamber this, stone-flagged below, heavily timbered above, small of window but with generous hearth flanked by ingle seats. Here too were vasty oak settles and a massive table where stood a buxom woman kneading dough.

At sight of these hard-favoured visitors the dame

frowned; beholding the Captain's face she curtseyed and, quick to heed his wistful smile, she dimpled and smiled also.

"What would ye, my masters?" she enquired, glancing from Jocelyn's hawk face to his companion's smoothly handsome features and thence to the door in growing apprehension. "Masters, what would ye?" she repeated.

"Aught you have, worthy a man's honest hunger, good dame," answered Jocelyn.

"Cogsnails!" exclaimed his companion, sniffing daintily potwards, "yonder breathes delectable savour!"

"Why, sirs, there be shin o' beef a-stewing, but I can serve ye wi' haunch o' venison cold, or ham, sirs, smoked, and a sallet new-plucked——"

"'Sheart!" exclaimed Florian, rolling eyes ecstatic. "Have at 'em and all, Mistress! Sweet soul, bustle, prithee bustle, lest we——" he paused, as borne to them from the sunny garden came a voice in song, very sweet and clear, then was sound of light feet and in flashed the singer and seemed to bring sunshine with her.

"Oh, Margery," she began, "oh, Meg, I——" but now, espying the strangers, she stopped in pretty confusion and stood a thing of radiant beauty from slim foot to shining hair; now, by one ear was silky tress tied with small bow of blue ribbon. She glanced at Captain Jocelyn, she looked at handsome young Florian and dropped long lashes only to raise them and look again. The Captain bowed and turned to doff his tattered cloak, Florian stared, scarce breathing, as one who saw a vision, then swept her such obeisance as was out of all match with his shabby seeming.

"Lady—lady——" he stammered. "Vision of loveliness——"

"Ha, lady, quotha?" cried Dame Margery. "Out on thee, young master! Thou, Cecily, fie on 't, begone to thy churn!"

"Nay, dear mine Aunt," answered the Vision serenely, "I am here to thine aid, so chide not thy dutiful niece. Shall I lay table for these—travellers?"

"No, no!" cried the Dame, patting flour from her

shapely arms. "Good lack, no! 'T will never do — I will!" But the Vision, nothing heedful, tripped lightly about the business, while young Florian watched her in very transport and the good dame, sighing, showed so strangely apprehensive that Jocelyn spoke her in his kindest tone:

"Abate your fears of us, worthy dame; my comrade and I are something better than we seem; i' faith, the worst of us lieth plain to sight, — dust and outworn clothes!"

He smiled, and Dame Margery, quick to sense the honesty of him, bobbed a curtsey and answered, murmuring:

"Your pardon, sir, but this is a tavern and she . . . there came four men but yesterday, and gentlemen all . . . yet so shamed, so frighted her — and my John away as now, I was forced to take the spit to 'em, ay, marry did I! They vowed to come again, and sir, I was afeared you was o' their services."

"Not so, mistress. Plain travellers we, intent on food and nought other."

"Then food ye shall have, sir, ay, and of the best, I'll warrant ye."

Thus presently seated at well-laden table in remote corner, the friends began their meal with hearty appetite, though Florian often turned to gaze through the open lattice where the maid Cecily moved and sang amid the flowers.

"Saw ye ever sweeter maid, Jocelyn?" sighed he, at last.

"Once!" answered the Captain. "Prithee pass the ale!"

"Heard ye ever name so sweet?"

"I have so!" nodded Jocelyn. "Essay this spiced beef; 't is rarely flavoured."

"But how, friend Jocelyn, how should maid so fair bloom in rustic alehouse, think ye?"

"Flowers spring where they will, Florian. And this venison deserveth well."

"And she beareth herself sweetly proud, like one of degree, Jocelyn."

"Why then, eat, man, for we 've longish ride afore us."

And, after some while, their hungers appeased, Jocelyn sighed and spoke in hushed tones.

"Florian, we are listed in venture that promiseth. Here, comrade," and he tapped the breast of his doublet, "is the wherewithal to our equipments."

"And who is the fortunate wight so blessed to purchase thy service, sir?"

"Our services, Florian! And 'sir' me not. She is a woman."

"Sayst thou? What's her will of us?"

"To snatch pigeon from flock o' carrion kites, lad."

"Well and good!" nodded Florian, bright eyes a-dance. "So feathers shall fly anon! But sir — that is, dear my friend, prithee when, how, who and what?"

"Briefly, Florian, we are by doting sister hired to protect — and mark me, in his own despite — a lordly fool from arrant knavish gentry. For thy 'how' of it, — hum! I suggest by force o' kidnappery, arts wheedlesome, or wile strategic. As to thy 'who and what' — this fool is, 't would seem, a peevish, pampered youth, my lord the Earl of Aldrington; yet, though a lord, there may be hope for him, since he is very young."

"Ay, and how must we set about it, Jocelyn?"

"As chance offers. For amongst these my lord's knavish friends and gossips are duellists of repute, comrade; gamblers desperate as skilful, with polished foists; fine cheats and sharpers delicate, yet all accounted gentlemen o' repute."

"O, rare!" murmured Florian, white teeth agleam. "To outcheat these cheaters!"

"Ay, so, we may show 'em some novel arts o' dicery, lad, a bale o' bristles, langret, gourd and gullam, the longs and shorts on 't, ha?"

"And for these duellists — thou, Jocelyn! Aha, thou and I!" And now, though his white teeth still gleamed, his smoothly handsome face took on such joyous ferocity that the Captain raised protesting hand; quoth he:

"Nay, Florian, here shall be moderation in fatality, for, and perpend! To kill rogue in Flanders may be very well, to slay gentlemen in Paris for point of honour is there esteemed gentle pastime, but here in England, he that in duels kills never so honourably is yet, in some sort, accountable for his dead. Thus, seest thou, an' fight we must, I counsel we effuse them only, wing them merely — sufficient to purpose. We must be philosophers of the sword, thou and I, to make of it pointed argument which shall persuade villainy to virtue and teach crass folly something of wisdom; so shall — " he paused to sound of hasty feet, and into the quiet chamber a man came running who, reaching the wide hearth, snatched thence a long-barrelled petronel or dag and with this fierce gripped, glared towards the open door, very desperately.

"Friend," enquired the Captain, "what 's to do?"

The man started and, espying the two, came hurrying, his square, honest face dark with trouble.

"Good, my masters," said he, quick-breathing and atremble, "I stand in ill plight, for yonder, afar, gallop riotous gentlemen three — to work shameful thing on us. For, lookee, masters, I may not bar door again 'em, since this is an inn; and how shall I withstand 'em, for these be gentlemen — very potent — and I but humble fellow to be ruined or 'prisoned at their pleasures! Yet an' they attempt the maid again, then I'll off-stand 'em, come what may." And he cocked the dag.

"Nay, faith," said Jocelyn, leaning across table, "here is ill thing for the like o' thee, good fellow — suffer me!" And he drew the weapon from the man's shaking fingers.

"But master, how then?" cried the man. "'T is all I ha' to our defence. What must I do now?"

"Art John Bly, the landlord, I think?"

"Ay, I am, sir," answered troubled John, looking into his questioner's kindly gray eyes.

"Well so, John," said the Captain, laying weapon on

the settle beside him, " should these troublous gentles hither come, do thou play host as is thy duty, and should they prove anyways riotous, leave them to us. How sayst thou, friend John?"

"Noble sirs," quoth he, snatching off his cap, "spite your disguisements, I do perceive ye for gentles both and am humbly grateful to your honours. But sirs, these lawless gentry be three and all very proudly wilful and passionate, ah, and of a violence, ah, sirs, a violence — "

"Excellent well!" laughed Florian and reaching his long rapier, slipped the worn balderick about him.

And now from the road was clatter of horse hoofs, laughter, loud voices and shouts of "Host! House-ho!" Whereat landlord John, his square face pale yet determined, hasted forth to his duties; but even then from behind the inn was loud hunting cry followed by a woman's scream and, as Florian leapt afoot, to them from the garden sped the maid Cecily, her peasant's wimple rent by lawless hand . . . a panting, weeping, desperate creature who, running for the stair, tripped and would have fallen but that Florian leapt and caught her. Now, looking up into the gentle, handsome face so near her own, she cried to him in pitiful gasps:

"Oh . . . let them not . . . harm me!"

"Death first!" murmured Florian, reverent of look and voice. As for the Captain, he sat where he was, elbows on table, chin on fist, nor moved he even when upon them burst a breathless gentleman, a person of splendour from plumed bonnet to gilded spurs who, checking pursuit, roared in full-throated glee:

"Oho, Frank, Harry, . . . aha, here's your timorous virginity cuddling beggar-rogue!"

But even as he thus roared and laughed, Florian leapt open-handed and smote this shouter on either cheek, two cracking slaps that drove him reeling to the wall, there to lean and goggle and gasp in shocked amazement, while Jocelyn drew the terrified girl beside him on the settle and smiling comfortably, patted her small, tremulous hand.

Then the place was full of stir and babblement, cloaks fluttered, spurs rattled, feathers flaunted. . . . Three elegant gentlemen, very arrogantly clamourous, postured and glared while their three lacqueys peered in at door and window.

"How now, Sir Thomas?" cried one, a tall, slim exquisite in short, purple cloak and small, dainty beard. "What is 't, Tom man?"

"Yon cursed fellow . . . struck me, Frank!" gasped the smitten one. "By heavens, he dared lay vile hand on me, — ha, 'sdeath, I 'll have his foul blood!"

"No, no, Tom! 'T is an impossible rogue, a very dog, a poor thing too contemptible for your steel. Call we our servants to whip him to his native ditch!"

But now the Captain arose and in his fist, landlord John's long-barrelled dag; quoth he in wheedling tone:

"Nay, gentle sirs, I cry ye temperance. I humbly beseech ye curb your so perilous ferocity —"

"Peace, dog!" cried Sir Thomas, cherishing his smarting cheek. "Yon base villain struck me and I 'll ha' blood for 't!"

"Well said, Tom!" cried the gentleman on his right. "The curs whine already!"

"Let 's swinge 'em roundly!" cried the gentleman on his left. "Have with thee, Tom!"

"Ha, so — let 's at 'em!" cried Sir Thomas, and out flickered their two blades. Only the third gentleman stood superbly aloof, arms folded; said he:

"I smirch not my steel with such dunghilly carrion, I!"

"Cogsnails!" laughed Florian, and his rapier flashed aloft in airy gasconade; but in this moment Jocelyn spoke:

"Hold me their fiery valour in check, *amigo*, whiles I warn these so rash gentlemen!" And he tossed the dag to Florian, who caught and levelled it at the rageful two with an airy dexterity.

"Stand, pretty poppets!" cried he gaily. "Stretch forth your ears, yet stir and speak not, lest my finger twitch ye harm."

And now, freeing his sheathed rapier of its carriages, Jocelyn crossed hands upon its heavy pommel and looking mildly on these gentlemen each and every, spoke:

"Sirs, heed now my words ere upon ye bloody perils and imminent destruction rageful rush. Lo here, gentles ungentle, my comrade and I! Philosophers twain o' the sword, we be, that go up and down in the earth, teaching base humans the humanities, as to wit, — the wisdom of Meekness, the saving grace of Humility and the like virtues. And this we do by insertion of chaste steel into carcase base, thereby letting Wisdom in and Roguery out. Now ye, sirs, are three — ye are young — ye are three young, base rogues that would to tender Innocence give shameful alarm. Therefore we philosophers twain do proffer ye two alternatives. Ye shall, all three, to Innocence, humbly kneeling, sue grace and meekly begone, or be forthright of this same baseness purged by steely inplantation and injection, — choose ye!"

"Ah-ha!" cried Florian gaily, uncocking the dag and tossing it behind him. "Fight now, fight or crawl hence for lewd, craven curs!" And plucking dagger, he stood, weapon advanced, slim body lightly poised, his smooth face fierce-smiling, agog for conflict.

A moment's deadly pause, then, with stamp of passionate foot, Sir Thomas leapt, all whirling steel and roaring ferocity, backed by his friend. And instantly was uproar, — a wild hurly-burly of clashing steel, trampling feet, fierce shouts and exclamations, an ever-growing tumult. And amid it all, young Florian leapt and swayed, so quick of foot and hands, so supple and dexterous of body, that his weapon seemed multiplied, dealing blows with darting point and close-sweeping edge, while Jocelyn, tattered cloak about left arm, watched those three twinkling blades, the one against the two, interposing his sheathed rapier in cunning feint or parry at such rare times he judged his comrade anyway hard pressed.

"Oh, aid — will you not aid him!" cried Cecily, in anguished tones.

"Not so, child!" answered the Captain. "'T would but mar a pretty bout; 't were to gild the lily — "

"Harry — Harry — " gasped a voice, "wilt see us — murdered?"

"Blooded, sir!" retorted the Captain, "an extransudation merely — "

"Harry — Oh, Hal — " wailed the voice; the third gentleman cast off his purple cloak, whipped forth sword, leapt to combat and reeled back, gasping, from the powerful thrust of Jocelyn's sheathed weapon. . . .

Jingling stamp of spurred feet, ring of steel, pant of laboured breathing — and then came sudden end — a rapier fell clattering, Sir Thomas, crying hoarsely, reeled to the wall, clasping bloody arm, whereat his friends, lowering their points, stepped back and leaned beside him in breathless, sweating dishevellment, their prideful arrogance quite gone. The Captain, sitting on corner of table, swung a long leg; Florian, wiping moist brow, frowned and, having fetched his breath, spoke:

"So, my poppets, bold mannikins that would raise riots and fright tender maids, is 't enough, then? Are ye done thus early? Then march, rustical bullies, off to your kennels. And you, sirrah Tom, speed before and do your bleeding outside. Begone! Lest I be minded to rid the earth o' such base, doggish knaves!"

And when these three gentlemen, their three lacqueys attendant, had departed very silently, each and every, came honest John with his buxom dame very earnest in their gratitude, but of the maid Cecily, the lovely cause of this to-do, no sign.

Therefore Florian stole out into the garden while Jocelyn talked with Dame Margery and landlord John; quoth he:

"Tell me, friend John, is not this tavern on my Lord of Aldrington's land?"

"Ay, marry is it, sir!" nodded John. "All the ground be his so far as eye may see hereabouts. But th' Earl be away to Court and London nowadays, since when things do be changing, sir — "

"Ay, from bad to worse!" sighed Dame Margery.

"Prithee how?"

"'T is Master Denzil, sir, my lord's chief bailiff, — he were ever a summat hard gentleman, but o' late 'e do seem harder —"

"'Specially to we folk in Southdean!" said Dame Margery.

"Raised the rents he have, sir!" sighed John. "Ah, and the market dues. And, sir, 't is told as he be minded to sell land hereabouts — ah, and the old 'Peck o' Malt' wi' it and all to Sir Thomas Vincent, him as your friend run through the arm so sweet and proper."

"Doth the Earl know o' this?"

"I' fegs, sir, 't is Master Denzil ruleth since the old lord died. Oh, but yon were the days, sir, in the old lord's time! But now —"

"Ay, now," said Jocelyn, rising, "I 'm for the road. But lookee, friends, 't is in my mind the good days may, peradventure, come again, — so bid Care hence likewise." Then, having paid the score, he donned cloak and hallooed to Florian, who came forthwith.

So they got to horse and away through the golden morning; the Captain very silent, pondering ways and means, but Florian glad as the day for, as they rode, his hand crept often within his frayed jerkin where, upon his heart, lay a little knot of blue ribbon.

## CHAPTER III

### TELLETH HOW ONE MASTER DINWIDDIE CAME TO TOWN

His youthful lordship the Earl of Aldrington sat up in bed, clasped his young temples and moaned, whereupon to him sped a soft-footed creature who bowed:

"Is your lordship awake?"

"Fool, can't ye see? Ay, I'm awake and would I were dead!"

"Ay, nay, my lord, no, no — "

"Ay, but I do, Mervyn. Was I so vastly drunk last night, was I?"

"Not so, my lord. I protest your lordship was no more than a little merry — "

"Ha, this shall account for my present woe!" groaned the Earl, cherishing pain-racked brow.

"Will your lordship be pleased to take breakfast?" enquired the soft-voiced Mervyn, his narrow eyes strangely at odds with the servility of tone, as he surveyed his young master's abject misery. "Will your lordship eat — "

"No!" cried the Earl, shuddering violently. "Curse all food! Curse everything! Where's Will Thurlow?"

"Your lordship's . . . head groom, my lord?"

"Who else, fool? Where is he, I say?"

"With his horses belike, my lord, though, as your lordship will perceive, I am seldom in his company, being your lordship's own bodyservant and gentleman o' the chamber — "

"Then go fetch him!"

"What — here, my lord? A groom! In your lordship's privy chamber — " The Earl uttered a peevish oath and snatching off his nightcap, hurled it furiously at Mervyn who bowed and, picking it up as it were some holy relic, placed it tenderly on the bed.

"If your lordship would but take somewhat, — a capon's wing, a sip or so of spiced Canary or mulled sack — "

"Malediction — no!" howled the Earl. "Go summon Will, mine honest Will; nay first, who was with me last night? Who attended me home?"

"Divers noble gentlemen, my lord, oh, indeed a many — your lordship being so run after and the admiration of the Court, in good sooth! Your lordship held noble company last night and among them chief, my Lord Riderwood and Sir Walter Fearn — " The young Earl moaned, frowned and sinking back amid his pillows, closed his eyes.

"What o'clock is 't?" he demanded, feebly.

"High noon, my lord. Will your lordship be dressed?"

"No, damme! Hence and bid Will Thurlow to me, and thereafter stay below stairs till I ring. Dispatch!"

"At your lordship's humble service!" sighed Mervyn, and again his eyes mocked his humility as he bowed and vanished, silent as ever. And after some while was clump of heavy boots, a thump on the door which opened to admit one clad in the Earl's handsome livery, a huge fellow, yellow-haired, blue-eyed and young who, blinking upon his young master's palely delicate features, pulled his forelock, bobbed curly head and spoke in broad South country speech:

"Wot be ee a-wantin' wi' I, young maister?"

"Come in, man, come in and shut the cursed door!" cried the Earl fretfully. "Now hither to me! Sit ye on the bed; sit, man, sit! Will, I 'm direly sick!"

"Which beant no'ow nowise to be marvelled at, m'lord," answered Will, shaking his head slowly.

"What d' ye mean, my rogue, what the devil d' ye mean?"

"As these yere furrin wines and gickyshaws don't no-how set sweet or proper on a English stummick, m'lord, and your innards being English, well — there y' are!"

"Will, 't isn't all the wine, no. Gad's life, man, I can drink with the best of 'em!"

"Ay, and wi' the worst too, m'lord."

"Ha, the worst, sirrah, the worst? Now, damme, what 'll

ye mean by the worst?" Will blinked sleepily and scratched his yellow head; quoth he:

"Well, young maister, I dunno,—only theer be my Lord Riderwood for one and for another—"

"Presumptuous dog, these be gentlemen o' quality!"

"Ay, but which quality, m'lord?"

"And my friends, jolthead, what's more!"

"Ay, more's the pity on't, young maister!"

"Bring me a drink, Will."

"This yer wine, m'lord?"

"No, to the devil with it! Water, man, water!"

So big Will, moving with a wondrous lightness, rose and brought the water, holding the goblet while his lord drank thirstily.

"Ha, by heaven, Will, there's naught so good as water— when a man be truly athirst."

"Ay, m'lord!"

"How dost like London town, Will lad?"

"Which, sir, for fine folks as wants a bullabaloo o' noise, and smells, and streets as goes every whichsoever way and folk as jostles, why there be no place to match it nohow. But for I—Lordy-Lord, gimme Aldrington and the good, green country! To be out arter the fish Exat way, you an' me, m'lord, like us used! Or prawns over to Birling Gap! Or galloping the Downs upalong High-and-over! Or sailing off Seaford! God bless us, that be life, that be!"

"Peace, fool!" snarled the Earl. "Hold your plaguey tongue!"

"Ay, sir!"

"And sit down again!"

"Ay, sir!"

"And,—hearkee, Will—"

"A-hearkin' I be, m'lord."

"Will, I've lost a vast deal o' money!"

"Ay, sir!"

"So much, Will man, that I dread to think on't."

"Ay, sir!"

"Never was such fiendly ill luck! Dice or cards, I cannot win!"

"Ay, sir!"

"Ha' done with your cursed 'ay sir!' Can't ye say aught else, fool?"

"Ay, marry an' I might, m'lord."

"Then a God's name — say it!"

"Why then, m'lord," said Will, blinking more sleepily than ever, "wi' dice nor cards ye cannot win and so it is ye lose — "

"Here's dizzard's babble!"

"I aren't done yet, m'lord. For ye lose because others do win and they wunt lose nor you can't win, until they've won all ye have to lose and, well — there y' are, m'lord!"

The youthful Earl glared at his young head groom and erstwhile slave and playfellow, and despite his guileless look and sleepy blue eyes, had an uneasy feeling that this golden-haired young giant was not the simpleton he seemed. And when master had glared thus on man and man had blinked on master awhile, master spoke:

"Will — dost think I — shall be ruined?"

"No, m'lord. But there's others as do."

"Others?"

"Ay, sir, there's m'lady Ione — "

"Tush!"

"And there be Penelope, as be now her maid."

"And thy sweetheart, eh, Will? And thou too great a numps to tell her so!"

"'T wouldn't be no manner o' use, I rackon, m'lord — Ay, she do be sweet lass, m'lord. But, sir, if ee don't never nowise win wi' cards or dice nohow, wherefore go on a-losing — "

"My good fool, a gentleman must gamble now and then!"

"But better then than now, m'lord."

"And you've no fears for my ruin, old Will lad?"

"Not I, my lord — nary one!"

"Art good, faithful fellow, Will, God bless thee. But . . . i' faith, Will, twixt you and me, I 've lost . . . ay, curse it, I 'm dipped so deep I dread my sister hearing on 't! And then . . . beside . . . come nearer . . . stoop your head! Hearkee, Will . . . besides the money I 've lost . . ." the young Earl's breath seemed to catch oddly and when he spoke again it was in gasping whisper. "Will . . . last night . . . I lost the . . . Aldrington Jewel!"

Here was a strange silence while master, blenching somewhat, stared up at man and man glared on master in speechless amaze and evergrowing horror.

"The Jewel!" said Will at last, and now he too was whispering. "You never mean . . . King Richard's Amulet!"

"Ay — I do, Will, I do . . . the Pelican in Piety —"

"Almighty God!" gasped Will. "'T is the Luck o' the Aldringtons! Who — how — Lord save us — how . . ."

"Nay, Will, hearkee," and now master, pale and tremulous, seemed almost pleading with man, whose blue eyes, no longer sleepy, held such bitter accusation, "hearkee, Will lad, it is not truly lost, 't is but in pawn; Riderwood holds it 'gainst certain monies owing —"

"Lord Riderwood —"

"He will return it to-night, Will."

"Be ee sure, sir?"

"He pledged me his honour. And . . . ha, damme and the devil; " cried my lord in sudden petulance, " no need is to glare on me so — ha, on me! How dare ye so presume, ye dog! Get off my bed — back t' your cursed horses! Malediction! Am I to be browbeat by my own groom, plague seize ye. Begone, d' ye hear? "

"Ay, sir!"

"And . . . on your life, no word to Ione, be secret or I — I cast ye off to the devil."

"No need for to threat me, sir. And which do mind me, sir, my Lady Ione she 've wrote a letter for ye."

"Why then, give it me."

"Which I can't, m'lord, seein' as 't is bore by a gentleman."

"Then go fetch it, I say."

"But, sir, 't is the gentleman do say as he must deliver to none but your own self."

"A murrain on the fellow! What manner o' person is he?"

"Right proper, sir, and saith he but lives to know your lordship."

"Ha, a well-mannered, seemly person is he?"

"Ay, sir!"

"Then give me my nightcap. Now go say he may present himself. And send Mervyn — nay, come you, instead." So away clumped Will and presently returned, ushering in a bowing, comely personage whose dress, though rich, smacked something of the country, as my lord was instant to perceive.

"You are new to London, sir?" he enquired.

"My lord, but this hour arrived and with here an epistle writ by your lady sister on my behalf." The young Earl graciously accepted the letter and, having read it, glanced at the bearer with a kindly tolerance.

"My sister is pleased to commend you to my notice and protection, Master . . . Master Dinwiddie."

"I am honoured, sir."

"She writes that you seek my patronage."

"'T is my very earnest desire, my lord." The Earl sank back amid his pillows and surveyed his petitioner at ease; this tallish, shapely person whose lean, aquiline face was lit by such arresting gray eyes, heavily lashed and, just now, very properly abased before my lord's searching regard and whose hands (too heavily gauntleted for my lord's fine taste) fumbled awkwardly with a hat better suited to cloddish squire on village green.

My lord having thus pondered the gentleman, from dark head to long, buckskin riding boots, was touched by his very evident diffidence and became the more gracious.

"Mr. Dinwiddie," said he languidly, "a sennight hence I wait upon Her Majesty," Mr. Dinwiddie bowed, "introduced by that famous gentleman and soldier, Sir Francis Vere." Mr. Dinwiddie bowed again. "On the which occasion, sir, yourself shall attend me if — ha — you will submit yourself to the care of Monsieur Dupont, my tailor."

"Your lordship is vastly generous!" murmured Master Dinwiddie and bowed yet again, while my lord sighed plaintively, hand to throbbing brow, and tall Will smiled broadly behind the great bed curtains.

"To-night, sir," continued the Earl, "hither to my house resort certain young gentlemen to sup with me and thereafter 't is like we may fall to this new game of Primero or toss a main or so at Hazard; you may join us, sir; I shall make you known to them."

"In faith," exclaimed Mr. Dinwiddie, in a transport, "I vow your lordship is so infinite condescending I am bold to sue like favour on good friend of mine, a gentleman, like myself, of the country, nobly descended, though little instruct in fashions courtly, a Mr. Florian Ferndale, my lord."

"He may come, sir. Ye shall be expected at six o'clock. Ye shall sup with me. Sir, my hand! So, for the nonce, farewell. Attend the gentleman forth, Will, and bid Mervyn to me."

So, with stolid Will attendant, the visitor descended to the courtyard, where spirited horse was being walked to and fro by a groom who at sign from his superior departed that Will himself might hold the stirrup; quoth he a little anxiously, and cap in hand:

"Cap'n Dinwiddie, sir — m'lord — 'e do be s' very young — owdacious young, your honour."

"Whereof old Time shall gently cure him, Will."

"Hows'ever sir, it do fair warm m'heart as you 'm here to give a eye to . . . things . . . and sich-like."

"Meaning my Lord Riderwood?"

"Ay, sir . . . And your honour is it sure as us rides for Aldrington to-night?"

"So sure as I live, Will," nodded the Captain.

"Why then, may your honour live long and die happy! Lord love us, I'm so j'yful as I dunno wot and, well — there y' are, sir."

# CHAPTER IV

## Telleth How and Why the Earl Left London Town

" Twelve o'clock! A fine night! And all 's well! "

The luxurious, panelled chamber was so still they could hear the solitary watchman go tramping down the deserted street with clatter of lanthorn and partisan, his heavy feet making strange echoes near and far, feet that paused again, remote, to another wailing cry of:

" Past twelve o'clock! A fine night! And all 's well! "

My lord the Earl of Aldrington uttered a pettish exclamation as he glanced from the money and scattered cards before him to the open lattice; his boyish face was darkly flushed, his eyes too bright and his air a little wild as, flinging back in his chair, he spoke:

" Twelve o'clock and a cursed bad night — for me! Eh, Riderwood? And it — it groweth late! "

" Not for us, Rick, 'sbud — not for us! Your true gentleman o' blood but begins to live when your dull, country clod and heavy cit lie snoring abed. So fill your glass, man; nay, I will — so, a bumper. Now shuffle and to 't again, Dick."

The Earl glanced at my Lord Riderwood with a certain apprehension, — a tall gentleman of a magnificence and entirely languid, yet a masterful, smiling personage whose oval face, small of eye and mouth but large of nose and chin, held that which awed the petulant boy to half-sullen acquiescence. Slowly and unwillingly he gathered the cards, then paused and, very conscious of Lord Riderwood's keen eyes and smiling mouth, enquired with a meekness:

" Pray, Riderwood, how much am I owing you and Malone to-night, so far? "

"Tush, my dear Richard! Fie, what matter betwixt friends? Some few hundred or so."

"Nay, but how much — you, Colonel?"

"Eighteen hundred and seventy-three angels, to be precise," laughed Colonel Malone, consulting his tablets. The Earl dropped his cards.

"So much?" he gasped.

"Fie, Richard man!" murmured Lord Riderwood, gently reproachful. "Here's nought to such wealth incalculable as thine."

"Ay, true, Charles, true!" nodded the boy, taking up the cards. "But," and here he let them fall again, "I lost nigh three thousand last week . . . And then, Riderwood, what o' the Aldrington jewel . . . the Relic? Hast brought it — "

"Be easy for that, Dick," answered Lord Riderwood, smiling tenderly into the boy's eager face. "'T is but in pawn, as 't were. Come, the cards — "

"Nay, but you promised I should have it back again to-night; you pledged your word — "

"Ay, 'sfoot, so I did! And my word is my bond, Richard. At the least, no man is so reckless to deny it, I think. I promised shouldst have it again and so thou shalt, dear lad, next time we foregather neath my humble roof."

"Nay, but indeed, Charles, I — you — since you so promised — "

"Nay, now, dear my Richard, wherefore that frown? 'Slight, 't would almost seem thou dost not trust thy Charles! Yet e'en were it so I 'd forgive thee, sweet lad, for thine own and so bewitching sister's sake. Come now, a health, I pledge ye the peerless Ione! And now to our game!"

"No, faith, Charles. I weary o' Primero; the cards are no friends o' mine, especially to-night."

"Nay but, Dicky-man, ye would so plunge!" wheezed the Colonel, glancing up from his tablets, "so very desperate bold, Dicky, and myself warned thee Riderwood was ever most hellish lucky Tuesdays and Fridays, be the powers! Thou 'lt mind how I warned thee? But an' the cards fail thee, what o' the bones? 'T is like the dice shall prosper thee and luck turn. How sayst thou, Dicky-man?" The young Earl glanced about him almost des-perately, — at the red-faced Colonel Malone, cyphering in his tablets, at Sir Walter Fearn, scowling fiercely over his game with the meek-smiling Mr. Ferndale in opposite corner, at Lord Riderwood's gentle complacency and at Mr. Dinwiddie, drowsing over his wine in great elbow-chair hard by.

"Oh, — have with ye!" he cried, setting his youthful chin.

So dice were produced; Colonel Malone laid by his tab-lets and took up the box.

"What shall we set?" he enquired, glancing towards Lord Riderwood. "A rial a main."

"Five!" cried the Earl, refilling his glass, "and let it be — angels."

"And — ten!" murmured Lord Riderwood, smoothing his perfumed hair.

So the game began, Colonel Malone boisterous and jovial, Lord Riderwood serenely languid, the Earl flushed and passionately intent — and — Mr. Dinwiddie outstretched slumbrous in the great elbow-chair.

Main succeeded main with varying fortune and then, once more, ill luck swooped upon the young Earl. . . . From red he grew deathly white, his eyes glared feverishly beneath slim, twitching brows, he dashed creeping moisture from his beardless cheek, he muttered passionate exclamations of dismay. . . .

It was as Lord Riderwood made to throw that his hand was gripped by sudden, pouncing fingers, — long powerful fingers that wrenched and twisted. Colonel Malone gaped dumb-smit, as did the Earl; Lord Riderwood whispered vicious oath as from his tortured hand dropped the hidden loaded dice; then he was whirled about to front a grim visage, eyes that glared, lips that curled from white teeth,

and smiling thus bitterly contemptuous, Captain Dinwiddie
spoke but — not in the awed, deferential murmur of the
gentleman new from the country.

"So-ho, base lord and sorry foist, I 've seen it better done
in camp a score o' times." Lord Riderwood was up and
away, but as he leapt in again, dagger a-gleam to smite,
Florian's outthrust leg tripped him in full career and he
crashed heavily face down, his left arm doubled under him
and so lay motionless and utterly silent; yet when his two
friends hasted to lift him, his pallid, writhen lips voiced the
agony of his broken arm. But he choked back the moan
and looking on Jocelyn twixt narrowed lids, spoke
murmuring:

"Liar! Rogue! One day I 'll — watch you die —
slowly — stab by stab. . . . And now — Malone, get me
— out o' this, a Gad's name — ere I — swoon."

Now when they were gone, Jocelyn turned to the Earl
who sat crouched miserably at the table, staring wide-eyed
on vacancy.

"So, my lord," said he gently, "having discovered these
fine gentlemen for merest rogues, I would have you — "

"Nay, sir," cried the boy haughtily; "these gentlemen
be still my friends — "

"Saints and martyrs!" murmured Jocelyn.

"Mr. Dinwiddie, these be men of condition, persons of
quality, gentlemen highly esteemed; to — to doubt their
honour at word of a stranger were to dishonour myself."

"Mighty fine!" nodded the Captain. "Howbeit these
same estimable persons robbed ye with pricked cards,
palmed false dice — there lie they yet, witnesses mute yet
sufficiently eloquent. So now, my lord, open those so
youthful eyes and I shall explain forthwith the how and the
wherefore. Here then are my noble lord's false dice, a
pair of barred catertreys, barred — that is, shaped longer
on the three-four axis, so that howsoe'er and how often you
throw them, they shall never show other than combinations
of one, two, five and six. Essay, my lord, and let your
faith in yon foisting gentry be shocked rudely hence.

Throw, sir, first with my lord's barred catertreys and then with these true dice. Then feel me these cards, here — and here again."

Unwillingly the young Earl made the tests and finding proof beyond all doubt of his late friends' roguery and his own folly, stared sullenly where Florian was collecting certain monies, who, meeting his frown, laughed gaily.

" 'Sheart! my lord," he tittered. " Yon gentle scourers, having small respect for our yokelly intelligence, played their cheats so openly that I am richer by fifty odd broad pieces — "

"Ha," cried the Earl, pettishly imperious. "And who . . . what the fiend are ye, that in guise of simple country gentlemen may outcheat these . . . these . . ." the youth faltered and ere he might find the just and proper word, Jocelyn drew forth her ladyship's first-written letter and unfolding it, set it before him.

"This should explain — somewhat, my lord," said he. The Earl read it through and instantly scowled blacker than ever.

"So!" he exclaimed with long-drawn, passionate hiss. " They fooled me!"

"Repeatedly, sir!" nodded the Captain. "And she entreats your return for the harvest, my lord."

"Ha!" exclaimed the Earl, smiting the table before him in fury of mounting indignation, "these . . . these that I ha' cherished and called friends . . . dared so deceive me!"

"And," murmured the Captain, "she yearneth for you home again, sir!"

"Damme!" cried the Earl, shrill with raging impotence. " They 've cheated me of thousands . . . money and . . . ah, God — "

"Tush, child, and hush!" said the Captain, taking up the letter with care.

" Child? " raved the Earl. " Ha, will ye dare — "

"Peace, boy!" said the Captain, refolding the letter and setting it back in his bosom. " Bleat not, thou poor shorn lamb, nor let tender gull his pinions plucked so futile flap and flutter! In a word, lad, repine not thy squandered gold; count it but payment for experience shall haply make o' thee wiser youth, nobler gentleman and kinder brother. Your sister begs you return home for the harvest but yearns for your presence sooner. Well, how say you?"

"That I go in my own time and pleasure, Master Dinwiddie and——"

"Spoke like a graceless, peevish boy, my lord." The Earl arose, very youthful-seeming but supremely arrogant, and pointed imperiously to the door.

"Master Dinwiddie," quoth he, with an icy haughtiness, "you have my permission to go! You may remove."

"Sweet lord," answered the Captain, with Italianate bow of bewildering complexities, "'t is so mine intent. Pray ring for your nobility's boots and horse."

"Sir, begone! I'm in no mood for your pleasantries."

"My lord, I was seldom more serious. Florian, pray ring the bell."

"Why . . . what black villainy is this?" cried the young Earl with sudden tremour, as Florian tugged gaily at bell-rope.

"My lord, merely I propose to carry foolish boy to doting sister and so be done——"

"Ha, by heavens, will ye affront me in mine own house——"

"Cheerily, sir, or any other where, in such sweet and proper cause." And now was tramp of heavy feet, the door opened and tall Will stood pulling his forelock at them, and . . . beneath one great arm his young master's riding boots.

"What . . . Will?" cried the Earl in angry surprise. "How come you here? Where is Mervyn?"

"Drunk and asleep, m'lord," answered Will, holding forth the boots invitingly.

"Then summon my grooms, and do you and they rid me o' these . . . these persons forthright."

" Which, my lord," answered Will, pulling forelock again,
" which can't nowise be done, nohow, sir."

" Ha . . . what d' ye mean, fool?"

" Which, m'lord, I means as here stands Cap'n Dinwiddie, m'lord, the Cap'n Dinwiddie as saved brother Tom's
life from them blood-bent Spanishers over in they Netherlands and . . . well, there y' are!"

" Well? Damme, and what now?" demanded the Earl.

" Which now, m'lord, the 'osses be a-waitin' so I'll go
and wait along wi' 'em, by your leave, m'lord!" So saying,
Will set down the boots and departed suddenly, but scarcely
had the door closed upon him than the Earl leapt thither
only to be caught and swung about in Captain Jocelyn's
powerful grasp.

" Gentle sir," quoth he, " beseech you remark, fond youth
perpend! Your lady sister, distressed by your follies
notorious and of your regeneration despairful, hath
honoured me with commission to pluck you from roguery
and ruin, and plucked, forsooth, you shall be. Thus, sir,
and with all the humility in nature, I supplicate your lordship to be incontinent booted, for we ride instantly to
Aldrington."

The young Earl looked from the Captain, grim and stern,
to Florian, grim and smiling, glanced despairing at the
bell-rope, murmured peevish oath and reached for his
boots. Thereafter, obedient to the masterful hand on his
shoulder, my lord descended the wide stair, glancing
furtively this way and that for the many servile lacqueys
that should be and were not, and so, silent and submissive
ever like one who dreamed, reached the courtyard where
stood Will with the horses.

And thus, still like one a-dream, my Lord Richard, Earl
of Aldrington, in the County of Sussex, mounted and riding
between the Captain and Florian, with stolid Will behind,
was borne rapidly away.

## CHAPTER V

### TELLETH HOW THE EARL CAME HOME

IT was in the dawn they saw the age-worn, battle-scarred tower and more modern chimneys and gables of Aldrington Chase rising above tree tops and all roseate with the spring of day.

But now the Earl checked his foam-spattered horse, and having stared gloomily awhile on tower and chimney, shivered and turned on Florian.

"Pray, sir," said he, meekly miserable, "suffer me a private word with Mr. Dinwiddie, an 't please you."

"With joy, my lord!" smiled Florian and rode on down the slope with Will; but even then the Earl was mute awhile, his young face very troubled.

"Alas," sighed he, at last, "money was not all I lost away there in London!"

"What then?" questioned Jocelyn with quick anxiety.

"'Twas thing, sir, no money may purchase! Indeed, 't is a thing beyond all price to us Aldringtons, more precious than aught else in the world, even life itself. There be ancestors of mine have died for it ere now and I . . . God forgive me, have lost it . . . the holy Relic we Aldringtons hold our fortune and honour! The Amulet! The King's Crystal! The Pelican in Piety given to my ancestor by Richard the King at the Siege of Acre. Since when it hath been worn by every Aldrington like Sir John, that, dying at Agincourt, sent it back here to Aldrington Tower by his esquire . . . And I — upon a night lost it basely at play — ha, no — 't was stolen from me by yon vile fellow Riderwood! The . . . Aldrington Relic. . . ." Here he gasped, and in his young eyes such anguish that Jocelyn instinctive reached long arm about his slenderness, patting his bowed shoulder, and young Richard, sensing this dumb sympathy, clasped this comforting hand, gripping it fast.

"Wert right!" he murmured. "I am a fool unworthy my high lineage, those knights and lords that so cherished this honoured Relic . . . and I to lose it in such base fashion. Oh, I am vile! I must return and win it back somehow . . . at any hazard. If ever my sister should know —"

"Nay, despair not, my lord, we must recover it."

"Ay, by God's light — if you but can . . ."

"Tell me, is 't of value intrinsic, easy of sale?"

"No, indeed, no! It is of small value save to us Aldringtons."

"Knoweth Lord Riderwood this?"

"Indeed, sir. 'Twas my sister first showed it to him. It was Ione told him how 't was the Aldrington Relic and very symbol of our honour and welfare."

"Knoweth she this fellow, then?"

"Very well. He was often here upon a time and hath a house beyond Hoove village, hard by the sea, a desolate place and old."

"Hum!" quoth the Captain and frowning, tugged at moustachio. "And prithee, was this lord so presumptuous to attempt aught in . . . as 't were . . . an amorous way, — sighings, tender looks, soft speeches and the like cursed audacities?"

"Ay, truly, he proffered marriage — ha, and he wretch I prove so dishonoured! Ay, he wooed, fiend take him! But, at the last, Ione so answered him, God be thanked, that incontinent he rode for London and I, being very fool, was persuaded to ride with him."

"Why then, my lord, for your lost Relic, here 's comfort — Riderwood, being cunning gentleman, shall seek its best market nor part with it to any save an Aldrington — at a price!"

"Ah, no matter the price, sir, I 'll pay gladly."

"Hum!" quoth the Captain and tugged his moustachio

again. "Sir, there is a price no brother may ever pay or — suffer paid!"

"Ah, you mean — Ione?" gasped the Earl. "Why, there it is. There lieth my fear . . . Ione is of such passionate devotions to this so honoured Relic . . . to win it from Riderwood's vile keeping she would . . . oh, God, she might even —"

"So?" murmured Jocelyn. "Then ere the which event it would become necessary my Lord Riderwood suddenly die."

"Ay, true — true!" cried the young Earl wildly. "But how? Who is there to match him? I saw him touch De Bergerac thrice in as many venies! He's vaunted cunning and deadly skilful as ever the great Saviolo himself."

"But then, my lord, I am Dinwiddie."

"Ay, ay — but 't is no answer."

"My lord, should you learn me better, you 'll know me for complete answer to much, and things a many."

"Even to . . . to Lord Riderwood?"

"Such answer, my lord, that I warrant him never to ask question more."

"But he . . . he hath killed divers times!" faltered the Earl. "I 've heard he hath secret thrust no man may parry . . . and you, sir —" here he glanced at his companion and was dumb, for in this face, suddenly grim, was that which killed all doubt; then as suddenly these narrow, glinting eyes opened, this fierce mouth curved to such transfiguring smile that the youth, leaning impulsively from saddle, reached forth an eager hand.

"Sir," said he, in voice eager as his look. "Oh, Mr. Dinwiddie, wilt honour me with thy friendship?"

"My lord," answered the Captain gravely, "right heartily!" And hand met hand.

"And now, friend Jocelyn, to such as do love me I am Richard. And faith, I owe thee overmuch for showing me the roguery of those I deemed friends, — but more shall I owe thee an' thou 'lt teach me the art o' fence, subtle tricks o' the sword, ah — wilt thou?"

" Willingly, Richard, an' thou 'lt be diligent to learn."

" Ha, that will I on my life! And then, besides, wilt aid, wilt counsel me how to win back the Crystal — The Amulet? "

" Hand and head."

" Why now, here 's mighty comfort to me, friend Jocelyn. Come then, let us home to breakfast."

So down the hill rode they together through the sweetness of this early morning, the new-risen sun bright upon them while birds made joyous babel near and far.

" Aha!" cried the Earl, bright eyes a-dance. " Friendship is right goodly thing, Jocelyn. How it comforteth a man! 'Sfoot, I grow joyful as the birds and feel as I had known thee all my days. . . . And if Riderwood's arm be broke no need is there to trouble for him till after the harvest. Come, let 's to breakfast — honest English beef and ale, Jocelyn, ale!"

At foot of the hill they came up with Florian and Will; thus rode they, all four, between lofty gates, neath an avenue of great trees and so clattered merrily into the stately courtyard of this so ancient and noble house of Aldrington, silent all at this early hour.

And yet one there was that heard, for out from wide lattice open to the fragrant morning leaned Ione who, espying her brother saluting her gaily, hat in hand, reached forth a white arm to him, crying joyous as the carolling birds:

" Oh, Richard, welcome, welcome home at last!"

# CHAPTER VI

## CONCERNETH THE LADY THAT WAS JOAN, AND DINWIDDIE A PHILOSOPHER

" AND so," said my lady, holding morsel of bread daintily above the lily pool where plump fish swam, " so you succeeded in this desperate enterprise I set you."

" Madam," answered the Captain, eyes furtively a-twinkle, " I am Dinwiddie! "

" Which is item I am not like to forget, 't would seem."

Here she dropped the crumb, whereupon was swirl and ripple of leaping fish, while the Captain, viewing all the generous shapeliness of her as she leaned thus near, so vivid and quick with young life, became abstracted.

" You also unmasked Riderwood for the villain I knew him. I 'm wondering how 't was done? " Here, finding the Captain silent, she turned on him with arrogance; " Sir, I spoke! "

" And lo," he answered with meekness, " all nature entranced stands awed and dumb, e'en as humble I."

" Shall I not be answered, Captain? I would know how you proved one so skilful and hatefully assured as Lord Riderwood a cheat so beyond all possibility of doubt or denial? "

" To such as myself, madam, the thing was patent."

" And prithee, what is yourself that can spy out roguery so instantly where all others are blind? "

" Purely myself! " he answered gravely. " Which is subject so vast I might expound you thereon to infinity; yet briefly, I know roguery when I see it since I have roguery seen full oft, have studied it, pondered it and am therefore in roguery sufficiently instruct."

" In fine, sir, a super-rogue? "

"I permit your ladyship to judge o' this!" And he commenced an obeisance of such intricacies that she turned away to frown at her fishes; yet having fed them three more crumbs, she spoke to him over her shoulder:

"Howbeit, Richard now scorns and bitterly despises the wretch, and for this my thanks."

"Your ladyship's gratitude sets me on very pinnacle o' bliss!" he murmured.

"Richard tells me the vile creature was hurt."

"'T was his misfortune to break an arm, madam."

"God be praised!" said my lady fervently. "I could wish him so many arms and legs as a spider and all broke!"

"Your ladyship is gentlewoman of a certain vindictiveness, 't would seem!"

"My ladyship, Sir Captain, detests and abhors all such men as he. So do I rejoice you so exposed him, to his eternal dishonour, and marvel you should do it with such ease, and he so deadly and feared, 't is my wonder!"

"Madam, I am Din—"

"Yes—widdie! 'T is known, sir, 't is fact admitted. And thus, knowing you for Dinwiddie, I would of Dinwiddie ask what Dinwiddie, in the dark profundities of the Dinwiddie mind, thinketh of my dear Richard?" The Captain bowed.

"That heaven hath blessed him in his sister."

"Sir, his sister humbly thanks your Stateliness and begs the Dinwiddie's so experienced judgment on her brother, his character."

"I am honoured that he hath named me friend."

"And here 's another wonder."

"Is this, indeed, so marvellous?"

"Sir, 't is very miracle!"

"How then, madam," said the Captain, having duly pondered this; "seem I so bitterly dislikable, of aspect so villainous, so harsh, repellent and altogether unlovely?"

"Nevertheless and notwithstanding," she answered, still busied with her fish, "I find your new habit well enough; 't is seemly and of a sombre sobriety in accord with your sober airs, your brooding visage, your mien of portentous gravity and age-old experience of this sorry world. In fine, sir, 't is sufficiently Dinwiddieish."

"Howbeit," sighed he, "within this mine age-worn body, this withered husk, the heart o' me is vernal yet, my Lady Joan." Now, meeting his whimsical look, she laughed suddenly, then:

"'Joan', quo' he!"

"Ay, Joan!" he nodded. "'T is sweetly English and suits thee better than the Greek, God wot."

"And now, sir," says she, a little flushed and stooping above the pool again, "there remaineth small matter o' business betwixt us. The sum I named — "

"Madam!"

"Is methinks too mean for such instant and notable service; therefore I — "

"Lady," said he, flushing, "pray know that as your brother's friend — "

"Tush, sir! The labourer is worthy his hire, a bird — "

"Your ladyship, no more o' this, I beg."

"Sir, a bargain is a bargain and — "

"Madam, the circumstances are something altered and — "

"Also, Captain, even the Dinwiddie must eat."

Now at this, receiving no answer, she turned and saw him prodding savagely at the grass with scabbarded sword and frowning so blackly that she instantly frowned also.

"Hoity-toity, sir!" she exclaimed, dimpled chin aloft, "I think you become mighty proud of a sudden!"

"No, madam, you merely anger me. Be pleased to suffer I go!" and he turned away.

"Remain, sir, and be assured your anger affronts me!"

"Why then, 't is not anger in vain, madam."

"And your money shall be paid you this moment. Lo, here — take it!" So, mutely obedient, he took the heavy purse and dropped it into the lily pool, meeting the flame of her amazed anger serene of eye and faint-smiling. And his gray eyes were wistful and his smile sad as ever, yet, it is to be thought, he was nowise unhappy.

"My lady Joan," said he gently. "be not angered with me, for your brother Richard hath pledged me his friendship and by his earnest desire Mr. Ferndale and I remain here his guests awhile, until . . ." he glanced from her vivid beauty to the glory of flowers, the winding walks and tall yew hedges that shut in this fragrant, peaceful haven.

"Well, sir, — until?" she demanded.

"Until Destiny shall spur us hence."

"And what of your money in the pool, here?"

"It shall be humble offering to the kind genius of this fragrant sanctuary."

"Art a strange man, Captain Jocelyn, and vastly unexpected!" said she, viewing him kinder, and with lovely head aslant.

"I am so!" he answered, shapely mouth a-twitch, "nor shall ever behold again the like of me."

"Oh, and indeed, sir?"

"Yea, and beyond all peradventure!" he answered gravely. "For in all this world there is of me but one and this one most singular."

"How, prithee, and wherefore — most meek and humble gentleman?"

"Lady, in me you behold the last o' my name and this a soul apart, remote and immune from all kinship, the veriest quintessence of every Dinwiddie that ever was, the epitome of my race, — of fortune none, of friends few, of deeds many but of dreams infinite."

"Dreams, quotha? Now methought thee man of action."

"And madam, that am I that dreamer am, for action is thought's expression and what be thoughts but dreams?"

"O' my conscience, Captain Jocelyn, you wax passionately eloquent on yourself."

"Verily," he answered, "for are not ourselves unto ourselves of ourselves the chiefest concern?"

"Why then, walk with me, sir, for i' faith, myself would of thyself learn thyself's so infinite dreaming o' thyself, — ay, and moreover, whereof cometh thyself's so vasty content of thyself?"

"By self-contempt!" he answered, as they wandered slowly on together.

"Ah, a paradox!" she nodded. "Prithee expound."

"As thus, madam," he answered gravely, his gaze roving, yet very conscious of her lovely nearness. "I then, scorning myself heartily within myself, find myself, ever and anon, so surprised to prove myself so greatly better than I had deemed myself that myself taketh therein no small solace. Thus I, that have so little, scorning the much, am with the little content."

"Why, 't is a mad philosophy, Master Jocelyn."

"Lady, 't is the philosophy of one Epictetus that was slave to gentleman o' Greece and, being in dungeon pent, scorned freedom and thus, in his soul, was free."

They had reached an arbour deep-bowered in sweet vines and sitting within this fragrant shade she beckoned him beside her.

"Captain Jocelyn," said she, sitting back the better to survey his comely though saturnine features, "you prove vastly different to my first thought of you."

"Shall I wear my heart o' my sleeve, madam?"

"Nay, but to so deceive me! To-day you seem soft-voiced philosopher — you that strutted into my life — a fierce, swaggering, reckless fellow, indeed the veriest bravo of Alsatia, a hireling bully for anybody's money."

"Now I protest your ladyship's blandiloquent adulation and flattery fulsome is sweetest incense to my self-esteem; it puffeth my vanity, it — "

"Flattery, sir?" she repeated, opening scornful eyes at him. "Are you so proud to be reckoned vile wretch to spill blood and work villainy for mere gain?"

"Beyond expression, madam. For 't was such base rogue you sought to your need, so, for the nonce, thine own base rogue was I."

"You mean," she demanded, viewing him with her clear level gaze, "that you but played a part?"

"God wot, lady! I was Dick Slash and Cutting Tom, with Sir Petronel Flash thrown in; — i' faith I was, methinks, the impeccable roisterous roarer and bully par excellence!"

"And pray," said she, eyes still intent but frowning, "what manner of creature are you now?"

"Now," he answered, his wistful gaze on the peaceful, sunny garden, "I shall study to be all you'd have me." Here was silence, she tapping slim foot impatiently the while she frowned at his averted face; at last she deigned him another question:

"How an' I bid you be — merely yourself, sir?"

"Ay, but — which one, lady?" he sighed.

"Heaven aid me! Art so various, sir?"

"Infinitely, madam."

"Then be of yourselves the poor best." Here my lady arose, shook voluminous petticoats about her shapeliness with gesture petulant though gracious and then, seeing the Captain had risen also, sat down again.

"Be seated, sir!" she commanded, and, meekly bowing, he obeyed.

"So then you refuse my service, sir?"

"Never in the world!" he answered and with such fervour that she frowned at him.

"Yet in your new-gotten high-mightiness you refuse a just payment — ah, how dared you throw it into the pool?"

"I saw no place so fit, madam."

"And you will not that I pay this money agreed and earned?"

"Pray believe so."

"And why? Because I am woman?"

"Because I am your ladyship's brother's friend."

"So then I'm done with you, sir."

"So then," he sighed, "tottering creation sinks in thunderous ruin —"

"Ha, will you mock? D' you dare flout me, sir?" she stormed.

"Rather do I grieve, madam, and —"

"Tush, sir! With your . . . tottering ruin, forsooth!"

"Most truly," he nodded. "For my creation was a noble dream, wherein I, that ever dream most daringly, so fearless dreamed that thou and I won of each other such respect as blossomed to a kindly friendship, a sweet and gentle amity —"

"Oh, never!" she retorted, sitting very stately. "I'll be friend to no man that holdeth me in his debt — and in especial — you!"

"And wherefore this distinction, my lady?"

"For that you, sir, are, God bless us, — Dinwiddie!"

"Ay, faith!" he nodded forlornly. "So have I been all my life, but for this I had plucked the moon from heaven and juggled with the stars."

"Oh?" she mocked. "Are we now humble? Doth humility rule awhile, most mighty, ineffectual gentleman?"

"Ay, truly, truly!" he sighed. "Thirty and seven years have I striven with life, flouted Death, battled with Circumstance, endured the peril and plague o' divers wars and am to-day dubbed — ineffectual! Lady, I am dumb!"

"God be thanked!" she retorted. "For you stifle me with ocean o' words. You jibe me, jeer me with solemn look, you confound me with phrases fantastical, and you toss away your money as it stung you! I prove you a man proud to folly, vain to extravagance, disputatious, obstinate, of words too many, of graces too few, overbearing, overweening, yet, over all a man — and so 't is, Sir Prideful Arrogance, I humbly bid you welcome to Aldrington Chase!" And rising swiftly, she sunk before him, down and down, in slow and gracious reverence, while Jocelyn sat there motionless, wide-eyed and, for once, bereft of all words.

"Lo, sir," said she, rising with a stately ease, "for your wordy ocean, my speechful cataract! Come now, let us go seek a gardener shall recover your so despised gold."

So forth they went into the balmy sunshine, pacing flower-bordered paths awhile in silence. And because of his dumbness she turned aside to smile at a flower and inhale its dewy sweetness, and thereafter hummed to herself softly but very gaily; but presently, glancing askance at him, met his look of perplexity and laughed.

"Prithee, why so strangely silent, so unwonted dumb?" she questioned, with something of malice. "Art drowned in my speechful torrent?"

"God wot, madam, that am I!" he answered, grave and wistful. "I pain to know if your so kind welcome hath in it anything of sincerity."

"In troth, sir, yes. For did you not promise me, though very lightly, that you would save my dear Richard from — himself? And I dream belike you may — or at the least, something offset the evil companionship of his latter days. For though methinks 't is labour for a Hercules, yet as I mind, you are — Dinwiddie! Sir, I would have him learn how a busy life, here in the despised country among his people, may be lived, ay, by even a fine gentleman to better purpose than wasted upon the wicked town."

"Hast faith in my powers, my Lady Joan?"

"Again, sir, you are Dinwiddie! So needs must my faith be absolute."

Now when they had paced some while in silence, Jocelyn spoke with tone and look strangely humble:

"Wilt stoop to mine aid in this?"

"With all my heart!" she answered and paused to turn and look at him. And thus stood they a long moment, eyes searching eyes; and presently when they had walked on again, though their words were few, they went in a new communion.

# CHAPTER VII

### Telleth of a Fight, a Witch, and a Warning

There was ring of steel within the orchard, clink and clash of foils in thrust and parry, where my lord the Earl, doublet and shoes off, was taking his first lesson from the Captain and making furious work of it, leaping and sidling, stabbing and foining until the blunted weapon was beaten from his wearied grasp and himself breathless.

"How — am I — Jocelyn?" he gasped.

The Captain shook grave head and picked up the foil while Florian, seated cross-legged hard by, and cracking nuts between strong white teeth, shook his head and smiled:

"Thou 'rt dead, friend Richard!" he answered. "Stark dead a score o' times. 'Sbud, any swashing Tom or Dick might ha' cut thee into small gobbets — "

"Peace, ha — peace, I say!" cried the Earl angrily. "Know, sir, I am not so unlearned! How say you, Jocelyn; speak, man!"

"See now," answered Jocelyn, proffering the foil, "this new art of fence, this rapier play, is not very delicate; 't is point contra edge, and point is ever the speedier and more deadly. Thus 't is art so precise that, ill taught, it is a menace — "

"Ill taught?" cried my lord, snatching the foil and scowling at it. "Damme, sir, seven masters have I had and amongst them De Bergerac himself — "

"And, faith, Richard, 't is what I feared for thee; seven methods be worse than none, 't is confusion seven times confounded — "

"Try me again!" said the boy sullenly. "See, 't was thus De Bergerac would have me stand! 'T is thus Signor Spinelli had me bear my point! And thus Herr Von Holz swayed me his hand — with a one — two and — "

"Thy foeman's blade through thee, alas — so!" quoth Jocelyn; and the Earl felt steel touch his ribs and stood back, scowling blacker than ever.

"Tush and the devil!" he cried pettishly and tossed away his foil, whereupon Jocelyn tossed his own after it and, bowing, turned on his heel, leaving the young Earl to stare after him somewhat abashed and exceeding amazed, while Florian, lolling against a tree, cracked another nut, on whom Young Magnificence turned, forthwith.

"Saw ye ever such curst fellow?" he demanded.

"But seldom!" answered Florian, smiling up into the angry young face.

"Would you affront me, Master Ferndale?"

"No, my lord!" answered Florian, munching.

"I say that yon Jocelyn is devilish touchy fellow!"

"He is so, my lord," nodded Florian, "i' fackins, he's so touchy we are like to be touching saddle anon, he and I."

"Sayst thou?" muttered the Earl.

"In faith!" nodded Florian.

"Then — ha, damme — he may to the devil for me!"

"To the devil, my lord? Why so he would, to keep his word. Ay — cogsnails, he'd scour all hell ere break his promise."

"Promise, sir? I' the fiend's name, what promise?"

"Well, I heard some talk of a jewel, my lord, a relic or what not."

The Earl's lofty arrogance wilted suddenly, the magnificent youth became a boy so troubled and pitifully distraught that Florian turned away and began to guzzle more nuts.

"Think you he — he truly meaneth to begone, Florian?"

"My lord, none may answer this save himself."

"We must stay him . . . we must! And prithee call me Richard. . . . We must not suffer him to go."

"For sake o' thy jewel, Richard?"

"Ay . . . and because I do truly begin to love him."

Florian turned and reading the truth of this in the boy's eager face, nodded.

"Well, he's a man. And thou hast legs, — use 'em, Richard, — to him, friend, and speak thy wish."

Thus, presently, unto the Captain, wandering thoughtful in the rose garden, came my lord, and the foils beneath his arm.

"Sir," said he, very flushed and somewhat breathless, "I was wrong! 'T was my curst temper! Jocelyn, forgive me . . . I'm an ass, a fool — "

"Yet very manlike!" said the Captain.

"Why then," cried my lord, hand outthrust with boyish eagerness, "prithee come try me again."

So in a while back went they, arm in arm, to find Florian drowsing in the sunshine. And once again the air rang with clink of quick steel, but now with laughter and cheery voices also, until came a liveried serving-man in panting haste:

"My lord," he cried, "gentlemen — four, to see Master Dinwiddie." As he spoke, was a trampling of horses' hoofs and into the sunny orchard jingled these gentlemen four who, swinging to earth, came with great strides, — four very sinister gentlemen cloaked to the chins, hatted to the eyes, who glared truculently, scowling on creation.

Jocelyn, bending his foil gently this way and that, watched them with the experienced eye of mutual appraisal; Florian, afoot now and arms crossed, surveyed them with a certain joyous expectancy, while the young Earl, extremely on his dignity, frowned on these arrogant strangers and spoke them in his haughtiest tone:

"'Sdeath, sirs! What means this intrusion — "

The four halted within a yard.

"Ha!" cried one, glaring ferocity and twisting rampant moustachio. "I take it you are my lord the Earl of Aldrington, ha?"

"Himself, sir, and demand the reason for this outrage, this unmannered — "

"My lord," cried a second, with martial stamp of spurred foot, "believe we mean your lordship no offense and nothing harmful. . . . You there!" he roared and stamped about to face the Captain, "which o' ye calls himself Dinwiddie?"

"To me, bowcock rufflers!" answered the Captain, foil gracefully a-flourish. "Hither bold, scowering bullies and win your blood-fee, an' ye may."

Four cloaks fluttered, four rapiers leapt glittering, and the four intruders sprang to instant and murderous action and were as instantly checked by whizzing foil and darting blade. . . . And now, instead of ring of blunted foils, of laughter and cheery voices, was clash and grind of weapons wielded with deadly purpose and in grim silence.

Back to back they stood, the Captain and Florian, light poised on agile feet, hemmed in by whirling steel, Jocelyn silent ever, plying his foil in lightning parade and counter-thrust at eye or throat, its blunted point a ceaseless menace, while Florian's long blade whirled and leapt what time he laughed and jeered as was his wont:

"Sa-ha, play close, my bully roarers! Stand to 't, Roguery! Aha, merrily all! And here's for thee, Dog's-breakfast!"

To and fro the combat swayed furiously, until arms began to weary, breaths to labour . . . then, crying hoarsely, a man reeled back from Florian's reddened point; dropping weapon to clasp his wound he leaned against a tree, staying the blood flow with one spread hand while with the other he plucked forth a pistol; but as he stood waiting a chance to shoot, the young Earl closed with him in desperate grapple to clutch that murderous pistol hand, wrenching, twisting, straining until the weapon exploded high in air, its bellowing report presently answered by shouts afar, a vague hubbub growing louder; whereat gasping voices cursed fiercely and cried sudden alarm:

"We're flammed! Off, lads—to horse ere we're beset!"

"Ay, the horses—the horses!"

"Back, Florian!" panted the Captain. "Let 'em away . . . 't were better so."

"Alack . . . 't is pity!" gasped Florian. "Yet each

beareth his own — particular smart — and this is my consolation."

Thus when my Lady Ione, petticoats high-kilted, came running, swift and graceful as any nymph of Arcady, it was to see three men scramble to horse and spur away at desperate speed; from which amazing sight her wide eyes turned where the Captain leaned against a tree, one arm behind him, while Florian, whistling softly, wiped his blade on a fallen cloak, and her young brother stooped above a sprawling fellow who groaned in answer to his fierce questioning.

"Saints ha' mercy!" she cried, recoiling from blood that fouled the trampled grass. "Who — who is hurt?"

"Villains four, madam," laughed Florian, bowing; "each and every, more or less."

"But wherefore? Who were they and what?"

"Roguery!" cried the Earl, hasting to show Ione the captured pistol. "But for me, Jocelyn had been murdered, ay, and Florian also, like as not . . . shot like a dog, Ione! The vile fellow had levelled pistol at Jocelyn . . . here 't is . . . was about to give fire when I leapt on the base villain! We fought right furiously . . . ha, 't was desperate business, I 'll warrant ye . . . the pistol explodes in my very ear and . . . well — here it is!"

"Richard!" she gasped. "Oh, my dear, you might ha' been killed!"

"Ay, true, Ione, 'sfoot, 't is gospel true! But tush, girl!" he exclaimed with youthful ostentation. "We men reck nought o' wounds or death in Friendship's cause. Yet here's the wonder on 't, Ione; here's the marvel, — friend Jocelyn fought them off with a foil, — a *foil*, Ione!"

"Nay," said the Captain, frowning a little, "here was Florian! Moreover, a foil is none so bad weapon."

"No, no, Jocelyn," cried the boy in passion of hero-worship; "on my soul I vow the like was never seen, — that two, and one with blunt foil, should outfight four —"

"But who were they, these four?" demanded Ione. "What doth it all mean? Who should dare such outrage here at Aldrington?"

"Ha, death o' my life, this will I know!" cried the Earl and turning about, stood agape, for the wounded man was up and stealing where his horse grazed. But now came Will Thurlow, flourishing a long staff and behind him a motley crowd of grooms, gardeners and servants male and female.

"Yonder,— ha, yonder he goes!" cried the Earl, pointing them to the fugitive. "Ho, Will, Jenkin, Sam, seize me the villain!"

"Suffer he go, rather," said Jocelyn.

"Go?" cried the Earl. "Not so, man. There be dungeons i' the old tower and none to lock there these many years. 'Sdeath, the murderous dog shall lie there — "
And away sped my lord, flourishing the empty pistol and shouting commands to his people while Ione, looking after him with troubled eyes, questioned Jocelyn over her shoulder:

"These wicked wretches dared venture hither seeking you, Captain Dinwiddie?"

"Evidently, madam."

"Then you become a menace, sir. You bring these murderous villains upon you even here in our peaceful Aldrington! Ah, Richard might have been killed!"

"'T was possible, my lady."

"And such bold villains, sir, having dared such violence once and failed, may adventure here again."

"Not so, gracious lady," answered Florian, "we've sated them; they sha' n't return."

"And yet they might!" nodded Jocelyn.

"And next time," said Ione, her gaze still averted, "my brother might not prove so fortunate, sir. How think you of it?" Here she turned for his answer but in this moment rose sudden clamour where the fugitive was taken, and thither she sped, leaving the Captain to stare after her, smiling a little grimly. Hardly was she out of earshot than Florian spoke, his handsome face grave and anxious:

"Art much hurt, comrade?"

"Naught to matter, lad!" answered the Captain and

showed his left hand dripping scarlet from the wound that gashed his forearm. "Twist me somewhat about it; a strip from the cloak yonder shall serve."

"So, and now," said Florian, as he deftly performed the operation, "come you and suffer I bathe it."

"Nay, 't is well enough," answered Jocelyn, crossing to where lay his doublet. "Go saddle our horses and bring such of our gear as lieth to hand. I 'll wait i' the copse beyond the park, yonder. Dispatch!"

"What, do we march, Jocelyn? Are we for the world again?"

"Ay, faith!" nodded Jocelyn, frowning and thoughtful. "Yon sworders were Riderwood's bullies, I guess, and shall never be content with this one attempt on me. So am I a menace in very truth, Florian."

"'Las, comrade!" sighed Florian. "'T was easy work this, gentle haven to such as thou and I. Ah, well, 't is Fortune's cursed spite on thee, Jocelyn; 't is the old Dinwiddie ill luck!" So saying, he sighed again, smiled, shook his head and strode away.

Then Jocelyn, glancing round about him very wistfully, muttered a rolling Spanish imprecation, laughed fiercely and took his course by shady ways towards the green twilight of the little wood where as he knew was bowery track leading to a leafy bye-lane.

Within this pleasant shade he halted and, leaning against a tree, began to ponder once again the perverse Fate had dogged him all his stormy days, wondering, as he had done so often, why Fortune should frown so persistently, making his efforts of none avail, his hard life little more than vain labour and himself scarce better than a beggar.

Now as he stood thus, scowling at adjacent tree as it had been curst Fortune's very self, a sudden cry and snapping of twigs aroused him and glancing hitherward he saw a white-headed old creature come tumbling down the steep bank to lie a ragged, soft-whimpering heap. So thither went he to kneel and lift that silvery head, speaking cheerily:

"How now, mother, art hurt?" For a moment she lay mute and dazed and now, despite silvery hair and ragged clothes, he saw she was younger than he had deemed and very neat of person, though her face showed haggard and fierce. At last she opened great, dark eyes that stared wildly and espying his rich attire, snowy ruff and silken doublet, shrank as in sudden panic.

"Ah!" she gasped. "Ye be o' the great folk and I hates 'em all!" Then, as if stricken by new fear, the fierce eyes were abased, the angry voice was schooled to dolorous whine: "Oh, kind maister, noble gentleman, suffer I go . . . I meant no evil. I came but for to gather me simples and yarbs. Ah, sir, don't ha' me took and prisoned again."

"Prisoned?" he repeated. "Nay, be comforted, none shall harm thee, poor soul." And speaking, he began to stroke her abundant, snowy hair with his stained left hand; now espying this hand, she cried out as one amazed and clasped it in both her own, staring on it wide of eye.

"The red hand!" she whispered. "Aha, 't is the Hand o' Glory!"

"Nay," said he, with his whimsical smile, "gory were better word, methinks!"

"'T is hand I ha' seen in my dreams and visions, a hand strong to serve as shall make service a glory . . . so art thou come at last, noble sir!"

The Captain rubbed his square chin, eyeing her a little dubiously.

"The fall shook thee, mother, ha?" he questioned.

"Mother!" she repeated softly, and down her thin cheek rolled a great tear. "'Mother,' says you! Oh, blessed word! None ha' named me so since my poor Rose was took,—'mother' says you! So now, good young maister, I 'd give ee mother's blessing an' ye 'd suffer me."

"Troth," he answered, "no man ever lacked for blessing more than I," and he bowed his head to her touch, but even then she hesitated.

"Kind maister," she sighed, "I be poor old Robina; folk do call me a black witch, they curse me, they fears me."

"So do not I," he smiled and stooped head lower. And when she had touched and blessed him, whispering, he sat back, looking down on her with his kindly quizzical smile.

"Art most unwitchlike witch, methinks," said he.

"Ah, my lord," she whispered, "there do be a witch-craft white as well as black! . . . And, ay me, yonder do lie all my yarbs abroad!" And she pointed where lay a great basket, its contents scattered by her fall. "And I be none so spry these days, young maister, my j'ints be stiff-like since they tormented of me."

"Tormented thee, poor soul?"

"Ay, racked me, they did. They had me to Lewes and put me to the question for sorcery. They said as I over-looked Joe Marsh's child as was a cripple and died sudden, said as I ill-wished un, they did. At first I denied of it, but the pain — ay, me — the pain gotten so sharp I couldn't nowise abide it and said aught they willed. So they was a-going to burn me — "

"And who are 'they', mother?"

"God bless ee, sir! They was Master Denzil and Sir Thomas Vincent and Maister Morton and other o' the gentlefolks. But Master Roger Netherby o' Friarsdean, him as 't is thought shall wed the Lady Ione, according to the old lord's wish, Master Roger, God bless him, wouldn't nowise suffer it; offered to pay good money or fight 'em all for me, he did. So to-day I be alive, sir, and all along o' good, brave Master Roger."

"Hum!" quoth the Captain, tugging moustachio. "And prithee wherefore art called witch?"

"Alas, my good maister," cried she, with despairing ges-ture, "for that I be wise where most be fools. I needs must see where others do be blind. I can likewise read the old magic o' running water, the smoke o' the fire. I ha' charms agin the axey and plague. I can cure ye cowpox and the scab, — ay, all manner o' ills wi' my yarbs. I knows sum-mat about birds and beasts, but more — ah, a sight more about men and women, aha! There be hands and some faces, like books, do tell me things, — and so 't is they fears me and I must go lonesome all my days. . . . Tell me, kind young maister, be these proud Aldrington gentlefolk friends o' thine?"

"Ay, truly."

"Then list ye and mark, good sir! I' the black smoke and red fire I 've seen peril threat 'em, — i' the running water is sound o' bitter tears. This proud lady and noble earl be no more than two childer, lost — lost and following lure to their woeful destruction . . . wandering i' the dark wherein be hands do lead 'em, poor innocents, to shame and death. Oh, blind!"

"Nay now, good soul, what wild words be these?"

"Truth, maister, very truth o' God!"

"Then speak me plain, — what know ye?"

"So much I dassent tell it . . . and none to believe me save them as would burn me as witch. . . . Hearkee, some one comes!"

"Ay, I hear. Yet speak, mother, speak!"

"No, no, I must away afore I 'm took. Only this — stoop, maister, stoop closer! Watch ye the Tower Garden o' nights."

"The Tower Garden? How, then, you know the place?"

"Ay, maister. Years agone I was maid to my Lady Ione's mother. So I bids thee watch!" Then old Robina scrambled afoot, glanced fearfully round about and hobbling to her basket began to collect her scattered herbs therein, while Jocelyn sat watching and wondering how much of truth might be in her wild talk until, seeing what painful labour she made to fill her basket, he rose and began to aid her.

And it was now that my Lady Ione, having ordered her wind-blown vesture and perfectly regained her breath, thought proper to appear.

So, all unhurried and very stately, she stepped into the sunny glade and stood dumb and motionless as if amazed and shocked at sight of old Robina, who stood dumb-struck, white head abased and gnarled hands fluttering; as for the Captain, he went on gathering up the herbs.

"Heaven and the saints defend us!" exclaimed Ione at last, recoiling a step. "I find you in strange company, sir! Know you what manner and sort of creature this is?"

"Faith yes, madam," he nodded, still busy; "she is of the defenceless sort, a poor woman very vilely used."

"Not so, Captain Dinwiddie; she is a notorious witch and infamous malefactor used too well."

"And you are trampling the poor soul's herbs, lady!"

Ione frowned and snatched back her shapely foot as if the Captain had struck it.

"Woman," she cried, turning on old Robina in a fury, "have I not expressly forbid you hereabouts? Answer me!"

"Ay, my gracious lady!" answered the old woman, curtseying, "yet I did but venture for simples that do grow only hereabouts. . . . I meant no ill, lady. I be a-going."

"Why, then, I'll carry thy basket, mother," said the Captain, reaching for it. But old Robina backed away, smiling up at him, and her great eyes were very bright.

"Nay, my kind, good maister," she answered gently, but shaking white head with fierce, determined gesture, "my leddy yonder shall be needing of ee more nor I . . . for see, ma'm, see — he hath the Hand o' Glory! And oh, my Leddy Ione, beware o' them as rides by night! Shame! Death! The woeful end o' your noble house! Prison and a grave! Beware!" Then she lifted her cumbrous basket and with gesture that might have been blessing or a curse, limped painfully away.

# CHAPTER VIII

## CONCERNING THE RED HAND OF ALDRINGTON AND MR. ROLAND FANE

QUOTH Jocelyn, gazing after old Robina's bowed form:

"Dost know yon poor creature, I think."

"Indeed, for wicked hag and black witch!"

"Sayst thou?"

"Ay, I do, sir! She is notorious these many years for damned sorceress."

"Hum!"

"Never dare hum at me, sir! I say she is vile hag and yet you must name her 'mother' forsooth! Ah, fie shame on you!"

"Shame?" mused Jocelyn, rubbing shaven chin. "She spoke of shame and, moreover, of death — of destruction and of those that ride by night. Now whom should these be, I'm wondering? Ay and what — "

"'Tis . . . 'tis wild creature! A mad creature . . . a frantic wretch — " gasped Ione and he wondered to see her deep bosom so tempestuous and rich colour all fled.

"Why, it seems they tortured her," he answered gently, "racked and maimed her, poor soul, and this is apt to set reason and sanity tottering. I've known it so in bloody Flanders in Alva's time. . . . Yet prithee, why should poor, mad creature's raving drive the colour from your ladyship's cheek, set those pretty hands ashake? Thou art the proud Ione, Lady Fane, of great and noble family; what may touch thee?"

"Nothing!" she cried, lovely head up-thrown. "Ah — nothing!" But, speaking, she turned her back on him and coming to a tree, leaned there, while Jocelyn viewed that shapely, drooping back with looks of anxious perplexity. Then she turned and taking off the rustic hat she wore, fanned herself therewith.

"The sun's so hot!" she sighed. "And plagues me vilely. And now let us go; Richard waits you."

"But then, madam, I wait here for my comrade Florian. And I had liefer bid my lord farewell by proxy. I beg your ladyship therefore tell him I — "

"Now what idle talk is this of farewell? You babble, sir! And Richard shall be in fury of impatience, — come!"

"But your ladyship must be pleased to remember how — "

"Oh, Captain Dinwiddie — tush!"

"How your ladyship hath discovered me for something of a menace — "

"Enough, sir!"

"As indeed I truly am, 't would seem. And thus I would but remove this peril, according to your ladyship's will."

"Then my ladyship wills ye remain, sir. And what's more, my ladyship commands — "

The imperious words ended in a gasp and she stood gazing at his stained left hand with expression of such fearful amazement that he glanced at it also.

"The Red Hand!" whispered Ione. "So this — this is what she meant! Said she . . . did old Robina tell you aught of the Aldrington legend?"

"Madam," he answered, shaking his head, "here's riddlesome talk beyond my wit. This hand o' mine showeth red for that, being mere human, an' steel insinuate, I must needs bleed."

"So then you were hurt? Show me! Come you and have it tended. . . . How, sir, do you hesitate? Will you gainsay me? What then, must I be humble to beg, sue, lead, supplicate and entreat your High Mightiness not to be gone? Must I kneel and implore you remain here at Aldrington? So then, behold me, sir!" And speaking, she was on her knees before him, had caught his stained hand, folding it between her soft palms as one who swore the ancient fealty oath; then, while he stood amazed beyond all speech, she rose, viewing him with her stateliest air.

"Well, sir, is 't enough?" she demanded. "Is your stubborn pride sufficient soothed?"

"'Slife, madam, I 'm all bewildered!" he answered, shaking his head in frowning perplexity. "I grope for the wherefore of such unnatural humility! What magic is there in all creation to bring such arrogant lady to her proud knees?"

"Her own will, sir, mayhap."

"So am I very fain to know this legend of Aldrington, this tale of a Red Hand, for of a truth—" he paused and turned as towards them through the little wood rode a handsome, smiling personage, nobly mounted, gaily clad, a gentleman rubicund and jovial, whose comely features were adorned by small moustachio and little dainty beard trimmed in the latest mode and so youthfully golden as made his heavy brows and deep-set eyes the older by contrast (or, at least, so thought the Captain).

Beholding Ione, this gay and sprightly gentleman was off his horse, had doffed plumed bonnet, bowed, caught her hand, kissed it, all in as many moments.

"Sweet coz," cried he in aggressive ecstasy, "by Venus her downy doves, I swear the passing days but perfect thee; thou 'rt a delight to the eyes, a vision delectable, a very joy!"

"And thou 'rt merry and fulsome as ever, cousin!" she laughed, freeing her hand from his lingering clasp. "Captain Dinwiddie, here stands Richard's and my only living relative and kinsman—our cousin, Roland Fane."

"Your servant, Mr. Fane!" said the Captain and bowed, keeping his stained hand out of sight.

"Yours devotedly, sir!" cried Mr. Fane and flourished. "You are strange to Aldrington, I think, Captain?"

"I am, sir."

"But here to bide a while, I trust, sir?"

"Indeed, cousin," answered Ione, "the Captain is Rick's friend and is with us for so long as he will."

"Oh, excellent, i' faith! Captain, I shall ha' the joy to know you ever better, I hope."

Again the Captain bowed to Mr. Fane's smiling flourish.

"Ione, fair coz, I saw good friend o' thine but yesternight, poor Roger Netherby, to wit — "

"And wherefore 'poor', Roland?"

"Why ha' n't you heard, child? Marry now, I thought 't was common bruit. The reckless fellow hath affronted the whole bench o' magistrates i' the matter of Robina Shaw, the curst witch. 'S body, he hath set all the neighbouring gentry by the ears, he hath so, i' faith! He proffered to fight each or all on her behalf, this black beldam! Gad's my life! Tom Vincent would ha' taken him up but for his green wound — "

"Dost tell me Sir Thomas is wounded? Why, how come this?"

"The tale is he was beset by divers rogues and swinged 'em roundly, I hear. But for thy Roger, coz, 't is a bullheaded lad, poor Roger that must some day be thine own Roger — eh, my Ione?"

"Here's idle gossip, Roland."

"Nay, but, sweet soul, are ye not good as contracted each to other? Did not your several fathers agree the match, you to wed Roger and Roger you — ha?"

"This was years agone and we but children."

"Yet I'll be sworn Roger yearns to hold thee to 't, ay, he hankers for thee, coz, sighs for thy beauties e'en among his pigs and cows, a fervent swain though bucolic — and determined — "

"Nay, I'll vow Roger is a true gentleman as any and a comely — "

"Ha, verily, verily, my Ione, a rustical Apollo he, yet fearful wooer, poor laggard lover that would yet dare not . . . and thyself such peerless creature conformed of such warm lovelihood that by Venus her girdle I vow and swear myself thy veriest slave adoring and — "

"Fiddle-de-dee!" she mocked. "Sure 't was not to prate me such folly you rode hither."

"Sweet coz, upon my life it was to drink me in eye draughts of thy beauty, to quaff thee till my senses reel—"

"And quaff wine with Richard between whiles—eh, Roland?"

"This too!" he laughed, kissing her hand again. "All the neighbourhood shall flock to greet him anon and I'd be first. Come, prithee let's to the dear lad forthright."

So, bridle on arm and full of jovial talk and laughter, this cheery gentleman strolled between them.

"Are you from London lately, Captain Dinwiddie?"

"Yes, Mr. Fane."

"Were you at Court?"

"Not I, sir. And you?"

"No, no, Captain, faith, no! A simple country gentleman I, a soul, sir, plagued with ambitions none, content to sit and watch this waggish world wag."

"'T is to be hoped it waggeth to your pleasure more than to mine, sir."

Now at this, Mr. Fane glanced up, sudden yet askance, and, meeting Jocelyn's serene, grey eye, answered impulsively:

"Supposing it doth not?"

"Why then," answered Jocelyn, his dreaming gaze now on the distance, "there be some that, by wag o' tongue or pen, may contrive this world shall to their own purpose wag. So, an' it wag to our disfavour, let us submissive wag with it or—see it wag for us."

"O' my soul now," laughed Ione, "an' the poor world must wag as wag your tongues, it shall wag itself weary, sirs!"

"Faith and troth, sweet coz!" laughed Mr. Fane a little boisterously, "I do protest your Captain is right philosopher, a pretty wit keen as his sword. A man of parts! A creature of sentiment, ha?"

"More," she answered, "more, an infinite deal, cousin, yet all's explained in this—he is Dinwiddie!"

And presently, coming forth of the wood, they beheld across broad, undulating park and far-flung blooming gardens the great house of Aldrington throned majestic on its three terraces,—gable and chimney, battlement, turret and the age-old, war-scarred tower, this house that had grown with succeeding generations from grim stronghold to stately home.

Mr. Fane halted and reached out a long arm.

"Aldrington Chase!" he murmured and his voice was no longer jovial.

"And yonder is Richard in the bowling alley with Mr. Ferndale," said Ione. "Come, let us join them."

So they went on again, Mr. Fane very joyfully eager for a game.

"And what think you of Aldrington, sir Captain?" he enquired gaily.

"That 't is right noble heritage, sir," answered Jocelyn, looking from this splendour to his questioner's so youthful-seeming, smiling face; "indeed so rich, so glorious that to possess it some men might peril their very souls."

"God's life!" exclaimed Mr. Fane, staring back at him beneath lifted brows; then he laughed and caressed his little, golden beard with long, white fingers, but the eyes of him, glancing askew, seemed older than ever (or so thought Jocelyn).

# CHAPTER IX

## DEALS, AMONG MORE IMPORTANT MATTERS, WITH A POETIC CAMPAIGN

MASTER RICKABY, High Steward of my lord's great house-hold, was in his glory, for to-day being the young Earl's birthday, the neighbouring gentry, more especially such as were blessed with marriageable daughters, had come flocking to wish him joy and bid him welcome home. Thus, resplendent in black velvet, with gold-tipped wand and chain of office and backed by gentlemen ushers and liveried serving men, Master Rickaby stood forth to welcome my lord's guests, regulating the depth of his bow according to the rank and status of each visitor, — a gracious nod to an esquire, a bow for a knight, a humble obeisance for a lord; yet to none did he bend supple back so profoundly as to handsome, smiling Mr. Fane (or at least so thought Jocelyn).

Therefore, amid the ever-moving splendour of raiment, swirling cloak and nodding feather, Jocelyn's keen gaze, roving here and there, never lost the flutter of Mr. Fane's velvet cloak, a very conspicuous adornment, high-collared and short, according to the latest mode, of a rich plum colour and adorned with much gold bullion.

So the great courtyard of Aldrington Chase rang to the clack of horse hoofs, it echoed to manly voices and feminine chatter and laughter; the wide lawns were athrong with radiant company, dainty visions in stomacher and farthingale who smiled and curtsied, splendid creatures be-jewelled and feathered, in starched ruffs, slashed doub-lets and padded trunks, who bowed and strutted, — all hither come to pay due homage to young Richard the Earl who smiled and bowed, yearning meanwhile for hawk and hound, laughed and talked and, between times, muttered peevish asides to Jocelyn.

Came old Sir John Clayton with his three ripe and dimpled daughters (riding demurely pillion); came my Lady Golightly (gallantly mounted and with four burly retainers to guard her lovely person on the road; came (as hath been said) Mr. Roland Fane, smiling and aggressively jovial as ever and with him Sir Thomas Vincent, stalking vainglorious, his wounded arm conspicuous in silken sling.

"Wounded, my lord? Ay, faith and small wonder!" quoth he, full-throated. "And 's bones, Dick, 't was rare, — two swashbuckling rogues curst ferocious! Yet I with-stood 'em, ay, marry did I, — with mandritta and rinversa, sa-ha! A tit for their tat! I invested with my imbrocata Italianata, 't is thrust I must learn thee, Richard — "

Thus much the Captain heard and edged tenderly forth of the glittering company and got him by yew-shaded allies to the seclusion of the Tower Garden, where rose the mas-sive, time-worn, battle-scarred keep throned upon its three broad terraces. And here, seated in remote shady corner, he took from his bosom a small volume and began to read.

But his glance often wandered from the page and always in the one direction, and thus he presently espied that he looked for, — the flutter of plum-coloured velvet, and part-ing the ivy stems, beheld Mr. Fane with the Steward ap-proaching on the terrace immediately below; and Mr. Fane, no longer smiling, seemed almost petulant.

"From London, — psha, this I know, man! But ha' they no papers among their baggage?"

"None, sir, none! And little enow o' baggage for gentles of condition!"

"Well, time will show!" murmured Mr. Fane, seating himself gracefully on the marble bench directly beneath the Captain's happily chosen lurking place. "Now for the paper, Rickaby . . . on his pillow, mind, where it shall not 'scape his eye!"

"Trust me for this, sir!"

"I do, Rickaby, I do, and shall not forget thee when

dawns the day and Fortune's sun change all the world — "

"Hist, sir! Hither cometh Sir Thomas . . . see, he wafts you. By your leave, I'll away to my duties, sir."

"Ay, so, Rickaby, and forget not the paper!" The Steward bowed and departed in the one direction as Sir Thomas Vincent, flushed and scowling, came striding from the other:

"Ha, Roland," cried he angrily. "I can learn naught o' the reason for his so sudden return, this flight from London! And no word from Riderwood! Is aught amiss, think ye?"

"Softly, my Thomas, softly!" sighed Mr. Fane, selecting a comfit from small, bejewelled box. "No news is good news, — in especial for such bold schemer as thyself — "

"Nay, but what o' yourself, Roland? You are pledged deep as any."

"Ay, but — merely to such small matters as but affect mine own humble concerns, Tom."

"You, why plague on 't, Roland, yourself was in 't long afore me!"

Having masticated his comfit daintily but with great apparent relish, Mr. Fane sighed gently and shook his comely head.

"No, no, Tom!" he murmured. "My interest was, and is, but in mine own affairs, no more, let prove other that can! England may be Catholic or Protestant — all's one to me, so Fortune on me smile. But enough o' this, Tom; tell me rather how speeds thy wooing o' my fair coz?"

"'Sdeath, I cannot tell!" growled Sir Thomas. "She's so curst capricious — and score o' gallants a-dangle e'en now! I left Phil Drayton sighing his poetry at her, and young Chantrey . . . and Felton . . . and divers others making sheep's-eyes."

"Tush! What matter for these since the valiant Robin holds aloof? Robin Netherby is thy chiefest rival, Tom."

"And yourself, Roland! You are forever at her beck — "

"Nay, I'm but her humble cousin. But Robin, by parental mandate, is her chosen swain, happy Roger!"

"A damned heretic dog!"

"Ay, true alas! And he defied thee, Tom! Thyself and all our worthy justices in matter of the witch,—flouted thy magnificence, Tom, hand on tuck—ha?"

"I'll have his blood for't yet!"

"And yon same witch, this hag Robina Shaw, is spy, as I hear, a creeping danger—"

"She shall be dealt with anon!" quoth Sir Thomas, rising. "Meantime, I'm for my lord's sherris sack."

"Have with thee, Tom!" cried Mr. Fane joyously, rising also.

For some while after these gentlemen had sauntered away, Jocelyn sat staring before him very pensively at nothing in particular; at last he too arose and, still avoiding the merry concourse, wandered away to the distant rose garden. Here, seated within the shady arbour, he opened his book again but instead of reading fell to new perplexity of thought, until a shadow fell across the page and, glancing up, he beheld Ione.

"Good Master Disdain," said she, curling red lip at him, "why must you steal away from us and our company? O' my life, sir, I marvel at your so great discourtesy!"

"And I, madam," he retorted, rising to bow, "I marvel how your ladyship should miss me so soon among so many." Ione stared, caught her breath in a little hiss, flushed, frowned, laughed suddenly and, sitting down, beckoned him beside her.

"Oh, sir," she sighed, yet with vivid lips upcurving, "how, a Fortune's name, may I help miss Nature's Paragon, Creation's Wonder—Dinwiddie—how? And yet, Sir Human Perfection, this flouting of our company—fie! There be ladies yonder with charms to allure any mere man. Yet you, being superman, do flee them for your own exalted company."

"And kindly Dan Chaucer," he answered, patting the book upon his knee.

"Dost rather choose musty old book to glad young beauty?"

"I' faith, my Lady Ione, I'm no squire o' dames and am grown beyond youthful dalliance, alas!"

"Hoary ancient, your pardon! But since poor creation feminine lures thee not, how of thine own nobler, lordly sex? Yon gentlemen now, see you nought in any to attract the so lofty Dinwiddie soul?"

"Yea, verily," he nodded, "their beards, my lady, their beards! Ne'er saw I rarer show, for here be beards of every sort and fashion, from spade to dagger and so artfully pruned I'm minded to attempt one myself."

"Never dare!" cried she, in mock alarm. "Indeed, you might show braver clean-shaven, methinks you should seem, perchance, something less grimly and——" She paused suddenly as into this wide pleasaunce paced a disconsolate figure, a tall, very shapely young gentleman, somewhat dusty from hard riding, who reaching the sundial, leaned there dejectedly, his wistful gaze upon the distant, joyfully clamourous company and who, wholly unaware of the bright eyes that watched him from the vine-bowered arbour, presently went wandering forlornly away.

"Saw you ever such rueful visage, sir?" laughed Ione. "I pray you who is the woeful gentleman?"

"Why, who but Robin, Mr. Netherby of Friar's Dene."

"So then do I give you joy, madam, right heartily."

"Oh, Sir Captain! And wherefore?"

"In that I read him for goodly gentleman and what's more, God wot, a very man!"

"Well, and what is this to me?"

"Much, lady, much—since he is thy predestined spouse."

"Enough, sir! 'T is idle chatter; I say 't is foolish gossip!"

"Yet 't was told me i' thy presence by Mr. Fane——"

"Roland is gossiping fool."

"Love you not this fair gentleman, my Lady Ione?"

"I love no man!"

"Ha!" murmured Jocelyn, pulling at moustachio.

"Nor ever shall!"

"Hum!" quoth Jocelyn, whereat my lady frowned at him.

"And now, sir," she demanded, "'stead of moaning at me, pray speak your meaning in fashion humanly. I say I love no man nor ever shall, the which sets you a-humming, and wherefore?"

"For that thou art so aptly fashioned to wifehood, and being by thy sire ordained to wed, wedlock becometh thy bounden duty——"

"Oh?" she mocked. "And what of love? It ne'er hath touched me and pray the holy saints it never may; 'tis a folly——"

"Hold, madam, flout it not lest it prove tyrant to trample thy pride, a giant to bear thee whereso he will. For love is of thee, in thee and waiteth sleeping but to wake soon!"

"Sayst thou, Sir Wisdom?" she laughed; and then, to flout his gravity, "Ha!" she mocked, pulling imaginary moustachio at him, "Hum! And since my love sleepeth so sound, think you Robin Netherby the man to wake it? See where he comes again, blind as bat and still i' the doleful dump!"

"'Tis comely gentleman, madam, and his countenance the very map of pensive lover."

"Why truly, 'tis a good soul, Robin," she nodded.

"'Tis a bold and honest, yet—simple."

'And only the great dare be simple," answered Jocelyn, watching where young Mr. Netherby wandered forlornly and so lost in dejection he would have passed them by had not Jocelyn hemmed loudly, whereat he glanced about and espying Ione in the arbour, bared his curly head and came glad-eyed and with great strides.

"Ione!" he exclaimed. "Dear my lady . . . " and stood dumb, twisting feathered hat in nervous hands while his honest, brown eyes looked the adoration he had no power to utter.

"Why, Robin!" she exclaimed, giving him her hands, "be welcome! Captain Dinwiddie, this is our good friend and neighbour, Mr. Netherby of Friar's Dene."

The young squire turned, and meeting his eager look, Jocelyn, wise in men, smiled and reached out his hand to have it gripped right heartily.

"Good faith!" exclaimed my lady, glancing from one to other beneath raised brows, "'t is like the meeting of old friends long lost."

"Yea, verily," answered Robin, flushing youthfully, "for my own part, at the least, 't is strangely joyous meeting, since I am one, God wot, that seems denied the power of making friends."

"And yet," said Jocelyn, "friendship may be born in a moment and, like love itself, for some reason that soareth high 'bove cold reason. I' faith, the best o' life cometh ofttimes all unsought."

"And thus saith Dinwiddie!" mocked my lady. "The veriest pedantical, pragmatical soldier that ever followed drum, and something mopish and solitary like thyself, Robin, so here 's a like should like thee well. Therefore be seated, most misanthropic gentlemen and, cheek by jowl, pragmatize upon the pros and cons o' life, rail upon the world and all in 't save your two noble selves. As for me, I 'll to my guests. Never look so disconsolate, Robin, bide till yon noisy company be gone, and sup with us. Meanwhile, here is Captain Dinwiddie a sage philosopher that preacheth better than any soldier I ever heard on, so Robin, an' you be doleful as you look, shalt find him passionate to comfort, counsel and advise thee."

"And, your ladyship," retorted Jocelyn, with profound obeisance, "I am bold to aver that should Mr. Netherby stoop to act on my poor advice, your ladyship shall call him husband within the year."

"How — how now?" she cried with sudden gasp. "Dare ye so presume? Are you Providence to thus dispose of me?"

"Fie, no, madam!" he answered, gently reproving. "I

am merely Dinwiddie, yet of Providence the humble instrument to achieve your father's will, mayhap."

My lady stared into the speaker's wistful grey eyes and, finding speech wholly inadequate, gnashed white teeth at him and swept away. Then Jocelyn, bowing to Mr. Netherby, sat down; and Mr. Netherby, returning the bow, sat down also and both very pensive and silent. But when Mr. Netherby had gazed a while on vacancy, sighing deep and oft, he spoke. Quoth he:

"Captain, 't is my hope we may indeed be friends, and my name is Robin."

Answered the Captain: "Robin, thy hope is mine; pray call me Jocelyn."

"Then Jocelyn, thy words, though well and kindly meant, have but angered her against me, I fear."

"The which is very well, Robin. For I have heard — better a woman's anger, scorn, nay hate itself than cold indifference. Now since in this great Circle of Life extremes must needs meet, hate shall be kin to love, anger to gentleness, cruelty to pity. Here's truth methinks should cheer and bring mighty solace."

Mr. Netherby uttered a sigh very like a groan.

"She is so beautiful!" he mourned, "so rich, and all the world to woo her, — why should she return my poor love?"

"For that love, properly managed, Robin, begetteth love."

"And 't was our several fathers' will we should wed."

"Then why not do so, like dutiful son?"

"Why not — ?" Mr. Netherby stared his amazement.

"Yea, faith, what's to let or stay you?"

"Alas, a thousand things!"

"Yet chiefest o' these is Robin, Robin! Ay, thy very self. Thou dost suffer Dare-I to wait upon I-Will."

Mr. Netherby sprang afoot, frowned, sighed and sat down again.

"'Slife, 't was very truth!" he nodded gloomily. "And here's my reason, friend Jocelyn. She is of the Old Religion and I am Protestant, so it is she scorneth me for heretic."

"Hum!" quoth Jocelyn. "And there be many proud Catholic families in this South Country — ha?"

"Ay, verily!" nodded the young squire, frowning. "I am flouted and named 'puritan' — behind my back."

"By such silken rufflers as, let us say, Sir Thomas Vincent."

"That same! Jocelyn, 't is a gag-tooth braggart must cross steel with me so soon as his arm be sound."

"And he wooeth my Lady Ione!"

"Ay — until he prove fit to twirl rapier, then his wooing shall end one way or tother."

"To-day, Robin, there met me a witch hight Robina Shaw."

"That I 'll swear is no witch, Jocelyn, but woman rarely gifted; man, I 've known her all my days."

"She told me how you saved her from dire harms by proffer o' gold or steel, the which maketh me glad o' your friendship, Robin. She also spake me dark warnings of danger threatening these Aldringtons. Know you of any such lurking peril?"

"Nothing!" answered Robin, his brow dark with quick perplexity. "Nought i' the world . . . except — "

"Ay, — except?"

"These late penal laws 'gainst the Catholics, forbidding Mass and the harbouring of priests. Yet here in our good South Country these laws bear but lightly, more especially on proud and noble family of such oft-proven loyalty as the Aldringtons."

"Hum!" quoth Jocelyn again. "This breedeth yet other question, Robin, to wit — the Aldrington Legend of the Red Hand, know you aught of it?"

"That do I; 't is famous hereabouts. This Red Hand is in the Aldrington escutcheon; some do name it the Bloody Hand of Glory, for 't was won in the Crusades by an Aldrington that lost his hand saving the life of King Richard. The story goeth that if the Bloody Hand appear in dream or vision, it bodeth ill for the family, an evil only to be averted by some penance or act of humility, and the Aldringtons were ever mightily proud . . . and to-day proudest of them all, I'll vow, is Ione, more especially to me, and 't is this puts me to such small hope o' my wooing — "

"Pluck up thy heart, man; she is woman and therefore to be won."

"Ay, but there be so many others a-trying, Jocelyn, and —'sdeath, yonder is one o' them, a wooer the most persistent he . . . Philip Drayton of Shalmeston. See, yonder they go!" Glancing whither his companion directed, Jocelyn beheld my lady walking very slowly beside a youngish gentleman rich, though soberly clad, whose stately head was bowed over a sheet of fair paper.

"Look now, mark him, Jocelyn, — devil seize him, he woos her before my very eyes."

"Nay, surely he reads a letter."

"Not so," sighed Robin. "'T is yet another of his odes, plague on 'em! 'T is some new sonnet he hath writ to her and thus he woos, for 't is well known she dotes on poesy."

"Aha, sayst thou, Robin?"

"Ay, faith, and thus he poetizes her whenso he may."

"Why then, my Robin, thou must out-poetize the gentleman."

"I?" exclaimed Robin, in dreary amaze. "Good lack, Jocelyn, I'm merest fool with a pen. I know more o' breeding horses and cattle than stringing verses, and there's the woeful truth on 't."

"Hast ever tried, Robin?"

"Once!" confessed the young squire, a little guiltily. "Only once! For she read me some ode Drayton had made to her eyes, and very indifferent I thought it yet she so mightily pleased thereat, seest thou, that I must needs fall too, plaguing my wits to pleasure her in like fashion, — and all to no purpose for, and spite of all my labour, I could never achieve more than poor couplet."

"Then prithee, Rob, since we are friends, speak me this couplet." Mr. Netherby flushed, scowled at his dusty riding boots, fumbled with his sword hilt and fixing his honest, brown eyes on remote distances, spoke, somewhat mumbling:

> "'Oh, eyes divine, wherein I see
> All that I hope and fain would be
> Bright stars —'

— and there I got me bogged, Jocelyn, stuck beyond hope!"

"Why now, this promiseth!" nodded the Captain, tugging at moustachio. "My friend it doth so. We should make somewhat o' this betwixt us. Let us endeavour it." And taking forth his tablets, he scribbled hastily, frowned, shook his head dubiously and recited thus:

> "'Oh, eyes divine, wherein I see
> All that I hope and fain would be
> Thy light doth glad this world for me,
> Oh, eyes divine.'"

"How think you of this, Robin?"

"Gad's my life, 't is like art magic! Those two lines cost me an infinity of painful labour, and by Heaven, you rhyme to them in the blink of an eye."

"Hum!" quoth Jocelyn. "This my line marcheth something heavily, yet with two more cantos it should serve. Zounds, Rob-man, but we'll out-versify yon poetical gentleman betwixt us. Her ladyship shall be bombarded with ode and sonnet, — by the week, the day, the hour, an' ye will." The young squire shook his head dismally.

"I take it mighty friendly in thee, Jocelyn, but 't would be deceiving her; moreover she'd find me out and —" he stopped, for his roving gaze had lighted upon Ione and her companion now seated afar, Sir Philip still intent on his reading, she leaning near like one entranced.

"A murrain on the fellow!" sighed Robin. "See how she hangs upon his words!"

"Thus shall she hang on thine, Rob."

"Then, by heaven, we'll do it! How can we contrive? And yet 't will be a cheat! And yet to good purpose! And yet again —"

"Now, hearkee Robin, in the duello, as dost know, 't is become the polite fashion that seconds fight beside their principal. So in this I am thy second, but 'stead o' murderous steel, grasp gentle quill in this behalf. If thy lady yearn for sonnets she shall ha' them, and thyself copy and get them by heart; thus, should she question thee, shalt be at no loss — how now, why dost scowl, prithee?"

"Yonder's my reason, Jocelyn, yon strutting complacency."

"Sir Thomas Vincent?"

"No, no, he's but a vain braggart; I mean yon smiling thing in his peascod-bellied doublet and vasty Spanish ruff — Roland Fane."

"Why, 't is a gentle, simple soul, a kindly philosopher, he."

"Ha! Dost think so, Jocelyn?"

"Hum!" quoth the Captain. "The gentleman told me thus much himself."

"And you believed him?"

"No more than methought necessary. You know him well, Robin?"

"These many years, — moreover, we are near neighbors."

"Is he Catholic, as seems the fashion hereabouts?"

"He was, and may be again, should the wind change and blow that way."

"'T will never change whiles Elizabeth rule."

"Ay, but she may die . . . "

Jocelyn glanced askance at the speaker with look suddenly alert and grim, a long, searching look, while young Robin, wholly unaware of this keen scrutiny, stared dreamily across the sunny garden. And now it was that my lady, having rid herself artfully of Sir Philip Drayton, crept soft-footed towards this bowery arbour and was about to surprise these two very grave and silent gentlemen with some laughing allusion to their portentous solemnity when she halted and stood rigid, breath in check, as the Captain spoke, his gentle voice softer than usual:

"Dost mean by murder, Robin?" The young squire started about, his eyes wide with horror:

"No!" he gasped. "By God — no!"

"And yet," nodded Jocelyn grimly, "the Queen may die so. Indeed, 't is very like, for there is a little man in Spain would have her dead this moment and hath offered large bribes for her killing, as he did for the murder of the Prince of Orange, God rest him! And if she die, we Protestants die with her, and this our England must writhe in blood 'neath the merciless heel of Spain, a second Netherlands, and I 've seen, ay, these many years, the bloody shambles Philip hath made there."

"God forbid!" exclaimed Robin fervently.

"The Queen's life is our one bulwark 'gainst Papistry with Philip and all his devilish powers behind. To-day, thank God, we are the freest people in all the world; so must the Queen live, lest England become a Spanish province and our freedom die. Ay, the Queen must live, but death, in divers stealthy shapes, hath been very near her and — hearkee, Robin, I tell thee this, Murder creepeth in her footsteps even now."

"Why then, God save her!"

"And her Majesty shall soon come South, Robin!"

"To — Sussex?"

"To Aldrington, mayhap."

"And why here, Jocelyn, why, o' God's name?"

"Wherefore not? Know you aught of peril for her hereabouts?"

"No, no, Heaven forbid! 'T is but that — there be many families of the Old Religion — very stubborn — very proud . . ."

"The Aldringtons?"

"Nay, Richard is no Recusant; he 's loyal, heart and soul, I 'll be sworne . . ."

"And her ladyship?"

"Why, 't is no more than pride with her, Jocelyn, — a tameless valiance of spirit. If — if therefore she speaks something wildly 'gainst the persecution of Jesuit priests or the Queen of Scots her 'prisonment — heed her not, seem deaf."

"Faith, Robin, no creature can be deafer than I."

"But, God's death, man . . . you'll never doubt her loyalty?"

"Never i' the world, lad. I do but fear lest her proud spirit be cozened by the artifice o' cunning roguery and used to her own dire peril. So now to bind and hallow our new-found friendship, let us take oath, here upon my dagger, that as we will spend our blood gladly to protect the Queen, so will we also shield this wilful lady from her own rashness, an' need be —"

Here, with swirl of silken draperies, Ione was fronting them, a creature tempestuous.

"Oh, gramercy for nothing, sirs!" she exclaimed scornfully. "For hear me proclaim the 'prisoning of Mary Queen of Scots is shameful injustice and the killing of our priests, those holy martyrs, is wicked murder —"

"Ione!" cried Robin, leaping afoot. "Hush thee, for God's sake! 'T is treason, should any hear — 't is death!"

"Nay," said Jocelyn, rising also, "here is no more than worthy evidence of a ladylike spleen —"

"Be silent, sir!" she cried, "I fear no one and care no whit who hears me, no, not even the Queen's Majesty herself. I am a Fane of Aldrington, as English as this earth I stand on; loyalty is in my blood. So, an' the Queen honour us here, I shall make my reverence — no matter what my heart shall say." Then she turned and swept away, leaving Jocelyn very thoughtful and Robin more woebegone than ever.

# CHAPTER X

## TELLETH HOW THE EARL DREW SWORD, AND HOW CAPTAIN JOCELYN USED IT

On sunny morning Jocelyn sat beneath a tree in the orchard writing busily, though, ever and anon, he lifted abstracted gaze to the blue sky, for he was in the throes of composition. From this poetic absorption he was roused by the rhythmic jingle of spurs where, light-treading despite long riding boots, came Florian, joyous as the morning. Quoth he:

"How then, art alone, comrade?"

"I was!" sighed Jocelyn mournfully.

"Yet I'll be sworn my Lady Ione came hitherwards a while since."

"Not here, why should she?"

"Well, she's forever a-seeking thee on some pretext or other."

"Well, I am her hired servant."

"Ha, cogsnails — yet might be her lord and ha' done with perils and hardships forever were you any other than — Dinwiddie!"

"Florian, lad, you talk like crass fool!"

"Ay, belike I do, for thou 'rt such contrary soul, Jocelyn, spending thyself to another's profit and the mending of any one's fortunes, all heedless of thine own. But thus it is I love thee, man! Verily in all this world is but one Dinwiddie that must serve, aid, comfort and fight for all grievous humanity — save only Dinwiddie, and here he sits patiently awaiting peevish lad that will not come!" And Florian motioned towards the pair of foils that leaned to hand against adjacent tree.

"Ha, my lord will not come, sayst thou?"

"Not he, faith! He's in's tantrums again this morning, oh, a mighty taking! He was foxed again last night, you'll mind. Rickaby tells me he hath knocked down one of the footmen, blooded his poll with a stool, kicked his dogs damnably, and cursed his sister so roundly that my lady, so saith Rickaby, cursed him back, and so left him silenced yet more furious than ever."

"Then must I presently go fetch him," sighed Jocelyn, glancing down at his tablets.

"And 'sheart, there's none but you can do't, *camarada*."

"Whither ride you thus early, Florian?"

"Hither and yon, *amigo* — "

"The 'Peck o' Malt', ha? To drink yet another stoup of ale with John Bly, eh, lad?"

"I'll not deny it," answered Florian, reddening.

"And how of this maid, this Cecily? 'T is young creature — "

"Neither am I a Methuselah, *amigo*."

"And she is beside, as I judge, innocent, Florian."

"As a flower, I'll warrant her . . . and, God forgive me, I — "

"Might be worse, lad, God wot! We ha' lived wild, thou and I, — camp and leaguer, a ravaged country, flaming towns and a starving people; here's an evil nursery for youth! Ay, you might be worse. Go, get thee to thine Innocent and let thy past be an armour to her purity."

"God love thee, Jocelyn, and so it shall — "

"But, 'swounds, lad! Why must ye ride so heavily armed?" For besides rapier and dagger, Florian bore two heavy pistols.

"Eyes, Jocelyn!" he laughed. "Aha, there be eyes that watch amid the green. Thrice o' late I've been pried on by lurkers in hedge and thicket."

"Sayst thou?"

"Ay, do I! Yesterday I spurred me sudden into the woods that border the road where it narrows twixt here and South Dene, yet saw no one, though sure am I these same rogues lurked therein. Now Jocelyn, 't is my belief these be Riderwood's bullies waiting chance at thee, a crossbow bolt to slay thee silently, a shot from petronel or caliver,—watching and waiting for thee, *amigo*."

"Why then, they shall wait, lad, for I budge not hence yet awhile. Meantime I lack a rhyme to the word, 'fiery'—"

"Nay, Jocelyn, cock's body, man, be serious! Howbeit to-day I 'll prove these stealthy villains, who and what they are."

"As how, prithee?"

"Marry, comrade, by strategy, but mum for this! Also I 'm pledged to dine with Robin Netherby at Friars' Dean beyond Hoove."

"Why then, bear him this!" said Jocelyn, drawing a packet from his doublet. "Say I hope to see him here anon. 'T is goodly gentleman, ha?"

"Of a truth, comrade, a stout, hearty fellow is Robin, though something indifferent at play o' rapier and dagger."

"Thou canst amend this, my Florian."

"Ay, troth! I go to hold a veney or so this morning."

"Then I 'll with thee so far as the house," said the Captain, putting away his tablets. "I 'll go reason with my Lord Richard." But hardly was he afoot than was distant baying of hounds from the stable yard and the young Earl appeared with two or three of his favourite dogs leaping and barking joyfully about him; but, halting suddenly, he turned and lashed at them savagely with the whip he bore, until they cowered yelping beneath the cruel blows and finally sped away, howling dismally. Then my lord came on again. He was clad for the road, splendid with silk and velvet, in bonnet bejewelled and feathered, in gold-spurred riding boots of perfumed leather; the rapier at his hip sparkled with gems and a great pearl adorned one ear, —a slim, radiant young figure marred by sullen visage.

So came he sauntering into the orchard and meeting Jocelyn's questioning look, scowled blackly in return, tossing aside his whip with a muttered imprecation; whereat

Florian winked askance, bowed with an airy grace and sped away joyous as ever.

"Well?" demanded my lord, scowling on the Captain, haughty and arrogant. "Well, I say?"

"No!" answered Jocelyn, "ill, my lord, vastly ill, by the looks o' you!"

"Ill, quotha — ill, forsooth?" cried the Earl, a little wildly. "Have you forgot who I am?"

"Nay, faith, sir, I know you for pettish boy, a sorry youth that God, for some strange whim, hath set very high i' the world with a great heritage, much wealth and vasty power for good and ill. But my lord, since so much is given you, much shall be expected of you. Thus, being so great a lord, strive to be better thing — a man of great life and worthy deeds — "

"Ha' done!" cried the Earl, in sudden frenzy. "Prate me no more; you shall preach and flout me no more. I say be silent! Ha, malediction! Am I not master here?"

"Of your great house, yea, my lord, though by chance o' birth only; of your regiment of servants, mayhap, when you be not drunken, but of aught beside — no, and least of all, yourself — "

"Will ye dare so affront me — me, Aldrington — and here? Will ye dare so? I'll not endure . . . begone . . . nay, my men shall whip you hence — "

"Besotted boy, babble not to me!" retorted the Captain contemptuously. "Rather go hide your young drunkard's head for very shame — "

"God's death!" cried the Earl and, whipping forth rapier, leapt with point advanced. But the murderous thrust was turned, the weapon wrenched from his grasp; he was seized by mighty arm, clasped, crushed and, writhing thus helpless, beaten with the flat of his own sword. So the Captain belaboured him very heartily until the wound in his arm opened, spattering them both with blood. But still that relentless arm rose and fell until at last, and despite all his pride and resolution, my lord uttered a gasping moan; the merciless blows ceased, and tossing my lord one way and the sword the other, Jocelyn stepped back and stood to fetch his breath and glance down where lay the Earl asprawl, his finery stained and dishevelled, his slim, young body shaken by great, noiseless sobs. Then Jocelyn turned to be gone and came face to face with my lady who leaned, pale and trembling, against a tree.

Speechlessly she pointed shaking finger and looking whither she directed, Jocelyn saw his left hand once again all red with blood and smiled grimly; quoth he:

" The Hand of Glory, madam! "

"I pray you suffer that I tend it," said she, very humbly.

"It is of no moment, my lady, and I am in haste—"

"But . . . sir, you cannot go thus."

"Madam, I can and must—"

"At the least my scarf. . . . 'Twill be small delay—"

"Ha, villain—devil!" cried a shrill, gasping voice. "Go where ye will, you shall not 'scape my vengeance!" And up sprang the Earl, in frenzy of shame and anger, his features contorted, his slim fists smiting the air. "You shall be brought back . . . to suffer—" The shrill voice broke and my lord was sobbing wildly in his sister's cherishing arms.

Then Captain Jocelyn turned and strode hastily away. And presently coming beside the little brook, he knelt to lave the blood from his hand in the sparkling water and to tie up his hurt, and so on again towards the house, more profoundly thoughtful than ever. Roused by a shout, he glanced around and saw big Will Thurlow, my lord's head groom, running to meet him.

"Oh, Cap'n sir," cried Will breathlessly, "John Bly do be come for ee, and arl of a sweat, wi' word o' Master Ferndale—hurted he be, shot, sir, so John do tell. This way, Cap'n."

Reaching the stable yard they saw John Bly still on horseback, his honest face very grave.

"Sir," quoth he, knuckling an eyebrow, "my dame do say can ee come drackly minute?"

"Certes!" nodded the Captain. "Prithee, Will, have my horse saddled. . . . Is Mr. Ferndale much hurt, John?"

"Why us bean't nowise sure, sir," answered the landlord, shaking his head, "thofe he were sa-prising bloody."

"Shot, was he?"

"Ay, sir, from they thickets where the road narrers—"

"Bide for me, John."

Hasting within doors, Jocelyn sped up to his sumptuous chamber, got into his riding boots, belted on rapier, turned for his hat and cloak and paused, for in place of his own lay Florian's. Muttering oaths, he did them on, caught up his pistols and hasted back to the stable yard, where Will himself waited with the saddled horse and talked with John.

"I do hope, sir, as it beant nowt serious-like," said Will, as the Captain leapt to saddle.

"Amen, Will, lad!" he answered, ramming pistols into holsters; then, whirling his spirited horse, quoth he: "Now, John Bly, let us ride; and spur, man, spur."

# CHAPTER XI

## In Which This Narrative Begins to Unfold

In the best chamber of the "Peck o' Malt" tavern, outstretched upon a great, canopied bed, lay Florian, pale as the sheets and swathed in many bandages; yet his eyes seemed joyous as ever and his pallid lips were smiling as he gazed up into the Captain's anxious visage.

"Ha, Jocelyn," said he faintly, "my artifice worked more shrewdly than I looked for . . . yet it succeeded to admiration! For, seeing me fall . . . out on me sprang these rogues and would ha' finished me with steel but for . . . a small sailorman that chanced to my rescue. So off they galloped for London . . . to give the happy news o' thy death, Jocelyn . . . ay — and took with them . . . thy cloak for witness . . . "

"Death o' my life!" exclaimed the Captain, frowning, "and will ye be forever leaping 'twixt me and imagined perils?"

"That will I!" answered Florian, with feeble though determined nod. "And 't is but tit for tat . . . so never scowl on me, *camarada*, nor look so grimly. I do but for you what you ha' so often done for me."

"Tush, man!" quoth Jocelyn. "Now could I curse thee right heartily — "

"Nay, softly, *amigo*, have a care! There be ears . . . more delicate than mine . . . hereabouts." The great bed hangings stirred, rustled softly and Cecily appeared, a slim, lovely creature who, despite flushing cheek and humble guise, fronted the Captain's keen gaze with head aloft and her blue eyes shy yet challenging.

"Oh, sir," she murmured, bobbing rustical custsey, "I am your honour's very humble servant."

"Hum!" quoth the Captain and tugged moustachio, for

in the high carriage of her little head he saw of humility no whit.

"Sir," said she, in the same shyly gentle murmur, "your poor friend lieth sore hurt."

"Troth, child," nodded Jocelyn, "'t is very determined fellow i' the matter of wounds; he was forever thrusting himself 'twixt me and danger and taking some scathe on my behalf yonder in Flanders and Brabant, and now, here in this peaceful countryside, he must be at it again!"

"Then, sir, methinks you should give thanks to God for such noble gentleman's love." Here she turned to young Florian with such look that his pale cheek flushed and his handsome eyes shone, while the Captain tugged moustachio harder than ever.

"Moreover, comrade," said Florian, almost apologetically, "this time 't is no more than pistol ball through my shoulder . . . I should be abroad again . . . in a day or so."

"Oh, nay!" said Cecily, shaking lovely head in gentle reproach. "Master Yaxby, the leech, vows you must not stir abroad this sennight and more—And there be Aunt Meg a-calling. By your leaves, gentlemen!" And she sped lightly from the room.

"Now is she not very flower o' God, Jocelyn?"

"Ay, truly!" nodded the Captain. "And—what beside, I wonder? But of these murderous rogues, didst know them?"

"Ay, marry did I, and for Riderwood's bravos all four, or at least those same that beset us i' the orchard at Aldrington. I . . . tried a shot and winged one . . . then they were on me . . . reft away thy cloak and . . . would ha' spitted me where I lay but up came a plump, small fellow but with vasty roaring voice and four-foot tuck, whereat they spurred off, as I say. So then . . . this little man staunches me my hurt very deftly and carries me here. And sure never fell man to tenderer care, for Mistress Cecily—"

"And good Dame Margery,—eh, lad?"

"Why, to be sure!" nodded Florian. "But—"

From somewhere near by rose a sudden, hoarse, re-sounding bellow:

"Host ahoy! Ale, messmate! More ale!"

"That," said Florian, smiling wanly, "should be my little man and a mariner by the sound of him—" Here the door opened and in bustled the buxom Dame herself, bearing something savoury in a pipkin.

"Lack-a-day!" quoth she, shaking her comely head. "Marry come up, and here's a pretty business, my master! Your poor gentleman comrade nigh murdered in 's gore and scarce a mile from the 'Peck!' Now, my poor soul—come sup this! Cecily, child, set his pillows—so! Come now, young master, I 'll feed ee this broth."

"Nay, good dame," protested Florian, glancing askance at the Captain's grim figure, "I can handle spoon—"

"So will I feed ee, come! And hast talked too much. Master Yaxby told as ee must be quiet and sleep. So come, I tells ee, sup this hearty and then the potion Cecily hath for ee. For yourself, sir," said she, turning to Jocelyn, "step ee below and shall find somewhat worth the eating, I 'll warrant me! Your gentleman friend must to sleep anon."

So downstairs went Jocelyn into the cosy kitchen where stood honest John Bly at well-laden table eager to serve him.

"Which this do be a proud day for we and the old 'Peck', master," quoth John, busied with carving knife. "To 'ave your gen'leman comrade wi' us and him such a proper, hell-fire sworder, 't is like a gardean angel he 'll be, in manner o' speaking."

"Have the riotous gentlemen troubled you o' late, John?"

"Sir Thomas Vincent rid up t'other day, called for stoup of ale, drank it, a did, but never ventured foot indoors,—mild as milk, sir, though scowled, a did—"

Here, in answer to another stentorious roar, the land-lord hurried forth into the garden with hasty apology, leaving his guest to eat alone; but presently, forgetful of the goodly viands before him, Jocelyn leaned back from the table and fell to a profound meditation. From this reverie he was suddenly aroused by a hoarse whisper behind him:

"*Bergen-op-zoom!*"

For a moment he made no move then, glancing over his shoulder, beheld a round, close-cropped head inthrust towards him through the open lattice, which bronzed face, round also, was lit by round, bright eyes; the nose too was round, being short and pugnacious and, lastly, the clean-shaven lips were round, being just now pursed upon the whispered word "zoom."

Having surveyed this face with leisured, calculating glance, Jocelyn nodded and made answer:

"The Kowenstein Dyke."

"Aha, i' the clout!" nodded the head, with a chuckle. "God save ee, my master."

"And you, sir."

"Thou'rt Captain Dinwiddie, o' Sidney's Zeeland Regiment?"

"I was, sir, but — "

"You was wi' Sir Philip at Zutphen, ha?"

"And also when he died, God rest him!"

"Ay, a sweet, proper lad yon. Him dead, you was in my Lord Willoughby's Company — ha?"

"Very true, sir. But who — "

"Ay, ye'll not be minding me, I reckon?"

"Why, no," answered Jocelyn, viewing the round face, feature by feature, "and yet memory stirs — "

"And, Cap'n, 'tis small wonder as I were n't sure of you, for last time I clapped eyes on ee was in the battle on the Dyke — ay, so! You was in rags and rusty steel, bleeding like stuck pig, Captain, and drownding in your armour. I be one o' they as pulled ee out, my brother Nat being t' other. A bloody business, yon Kowenstein, a bloody, bloody business!"

Jocelyn rose.

"And it was you," said he, crossing to the speaker, "it was you hauled me back to life!"

"And brother Nat! We was in the boats that day, and seeing you shot down, hove ee aboard and got ee back to your company—"

"Prithee, whom have I to thank?"

"Well, master, I be Nick, do ee see, Cap'n Nicholas Fell o' the *Rose*, pink and well beknown to my Lord Willoughby and your old comrade, Sir Roger Williams."

"Zounds, man!" exclaimed Jocelyn, clapping both hands on the little seaman's broad shoulders. "I know thee now, ay, and from many others besides Stout Roger. And 't was thou saved me—"

"And brother Nat. Out yonder he lays a-starn o' me, hove short. Twins be Nat and me, ay, and like each other as two peas—save as Nat be longer-sparred and a hairy figurehead to un."

"Why then, let us have him in!" quoth Jocelyn, peering into the sunny garden. "Nay, I'll out to him." So, forth of the wide casement he clambered and in company with the little sea captain came to a shady corner, a grass plat screened by hedges where flowers bloomed and bees hummed drowsily. And here, asprawl in the sun, lay a lank, bony fellow whose lean visage looked forth sleepily, below, above and through ferocious tangle of hair, moustachio and beard. From this hairy giant, Jocelyn glanced at the small, plump Captain and round about in some puzzlement, whereat the little Captain questioned him in hoarse whisper:

"Anan, sir? We'm secret here! What d'ye look for?"

"Your twin brother."

"Why, sir, he lays afore ye,—being as I said somewhat longer fore and aft and figurehead hairy, but otherwise the very spit o' me. Ay, this be brother Nat, sir, and Nat, here he be—Cap'n Dinwiddie hisself, lad!" The tall man was afoot in single, lithe movement and meeting Jocelyn's friendly look, smiled, made a leg and having shaken Jocelyn's outstretched hand, sat down again nimbly as he had risen.

" Us heered as you was killed, sir!" said he sleepily.

" Faith, I 've been dead frequently by report, and dead I should be like enough this time but for my young comrade that you succoured, I think."

"Ay, sir, how doth the gentleman?"

"Well enough, thanks to you."

"Why then, sir," said the little Captain, seating himself on the grass, " if you 'll bring up here, my master, under my lee, us 'll open the matter forthright, eh, brother Nat?"

" Ay!" mumbled tall Nat drowsily.

"Sir," said Captain Nick, lowering his voice again to hoarse whisper, "us had word o' ye in Flanders, Brabant and the Netherlands. Now yourself, having been chose for special mission, do know as there be somewhat afoot in Spain, Flanders and Paris . . . and now in this South Country against the life o' Her Majesty. Yourself likewise will know of one sent out o' Spain for this rank purpose that, being close followed and pursued, got himself into the Fleet Prison for safe hiding, ha?"

" I also know he was not there!" answered Jocelyn.

"Ay, but, sir," whispered the little Captain, his round eyes glancing hither and thither very watchfully, "this, mayhap, ye do not know — that 'stead o' one, came three!"

" 'Sdeath!" muttered Jocelyn.

"Master, your friend Sir Roger Williams followed one o' these three but lost him in London. Yourself followed another and likewise lost him, but Nat and I followed the third and, by good hap, laid him aboard and took him. Eh, Nat, eh?"

" Us did so, Nick!" mumbled Nat slumberously, but eyes quick and bright beneath wide hatbrim.

"Where is he?" demanded Jocelyn grimly.

"Safe-trussed, hard by — "

"You searched him?"

"From trucks to keelson, sir, and i' the lining of 's left

boot us found — this!" And from the breast of his sea-stained jerkin, the little Captain whipped a small, thin sachet of oiled silk, and from this a folded paper, the which he gave to Jocelyn who, smoothing it out, peered at it closely and at arm's length, holding it against the light, but saw it for no more than blank sheet of paper without vestige of writing.

"And what do ee say to that, my master?" quoth the little Captain. Jocelyn frowned and shook his head. "A blind, eh?" sighed the small mariner. "A lure to lead us astray from the true quarry, ha?"

"Or writ secret!" murmured Nat.

"Ay, mebbe so, lad, mebbe so, thofe 't is beyond we. How sayst thou, Captain Dinwiddie, sir? I've heard as you've some secret elixir for such hid writings, to prove 'em, ha?"

Frowning still, Jocelyn glanced at the speaker and from inner pocket drew a small phial; opening this, he poured a spot of its contents upon corner of his kerchief and therewith gently dabbed this so innocent-seeming paper while they watched very intently, for the slumberous Nat had propped himself on bony elbow. So passed a long minute; then Jocelyn shook his head, Captain Nick cursed softly and brother Nat yawned, for the paper remained blank as ever.

"So then, 't is flam for sure!" growled Captain Nick, while brother Nat fell back upon the grass but with eyes alert 'neath hat brim, and Jocelyn, folding the paper, thrust it with seeming carelessness into his bosom.

"And now for the bearer!" said he, rising.

"Why, 't is a dumb dog," growled Captain Nick, rising also and tightening his broad sword belt. "Nary a word out o' him so fur. Yet he may speak, for brother Nat, having been something tortured by the bloody Dons, knoweth divers ploys shall persuade ye most stubborn to discourse. But first, Cap'n Dinwiddie, sir, this letter from my Lord Willoughby!" Jocelyn took the missive he proffered and, breaking the seal, read this:

To Jocelyn my comrade and singular good friend these: The wind at last blowing fair for foulness, the bearers of this, come to your command both and each. Trust them as yourself. So God aid and prosper loyalty. Thine as ever.

"Ye know the hand, sir?"

"And word!" nodded Jocelyn, tearing the letter very small. "Where lieth your vessel, friend Nick?"

"Off Shoreham, sir, hove short and, like Brother Nat and myself, instant to sarve ee. There be Spanish soldiers landed in Ireland, three companies, and many more ready to sail, and with these, three French regiments, 'tis said. You know o' this, sir?"

"Ay, I know!" answered Jocelyn. "And now for this messenger; I'm fain to see him."

"Ay, ay, sir; we've got he t'other side the five acre in John Bly's old barn."

"How, you know John Bly then?"

"Marry, that do we, sir! We was old shipmates and born hereabouts, do ee see."

"And did you tell John aught o' this business, Captain Nick?"

"Nary a word, sir. Least said, soonest mended, so mum it is, master."

"Good!" nodded Jocelyn.

"Us hath word, sir, as you be at Aldrington, the Great House?"

"Ay, verily. And you, being native here, should know the young Earl."

"By sight, sir. 'Twas his father the old lord as us knew better. Our father, God rest him, used to farm Aldrington land, years agone. And lookee, the proud Aldringtons be Papishers, a Catholic family!"

"Yet not suspect as traitors, surely?"

"No, no, I'll warrant 'em loyal enow. But then, damme, no proper Englishman can be a Papist these days when besides Rome and the Inquisition it means bloody Spain also, with a pox on't!"

Thus went Jocelyn between small, talkative Nick and big, silent Nat, until they reached a barn long out of use and very remote and hidden, being all set about by dense thickets. Being come within this desolate ruin, Captain Nick led the way to a certain shadowy corner and halting, suddenly gasped a rolling sea oath, for the corner was empty.

"Lord, smite, shiver and sink me! Lookee, Nat!"

"Ar!" quoth Nat.

"The hell-fire rogue's slipped his moorings. Stand by, Nat, stand by! Veer, lad, veer and cast about; the black swab be likely hereabout yet." Now while the brethren sought their fugitive with profane diligence, Jocelyn took up a length of stout cord that showed many cunning sailory knots, and was yet staring at this when back came these two brothers, the one cursing very hoarsely fluent, the other grimly dumb.

"See here, comrades!" said Jocelyn. "These bonds were clean cut, the which argues your prisoner found some friend to aid him. How think ye?"

"Snoggers!" quoth Nat, spitting disgustedly.

"'T is woundy marvel!" growled Nick. "Who should aid the dog?"

"Belike one that expected his coming. That he was looked for, we know. Canst describe him, Captain Nick?"

"Ay, I can so. A youngish, smock-faced fellow, buffed and weaponed like an officer, and a feather in's bonnet very brave, eh, Nat?"

"And a scar o' the chin."

"Ha!" nodded Jocelyn. "Youngish, clean-shaven, and a scar on his chin. Was he tall and vigorous, or —"

"Slimmish, sir, and no great size. Ha, 'sblood, would I had my fingers on's neck again! Ah, well, good lack and how now, my master?"

"It is for me to do what I may, Captain Nick. Meanwhile, get ye back to Shoreham."

"Shoreham it is, sir. You shall hear on us at the Crown and Anchor Inn." Then back went they to the stable yard and there the two mariners swung to horse and presently galloped away, bumping and rolling in their saddles like the sea dogs they were.

Returning to the kitchen, Jocelyn found it deserted and crossed to the wide hearth where logs smouldered; bending to the fire, he drew the folded paper from his bosom and placed it very carefully where the warmth might reach it.

And slowly upon that white and seemingly empty paper marks began to form, lines of bold writing that grew more distinct until he could decipher these words:

Ione, Lady Fane, thou art the chosen. For it is now certain the woman Elizabeth shall come to Aldrington. Thus, unto thee, noble lady and faithful daughter of Holy Church, is given the happiness to aid the Religion. He that beareth this shall be thine instructor therein, to his guidance submit thyself and also to our good and trusty son, Philip Drayton of Shalmeston. To this holy work are pledged the noblest in England, as: the Earls of Arundel, Northumberland, Worcester, Cumberland, Viscount Montacute, Lord Dacres, Vaux and very many else. Be it also thy duty to add unto these proud names that of the noble youth the Earl of Aldrington, thy brother. Lift up thy heart, nothing fearing. Be thou faithful in this work of salvation to win England back into the loving arms of Holy Mother Church, so shall thine be the blessing of Heaven now and hereafter.

Amen.

Having read this missive, Jocelyn made as if to burn it, then paused and folding it small, thrust it carefully into the breast of his doublet and stood thereafter staring down sombrely at the fire. Lost thus in thought, he was roused by the entrance of Dame Margery who, seeing his troubled look, smiled and nodded cheerily:

"Take heart, my master," said she, stirring the logs to merry crackle, "your poor friend sleeps sweet as any babe and shall be well anon, I'll warrant him! And a shall lack for nought; us'll care for ee, ay, marry will we."

So when he had thanked her, he stepped out into the yard and finding John with his horse ready saddled, mounted forthwith like one in haste, then reining in the mettled animal, turned to glance down into the landlord's honest face.

"Hast had much custom to-day, John?" he questioned.

"None so much, sir — though there came divers o' the gentry to be sure. 'Smorning came Squire Twyfoot and 's man, journeying for London. Ay, and 'sarternoon who should ride up but Master Fane."

"Mr. Roland Fane? Hum! And stepped he indoors?"

"Ay, marry, sir, and drank stoup o' my best, and mighty pleasant too! Smiled, a did, laughed and talked wi' me and my Meg that merry — and him such great gen'leman and own cousin to th' Earl hisself, and yet so friendly as any ordinary man!"

"Talked, did he, John?"

"Ay, o' the crops an' the fishing, and if I'd been along to Shoreham to-day, which I had, and whether any strange ships was come in, or if I'd chanced to see Sir Philip Drayton thereabouts, and drank his ale, Lord love ee, hearty as any Tom or Dick, a did!"

"And had you seen Sir Philip Drayton at Shoreham, John?"

"No, sir. But Mr. Fane 'ad n't been gone long afore drownd me if Sir Philip don't come a-riding up — "

"And did he step in also, John?"

"Ay, he did, sir, and calls for — Rhenish! But me not 'aving no wine, he takes ale instead, though drank precious little on 't, a did. Then I hears a hail from the gardin and there's Cap'n Nick and his brother Nat as I sailed along wi' afore I were married — "

"And when did Sir Philip Drayton leave?"

"I can't rightly say, sir, for when I come back from the gardin, 'e were gone, but setting on his 'oss at the door were Maister Denzil, th' Earl's head bailey."

"And did he call for ale, John?"

"Not 'e, sir, dang 'im! Scowled, a did, and bade me call Maister Fane, and when I says as the gen'leman be gone, a cursed me and galloped off."

"And methinks I'll do the like," nodded Jocelyn. "Tell Mr. Ferndale I shall see him to-morrow, — and now here's for thee, friend John!" So saying, and despite the landlord's protests, Jocelyn tossed him money and turned to ride away, then checked to the beat of rapidly approaching hoofs. Upon the road into the tavern yard galloped Richard the Earl, while behind spurred Mr. Roland Fane.

Reining up his foam-spattered animal, my lord sprang to earth, a wild-eyed, passion-shaken boy, and seizing Jocelyn's horse by the bridle, pointed imperiously towards the tavern with his whip.

"Sir," cried he breathlessly, "I must ask your favour to — step indoors with me."

"To what end, my lord?"

"This you shall learn anon — pray come!" For a moment Jocelyn hesitated, frowning and a little dismayed, then perceiving Mr. Fane's rapid approach, he dismounted and followed my lord into the wide kitchen, while honest John stood gazing after them awed and dumb.

Hardly were they entered than my lord tossed by hat and cloak, drew off his gauntlets and faced the Captain, very pale but desperately determined.

"Captain Dinwiddie," said he, youthful chin outthrust, wide eyes bright and steady, "you struck me . . . you shamed me to death . . . so now you shall kill me or . . . I you! Pray have the goodness to draw and stand to your ward, sir." And out flickered his sword; but Jocelyn, stepping back out of distance, folded his arms and shook his head.

"My lord," quoth he gently, "this were folly —"

"Ha, devil," cried the Earl, "wilt mock me yet?"

"Not I, my lord. Neither will I fight."

"Ay, but you shall!" cried my lord, levelling his blade. "Oh, villain — fiend — base fellow . . ."

"Whatso your lordship willeth," sighed Jocelyn; "howbeit, I am no murderer."

"Must I strike you?"

"Even so, I will not fight —" But now entered Mr. Fane, somewhat dishevelled with haste.

"Heart alive!" he exclaimed. "What's to do?"

"As I told you, Roland, Captain Dinwiddie dared to . . . strike me and I'll see blood for it —"

"Nay, sweet lad, be warned!" cried Mr. Fane in whee-dling tone. "Thou'rt but mere boy and —"

"God's death, sir! I'm a gentleman also —"

"Why, true, Dicky, true! But so young! Nay, be-seech thee, coz, have a care —"

"I care for nought, Roland. An' he kill me — so much the better. Captain Dinwiddie, draw!"

"Nay, but Rick," pleaded Mr. Fane, "oh, sweet coz, this Captain is skilled swordsman —"

"And what then? The villain . . . struck me! Cap-tain Dinwiddie — to your ward, I say."

"My lord," said Jocelyn, backing away, "you do but waste your breath and my time —"

"Fight, sir!" cried the Earl, brandishing his rapier. "Fight, or by my salvation, I'll have you published for craven cur and cowardly villain!"

"Why then, my lord," answered Jocelyn, serene as ever, "pray set about it; meanwhile I will away to my business —"

"No!" cried the Earl wildly, "I say I'll not endure such vile disgrace, I'll die first —"

"Stay, sweet lad," quoth Mr. Fane, gently interposing, "peradventure our Captain will crave your pardon?"

"Ay, faith, and with all my heart!" nodded Jocelyn, but with voice and look so disarming that the youth, lower-ing his sword, stood mute, — only his breath came in sound very like a sob. "For verily, my lord," murmured Jocelyn, "sorry am I indeed. And so, for sake of our one-time kindness, I would have you think the best o' me. Fare thee well, my lord."

"Aha, excellent!" laughed Mr. Fane gently. "Well said, Captain! 'Tis silvern tongue can wipe out such affront. Yet, after all, a blow is no great matter, and you

Richard, as first gentleman in all this South Country, the proud Aldrington, may stomach it — nay stoop to forgive e'en a blow from such deadly swordsman as this warlike gentleman, let the world scoff and jibe as it will, — "

With a high-pitched cry of fury, the Earl snatched up one of his gauntlets and hurled it into Jocelyn's face.

"Now!" cried he. "Is it enough?"

"Perfectly, sir!" answered Jocelyn, bowing. "I bid you farewell!"

"How?" gasped the boy. "Wilt refuse me yet?"

"My lord," answered Jocelyn, a little grimly, "I am one that dare refuse fight to any man."

For a moment his lordship stared dumb, then, catching up the leathern ale-jack from the table, dashed its contents into the speaker's face.

"Now," he panted, falling on guard, "now . . . doth this suffice?"

Very deliberately Jocelyn drew forth his kerchief, wiped his face, looked reproachfully into the young Earl's wide eyes and, turning to depart, saw Ione standing on the threshold and in her eyes such radiant look as he had never seen ere now, and when she spoke her voice, low and sweetly intimate, matched the wonder of her eyes.

"Captain Jocelyn," she murmured, "at last, methinks I do behold thy worthiest and very noblest self!" So saying, she stripped off embroidered riding glove to reach him her hand. "Sir, well knowing my brother's devilish temper, I have ridden hither, nigh frantic with dread, fearing you should prove less brave and worthy gentleman than I find you. And, sir, for all the bitter affronts I saw you endure with such a valiant patience, my gratitude goeth beyond any words."

Dumbly the Captain took that slim, white hand, stooped reverent head and kissed it, saw the radiance in her eyes bright as ever and stood speechless still. Then spoke the young Earl, low-voiced and sullen:

"Ione, you forget — I am Aldrington, and he dared strike me."

"And I would to God," she retorted, "there had been such man to strike Aldrington whenso needed —"

"Nay, but my sweet Ione," cried Mr. Fane, flourishing gracefully, "my loved and lovely soul, our Richard is by God's grace one of the great ones of the earth and — to strike such —"

"Pray, silence, Roland. Hearken — one gallops on the road! Who should ride so desperately?"

The drumming hoofs drew nearer, clattered into the tavern yard and stopped. Then in the doorway stood Will Thurlow, looming gigantic and, though he addressed the Earl, it was on Jocelyn he fixed his troubled gaze:

"M'lud!" he cried. "Oh, m'lud, they be a-murdering th' owd witch! Tormenting of her! They be a-going to drownd old Robina Shaw over to Westover —"

"Well, and how then?" enquired Mr. Fane. "A witch is a witch and —"

"For shame, Roland!" cried Ione. "Dame Shaw was my nurse. . . ."

Even while she spoke, Jocelyn stepped out into the yard where John Bly, more awed than ever, brought his horse.

"'T is a-dreaming I be, sir!" said he, as Jocelyn swung to saddle. "First — my lord th' Earl and now — my leddy! I' fegs, 't is a-dreaming —"

But spurring his horse, the Captain leapt away at a gallop; once only he paused to ask his direction of a be-smocked rustic and then on again at the same desperate speed. And thus he was presently aware of a distant sound, a hoarse and ominous murmur that swelled gradually to a babblement of fierce shouts and cries, a wild and awful clamour.

# CHAPTER XII

## WHICH IS CHAPTER OF ACTION

REACHING the brow of a hill, the Captain suddenly beheld that which drew a fierce oath from him as he plunged headlong down the steep declivity, — a scene all too common in these bad old days, — this :

A village green with a dark, deep pool beside which stood that dreadful instrument of torture called the ducking stool. And this a massive chair suspended from a movable, transverse beam ; and clamped fast within this swinging chair a dripping, faintly wailing shape of misery that, poised for a moment thus above the fierce-eyed clamourous throng, was plunged suddenly down and down into that deep pool, only to be hove aloft once more, gasping and half drowned, for the crowd to gape and jeer at, ere down swayed the beam again and the wretched creature's feeble supplications were choked as her white head vanished beneath those dark and stifling waters.

And then the crowd was split asunder where the Captain rode, plying whip right and left at such as would have stayed him. So he won through and leaping from saddle, began loosing the moaning, half-dead creature from her cruel bonds.

"Hold there!" cried an arrogant voice. "Let be, I say!" Captain Jocelyn never so much as glanced up and had nearly freed the swooning old woman when a powerful grasp wrenched him about to behold a tall, somewhat ponderous personage, who scowled and spoke in loud-voiced authority:

"Who are ye dare meddle here? 'T is a vile witch very rightly adjudged to the water — " Now here, beholding the Captain's deadly ferocity of look, the speaker faltered and recoiled, then cried out harsher and louder:

" Let be, I say! Hence, and meddle not with the law's
authority, or I 'll ha' some of these good fellows toss ye
into the pool, along of this cursed witch, for I am Reginald
Denzil, head bailiff to my lord, the Earl of Aldrington!"

" Ha, sayst thou!" murmured Jocelyn.

" Ay, I do say so, and—" A jingle of spurs, a swirl of
fluttering cloak, and Mr. Denzil, reeling to the buffet of
the Captain's iron fist, was instantly kicked splashing into
the pool by the Captain's heavy boot, whereat rose a
fierce clamour of hoots and outcries, a wild and menacing
uproar. But, all unheeding, Captain Jocelyn turned again
to free that pale, still form that hung dripping in her woeful
misery. . . . A stone, hurled by some mighty peasant
hand, smote him bleeding and half-stunned to his knees, but
up he sprang, sword and dagger agleam, to front his raging
assailants, and so stood fierce and grim, one against the
multitude. But the many held aloof and what avail even
his deadly steel against the missiles that began to batter
him? Twice he was beaten to his knees and twice he arose,
blind with trickling blood, yet resolute still. . . . And now
faint to his ears came words:

" Ah, noble maister—oh, God o' pity, save him . . .
shield him . . . in thy wings, O Lord. . . ."

And now, even as his senses failed, he heard vague shouts,
espied three figures, dim and afar, that rode very furiously;
and then, reeling to that chair of torment, clutched at it
blindly, set protecting arm about old Robina's shivering
form, and smiling through his mask of blood, spoke:

" Courage—old mother! Methinks—thy prayer is
—answered. . . ." And speaking thus, sank weakly to
his knees, to his face and lay very still and mute.

# CHAPTER XIII

## WHICH IS CHAPTER OF TALK WITH MENTION OF DESTINY'S JADE

HE opened his eyes to the cool sweet solace of water, to feel a cherishing arm about him and his aching head softly pillowed; then he was aware the young Earl knelt beside him, pale-faced and anxious, his voice very pleading and insistent:

"Jocelyn! Oh, Jocelyn, speak to me! God's love, man — speak!"

"Ah, my lord . . . prithee, how doth the old dame?"

"Well enough. Ione hath cared for her. . . . But how is it with thee, friend? Ha, by God, I'll ha' this cursed village destroyed; it shall burn and these villainous folk go homeless!"

"No, no, my lord."

"Ay, but they shall! I say I will! And prithee, call me Richard. And Denzil shall to prison, damn him —"

"Nay, but, Richard, I . . . kicked him into the pool —"

"And the rogue set these village scum to murder my friend!"

"Am I truly thy friend, Richard?"

"Ay, before God! Ay, Jocelyn, even when I entreated thee so vilely, I loved thee in my heart . . . and now truly do I love thee better than ever!"

"Why then, dear lad, in friendship to me . . . seek no vengeance on these folk, for —" the pleading voice faltered.

"Ha, God's mercy! What now, Jocelyn — art faint?"

"A sup — o' cordial — Dick. . . ."

"Ay, I'll go fetch it! Look to him, Ione!"

Now presently, his faintness passing somewhat, Jocelyn became aware that the softness pillowing his battered head moved gently and, glancing up, looked into Ione's lovely face bent over him, its proud beauty tempered by a strange, new kindness.

"My lady . . . Joan!" said he, wondering, and made to rise, but her gentle touch on his brow stayed him.

"Rest you!" she murmured.

"And in this most unheroical posture!" sighed he, with his wry and wistful smile. "By my faith, I had rather front Spain's famous pikemen than English rustics!"

"'T is great marvel they did not kill you. And all for an old creature that is a black witch!"

"Ay — she is old!" he murmured. "Also she hath suffered overmuch."

"And yet — to hazard your life so wantonly!"

"Well, hath it not won back my Lord Richard's friendship?"

"And mine!" said she, stooping yet closer above him.

Now as she spoke thus, he moved the better to see her face and she, meeting his searching gaze, flushed hotly, averting her face as in quick confusion, and he felt all her loveliness shaken by a sudden tremor while now those slim fingers were plucking nervously at a fold in her habit. Perceiving all of which, Jocelyn, about to speak, drew a deep breath instead and gazing up at a white cloud above them, answered in tone of such airy levity that she started as if with sudden hurt.

"Why then, sweet madam, here's dainty paradox — in that by my abasement I soar. E'en so my hurts become joys, bruises my pride, defeat a notable victory. . . ." The jocund voice faltered and he scowled at the white cloud until, becoming conscious of her scrutiny, he contrived to smile.

"Sir," said she, a little breathlessly, "you . . . you make jest of my proffered friendship, I think?"

"Ah, never!" he sighed. "But pray you, consider my situation, — bruised and battered, a dolorous object in pitiful, ladylike lap —"

"Would you also scorn my pity?" she demanded, looking from him to the dark pool and frowning in her turn.

"Not so, my Lady Joan, for Pity is sweet and tender virtue, though to me a gentle stranger so seldom met withal that I know not how to welcome it." Now at this she sat so silent and so very still that he glanced askance at her averted face.

"'T is like enow I should ha' been less an object for pity had our right gallant Robin Netherby chanced beside me. . . . How think you, my lady?"

"That my brother Richard tarries a weary while, sir."

"And I find myself greatly recovered, madam—"

"Indeed, I think you are!" she answered, her gaze still averted. Here the Captain made to rise, whereat she instantly caught him by the hair, she even tweaked it viciously, though her voice was gentle when she spoke:

"Ah, beseech thee, lie still, thou poor stricken wretch."

"With all my heart, madam," he answered humbly, and lay there in very blissful content, despite his bruises; and for some while not a word between them.

"This is vilely tedious!" sighed she.

"Alack! I fear it must be," he murmured contentedly. Here ensued silence so long that at last she questioned him petulantly:

"Have your so grievous hurts made you dumb, sir?"

"Not altogether, my sweet ladyship."

"Then I pray you, sir Captain, if yet remain in you sufficient of strength, resolve me the profound riddle,— what manner of strange creature is this Dinwiddie?"

"God only knoweth!" sighed Jocelyn. "Let us call him the poor jade of Destiny must struggle blindly on, heavily burdened, through quag and mire and thorny ways, 'neath the goading spurs of Circumstance,— on and on, I scarce know and care not whither—"

"Care not?"

"Of what avail?" he answered. "Yet all journeys must end at last, God be thanked!"

"Ay, but where, Jocelyn,— where?" she whispered in awed inquiry?"

"In Ultima Thule, my Lady Joan, that Magic Vale where

the lost is found and our noblest dreams, so long forgot, do meet us in blessed reality and we thereby grow young again, glorious and perfected at last." Now at this, she looked down on him like one amazed and when she spoke it was in accents once again hushed and tender.

"Here is strange thought!" she murmured.

"And yonder," he sighed, "cometh my lord to end your ladyship's tedium."

Sure enough, the young Earl came hasting and now with divers of his gentlemen attendant.

"Oh, Jocelyn," cried he breathlessly, "on my soul, there's no wine nor cordial in this accursed village, seek how I will! So I've sped some of my people a-gallop to Aldrington —"

"Grammercy for thy trouble, Richard, but I'm well enough without — faith, I can ride an' thou 'lt help me up."

And so, despite the protestations of my lord and his gentlemen, the Captain presently got to horse and sitting thus, glanced about him.

"Now prithee, Dick, what of my old witch?" he enquired.

"Away to Aldrington in Will's care," answered the Earl. "Henceforth no man shall dare harm her, Jocelyn man, witch or no, for thy sake, dear my friend."

# CHAPTER XIV

## Telleth of Peril and Captain Jocelyn's Counsel

Captain Jocelyn, sitting remote and solitary in the arbour, busily versifying, was pondering the just rhythm of a line when, chancing to lift his gaze from the paper on his knee, he beheld my Lord Richard approaching. And the young nobleman's delicate features seemed greatly troubled and, espying Jocelyn, he so far forgot his wonted dignity that he came running to seat himself breathlessly at his side.

"Oh, friend," quoth he, so soon as he had breath, "'t is a plaguey world, a mere dog-hole of a world!"

"Hum!" quoth the Captain, glancing keenly at my lord's woebegone face as he put away his writing. "Howbeit, Dick, the thrush i' the coppice yonder thinketh otherwise; hark to the merry, pretty fellow, how joyous he sings."

"Why, 't is but a fowl!" sighed my lord, shaking doleful head. "But as for me, I am Aldrington and therefore full of cares and what is more — a sorry fool."

"To be 'ware of our own folly is beginning of wisdom, Dick."

"And at the least I grow wise enough to see thou must never leave me, Jocelyn." Now at this the Captain tugged moustachio, his look pensive and a little troubled.

"I shall bide so long as dost need me, Richard," he answered, "or — until Duty calleth me hence."

"Ay, but, Jocelyn, what mean you by 'duty'?"

"To keep this land of ours from the bloody claws of Spain, Richard, as every Englishman should."

"Why, so we will, by God! We want no Spaniards in this England of ours."

"Yet many Englishmen do! Hearkee, Richard! There is a plot for sudden landing of Spanish soldiers under Parma and general rising of all English Catholics to set Catholic Mary of Scots on the throne, backed by King Philip's might, thus making England a Spanish province —"

"Nay, but what of Her Majesty — what of our Elizabeth?"

"She is to be murdered, Richard."

The young Earl rose suddenly and stood mute, staring so wildly that Jocelyn questioned him in quick amaze:

"'Sdeath! What ails thee, lad?"

"Death!" whispered the boy, shivering violently. "Ay, my death, perchance! The Tower! Mayhap the rack — torment! Oh, kind God, aid me! They — they snared me —"

And now Jocelyn had risen and, drawing the Earl's trembling arm within his own, walked with him beside this chattering rill, on and on until they reached the shady coppice, and here remote within this leafy solitude, paused and spoke.

"My lord, dost count me thy friend?"

"Ay, with all my heart!"

"Then suffer me to share thy trouble. Trust me — an' thou wilt."

"Oh, Jocelyn," whispered the boy glancing fearfully about, "this were to trust thee with . . . my very life. . . . And thou art a — heretic!"

"'T is true I hate Rome and all its works," nodded Jocelyn; "yet am I thy friend. And yet again, being so great a lord, lad, hast doubtless many friends more powerful than I —"

"None that I dare trust."

"Your lady sister — Ione?"

"No, by God! 'T would never do . . . she is so passionate for the Faith, 't is of her will alone these Jesuit Fathers steal here so oft a nights to celebrate Mass, for I'd ha' none of them. No, thou art the only one I can or dare trust . . . though, being an Aldrington, I am Catholic and thou a . . . a damned heretic."

"Yet are we both Englishmen, Richard."

"Ay, truly, truly!" whispered my lord. "So if the curst Spaniard threaten — our England shall come before religion. So now . . . hearkee, Jocelyn! Ever since my birthday, I have been sore troubled, so turned I something sottish again, for when a man is a little drunk, Jocelyn, his troubles seemed eased. And my trouble was a letter I found on my pillow . . . this!" Again the Earl glanced fearfully about and drawing a crumpled letter from his bosom with quick, furtive gesture, thrust it into the Captain's ready hand.

Smoothing out this paper, Jocelyn read and instantly glanced furtively around in his turn.

"Know you this hand?" he questioned.

"No, 'tis strange quite, Jocelyn."

"Let us sit down, Richard, here beside the rill, where none may easily surprise us." And now, seated thus side by side, Jocelyn read the letter a second time, studying its every word, these:

To Richard Fane, Earl of Aldrington, Baron Shere, Viscount Fording etc.: these. Right noble lord, it is now assured the woman Elizabeth shall come to your home at Aldrington. Be you ready therefore to strike for Queen Mary and the Religion, according to the oath sworn and signed by your lordship, which oath and signature we have in secure keeping.

"Swore you any such oath, at any time, Richard?"

"Never, as God seeth me — never!"

"Signed you any such paper, then?"

"Jesu aid me! I hardly know . . ." gasped the trembling youth; "unless it was some paper I signed for . . . for Riderwood . . . at his behest — "

"Riderwood? Nay, but think, lad, think! This document itself is enough to bring your head beneath the axe — think!"

"Alas . . . oh, Jocelyn!" groaned the Earl. "I had

forgot all about it until I found this letter . . . I signed so many papers . . . scarce heeding what . . . gaming losses, Jocelyn — "

"Nay, but this was some paper, I guess, pledging yourself to abet the Queen's murder . . . think, Richard, think! What like was it?"

"There was one I mind vaguely . . . a small paper with writing that began . . . 'For the weal of Catholic England and the Cause' — or somewhat thus."

"This would be it, like enough. How was it worded?"

"Alas, I cannot say. I scarce read it, I . . . I was something drunk. But 'twas at Riderwood's lodging in London and commenced: 'For the weal of Catholic England and the Cause' — "

"Who was there with you beside my Lord Riderwood?"

"None save the Colonel and Tom Vincent and they both far more drunken than I — "

"Did these sign the paper also?"

"I . . . cannot say."

"Did my Lord Riderwood?"

"I cannot tell this either."

"Saw you any other signature beside your own?"

"None that I can mind." Jocelyn frowned at the paper in his fist and sighed.

"My Lord Richard," said he, "you bear a great name that your ancestors have made honourable; to-day by your folly this proud name is perchance being used by traitors and murderers to lure others to damnable treason — "

"Ah, God — God forgive me!" gasped the Earl, covering his face with twitching hands. "Oh — despise me for fool an' you will, Jocelyn, scorn my unworthiness an' you must, but, ah — believe me loyal to Her Majesty; never think me traitor and . . . do not leave me." Now at this cry of despair Jocelyn's frown vanished and when he spoke his voice was kinder:

"Nay, how shall I judge thee, lad? Thy sin is no more than youth. Thou 'rt too young, too rich, too solitary. Now is the time for thee to turn from boyish folly and quit thyself like a man, be bold to vindicate thine honour and prove worthy thy nobility.   And here am I, thy friend, to aid thee how I may — ''

With cry of sobbing gladness, my lord turned and clasped the Captain in his arms and with face hidden thus spoke like one that prayed:

" Now do I thank God and the saints for thee, Jocelyn, and here do swear me to strive for better life, keeping my honour bright . . . and bold to meet what is to be, as a man should, ay — like man worthy thy friendship.''

" Why, Richard . . . why, Dick!'' said the Captain, laughing oddly, " seldom, I guess, was friendship more strangely welded!   Come now, let us hold council of war, and first of this letter.''

" Ay, shall we burn it?''

" No, no; rather will we make it a weapon to smite villainy.''

" Ha, with all my heart.   But prithee how?''

" As thus:   You shall this hour write two letters, the one to your cousin Mr. Fane and other to Sir Thomas Vincent, bidding them here to dine or sup.   Then you shall, over the wine, show them this letter, vowing it vile slander come you know not whence or how.   Swear you remember signing no treasonable document soever and that unless you see such with your own eyes, you 'll to London forthwith and place this paper in Her Majesty's own hand for proof o' your loyalty.   Now this threat methinks shall cause such stir that the document with your signature must needs be produced to fright and compel your silence, and once we know where to come at it, we must contrive its destruction one way or t' other, ha?''

Up sprang the Earl in youthful transport.

" God's light!'' he exclaimed.   " Ha, Jocelyn, I 'll do 't — I 'll away and write these letters this moment. . . . And yet wherefore to Roland; 't is quiet soul content with country ploys and knoweth nought o' the matter; wherefore to Cousin Roland?''

" Hum!'' quoth the Captain, tugging moustachio, " he

is gossip to Sir Thomas Vincent. Howbeit, write him also, ay, see he come without fail; 'tis a shrewd gentleman and —"

Upon the drowsy stillness broke a cheery view halloo, and towards them strode Robin Netherby, his comely face bright as the day.

"What, Dick!" he cried gaily. "How doth our wounded squire o' witches? Ione tells me the Westover folk nigh killed him. How goes it with thee, Jocelyn?"

"Nay, rather — how speeds thy wooing, Robin?" The young squire flushed, whereat my lord leapt afoot and laughed.

"Troth now," said he, "I'll away to my letter-writing, for love's a plague I'll not endure talk on till I needs must. Love? A murrain on't! Ay, by heavens, Jocelyn, stare an' ye will but I vow there be a many ladies, old and young, would woo and wed me for my name, but never a one for myself! Ask Robin! — So I'll none o' them, I."

"True enough!" nodded Robin, as my lord hurried towards the house. "Such lofty estate hath its trammels. Though by the old lord's will, Dick was contracted to the lady Philippa Mereworth, e'en as Ione to me. . . . And speaking of her — ah, Jocelyn, thy verses ha' changed her to me out of all knowing! . . . She is so kind, of such sweet humility that I am all amazed."

"Why then . . . it is very well, friend Robin."

"Yea, verily . . . and yet, — when I read to her these verses — thy verses, Jocelyn, she looks on me with eyes of such awed wonderment that I am ashamed to so deceive her, and when she questions me I scarce know how to answer her."

"And yet, Robin, if by such innocent deceit you may save her from wedding less worthily or . . . or other ill chance, this deception shall prove veriest blessing."

"And yet, Jocelyn man, should she find me out as, being of wit so infinite nimble, she may — oh, God save us! How then?"

"Hum!" quoth the Captain gloomily. "For my part,

I have never known husband yet that wrote sonnets to his wedded wife."

"Wife?" repeated young Robin, drawing deep breath. "Faith now, though she truly showeth so kind o' late . . . yet . . . it seemeth impossible . . . somehow . . . that she should ever be . . . my wife!"

"Nay now, Rob man, I protest here is no proper amative spirit! Fie on thee, laggard! Now is the time to . . . win and wed her, whiles yet she wonders and joys in thy seeming new-found gift o' verse. Thou must vow love for her thy inspiration."

"Ay, I know it, Jocelyn, I know it. And yet 'sbodykins —even now she seems so . . . as unapproachable as ever! Now though I would joyfully dare death and the devil to clasp her so much loveliness, to kiss — why, what ails thee, man?" he questioned, somewhat startled, for the Captain had risen to his feet very suddenly. "How, do thy hurts plague thee, Jocelyn?"

"Somewhat, Robin," answered the Captain, his face averted. "Also I have other new verses for thee; come with me and I'll read them over to thee, friend."

# CHAPTER XV

## Which Is Chapter Mainly Suggestive

Propped by many pillows, Florian sat in the sunshine beside the open lattice; his comely face was somewhat pale and thin, but his eyes were quick with young life and the joy of it, and now showed yet gladder and brighter as they met his friend Jocelyn's welcoming smile.

"Cock's body, man!" said he, clasping the Captain's hand in both his own, "I joy to see thee, ay, marry, with all my heart. 'T will be black day for me should I ever lose thee."

"Shall be small chance o' that, lad, whiles life be spared us."

"Ay, God wot! But Jocelyn, hast ever held thy life so plaguey cheap — in fight or out, bloody Flanders or bowery England, thou must be for thrusting into perils on some behalf other than thine own, and now 't is for haggish beldam of a curst witch! Who'd dare a mob in such vile cause, who'd adventure life and blood in such sorry business save Dinwiddie? Ha, glorious folly! Would I had been there to suffer with thee. And — cogsnails, they battered thee! Thy grimly old mazzard beareth the marks yet! The villains nigh killed thee, I hear?"

"Ay, troth, they did so!" answered the Captain, a little ruefully.

"Aha — 'snoggers, man, to think on 't! You that ha' lived through so many bloody frays and seen so many die, to be all but slain by a parcel o' yokels! Oh, the antic mockery on 't!"

"Howbeit, Florian, this witch, that is no witch, showeth hearty again and is in my Lady Joan's care henceforth, so all 's well."

"Save for thine own bruises, Jocelyn. For thee the wounds, the buffets, the steep and flinty track, — and what beyond?"

"The mountain-top, lad."

"Methinks 't will prove lonely there, *amigo*."

"Well, I am used to loneliness, Florian. Moreover, you will be there; we achieve or fail together."

"Ay, truly!" murmured Florian, yet glanced, almost furtively, down into the garden where one sat spinning amid the flowers, hidden from all eyes save his, while the Captain, leaning back in his chair, grew thoughtful.

"Florian," said he suddenly, "know you why I am in England?"

"No more than you ha' told me, comrade, the which is little. Yet well I guess 't is hazardous, since yourself was chosen for 't."

"You know of this devilish Spanish plot?"

"Ay, I do. And what then? Dost need me? I am mending apace and could — "

"Tush, lad! My need o' thee is on this wise, — to play the sick man, to seem feeble yet be wary, and to heed well all that come and go hereabouts, for there is somewhat a-brewing or I lose my guess."

"What, is the game afoot?"

"Ay, comrade, and so am I!" nodded the Captain, rising.

"Nay, now, yet bide awhile, Jocelyn. Leave me not to solitude so soon."

"Solitude quotha!" smiled the Captain. "What, then, of good Dame Margery, what o' the maid Cecily and honest John?"

"Busied wi' house matters. Come now, let us talk awhile."

"Hum!" quoth the Captain and sat down again.

"Jocelyn, when a man lieth sick, strange fancies come into his head and I ha' been plagued o' late concerning the future, what it shall bring for you."

"Age!" sighed Jocelyn.

"Forsooth, Jocelyn, yet what more? Tell me, for all

your years of hard life and so desperate ventures, what have you to show?"

"A serene and contented mind, lad."

"Nay, but spiteful Fortune hath plagued thee scurvily all thy days, man."

"True enough, Florian. But he that hardship hardily endureth may prove better man than Chance's favourite or Fortune's pampered pet."

"Mayhap, comrade. But what have the coming years in store for thee?"

"Nay, who shall tell me this, Florian?"

"I will, *amigo!* And first,— 'spite all your valour, your wit and wide experience o' the world, you are to-day a homeless man and well-nigh destitute."

"And there's the wonder on 't!" sighed Jocelyn, shaking his head ruefully.

"No wonder at all!" retorted young Florian. "Since you, forgetful of your own good, have ever been the champion of lost causes, wasting yourself in luckless ventures to save others, 'stead o' seeking your own happiness and—"

"Now hold there, Florian! Happiness, as I do think, cometh but by service. Ponder this!"

"Why, 'twere strange happiness, methinks, *amigo.* Tell me now, when your plots and counterplots are ended, your mission accompt,— how then?"

"I shall doubtless serve England and Her Majesty in some other fashion."

"Oh, verily! Yet wherefore not serve thyself also?"

"As how, my Florian?"

"Be done wi' your roving and fighting and— get you a home."

"A . . . home?" repeated the Captain, and so wistfully that Florian leaned from his pillows to view him eagerly and went on more softly:

"Ay, a home, Jocelyn! A wife! Children!"

"Why, a home would be very well!" muttered the Captain, his gaze abstracted. "Ay, truly—" Here, chancing to meet his companion's eager look, he sighed, smiled wryly and shook his head. "But wherefore saddle me with wife and children, comrade?"

"For that to wed is man's duty to himself and the world, and no place is truly home — without children!"

"Why then, lad, prithee where's the woman shall so favour me that am indeed a homeless man and destitute?"

"Well, old friend, there is . . . Ione, Lady Fane."

Now at this the Captain started, changed colour, glanced at Florian, glanced away and sat dumb, while his companion continued more lightly, though in his eyes that same bright eagerness:

"'Is she not beautiful?' says I to you. 'Florian,' says you, fixing me with eye o' dreamful ecstasy, 'She is beyond all peer!' 'Also,' says I to you, 'is she not proper woman as women go, and richly apt to motherhood? And do you not love this sweet lady with passion deep and reverent—'"

"Ha' done!" said the Captain in low yet terrible voice and with look of such cold ferocity that Florian's pale cheek glowed with sudden painful flush and he stared wide-eyed and speechless. Then the Captain, upstarting to his feet, clanked and jangled up and down the wide chamber, cursing very fervently in three several languages until, noting his young companion's utter dismay and woeful dejection, he choked back his bitter reproaches and stood dumb, scowling on vacancy. At last he sighed and laying hand upon Florian's drooping shoulder, spoke in his old, kind voice:

"Forgive me, lad! But faith, you touched me on the raw! For I do confess e'en I have had my dreams — of late, that must be no more than merest idle dreams—"

"But wherefore so, Jocelyn? For I dare avow she loveth thee in her secret heart, and where shall she find ever again such man as thyself—"

"Ha—folly, comrade! Also I am . . . bitterly, a-striving to wed her with one more proper, according to her late sire his will—"

"Mean you Robin Netherby?"

"Ay, I do.  And why a plague must you raise talk o' such matters?"

"For that I would ha' you wed and settled . . . lest I lose you."

"Nay, faith, lad, so soon as my mission be done then, an' the Queen need us not, we'll march together again, thou and I 'gainst Spain and——"

"Alas, Jocelyn, this were impossible."

"Why . . . what . . . Florian, how so?"

"Jocelyn . . . old friend, three days since, I was wed to my adored Cecily."  The Captain stared mute with astonishment.

"Married?" he exclaimed.  "Thou?  A beggarly soldier wi' nought but his sword——"

"Not so!" cried Florian, his eyes sparkling.  "I am better creature than any soldier,——I am a husband!  Also, beside my sword, I have two hands shall win me a home worthy my sweet wife!"

"A home!" murmured the Captain.  "Children!"

"An' the kind God so bless us, Jocelyn.  Oh, this surely were better than living but to slaughter my fellowmen in quarrels scarce known, and dying at last in muddy trench."

Now at this, the Captain sat so long in gloomy abstraction that at length Florian questioned him again:

"Well,—— how say you?  What o' yourself, comrade?"

"Why, I say," answered Jocelyn, rising to grasp his friend's so ready hand, "God prosper thee, Florian lad, thee and thine in all manner of ways so ever.  As for me, I'll to my duties——"

"Nay, but wilt not speak with my Cecily first?  Suffer that I call her——"

"Not now, lad, not now.  To-morrow an' ye will.  For . . . dost not see, in getting herself a spouse she hath stole away my friend——"

"No, no, Jocelyn, now am I more than ever thy loving friend . . . and she also; there be two of us.  Suffer that I call her."

"To-morrow, lad.  And now, farewell!"

# CHAPTER XVI

## DESCRIBETH A SMALL, GREAT LADY

JOCELYN rode slowly by leafy ways, avoiding the main road, alert and watchful as ever, but heavy with thought, musing on this wise:

So then, Florian was lost to him at last and he must go henceforth more solitary than ever since, in all the world, friends had he but two, young Florian and grey-headed, hard-smiting, shrewd old Roger Williams. And Florian was good as parted from him already. Well, certes, better this way than by steel or bullet. And he had loved the lad and should do still, though their ways must lie far apart henceforth. . . . To wed and beget lusty children! To make a home hereabouts in this well-loved England! The very soul of him was thrilling to the thought, sick with the fierce yearning had grown so mighty of late, plaguing him with such visions of deep and abiding happiness that must be but the very shadow of a shade, the Dream Glorious never to be realized except mayhap in that Magic Vale where all things were perfected . . . as he had dared suggest to her.

And now, while his horse plodded on, how and where it listed, he spoke her name aloud, voicing all the yearning passion of tenderness her ears should never hear:

"Ione! Joan beloved, somewhere, somewhen, peradventure in that future time when Death shall crown us with a greater life, we shall meet at last and — "

The vague mutter of a voice roused him to instant alertness, his right hand clapped down on holstered pistol butt, and, his keen eyes scanning the leafage to left and right, he rode on through this peaceful English countryside, grimly vigilant, as he had done many a time in battle-fouled Flanders when Death lurked imminent.

Thus presently, turning a bend in the lane, he saw this narrow thoroughfare blocked by horses, men and a huge vehicle that had lurched sideways through the hedge. Twelve or more stalwart fellows were these who sweated and panted about the tumbled carriage; and the men showed brave in rich, albeit dusty, liveries and half-armour; the coach was huge, springless and clumsy, but gaudy with paint and gilding, and its six tall horses showed sleek and fat. Now, perched hard by upon a large cushion, was a very small, ancient lady, bejewelled, belaced and in mighty farthingale, a wrinkled, sharp-featured, very arrogant personage, who surveyed horses, coach and panting men with cold ferocity and cursed them, one and all, with such vehement eloquence that Captain Jocelyn, drawing rein, surveyed her with no little awe and astonishment. Hearing the clink of bridle and spur, this little, ancient lady turned on him, quick and birdlike, and beckoned him nearer with one small, imperious finger.

"An hour, sir!" she snarled. "By all the fiends in hell, a mortal hour have I kicked my heels here and my stout, fatling fellows yonder ha' n't moved it one jot! A plague seize 'em, a murrain, a pest, a pox! And I here a-languishing! Oh, Satan! Sir, I am an aged creature, feeble and frail, forlorn and lost, ditched and damned by mine accursed varlets' uncare. Do you aid me instantly!"

"Madam," answered Jocelyn, bowing low to hide his smile, "with all my heart, but —"

"Ho, my master, to th' fiend wi' your 'buts'! Diccon man, ha, Diccon, thou misbegotten varlet rogue and rascal, make me known to this person!" At which shrill summons came one somewhat more resplendent than his fellows, who bowing, announced somewhat gaspingly:

"Sir, behold the noble Lady Ursula, Countess of Hartesmere."

"So, my master!" nodded the Countess. "Now tell me how far am I from Aldrington Chase?"

"Some five miles, madam."

"And my pestilent machine bogged, — with a curse!

What must I do? How come there, how? Pronounce, sir!"

"Well, your ladyship may 'bide for your carriage and ride, or walk, or suffer my horse to bear you — "

"Art fellow o' decision, I judge. And thy lank visage showeth honest and liketh me well. Your name, sir?"

"Captain Jocelyn Dinwiddie."

"'T is good, Old World name. Aid me up!"

"How then, will you trust so to a stranger, madam?"

"No, addlepate, to thy face. And I'll not ride pillion and no pillion saddle. Afore ye, sir — up!" So, reaching out long arms, Jocelyn swung this small, imperious dame to the saddle before him, where she settled herself serenely, ordering her voluminous petticoats with deft pattings of small, begemmed hands and kicks of surprisingly pretty foot.

"Ay, ye may look!" she nodded, seeing Jocelyn glance down at it; "my foot won infinite praise at wicked Harry's court. And I don't fal-lal my legs with these new and wanton Spanish silken hosen, — not I! One might as well go naked-legged! Though my niece Lady Fane doth affect 'em, as I hear, and so would my naughty grandniece Philippa, an' I suffered it."

"So doth the Queen, madam, they say."

"Well, she is — the Queen! Ho there, Diccon — Jenkin — Wat, see ye bring yon machine to Aldrington this night or your bellies shall suffer all, — no ale! By the devil his dam, not a drop! Now forward, my master!" So Jocelyn set off at gentle ambling gait, while this small but so domineering lady plied him with imperious questions.

"You know the Chase?"

"I am staying there, lady."

"Ho! A friend o' young Richard's?"

"He doth so honour me, madam — "

"Bah! 'T is a whelp, a cub, a curst imp! And a drinks too much for's years."

"Nay, madam, I protest you are unjust and — "

"Malediction, sir! I'm his aunt! And I know! These Aldringtons, with their pride and papacy! And what o' my lady Grave-airs, Madame Stately Touchmenot, with her red hair and long legs, — what of Ione Fane? Suffers she such male thing as thyself to breathe in her man-scorning presence — ha?"

"Madam, I — "

"'T is a proud and pranking baggage, that, scorning man and honest wedlock, flouteth Nature — "

"Madam," quoth the Captain, wincing, "madam, I beg — "

"What 'll ye beg, man? You ha'n't the look of a beggar. And never beg of a woman, — take! It shall spare a vasty waste o' wordy wind and womanly wiles and hypocrisy; it saves her face, spares her false modesty. As for this Ione, she's all good, warm flesh and blood yet acteth like airy sprite wi' no bowels, making scorn o' wedlock, forsooth! Tinkles instead wi' music, sighs o'er faddling rhymes! Courts men's souls and scorns their bodies, oh, Beelzebub! A modest, coy hypocrisy damned — "

"Hold, madam! I must demand you speak more truly of this most sweet and gentle lady or — "

"Demand, quotha?"

"Ay, demand — "

"Why, so you may, and your great, male chin a-jut in my face! Demand, sir, and demand, yet I'll speak how I will — and there's for ye, plague on't! This tongue o' mine waggeth to no man's order nor ever did, — no, not even to Harry the King! And he was man o' the malest and frighted the Pope o' Rome, a did. A rogue yet a man was Hal and might ha' been great but for — himself. And for Ione, this gold and ivory fool, this so stately wretch with her stork's legs, she was to ha' wed young Robin Netherby, a bravish lad yet something of a jack-pudding or he'd ha' wived her ere now. Lord! Men were men in my day; ay, and women women, that loved a man or hated a man and no deceitful muling and puling about it like — "

"Madam," said Jocelyn, reining up his horse. "I will now beg of your ladyship to get you down."

"Down where, man, where?"

"Upon your two feet —"

"How, — in this leaf and twiggy desolation? Never dare think it."

"Then I must do so —"

"Ha, wouldst desert me, villain? Attempt it, scurvy fellow, and I'll claw thee, clutch and cling so thou'lt call on Saint Michael to aid thee."

"Hum!" quoth the Captain, looking down into the small, fierce, elfin face so near his own with such rueful puzzlement that the Countess laughed sudden and shrill.

"Come now, my bold fellow!" she taunted. "Have at me."

"Faith," said Jocelyn, shaking his head, "were you but younger, madam —"

"I'd ha' had ye kissing me ere now," she tittered.

The Captain gasped, then seeing the dancing imp of mischief in this ancient lady's so strangely youthful eyes, he laughed full-throated and she with him, then tapping his lean cheek with her own small finger, she waggled it derisively beneath his nose.

"So, then, ye love Ione — ha? This creature that would seem a saint, spite the lurking passion of her telltale eyes and hot red hair —"

"Not red —" he began, then flinched and was dumb at his companion's screech of laughter.

"Red, my poor witling!" she cried. "Red, my nousless numps! Red as fire! Red as sin! Red as the burning pit o' shame! Red, I say!"

"Well, the Queen hath red hair," he muttered.

"Ha, and knoweth Ione o' thy love, Sir Captain?"

"No, madam —" he answered, before he could check himself and flinching to his companion's expected screech of laughter, saw she was looking up at him with shrewd and calculating gravity.

"And wherefore hast not told her this?"

"Madam," said he, a little stiffly, "I pray your ladyship, no more o' this."

"And your name is Jocelyn and you are a soldier?"

"Yes, madam."

"Hast fought for those poor, valiant Zeeland folk?"

"With all my might, lady."

"Art therefor of small fortune, belike?"

"Of none, madam."

"Dinwiddie is a good name. Of the West Country, methinks?"

"Devon, madam."

"Jocelyn is better yet. Thy people, kindred?"

"Dead, alas, or I might remember!"

"So, thou'rt young and I am old, and both of us solitary; thus are we akin, Jocelyn. Alas, I never had a son. . . . Ah, well, God knoweth best, they say, — mayhap I should ha' spoiled him. . . . Yet I ha' grieved to feel the son I never had clasp his man's arm about me; 't would ha' been mighty comfort in my age and loneliness, ay, me!" And nestling within the Captain's bridle arm, she laid her small, bedizened head upon his breast, all heedless of her great collar of rich lace.

"Art a something grim and gloomy creature for thy years, Master Jocelyn," she murmured, "and wherefore?"

"I have lived hard and seen so many die too easily, Countess."

"Why men must die an' they will ha' battles to their amusement, foolish one!"

"Ay, but not women and little children."

"Tush, boy!" she sighed. "Loved I a man, I should not fear to die with him. As for little children, dying in their so tender innocence, they but fly back to the God that sent them." Now after this they went a while in silence until, reaching a gentle eminence, Jocelyn reined up his horse.

"My lady," said he, pointing, "yonder riseth Aldring-ton Tower."

"So soon?" she sighed. "Plague take it!"

" Shall I set you down, my lady? "

" Nay then, art ashamed to bear me in thine arms, boy, for that I am wrinkled and old? "

" Now heaven forbid, madam," he answered hastily. " For indeed, you honour me."

" And your eyes show so honest that I must needs believe it," she nodded. " Come, boy, dost find some little kindness for me in your heart? "

" Ay, truly, madam, for I prove you strangely tender, despite your . . . your seeming — "

" My hell-fiery and furious showing and curst tongue — ha? Say, it, man, say it — for as I do know, 't is an acid tongue, venomous as loathed asp — ha? "

" 'T is something shrewd, my lady."

" Shrewd, forsooth? Wouldst bubble and play me the damned courtier now? "

" Not I, madam. For verily a woman that may love a man and die with him all unfearing, is high 'bove my poor praising, — in age, as in youth, she weareth a beauty may never fade."

" Ah, Jocelyn, ha' done or ye'll make me to weep! Yet 't was so woman loved in my day — when the world was younger and better."

" Why then," sighed he, " I would to God I had lived in such day."

" For this," said she wistfully, " I 'd kiss thee an' I might reach so high." Here the Captain glanced down and seeing the look in her bright eyes, bowed to the quick, soft pressure of her lips.

" 'T is so thy mother might bend from heaven to kiss thee, boy," she murmured.

And so, in this strange communion, they rode on again through sunlight and shadow and came at last into the great courtyard at Aldrington, where nothing stirred and silence brooded this sunny slumberous afternoon until, and here, to Jocelyn's no small consternation, the aged Countess fell to screeching in voice extremely loud and shrill!

" House — house — ho! Where a plague are ye all?

House . . . House, I say! Ten thousand devils, must I wait!"

But now came Master Rickaby the steward, this stately person, his wonted dignity somewhat marred by breathless hurry, yet bowing to his very knees at the mere sight of this so fierce, small, great lady, who instantly shook tiny fist at him whence she sat still perched before the Captain.

"Your betters, sirrah!" she cried arrogantly. "Where, minion, where is my nephew, the Earl? Where her ladyship? Speak, jolt-head! Where, I say — "

"Here, loved mine Aunt!" called a smooth, clear contralto voice, and Ione, suddenly appearing, stood as suddenly still and mute with surprise to behold her aged relative thus precariously perched.

"'Ods' wounds!" snarled the Countess, scowling. "Why must ye gape on me, madam, as I were some eye-blasting monster 'stead o' thy lady aunt, reverent with years — "

"Gape, Aunt — I!"

"Ay, like fish a-perishing, madam! Here was I utterly lost and cast away but for my gentle Jocelyn. Ay, ye may stare, child — my carosch in plaguey ditch, murrain on 't, and I were there with it, languishing this moment but for this my sweet friend Jocelyn." At this Ione, in the act of descending the marble steps, checked her stately progress to catch her breath and open her blue eyes wider than Nature. Whereat the Countess nudged Jocelyn slyly and bade him set her down.

Scarce was she afoot and had shaken out her petticoats than came Richard the Earl, breathless with hurry to make his reverence and be pecked on either cheek.

"And now, children," quoth the Countess, "or ever I speak another word, bring me indoor to a seat wi' cushions, for Jocelyn's saddlebow is plaguey hard to such ancient bones as mine. Come ye now, and you too, Jocelyn."

So they brought her into my Lady Ione's bower and there, throned amid divers cushions, the aged lady looked from Richard to Ione, where they stood respectfully in her presence and bade them be seated.

"Well, my naughty ones," she demanded; "where have ye hidden her — where?"

"Madam?" inquired my lord, looking his astonishment.

"Hidden whom, prithee, dear Aunt?" enquired Ione, with a certain lofty demureness.

"Oho!" cried the little Countess ferociously. "Now fie, and out upon your mock innocence, girl, wi' your great, long legs —"

"Aunt, for shame —"

"Tush, girl! I say your legs in their wanton silk stockens, — oh, I see 'em! Remain seated, Ione, and answer me forthright. Whom should I be a-seeking here wi' blood and sweat and bitter tears but Philippa, my naughty runaway, your cousin! Philippa, my niece, my ward, my chick, my one ewe lamb, the pet o' my lonely age. And the cruel wretch is fled away, vanished, — the naughty, wicked piece! And where should she flee but hither, as aforetime. So where have ye hid her? Speak, i' the name o' God! Speak — ha, confusion and the blight! Will ye stare and be dumb as so many stock fishes? Speak, — where is Philippa? Speak, I say, or —"

"Nay, but, madam," cried Ione, "how may we speak except you be silent and —"

"Silent? Ha — silent? How i' the fiend's name may I be silent and my poor heart beating like a snare drum? Ay, and my bowels all a-quake —"

"Aunt!" cried Ione.

"Madam," cried the Earl, "indeed . . . good faith, I do protest Philippa is not here —"

"Not here, boy — not here?" screeched the Countess. "Will ye dare tell me so, and I ha' journeyed all these weary miles! And my carosch in a ditch, with a curse!"

"Alas, sweet Aunt!" said Ione, showing more stately than ever. "I grieve your so great labours be all in vain, since our cousin is not at Aldrington —"

"Truly, madam," said my lord, "we ha' n't seen Philippa since last time she fled you, nigh a year agone —"

"Ho, malediction!" snorted the Countess. "Will ye

dare put me off with such flummery? 'T is hither she ever flees in her devilish tantrums. So tell me she is safe with ye and — I'll forgive your base deception, only tell me the sweet lamb is safe."

"'S life, madam!" exclaimed my lord anxiously, "I would to God 't were so, but upon mine honour she is not at Aldrington, nor have we seen her hereabouts."

Now at this the little Countess seemed to shrink amid her cushions, she wrung her hands and moaned in quick despair.

"Ah . . . then the dear God aid her innocence! Richard, dear nephew, what must we do? You that was to ha' wed her some day — do somewhat now — now! Lost!" wailed the aged lady, raising clasped hands towards heaven. "My white maid! My little, lost lamb — oh, God, shield her from harm and evil . . . shame . . . " The wailing voice was choked in sobs, the indomitable old head was bowed at last, the clasping hands fell apart . . . therefore, while my lord stood in frowning dismay and Ione, rising, clasped this little desolate form in sheltering arms, the Captain spoke:

"Pray, Countess, what like is this lost lady? Showeth she tall, dark —"

"No, no, friend Jocelyn, sweetly small is she, a most tender-seeming thing all pink and white, dark-eyed yet more golden than Ione —"

"Ha, by my soul!" cried the young Earl. "All Sussex shall be searched; ay, all the South Country! I'll have three hundred men horsed and away this very hour. Come, Jocelyn!"

"No need is there for this, Dick," said the Captain, rising, "since I do verily believe this errant lady is found already."

"How then," questioned Ione, with quick, strange look, "you know where she is hid, you?"

"Or I've no eyes i' this head o' mine," he answered, reaching for his gauntlets.

"And thine eyes be very quick and sure!" cried the Countess, reaching him her two hands with eager, pleading gesture, "thine eyes a woman may trust to — even woman younger and less wise in men than I, God bless them! Tell me, is my sweet innocent safe and well?"

"Both, madam."

"Ah, the vile, ungrateful little traitor, and I in tears for her! Go fetch her, Jocelyn man, carry her hither to me, — go this moment! Ah, Sir Honesty, show me the child safe and all unharmed, and Ursula of Hartesmere is more thy loving friend than ever — go!" So Jocelyn bowed and meeting Ione's glance, marvelled to see her eloquent eyes regard him so disdainfully and her black brows so knit against him and, thus wondering, cast riding cloak about him and strode off on his mission. But ere he reached the stable yard my lord came hastening after him.

"Jocelyn," said he, slipping hand within his arm, "I'm minded to ride with thee."

"Nay, Dick, what o' your aunt; she is old and —"

"My aunt?" exclaimed Richard with eloquent gesture. "Oh, God save us! She is plague groweth stronger with age. She —"

"Why, then, pray tell me of her niece, this runaway —"

"Philippa? She is Viscountess of Mereworth and must wed me one day, poor maid! But, Jocelyn, where doth she bide —"

"Love you her, Richard?"

"Ay, well enow."

"Enough for what?"

"To wed her as they say I needs must, some day."

"Hum!" quoth the Captain and tugged moustachio.

"Ha, Will!" cried my lord, as the big fellow came to wait on them, "a horse for Captain Jocelyn and saddle Black Roland for me."

"Nay, Dick," murmured the Captain, "for this occasion I pray you suffer I ride alone."

"Oh, as you will!" answered my lord, scowling in sudden petulance; now this reminding Jocelyn how Ione had also frowned on him, he mounted and rode away, not a little puzzled and thoughtful.

# CHAPTER XVII

### Telleth How the Viscountess Philippa
### Became Cecily and Wherefore

DISMOUNTING at the "Peck of Malt" he called John to tend his horse and crossed the yard, scarce heeding the rough-clad hairy fellow munching bread and cheese on the settle beside the door, and who stared after him with such very shrewd, bright eyes and thereafter beckoned honest John with the evil-looking knife he held and spoke in husky voice:

"Brother, yon gen'leman, be he biding hereabouts?"

"Ar, Tinker, at Aldrington wi' my lord th' Earl."

"Wheer be yon?"

"Fower mile along the road, mebbe."

"Thankee, Brother. I'll take another pint, your ale be mighty good."

Meanwhile Jocelyn, mounting the stair, opened a certain door to see Cecily start up from where she had been kneeling beside her young husband's chair and who, at the Captain's muttered apology, made him a very graceful, extremely demure curtsey; said she sweetly:

"Sir, I do rejoice to see you, for my Florian hath been a-grieving for you, and his friend is truly mine, I do hope."

"Why then, pray call me Jocelyn," said the Captain, advancing to take the pretty hand she proffered. "But how must I name you?"

"Why, sir, an' you be formal, — Captain Dinwiddie must call me . . . Madam Ferndale, but an' you can love me as your dear friend's wife, — I am Cecily."

"Ay, but," said he, glancing down at the small, capable

hand that clasped his own so firmly, "wherefore not — Philippa?"

The great dark eyes opened a little wider, the delicate brows twitched in sudden frown.

"Ah! So, then you know?" she murmured.

"I learned within this hour, madam — "

"How now?" laughed Florian happily. "What knoweth our solemn old campaigner?"

"That which I have oft been minded to tell thee of late, dear my husband, but 't is matter so small and our love so great . . . yet now needs must I — "

"Why then, speak, dear mine heart."

"Well, then, loved man, thine arm about me — so! Thy dear head upon my heart — thus! Though truly 't is none so great a matter, my Florian, only that I am not . . . not only thy very humble, true-loving Cecily, with few friends and never a groat of money, but — " here, meeting his look of adoration, she stayed to kiss him.

"Ah, love," he sighed, "God knoweth I seek no more of life than thine own sweet self. To know thee poor and destitute — why, 't is my very inspiration to mighty doing on thy behalf, to make us a home, to work and strive and perchance win some little fame to thee and thy glory."

"Why, so thou shalt, strong man of mine, for verily thy meek and humble Cecily am I henceforth, thank heaven! Yet I needs must tell thee that in those sad, empty days, or ever God suffered me blest sight of thee, I was indeed Philippa, Viscountess of Mereworth and divers other manors and estates I scarce do wot of, but — "

"Now forfend it, God!" exclaimed young Florian, gazing up into the lovely tender face so near his own with look of such amaze and growing dismay that she kissed him again, laughing a little unsteadily.

"Nay, hush thee and listen, my Florian," she commanded. "In those dark and dismal times I was wretched creature very unhappy and — oh, wilful! For, sweet husband, being desolate, I yet dreamed of love as a maid will, but a love so wondrous in its perfection that I began to

fear it was but an idle dream indeed. For I was rich and
many came a-wooing, yet love came never. So fled I a-seeking it, my perfect love, nor found it till thy dear eyes looked
down in mine. So I am thy wife to joy and suffer with
thee, to be poor or rich with thee, to comfort and aid thee
and to love thee alway, my husband. Ah, now see how eloquent true love hath made me and wiser than all my books
and school-men, — so prithee kiss thy wordy wife therefore." But Florian sat a while mute with wonder and dismay.

"And I no more than sick and beggarly soldier!" he
groaned at last. "Oh, man Jocelyn, what must I do?
Counsel me, friend."

"Why, kiss her, for sure!" said the Captain. "Ay, kiss
her, man, thy heartiest, thanking God."

"But . . . but so great a lady . . . my little Cecily
. . . of such lofty rank!" stammered Florian.

"Nay," she answered, "I am thy wife, no more and no
less! Is't not so, Jocelyn?"

"Why, truly, truly," answered the Captain, "an' ye be
duly wed, according to Church, the canonic law — of the
which I do know less than nought — "

"That is she, good my master!" cried Dame Margery,
peeping in at them round the door. "By your leave here
come I, Captain, for to tell ee this very thing. Wed she be
by Parson Gelpin hisself over from East Bourne. And ah,
sir, my lady Philippa do seem a'most like my own flesh and
blood, for 't was I first took she from her mother's arms —
a died that hour, sweet soul! So I was her nurse till I
wed my John. Ay, by the pyx, she be married fast enow,
I'll warrant me! And wherefore not? Marry come up!
Why should a not wed where a loves? And sweet Master
Florian be right fair and proper gentleman, by's look — "

"Verily, my good Margery!" answered the Captain.
"But what of her lady aunt, the Countess of Hartesmere?"

Now, at mention of this small, so formidable personage,
the good dame's defiant air vanished and she glanced about
uneasily.

"God save us!" she muttered.    "Good Master Jocelyn, what o' she?"

"Dame, she is at Aldrington."

"Lord love us all!" exclaimed the buxom hostess, clasping her hands.

"Come you from her, Jocelyn?" demanded Florian's little wife, caressing her young husband's thick, curly hair.

"Yes, Cecily.    She bade me bring you to her instantly."

"She would!" sighed Cecily, yet smiling tenderly also. "For oh, 't is most determined aunt and fierce, yet loveth me right well.    So prithee, Jocelyn, bear her my love but say that if she so yearn for sight of her truant niece, she must hither to us that she may grow to love my dear husband.    Say this for thy friend Cecily that loves thee, Jocelyn, for her husband's sake and thine own wise, gentle self."

"Ah, my Cecily,—beloved wife!" murmured young Florian; now presently, turning in the doorway, the Captain saw him on his knees with his long arms, so terrible in fight, fast girt about her slender loveliness.

Then, sighing, Jocelyn went his way, so full of yearning fancies that he rode off with no word for John nor heeded how the hairy tinker fellow had vanished.    Still adream, he rode through the mellow afternoon sunlight, yet so instinctively watchful that suddenly in one lithe movement he was out of the saddle, crouched behind his horse, pistol levelled at a certain bush for, with no wind abroad, this bush was astir, rustling ominously.

"Out!" he commanded.    "Come out or I fire!"

"Old war dog, have with thee!" chuckled a voice softly, and forth of the leaves started a swart, grimy fellow in ragged homespun and girt about with a leather apron. "Well met, Jocelyn lad!"    And off came a ragged cap, showing a close-cropped, grizzled head.    Jocelyn lowered the pistol and reaching out eager hand, he spoke in glad welcome, albeit in a murmur:

"Roger man, well met!"

"Ay, 't is myself," nodded the other, as their hands

gripped, " and for the nonce, look you, a tinker. Come your ways wi' me where we may talk."

" Why then, have with thee, Roger."

So, leading his horse in amid the boskage, Jocelyn followed Sir Roger Williams, this redoubtable and famous soldier, whither he led.

# CHAPTER XVIII

## Concerning One Sir Roger Williams, His Mission

"And look you," quoth Sir Roger, as they trudged ever deeper into these dense woodlands, "after the mud and blood o' the Low Countries, I prove a tinker's life one of marvellous ease and comfort, Jocelyn."

"And how long hath known such ease, old comrade?"

"Since I turned my back on London, four days since."

"Saw you the Queen, Roger?"

"Ay, I did! And had of her, for my twenty odd years' hard service, a tweak o' the ear, py heavens! Not so much as a cloak to cover me, and I in rags and rust, look you! Nor horse to bear me, nor stiver to my purse, and that empty as ever. And when I would ha' pled the cause of her poor soldiers starving and naked i' the Netherlands — a raged at me, ay, and railed on me right bitterly, for plaguing her wi' my letters."

"Spoke you of this Spanish plot, Roger?"

"Ay, and she damned it for stale news, vowed she'd heard enough on't from yourself, Jocelyn. 'This Dinwiddie, I know him,' says she; ''t is a watchdog bays the moon and snarls upon imagined dangers. For,' says she, 'I've 'scaped death by fire, poison and the axe, by steel and bullet, and think ye I shall perish by such mean thing as little Spanish Philip? Go to!' says she. 'If ye must be finding out yet more plots against my life, 't is for Dinwiddie and you and Frank Walsingham in especial to counterplot to my deliverance and salvation. Now go hence about it,' saith she, patting me o' the pate, 'away, my mad Welshman, for I've matters o' greater moment.'"

"Gloriana!" nodded Jocelyn gravely. "On my life, Roger man, 't is a strange, great soul, a valiant spirit bred

'mid intrigue and fostered by constant dangers; small wonder she hath outgrown fear. Gloriana! Sure, 't is the
most hated, best-loved Queen that ever was."

"True enow!" growled Sir Roger. "A woman bold
as man yet veriest woman, full o' contrairiness, can cog and
cozen and weep or curse all men dumb,—wise as Solomon,
yet stuffed wi' foolish whim-whams, peevish as any green-
sick wench, yet aggrieved for her fading youth and—no
sense o' gratitude! And there's your Gloriana! And yet
is she woman, and so, look you, we fight and starve and die
for her!"

"Well, Roger, can a man die better?"

"Ha—hum!" snorted the knight, pausing beside a little
noisy rill to shift his tinker's pack from one sturdy shoulder
to the other. "For my own part, look you, I'd liefer live
a jolly tinker, as mark this song I made, Jocelyn!" And
forthwith, as they tramped on again, he sang these words
in hearty, tuneful voice:

> "Ho the tinker bold doth no whit lack
> So I'll like tinker, trudge it,
> And every lousy care I'll pack
> Fast in my tinker's budget.

"And yet, alack, Jocelyn man!" sighed he. "Soon must
this care-free tinker rogue become again poor soldier and
care-harassed gentleman, oh, the pity on 't!"

"Nay, what's to do, Roger?"

"Much, I suspect, yet the how and what we can learn
but by following this chattersome brook."

"What brings thee here into Sussex?"

"Love for thee, lad, among other matters. To warn
ye, Jocelyn, as you be marked for death, but this is by you
expected, ha?"

"Hourly!" nodded the Captain. "But how especially?"

"As thus, Jocelyn. In days two or three shall come
divers gentlemen to Aldrington and of these one, a ripe
sword-master called Captain Charles Vince. Himself in-

tent on thy killing, look you, shall provoke thee to duello. 'T is a prime rapier and dagger man, black-visaged, tall, lacketh half an ear, and called Vince."

"I shall know him!" nodded Jocelyn. "And what now?"

"We shall follow this brook till it bring us beyond Hoove village, where hard beside the sea is a tavern named the Anchor where doth wait us the wisest, subtlest man in all England."

"And this I guess the Secretary of State, Sir Francis Walsingham, eh, Roger?"

"None other, py heavens! For hath not his policy anent Spanish Philip's lying treachery in the Netherlands proven true? Had but the Queen and timorous Cecil acted as and when he advised, — ha, to-day the Netherlands were free o' Spain, England secure and thousands alive that now lie mouldy bones."

"True enough!" sighed Jocelyn. "Leicester and his levies marched too late — "

"Ay, and moreover, look you, Leicester shall never be match for the great Parma."

"And prithee, Roger, how go matters in London and the North?"

"Well enow. Frankie Walsingham hath smelt out the English conspiracy, Babington and his fellows be all known and can be taken when he will, ay — so soon as matters show ripe, for — in thine ear now — the Queen o' Scots is deeply implicated! A little more time and she shall dig her own grave with her pen."

"Sayst thou, Roger!"

"Ay, it needeth but time and patience. But for this curst Spanish plot, there's much to learn. Mendoza in Paris is great with the King, Philip in Spain hath bought the Guises, Parma in Flanders marshals his veterans. Verdugo in Ireland waits but the word to invade us — and all this for the killing of our Bess and the woe of Protestant England, God aid us! . . . And now, Jocelyn, how stand matters here i' the South?"

"Neither ill nor good."

"So? How then o' these great Papist families and, more especially, the greatest of 'em all — how showeth the young Earl of Aldrington?"

"He is as loyal to Her Majesty as — thyself, Roger."

"And his sister, the Lady Fane?"

"Shall prove faithful as — myself."

"Ha-hum!"

"How then, Roger, d' ye doubt them?"

"Nay, lad, how should I? Yet there be rumours, look you to the contrary."

"Whence are these rumours, man?"

"Ask of Frank Walsingham an' ye will, for this same babbling rill hath led us aright; lo, yonder the Anchor Tavern, Jocelyn."

# CHAPTER XIX

### Telleth of Sir Francis Walsingham and How Captain Jocelyn Pledged His Head

WITHIN a small, dim chamber a man stood gazing forth of the inadequate window, its casement open to the warm, fragrant afternoon, — a slim man in a furred cassock; his pale face, lean and careworn beneath graying hair, was lit by large, mournful eyes that yet were bright and steadfast; his nose was dominant, his lips showed compressed above the jut of a resolute chin.

With musing gaze still sadly intent upon the sunny world beyond the lattice, he spoke in voice soft yet resonant.

"It was yourself, Captain Dinwiddie, brought Her Majesty the first news of this Spanish plot, despite two desperate attempts on your life — "

"And look you," snorted Sir Roger, "get no more for his pains than I, Frank!"

"Who serveth the Queen must look for no recompense!" answered Walsingham, turning from the window, his melancholy eyes seeming sadder than ever.

"Ay, py heavens!" growled Sir Roger. "Yet such as Chris Hatton ha' waxed fat — ask his Grace of Ely — ha! For Chris, look you, was ever a smock-faced gallant and a tongue o' velvet."

"Verily!" nodded Sir Francis. "A mere courtier. But we be servants of the Crown and of this England that soon must lie prostrate 'neath damned Philip's bloody shoe, or by God's will, stand higher and prove more mighty than she hath ever been, — her fate is in the balance, sirs — "

Here he fell silent and crossing to a table whereon lay many papers, sat there a while, staring moodily towards the narrow casement, his pale face showing more haggard than ever in the westering sun's mellow radiance; then sudden as he had paused, he spoke again:

"Three days since, a ship put into Rye and among the passengers two, one an Englishman named Ralph Storey and one Pietro Vespucci, an Italian soldier of fortune, that speaketh English and calls himself John Ford, yet both emissaries of Spain. They were permitted to land unchallenged and thus, unsuspecting, journeyed hither. Last night I had them apprehended. They are now travelling Tower-wards but their papers and effects are here. Now, sirs, my intent is that ye shall, disguised in their habits and with their papers for credence, pass yourselves off as these same secret agents and so learn the reason of their presence here in Sussex and who of the Catholic gentry hereabouts are concerned in this damnable plot against the Queen's life. Well, how say ye? Is 't agreed?"

"Bodykins, with all my heart," quoth Sir Roger. "We be ready, Frank, on a condition—"

"Ha, a condition, sir?"

"That we be held exempt in any matter of a corpse or so, a slit throat here and there, look you, should it come to 't."

"Agreed, Roger man; ye shall have carte blanche, though I'd liefer ye use your wits than steel or dag. Yet an' it must be sword or bullet, such as die so ye shall but save from death less kindly. For I tell you, gentlemen, afore God, here is no time to palter or be lenient as heretofore. No! Henceforth all proven traitors shall to the axe, be they high or low, man, woman, or maid!"

"Ay, with all my heart!" nodded Sir Roger.

"Within the closet yonder, sirs, ye shall find the cloaks and habits of these—"

"With submission, sir," said Jocelyn, "I would suggest that such disguise for me were worse than useless, since I am known hereabouts. I shall contrive better as my mere self."

"How think you of this, Roger?" sighed the State Secretary.

"That my old comrade is i' the right on 't, Frank. But for myself, that was erstwhile lousy tinker, I 'll go transform into this Italianate soldier that calls himself John Ford, pox on him!" So saying, the grim veteran of a hundred battles strode off about the business, the while Sir Francis Walsingham sat brooding silently awhile; and Jocelyn, knowing him for the grim veteran of so many secret intrigues, deadly stratagems and counterplots, and beholding now his astute, indomitable features, felt he was a match even for that master of duplicity, Philip the Second of Spain.

"Sir," said the Minister at last, fixing his keen gaze on Jocelyn, "you are living at Aldrington, the which is well . . . but the Lady Fane is of a beauty renowned."

"And with justice, sir."

"She is also of a bold, high spirit."

"Truly, sir, a valiant-showing lady."

"She harboureth priests against the law."

"Yet have I seen no priests at Aldrington, sir."

"She hath been heard to speak treason and to rail upon Her Majesty very contumaciously."

"Mr. Secretary, she is very proud and, being young, speaketh but on random impulse."

"She hath been in correspondence with Mary Stuart!"

"Yet, sir, for her loyalty I would pledge you this hand o' mine."

"Take heed, sir, take heed!" murmured Walsingham, his stern features grimmer than ever, and tapping long finger on a certain paper that lay on the table before him. "Come you and read me this — aloud!" So Jocelyn arose and looking upon this paper, read forth these words inscribed in a crooked, disguised hand:

"'In *re* Ione, Lady Fane. She hath been heard to condemn the Queen's Majesty her policy touching Mary Stuart late Queen of Scots, vehemently protesting against the present imprisonment of the same. She frequents the company of Sir Philip Drayton of Shalmeston and other notorious recusants.

" 'She holdeth midnight mass secretly with divers other Papistical abominations. She practiseth upon her young brother the Earl, to draw and seduce him and his powers to the interest of Mary Stuart.' "

"Well, sir?" demanded Walsingham, as Jocelyn laid down the paper, " how say you to this? "

"That this lady hath an enemy, sir."

"Ha, and a friend, 't would seem, sir, to champion her cause, eh, Captain Dinwiddie? "

"Howbeit, Mr. Secretary, my head is yet pledge for her loyalty." Sir Francis Walsingham's furrowed brow darkened in quick frown, his keen eyes narrowed to luminous slits, his grim mouth thinned to sinister, down-bending line.

"She is beautiful!" said he, in tone menacing as his look. "And you are a man . . . younger than I had thought. Now — heed me, Captain Dinwiddie; whoso showeth mercy on any traitor in such time as this perils England and shall die the traitor's death!"

"So shall you trust me, Mr. Secretary, or — "

"So will I, sir, for I have eyes and ears that watch unceasing and in many places — "

"Enough, sir!" said Jocelyn, with disdainful gesture. "Your England is mine also. No need is here for threats. An' this lady prove indeed false traitor, let my head fall with hers — or when ye will."

"So be it, Captain!" sighed Walsingham and fell again to gloomy meditation nor spake until back came Sir Roger, his shabby person quite transfigured in velvets, his brawny throat encircled by vasty ruff, his moustachios fiercely upcurled, and beard peaked.

"Py heavens, look you!" quoth he, spreading wide his ample cloak. "Your Roguery goeth better dight than honourable soldier! Wounds, nakedness and starvation in Flanders — "

"And here," quoth Sir Francis, "here be your letters of credence, Roger. One to a Master Twyfoot, merchant at

Lewes, one to Sir Philip Drayton at Shalmeston Manor, one for Mr. Fane at Kingston Buci, and this other for Lord Afton beyond East Bourne. In the yard below you shall find a horse chosen for speed and endurance, Roger. Ye may get news to me in London or Greenwich, either by means of a Mr. Trenchard at Lewes, or John Catesby in Shoreham. Lastly, sirs, the key or passwords are: 'Saint George for Santiago', — but this ye shall see for yourselves from leisured study of these treasonable papers. Yet one thing more. Ye have been chosen for this perilous mission being each of an oft-proven valour and cold, resolute judgment, since upon your wits and courages hang the Queen's life and perchance the fate of England. Also, since this is truly matter of such vast import, past experience should warn ye, your great work achieved, to expect little of honour and less of profit therefore. Yet for you as for me, the weal of England cometh first and shall be guerdon sufficient. And now, gentlemen, here's my hand. God save and prosper ye — farewell!"

And presently getting to horse, they set forth slowly, knee to knee, through the glow of sunset, reading these treasonable papers and letters that Walsingham's ceaseless vigilance had so lately intercepted; and having perused and studied each word, they fell to low-toned communion. And now it was that Jocelyn told his comrade in arms of young Richard the Earl and his folly and therewith his own suspicions and schemes, whereto Sir Roger hearkened with lowering brow, keen eyes watchful and intent, the while he plucked tenderly at his new-trimmed beard. . . .

And thus walking their horses, they took council together how best to make King Philip's murderous plot and mighty scheming of none avail.

"For, look you, old war dog," muttered Sir Roger grimly, "'twas by the hand of hired fanatic this bloody Philip murdered the noble Prince of Orange, as ye'll mind, and, by God, so shall he not slay our niggardly Bess, though we die for't all unminded — ha?"

"Amen, Roger!" nodded the Captain.

# CHAPTER XX

### IN WHICH IS FURTHER MENTION OF THE
### CAMPAIGN POETICAL

SHADOWS were beginning to creep when the Captain came jingling up the terrace steps and halted instantly at the sound of music. Crossing softly to an open window, he beheld Ione seated at a clavichord and singing, sweetly murmurous, words written upon a sheet of paper, words indeed that he knew very well, since they were his own, and instinctively he turned to be gone, but this tender murmur swelling suddenly to rich, full song, he paused to watch and hearken a while, lured by the unexpected glory of this voice so passionately tender that it seemed to make these words it sang far more beautiful than he had ever dreamed. Thus stood he (that so loved music) as he were entranced until this singing was drowned in sudden, harsh discord struck by petulant fingers and then, as if aware of the silent watcher, my lady glanced up quickly and saw him.

"Out upon 't!" she exclaimed, frowning. "Here sit I and would fain set me sweet music to sweeter words, yet can make nought o' sufficient worthiness to match them or pleasure me. . . . Ah, but you, Sir Captain? You have tarried shamefully on your errand."

"I was kept, madam."

"Found you my cousin Philippa safe and well?"

"Indeed, my lady. I found her happily wed."

"Wed? Little Philippa!" My lady's full, red lips parted speechlessly, that is to say she gaped in sheer amazement while the Captain, taking off his hat, leaned in through the open lattice and nodded confirmation.

"Philippa? Wed?" gasped my lady again. "Who is the man? Ah, what villain hath so dared? And she to have married Richard himself! And to thus defy Aunt Ursula! Oh, my soul! Here shall be mighty to-do anon!"

"Faith, so think I, madam. For, alas, her spouse is poor gentleman, barren of all things save a dauntless courage and high honour — "

"Ah, he sounds like — yourself, sir."

"My Lady Ione, you honour me." Here she turned back to the clavichord yet touched no sound therefrom but, with face thus averted, questioned him a little breathlessly:

"Is it perchance . . . that little, pretty Philippa hath been so strangely honoured to . . . win and wed this Perfection of Nature . . . Dinwiddie?"

"I?" exclaimed Jocelyn, in tone of such stark amazement that Ione, stealing glance at his astonished face, laughed suddenly, then as suddenly flushed hotly and bowing her head, played a few chords of music very softly.

"Nay," said she at last, "it were hard to imagine you a benedict, or that our peerless Dinwiddie should ever stoop to the folly of love."

"Ay, true!" said he, heartily. "I'm nothing fitted for such tender ploys; my tongue inapt for th' accepted dicta of sighful gallantries. 'Sdeath, I should make but sorry business on 't! And faith, I had liefer be ragged soldier than indifferent lover, indifferent loved — "

"Why then, since you are not husband to my poor cousin, who is he?"

"This, madam, you shall doubtless learn anon from your lady aunt. Pray you, where may I find her?"

"Troth, sir, not here! For when you came not, she commanded poor Richard forth, got herself to horse, and with him and divers of his gentlemen, galloped in quest of you."

"The Countess?" he exclaimed. "So old and on horseback? Now here's brave spirit! Oh, admirable!"

"Sir, my lady aunt, despite her age, is notable lady, indeed a very . . . personage."

"Ay, upon my soul, that is she!" quoth the Captain impulsively. "I would to heaven she were younger."

"Oh, sir! And wherefore, beseech you?"

"For that 't is noble woman, great of soul — "

"And tongue, sir, like serpent's sting, you'll mayhap ha' noticed."

"Yet 't is woman a man might love and honour."

"What man, I pray you? 'T is never — yourself?"

"Ay, faith, my Lady Ione, even I."

"Oh, wonderful!" mocked Ione, viewing him with quick smile. "So Dinwiddie could love that small ferocity, mine aged aunt. Come you in, wondrous man, and I will tell you wonders yet more marvellous."

But when he was seated opposite her on cushioned settle, she remained mute awhile, her slim fingers waking soft chords from the whispering strings what time she viewed him with level, dispassionate gaze, a look of such puzzled wonderment that when at last he questioned her, it was in tone wistful as his long-lashed, grey eyes:

"Well, madam?"

"Indeed!" she answered, with quick, determined nod, "so well that I'm all amazed and, like Richard, would fain know thee mine assured friend."

"My lady, this have I ever been."

"Why then, shalt 'madam' and 'my lady' me nevermore. I will be Ione to thee henceforth — nay, this am I for others — do thou call me Joan. I mind 't was so you named me for yourself! And now, to tell you of this marvel, — nay first, what of Mr. Ferndale; he is hurt, Dick tells me?"

"It is none so dangerous, God be thanked!"

"You much affection him, I think?"

"He is my friend, lady, and these be very few. But what o' this promised wonder, pray?"

Instead of answering, she played a few more bars of music very softly and, thus playing, spoke:

"I become ever more grateful to my Lord Willoughby."

"And prithee, why to him?"

"For that, when I sought his advice how best to free Richard of Lord Riderwood his wicked company, asked of him a bold fellow able to cope with this so evil and dangerous man, my lord in his wisdom sent me — Din-widdie."

"Know you my Lord Willoughby well, madam?"

"Very well.  I also know this new ballad they have made to his glory!"    And forthwith she sang in rich, clear voice:

> "'Ho, for the brave Lord Willoughby
> Of courage fierce and fell.
> Who would not give one inch of way
> For all the devils in hell.'

"This was writ of his bravery at Zutphen, I think.  Were you at Zutphen?"

"Yes, madam."

"Then you shall tell me of it, — "

"I had liefer hear you sing."

"Then belike I will.  Yet now I am to thank you for working such marvels in Richard; he is changed past belief, he showeth so manly these days, so kindly gentle, and can scarce bear thee from his sight!  I pray God this change in him endure."

"Never doubt it, madam; my Lord Richard hath found his manhood."

"By reason of you, Jocelyn!  So shall I call you Jocelyn, Jocelyn, henceforth.  Now for these other marvels, — and the first is — yourself, Jocelyn!  For I mind me how you said you were of character various and, by our Lady, I must needs believe it!  I've known you by turns — a bravo ready to smirch your steel for base hire, a courtly gentleman, a grim soldier dourly dumb, an euphuistic pedant with words amany, a grave philosopher, a wicked heretic, a kindly friend, a brute can thrash tender boy, a sad-eyed man, a wistful, solitary creature . . . thus much and more I prove thee, Jocelyn.  Now which of all these is thee, thy one truest self?"

"Neither and all," he answered, smiling.  "I am Din-widdie."

"And," she retorted, "Dinwiddie hath so vaunted himself the peerless perfection of all human concept that I was wont to mock this paragon, but — to-day am I all meek humility!"

Now at this he eyed her so very dubiously that her vivid lips curved to quick smile; then, sighed she:

"At the least, to-day I am sufficient humbled to doubt mine own judgment and woman's wit."

Here Jocelyn laughed suddenly.

"*Mirabile dictu!*" he exclaimed. "'T is miracle indeed!"

"Verily!" she nodded. "'T is the first time ever I heard you laugh!"

"But what now," he questioned; "what is there in all creation should work such world-shaking marvel?"

"Robin Netherby!" she answered, softly murmurous, and laid caressing hand upon certain close-written sheets of paper; now perceiving what these were, the Captain tugged moustachio and muttered:

"Hum!"

"Yea," she answered, taking up these manuscripts very tenderly, "here is the greatest miracle of all, — he, that methought dumb, speaketh with a sweet eloquence few shall ever match! Robin Netherby hath a great soul! And here is the other marvel, — that you, Jocelyn, on such short acquaintance, should be 'ware of this, whiles I, that have known him all my days, little guessed it and nothing esteemed him — until now! Indeed, we do sometimes entertain angels unawares or toss aside the seeming pebble that is truly peerless gem! For I do tell thee in this same Robin, that seems no more than simple gentleman, doth burn a spirit lofty and poetic."

"Art . . . sure?" murmured Jocelyn.

"I am as sure of it to-day as you were sure of it a sennight since. Robin hath writ me lines more beautiful than any ever penned me!"

"Why, I've heard Sir Philip Drayton is a poet and — "

"He? 'T is but a rushlight to the sun, Jocelyn! Here are the verses; you shall read and judge, — nay, I will — for they are very ill set down; Robin is no pen-man."

So, unfolding one of these papers yet not looking thereon, she recited the following stanzas, sweet-voiced and tender:

> "Oh, eyes divine wherein I see
>     All that I hope and fain would be
>     Your beams light all my world for me
>     Dear eyes divine.
>
> "There is a glory of the sun
>     When day begins to peep,
>     Rapture of stars when day is done
>     Ere gentle Luna, one by one
>     Doth kiss them into sleep.
>
> "But fade the day to deepest night,
>     Though sun, moon, stars refuse their light
>     Ye still should make my dark soul bright
>     Ye eyes divine.
>
> "And might I in your radiance see
>     The light that should but wake for me,
>     Then very man of men I'd be,
>     Oh, eyes divine!"

"Well," she murmured, deep eyes adream, "it was this poem I would set to music yet can contrive none sweet enough. What say you of it?"

"Why . . . it hath merit!"

"Merit!" she repeated softly and then her eyes, dreamy no longer, flashed scorn at him. "Merit, quotha!" she exclaimed and curled red lip at him. "What mean you with your 'merit', forsooth!"

"That 't is not overlong, madam, and therefore—"

"Enough, sir!" she cried disdainfully, refolding the script with an elaboration of tender care. "I perceive that even Dinwiddie hath his limits! Talk not of poesy, sir, prattle rather of your swords and cannons and musketoons, and if you must speak—name me 'madam'!"

"Faith," he answered, somewhat ruefully, "I have never as yet dared name you aught other. And for these verses I do think very well of them—here and there."

"Here and there!" she repeated, in growling indignation. "Captain Dinwiddie — sir, I do find you no better than iron-headed soldier! Yet I tell you of these verses that Sir Philip Sidney, no, nor Spenser himself, hath ever writ sweeter, purer line."

"Yet were these same gentlemen soldiers also, my lady. And for mine own part, I protest these verses do rhyme very well, with just rhythm o' dactyl and spondee, — they trip, lady, they — "

"Be silent, sir, you know not whereof you speak! Moreover, such laggard, would-be praise offends me. Though 't is grievous to find ye so lacking in all perception of this gentle art of poesy, for I do think it the noblest of all the arts. . . . And . . . afore Heaven!" she exclaimed, shooting at Jocelyn quick, keen glance, "an' Robin can write thus and is indeed such man to conceive such images, I may yet fulfil my father's will and suddenly wed him!"

"The which, madam, should prove thee wise as dutiful, since Robin is, forsooth, very proper gentleman — "

"Tush!" cried my lady for no apparent reason, and frowned; then, gathering up these so precious papers, rose to her feet; quoth she:

"There are here divers other verses I had meant to read for your delight, but I find Dinwiddie, this paragon, so pitifully lacking in all sense poetical that 't would be but vain labour."

"Yet, madam, even Dinwiddie might learn, with time and patience . . . of you, mayhap."

"Nay, sir, my patience is all fled. And yet, if Dinwiddie be sufficient humble — " she paused suddenly and turned, as in at the open casement came the smiling, comely face of Mr. Roland Fane.

"Greeting, sweet coz!" cried he gaily. "Thou thing of beauty, that Beauty's self transcendeth, fair greeting! Captain Dinwiddie, sir, your slave! Prithee, where tarrieth my lordly Rick? The sweet lad hath writ, bidding and commanding me to supper."

"And you are expected, Roland," answered my lady, beckoning. "Come you in, Dick hath but ridden forth to try a new cast of hawks."

Mr. Fane entered with all his usual smiling grace, took possession of Ione's two hands, kissed them, pressed them to his heart and was for kissing them again, when came a tap on the door and, receiving permission, the stately Master Rickaby presented himself and, gold-tipped wand of office gracefully aflourish, announced:

"Sir Thomas Vincent for my lord, your ladyship," and having ushered in the gentleman, flourished and departed. Sir Thomas strode forward, loud-voiced, bold-eyed and somewhat flushed with potations as usual.

"Madame," cried he, with capering bow, "ha, Lady . . . vision o' joy, hear me vow my bleeding heart at thy lovely feet, ah, prithee — " Here, chancing to meet the Captain's intent gaze, his speech ended in a gulp and his eyes widened.

"Why, Sir Thomas," laughed Ione, noting his stricken look, "ha'n't you met Richard's friend, Captain Dinwiddie?"

"No, madam . . . yes . . . somewhere . . . " stammered Sir Thomas.

"Indeed, sir," said Jocelyn smoothly, "at a tavern called 'The Peck of Malt' . . . we talked philosophy, you'll mind."

"Phil-osophy!" repeated Sir Thomas, his prominent eyes goggling. "You? Ha — in a buff coat and — a ragged cloak, 't was yourself — "

"One of my selves sir," nodded Jocelyn. "Our debate grew warm until my friend Mr. Ferndale, with argument pointed and a logic resistless, won you and your gossips to our way o' thinking."

"Ha! Now by the fiend, sir," quoth Sir Thomas with grandiloquent flourish towards his wounded arm, "were I but sound, you should incontinent answer for — "

"Hold, sir!" said Jocelyn, smiling. "'T is evident we be at cross purposes — for Saint George, as you should know and as Mr. Fane can tell you, Saint George is for Santiago!"

The book of music that Mr. Fane had been idly studying slipped from his stiffened fingers and lay unheeded; Sir Thomas Vincent, recoiling, whispered a startled oath, while my lady glanced in wonderment from one intent face to the other.

"Heaven's light!" she exclaimed. "Pray now, what riddle is here?"

"Mayhap," smiled Jocelyn, "Mr. Fane shall tell you this, madam."

But Mr. Fane, his nimble tongue for once unready, merely fumbled awkwardly for the music book and, contriving to smile, shook his head.

"Why then, madam," said Jocelyn, his smile a little grimmer, "perchance Sir Thomas shall resolve you this rebus."

"Faith and troth," muttered Sir Thomas, frowning, "I scarce do know . . . some matter politic, madame, some — " here, meeting Mr. Fane's warning glance, he fell suddenly mute, whereat my lady grew but the more determined.

"Come, speak, sirs!" she commanded. "What mystery do you make together?"

"Naught, sweet coz," laughed Mr. Fane. "Naught i' the world! 'Twas but some jest of the Captain, a jape — no more, a thing of airy nothingness — "

"Indeed, my lady," said Jocelyn lightly, but scanning her lovely face with a grave anxiety, "this said I, hand thus upon my heart, — now prithee heed, madam! 'Saint George,' quoth I, 'is for Santiago!'"

For a long moment she gazed at him with look of such evident mystification that the Captain's stern mouth twitched; he drew a deep breath like one relieved and smiled, whereat she instantly frowned on him.

"Folly!" she exclaimed angrily. "Or do you mock me, sir?"

"On my life, no, madam!"

"Why then, if this be your wit, 't is jest beyond my poor understanding!" Now here, for the second time, Jocelyn laughed very happily and seating himself at the virginal struck thereon resounding chords and forthwith sang, glad-voiced:

"So rest ye, worthy gentlemen
    Let nothing ye dismay
    What not now is, is yet to be
    That all the world one day shall see
    And this doth lie twixt you and me
    Till dawns the fateful day."

"So then," said my lady, eyeing him askance beneath puckered brows, "Dinwiddie hath a gift of music?"

"Occasionally, madam," he answered, running his sinewy fingers lightly over the keys, while he watched where Mr. Fane and Sir Thomas sat in the deep window recess, their heads very close together.

"And wherefore now?" she questioned, soft-voiced.

"Ah, my lady," he answered as softly, "'t is for that the heart o' me rejoiceth."

"Oh! And why, Jocelyn?"

"For such reason that, though marvellous good reason, 't were out o' reason to speak on."

"Enough o' your plaguey riddles, sir!" she sighed. "Instead, play me this new air of Master Giles Farnaby."

"Nay, alas, madame, I should but fumble it and I love music too well."

"Why, an' this be so, Jocelyn," she murmured, "I would you might hear Queen Mary of Scots, poor lady, for she playeth the clavichord to admiration!"

"My lady," he answered, eyeing her very anxiously again, "Queen Elizabeth of England plays it so marvellous well that we name it the 'Virginal' for her sake. . . . Doubtless you shall hear this same instrument sing to her touch when she cometh . . . to Aldrington."

"Is it so very certain she will come here, Jocelyn?"

"Not certain, my lady, but very like." Now at this,

Ione was silent, fluttering the pages of a music book she had opened while her troubled eyes glanced, almost furtively, at those two muttering gentlemen in the deep window recess, and when at last she spoke, it was in a whisper:

"Then I would to God——" she paused suddenly, for upon the air was sound of many horse hoofs, and when she spoke again it was to deride him: "Lo, sir, my lady aunt! Methinks I hear her wonted screech,—and she comes hotfoot to seek thee, Jocelyn, thine aged love! Aha, leaps not thy heart responsive? Come then, let us go meet her."

So Jocelyn rose forthwith, but ere they could reach the door, it swung wide and the old Countess stood upon the threshold.

# CHAPTER XXI

## WHEREIN THE COUNTESS, THIS SMALL GREAT LADY, VITUPERATES

THE aged lady of Hartesmere swept in upon them and scarce heeding Sir Thomas Vincent's deep obeisance or Mr. Fane's elegant flourishes, instantly pinned Captain Jocelyn by the girdle and shook at him in a very fury of exasperation.

"So, art here at last, Sir Slug!" she cried. "Do I see thee, Snail? Ha, what the plague, must you creep, must you crawl like accursed tortoise, and I swooning sick in passion of expectancy? Oh, Beelzebub and the pit! Where is my Philippa — speak! My beloved child, are ye dumb? Ha' you brought her? Is she here — "

"Madam," he answered, setting his hands gently upon the two small fists that still tugged at him. "She is not — "

"How, is she sick? Oh, God! Doth she ail — "

"She was never so well — "

"Then why did ye not carry the wicked rebel back to me as I commanded?"

"This I shall tell you alone, madam — "

"Alone?" she repeated faintly, then, seeing how he smiled, the dawning horror in her eyes vanished and she turned on the silent company.

"Away!" she cried imperiously. "Avaunt ye! Be-gone — nay, bide ye, ourselves shall remove. Ho, Richard, if my carosch be here, with a curse — order it to the door. . . . So, follow me, sirrah!" And with one small claw yet fast in the Captain's belt, she haled him forth. She brought him along the terrace and so into the secluded Tower Garden where rose the ancient keep, its scarred

battlements soaring aloft into the splendour of sunset;
here, seated upon carven stone bench, she motioned Jocelyn
to stand before her.

"Now," she demanded, frowning up at him very ferociously, "why did ye bring her not?"

"For that no man may come betwixt husband and wife."

"Wi — fe?" repeated the small lady in hoarse whisper
that rose to sudden, passionate screech. "Ha, wife, d' y'
say?"

"And husband, lady."

"Will ye dare tell me the wicked wench hath dared to
— wed?"

"An' your ladyship will suffer me — "

"Who — who is the black villain hath so won upon her
innocence? Where is this foul reptile, this cockatrice, this
base runnion — where?"

"Nowhere, madam. Instead, your niece, right fortunate
lady, hath won to herself a husband, by Nature most richly
endowed with graces o' body and noble qualities o' mind,
verily a gentleman that lacketh for naught under heaven
save base money — "

"Ha, then, 't is a beggar! A needy starveling rogue!
A lackpenny mumper! A shotten herring! A mere slub-
berdegullion knave, a — "

"Oh, cry you mercy, madam! Now prithee, take a
breath — "

"A pox on the wretch! A murrain, a plague! I 'll have
him to prison — whipped at the cart's tail! Tell me, who
is this thrice damned villain?"

"My comrade, madam."

"How . . . what — "

"A right valiant gentleman that honours me with his
friendship — "

"His name — his villainous name?"

"Florian Ferndale — "

"And this black rogue — "

"Nay, madam, — this noble gentleman — "

"I say, this ravisher of innocence — "

"Nay, madam, — this reverent spouse — "

"Malediction! Will ye suffer me to speak?"

"Yea, lady, though not to defame — "

"So you dare avow this . . . wretch your friend?"

"Heartily."

"And he is . . . poor, you tell me?"

"Nay, madam, I said he is rich in all things save base money."

"Palter not with me, sir. And now I mind how ye did confess your own poverty to me. So then, — here was plot twixt ye penniless comrades to trap my little Philippa into wedlock and share her fortune, you and he — ha?"

For a moment Jocelyn gazed down at her in speechless wonderment, then instead of the expected angry denial, he spoke in voice gentle and wistful as his look:

"Can you verily so believe, madam?"

The fierce old eyes wavered, the indomitable head bowed itself, and for once this speechful lady was dumb. . . .

All about them the shadows were deepening to a twilight hushed, very still and fragrant with warm, dewy scents, and now faint and far within this fragrant dusk a bird piped so sweetly mournful that Jocelyn, glancing thitherward, held his breath to listen.

"Well?" demanded the Countess suddenly. "Well, man?"

"Not so," he answered, "all's amiss, for I have read your ladyship wrongly. But then, in my life have been so few women — "

"Oho! And will ye pose for saint now? And — to me?"

"God forbid. But my days ha' passed in camp and leaguer, with little chance for easeful dalliance."

"And think ye then to read the close thoughts of such as I that am old in experience of courts and cities?"

"Nay, faith, madam. I did but judge you gifted with a wit to know the hidden good at the heart o' things."

"Being no bat I can see as far as most!" she retorted.

"Ay," he nodded, "no farther than the multitude and

't is a blind world, alas! Howbeit, I 'll now discharge me
of my message, to wit, madam: Your niece, the lady
Philippa, now Madam Ferndale, sendeth all dutiful greeting and bids me say that an' you so yearn for sight of her,
you shall behold her to-morrow especially in the hope you
may grow to love her so dear husband—"

"Bah! This moment," exclaimed the Countess, rising
in her quick, impetuous manner, "you shall bring me to
her."

"Ay, to-morrow, madam."

"This instant, sir."

"Madam Ferndale named to-morrow, my lady."

"What then, am I defied?"

"And for excellent good reason," he answered, bowing;
"my good comrade Florian yet languishes of a wound he
took in my defence and needeth quiet—"

"And he is soldier also?"

"And valiant, madam."

"Yet the rogue hath won more by trick o' vile, deluding
tongue than ever with his sword, and—"

"Hearkee, madam! This Florian, this gentle friend
of mine, stooped to wed your run-away niece, deeming her
no more than humble tavern maid. So, pray you, be done
with your empty pride and thank God she is safe wed to so
honest a gentleman. Now will your ladyship walk indoor;
supper should be ready anon—"

"A moment, sir. Your friend thus richly wived, what
of yourself?"

"Spain yet maketh bloody havoc in the Netherlands,
madam—"

"Also I 've yet another niece, Captain. Ione is also rich
and, spite her long legs, fair—"

"Madam, you offend me—"

"Why then, sit you, Jocelyn. For by God's good light,
I do believe your heart is honest as your eyes! So sit ye
here beside this desolate, old woman and tell of Philippa, her
marriage." But presently as they talked came the Earl
with Ione to bring their small, formidable aunt with all due

ceremony in to supper.    Yet even so my lord contrived to whisper the Captain:

"Ha, Jocelyn, plague on 'em, Roland and Tom Vincent ha' been at me to know wherefore I summoned them.    I bade 'em wait till after supper."

"Why then, hearkee, Dick!    To-night the unexpected may befall and I would have you prepared; come where we may speak unheard."

## CHAPTER XXII

### Wherein This Narrative Begins to Wax a Little Grim

Supper was over and the four gentlemen sat to their wine at a table drawn before the fire of sweet-smelling logs that flickered on the wide hearth. A noble fireplace this, a thing of beauty brave with carving, above which was the Aldrington escutcheon, deep-graven, rich with colours and tinctures red and blue, or and argent, where upon a field azure, gules and larger than life, the famous Bloody Hand glowed conspicuous in the soft radiance of many candles that woke gleams in the stands of armour that stood against arras-hung walls and made mystery of the huge carven roof beams high overhead.

But it was with his musing gaze on this great Red Hand that Jocelyn now sat, albeit very attentive to the conversation, none the less; and thus presently he heard that which he had expected and lifted goblet of fine Venetian glass to his lip, still gazing up at that great Red Hand, while Mr. Fane, reaching for his wine, spoke:

"Well, Rick, sweet lad, you wrote bidding me here to advise you on a matter, — so then here am I, replete with princely fare, jocund with peerless wine and bubbling with love and benignity and passion to serve thee, — speak!"

The boy hesitated, glanced from Mr. Fane's smiling face to Sir Thomas Vincent's lounging bulk and smote the table with his fist.

"Bodykins!" exclaimed Sir Thomas, forgetting to lounge.

"God ha' mercy, Richard!" quoth Mr. Fane, starting; "'sfoot, but you nigh upset my wine and to lose one precious drop were sinful shame — "

"Wine, sir, wine?" cried the young Earl a little breath-lessly. "What is this to the Aldrington honour? I have been defamed, sirs, by some nameless, lying villain!"

"Good lack, Richard! What's here?"

"Villainy, Roland! Thus it is I'd ha' you advise me what to do i' the matter, — and you, Sir Thomas, ay — and you too, Jocelyn, — as I say i' the matter of a lying, scur-rilous letter that would impeach mine honour as a loyal gentleman and servant of Her Majesty the Queen. . . . And for this letter — 't is here, see — read it for your-selves!" And speaking, he thrust the letter upon them. Having read and passed it from hand to hand, all three, there ensued a long moment of silence, wherein Mr. Fane sipped his wine with very apparent relish while Sir Thomas glared at nothing in particular and Jocelyn gazed at the Red Hand again.

"Well?" my lord demanded. "How now, sirs?"

"The question is," said Sir Thomas, his glance still wandering vaguely, "how and wherein doth this writing lie —"

"How?" cried the Earl angrily. "How, sir, but in every villainous word! I am — Aldrington! And where's the rogue dare avow any Aldrington faithless to his liege lord? Loyalty to the Crown is our tradition and very creed —"

"Nay, but Richard — dear lad," murmured Mr. Fane, smiling, "if — and mark me, I do but say 'if' — it should prove thou hadst indeed set thy hand to some such —"

"I never did, Roland! No, not I, nor would I ever so dishonour the name I bear. I say before you all three I signed no such treason 'gainst Her Majesty nor ever will —"

"Nay, but my lord," said Sir Thomas, "sure you must ha' forgot —"

"Sir, I should never forget such vile thing as this!"

"And yet, my lord Richard, I've the memory of a certain night in London — at Riderwood's house and we all merry . . . and your lordship, as I can swear, did verily sign —"

"Never!" cried the Earl furiously, thumping table again until the glasses rang; "never did I set my name to aught of treason against Her Majesty! And by God, sirs, so sure am I o' this that to-morrow I ride for London and will set this vile letter in the Queen's very hand for proof of my loyalty, — ay, to-morrow, — by God!"

Sir Thomas half rose from his chair and sank weakly back again, his eyes goggling and heavy lips apart in speechless dismay; Mr. Fane set down his cherished glass so awkwardly as to spill its so precious contents all unheeded.

"Richard!" he exclaimed, in voice no longer sleepy, "Oh, Dick . . . wouldst destroy thyself?"

"Nay, I would vindicate my honour of this wicked slander."

"Art mad, cousin, art surely mad! The Queen and her council have small mercy on traitors real or imagined in these bloody times! Show her this letter and by Heaven, she shall show thee a dungeon i' the Tower . . . ay, the rack, belike, and thereon twist and wring a confession from thy young bones, lad. Think on this —"

"Well and 't were better so!" cried my lord. "Better die in honour than suffer the Aldrington name to bear such black stain unrefuted —"

"Richard! Oh, Dick lad — here's madness!"

"Mad or no, Roland, to-morrow I ride to Court and with fifty, ay, an hundred o' my people, armed to bring me safe to Her Majesty! To-morrow I'll see the Queen, I say, and clear mine honour of this foulness or perish i' the attempt. And this will I do — except I be shown this damnable treason signed by mine own hand — and this can never be, since I signed no such —"

"Why then, my lord," said Jocelyn, speaking for the first time, "if, as Sir Thomas avers, such paper doth actually exist, shown unto you it shall be; — how say you, sirs?"

"Ay, for sure!" cried Sir Thomas. "Ye shall see it, Richard, with your own eyes — and how then?"

"This shall depend on ourselves, gentlemen, and — one

other!" said Jocelyn. "Howbeit, this paper must be produced at once."

"Impossible!" said Mr. Fane. "It is in London and —"

"Then it must be brought hence posthaste."

"Sir," drawled Mr. Fane, "Cousin Richard may see it very well — in London!"

"True, sir," nodded Jocelyn, "but then, here in Sussex, there is one must also see it, nay, hold it henceforth and thereby hold my Lord Richard."

"Meaning your honourable self, Captain?"

"Not so, Mr. Fane. I mean one that, for the nonce, calls himself John Ford."

Now at mention of this name, Sir Thomas rose from his chair, whispering an amazed oath, and sank down again. Mr. Fane leaned across the table, staring on Jocelyn with eyes half-closed, his lips upcurled in strange smile, his delicate nostrils a-quiver, and when he spoke it was in breathless murmur:

"Ah, then . . . he is safe landed . . . here in Sussex?"

"At Shalmeston," nodded Jocelyn, "with Sir Philip Drayton."

"Is this certain, sir? Did you . . . see him?"

"Indeed. He appointed to meet with us here to-night."

"Here? To-night?" exclaimed Mr. Fane, like one aghast. "Coming here, say you? Why then . . . I'll away."

"And wherefore?" demanded the Captain. "Why leave us in such strange haste? John Ford perchance shall ha' news of the utmost moment to all concerned —"

"'Slife, sir, and there's my reason for departure!" laughed Mr. Fane, his joviality a little more aggressive than usual; "for, pray perceive me, Captain, I am no whit concerned in anything under heaven save the well-being of one — *me mihi*, mine humble self, to wit. I am a philosopher sitting apart to watch the world wag as it will —"

"And yet, sir," answered Jocelyn, shaking his head, "you would seem to be deep in a certain matter and as much concerned therein as Sir Thomas here, or Squire Twifoot, or Sir Philip, or Mr. Chantrey, Lord Iford or Sir Guy Felton, to name a few."

"Not I, Captain, faith and troth, not I!" laughed Mr. Fane, rising. "Catholic or Protestant, this Queen or that, the Pope or Spanish Philip — all's one to this airy sprite calls itself Roland Fane. I've no ambitions save to live and let live, to 'scape dull care, to hover and flit — a very butterfly, God wot! So if there is to be here any criminations politic, I'll to my own quiet ingle. So, Cousin Rick and gentlemen, I bid — "

A sound of hasty feet in the remote dimness of the great hall, and Sir Philip Drayton came striding, his usual stateliness marred by nervous hurry, his darkly handsome face pale and haggard. With bow and a breathless word for the young Earl, he turned to Jocelyn.

"Captain Dinwiddie," said he, "it seems I am to salute you as a friend and zealous worker for the Cause. John Ford speaks well of you — "

"Comes he with you, Sir Philip?"

"He should be here anon, sir, but just now — " Sir Philip paused to close his haggard eyes and press a hand to his lofty but narrow brow, and Jocelyn saw his hand was shaking, "just now he is delayed . . . murder, gentlemen!"

"How, Philip, how?" gasped Sir Thomas. "Who — "

"Murder?" cried the young Earl, then, starting to the crash of breaking glass, turned where stood Mr. Fane, staring down at the fragments and the dark stain of his spilled wine.

"Alas, gentlemen!" sighed Sir Philip, sinking feebly into the nearest chair and passing tremulous hand across his eyes again. "I . . . I am unused to sudden death . . . I scarce know how to tell of it . . . murder! Oh, horrible! And in my own house — "

"Who, Philip? In God's name, who is dead? Speak!" cried Sir Thomas, his ruddy face grown suddenly pale.

"Walter Ringrose!"

"God!" exclaimed Sir Thomas, crossing himself. "One o' the three secret envoys from Spain? And murdered! How, man, how?"

"First drink you this wine, sir," said the Captain, tendering a glass to Sir Philip, who emptied it thirstily.

"Sirs," said he, staring before him wide-eyed, "you know how these three valiant men came out of Spain, each devoted to single great purpose. One of these is John Ford that will be here anon; one was Pietro Vespucci that vanished by the way and hath not been heard of, and the third was Walter Ringrose that landed safely last week but was captured hereabouts by two sailormen. Himself I found means to rescue and hide in my house at Shalmeston. He was, it seems, very well acquaint with John Ford in Spain and greatly anxious to see him. So seeing Master Ford was gone to friends at Shoreham, thither rode I and found him as eager to meet his friend, Walter Ringrose. But hardly were we mounted than cometh Master John Catesby, one of the burgesses, to see me touching certain smuggling affray and I, not wishing to keep Mr. Ford, bade him ride on to Shalmeston alone. But he, being strange to the road, agreed to wait. My business done, after prodigious delay, I summoned John Ford and together we rode to my house . . . and sirs . . . there . . . in my own closet . . . we found Walter Ringrose . . . lying beside an open casement . . . upon his back . . . dead and staring, — ah, staring. . . ."

"Holy . . . Saints!" stammered Sir Thomas, glancing about him very wildly. "We are betrayed! 'T is the work of Walsingham's cursed spies! What . . . what a God's name shall we do?"

"Command yourself, Vincent!" said Sir Philip, with look and gesture not lacking in a high nobility. "Have faith in the Holy Cause to which we are pledged so long as we have life, — to sweep heretical blasphemy out of our England, to snatch The Religion from under Tyranny's bloody heel, to avenge our martyred saints, the sweet blood of young Father Campian and others . . . others —" the

deep, fervent voice was hushed to the sound of heavy feet, as
John Ford was announced and all eyes turned to behold this
newcomer.    A bold-eyed, sturdy fellow, though of no great
stature, his lean visage more grim by reason of upcurling
ferocity of moustachio and sharp-pointed beard, an as-
sertive man who swaggered a little, left hand upon the
pommel of his long rapier, right hand wafting bonnet gracefully; yet as he approached, despite bravery of attire, his
grimness became the more manifest.

"Master Ford," said Sir Philip, rising, "Captain Din-
widdie you already know; these other gentlemen are my
Lord Richard Fane, Earl of Aldrington, Sir Thomas
Vincent, and Mr. Roland Fane of Kingston Buci."

Master Ford bowed and, doing so, dropped a glove which
Sir Philip stooped to pick up but recoiled suddenly with an
exclamation of horror:

"Your quest . . . ended successfully then?" said he,
pointing unsteady finger down at the gauntlet that showed
a dark and awful smear.    Mr. Ford, also glancing at this
betraying stain, curled his moustachio and nodded.

"Ay, sir, there is one villain less!" quoth he and taking
up the gauntlet, tucked it into his belt.

"But what," cried Sir Thomas, in ever-growing alarm,
"what is all this?    Who . . . who killed this man Ringrose—"

"Doubtless, sir, one of those that dogged him overseas."

"Why then, think you we are betrayed . . . in
danger?"

"Ay, certes!" answered Mr. Ford, scowling.    "Can
such vasty achievement be done without peril?    No!"

"Why then, good Master Ford, what . . . what must
we do . . . how avoid such peril?    How?"

"Be wary, sir.    Bring in such great names as we may,
and—ha, above all, see that none seek to evade the issue
or turn cat-in-pan!    And this bringeth us to the reason for
our meeting here . . .    My Lord of Aldrington, word
reaches me that you, having set your hand to the pact,
would now deny it,—"

"I do deny it!" cried the boy, very pale but very resolute. "I deny that I ever set my hand to any treasonable paper soever or that an Aldrington could be so base to dream treason against Her Majesty——"

"My lord, your signature is sworn to, I 'm told——"

"No, no!" cried the young Earl wildly. "I say I never did. I swear and vow——" here, meeting Jocelyn's serene gaze, he grew calmer and sidling nearer his friend, strove to speak more naturally. "Gentlemen, your schemes touch me no whit,—only this: I am, now as ever, loyal to Queen Elizabeth, and to prove this I shall ride to her Majesty and set my accusation in her own hand . . . except you show me this damnable treason signed by me."

"'Sdeath!" exclaimed Master Ford, scowling from one set face to the other. "Ye hear this, sirs? Let the paper be shown him; this shall bind him fast or it shall send him to the question and death, ay—torture and the axe. Show him the paper instantly!"

"Sir," said Jocelyn, "it seems this document is in London."

"Then let it be brought thence, forthright. Who holds it?"

"Mr. Fane shall tell you this," murmured Jocelyn.

Round upon the silent Mr. Fane swung the scowling Ford.

"Well, sir?" he demanded. "Mr. Fane, I say—well? Speak, sir! Who is the custodian o' this so important document? Answer, sir."

"To my poor belief, sir," answered Mr. Fane lightly, "it is with my Lord Riderwood, but——"

"Then pray acquaint him with the matter, Mr. Fane; summon him to produce this document forthwith."

"Nay, sir," smiled Mr. Fane, "you have me wrong; I am nowise concerned in this matter. I meddle not with State affairs; the merest idle, wholly indifferent spectator I."

"Ha, 'sblood!" cried Master Ford, with passionate gesture. "Then why do I see you here?"

"Having eyes, sir," tittered Mr. Fane. "And I am to-night dear my cousin Richard his guest."

"Then, Mr. Fane, guest or no, here is no place for spectators to-night, idle or otherwise. As for this paper, how soon can it be here?"

"In two days," answered Sir Thomas, "ay, two days at latest."

"'T is a case for speed and hurry, sir."

"How think you, Mr. Fane?" enquired Jocelyn.

"That Riderwood will be hurried by no man," murmured Mr. Fane.

"Howbeit," cried the Earl, "after two days I ride to the Queen's Majesty."

"So!" cried Ford, glaring about him. "My lord had best hurry, methinks, lest he and all of us be hurried to the Tower —"

"He shall, he shall!" cried Sir Thomas passionately. "I ride to him myself at dawn."

"Ay, but then," said Mr. Fane, "what shall let cousin Richard from galloping to the Queen at dawn also?"

"I will!" cried Mr. Ford, with a flourish.

"You?" demanded my lord haughtily. "And, pray, what shall prevent me calling my people to have you dungeoned for vile traitor?"

"This!" answered John Ford and, with the word, his dagger glittered in the candlelight. My lord sprang for the bell, but Jocelyn's touch and look stopped him.

"Under the circumstances," said the Captain, "I venture to think that even my Lord Riderwood, this deliberate gentleman, may be induced to unwonted speed."

"He will!" cried Sir Thomas. "By God — he shall! I ride to him this very night. Come, sirs, I'm for the road."

Sir Philip Drayton rose, a stately yet mournful figure, and fixing his haggard gaze on the young Earl, sighed deeply and spoke:

"My lord, friend Richard, as you'll mind, I knew and loved your noble sire passing well, for he was a great and valiant gentleman, being one of the few that in King Henry's blasphemous days was bold for the True Religion, a Catholic he that dared be so even in King Henry's very presence, putting The Religion before Royal Favour, lands, ay—life itself. And Richard, you are his son,—what wonder I judged you utterly devoted, faithful and steadfast as he. But God forbid I should force you or any man to that his soul abhors. Therefore, as your friend, I, for one, will never hold you 'gainst your conscience, only—"

"Sir Philip, by your leave," quoth Mr. Ford, "this goeth beyond yourself or friendship. My lord here threatens us one and all; he is become a menace and, as I see it, must be dealt with thus: That having signed the pact, by the pact he must be held,—his life for ours, blood for blood, or—"

"Nay, hold!" cried Sir Philip. "My lord, I pray you suffer I speak him word apart," and beckoning Mr. Ford out of earshot, he talked softly but with a passionate vehemence, then turning to the young Earl:

"My lord . . . Richard," said he very earnestly, "by my urgent desire for your good, Master Ford will stay a while to discuss the posture of affairs with you more roundly than I might ever do—"

"Yet to none avail, Sir Philip," cried the boy. "I am Aldrington and stand faithful to Her Majesty's Grace. And sir, the Earl my father dared King Henry for his conscience' sake, but he was never a traitor, nor will I ever be, so aid me God!"

"And may God have you and us, my lord, in his tender care!" sighed Sir Philip. "Farewell! Now, gentlemen, shall we go?"

For a long moment, after all sounds of their departure had died away, the Earl stood, youthful face pale and very troubled, staring down at the huge log that smouldered on the wide hearth; then he started and drawing a pace nearer the Captain, turned to front Mr. Ford, and in that moment, caught his breath, amazed beyond speech. For indeed Master Ford, magically transfigured, was regarding him with such eyes and such smile as his own father might have done; also when he spoke, his voice seemed heartily kind:

"Now, py heavens, this is well and passing well, my lord! Wert right, Jocelyn, wert right, old war dog; he rings true metal, no crack here, look you! All doubts or apprehensions be ended. My lord, I hail you as valiant gentleman and loyal servant of Her Majesty Elizabeth, — of Gloriana, our Bess."

"But, nay, but," stammered the boy, "but Jocelyn, I thought . . . he showed so fierce but now . . . so deadly — "

"Faith, Richard, and so he is — 'gainst all Spaniards and renegade traitors," nodded the Captain, "for he that speaks is none other than Sir Roger Williams — "

"He?" gasped the Earl. "He that defended Sluys so bravely . . . that led the storming-party at Axel, that cut his way through the Spanish camp before Venlo? Oh, Sir Roger, I do joy to see thee, sir; I am truly honoured! Pray give me your hand! Now sir, prithee sit! Here's wine of Burgundy. Rhenish, sack or *aqua vitae* . . . be seated, sir, and oh, prithee tell me of your fights and battles . . . Ay, and what you do here at Aldrington . . . oh, and your glove sir . . . the blood there on your gauntlet."

"Jocelyn, knoweth my lord aught of our suspicions?" enquired Sir Roger, seating himself at the table.

"Something, Roger."

"Sir," cried the Earl, all boyish eagerness, "I would fain be honoured by your friendship, therefore I . . . I would have you . . . I must needs confess myself arrant fool. When Jocelyn found me in London I was . . . drunken sot, a poor gull. . . . And in my beastly folly signed my name to this vile paper, scarce knowing what I did . . . being vilely drunk and trusting to rogues methought my friends . . . yet meaning evil to none, most especially to the Queen's Majesty. It is this paper they hold against me."

"Why then," quoth Sir Roger, scowling at the wine in his goblet, "'t is this same paper we must destroy."

"Ah, Sir Roger," cried the Earl, "it was to this end my good Jocelyn here schemed this meeting to-night."

"Well, my lord, I am here!" nodded Sir Roger. "And having seen you, heard you, look you, I am convinced o' your truth and loyalty. And knowing my comrade Jocelyn as I do, marry, but 't will be strange an' we do not betwixt us win back this cursed paper, one way or t' other."

"Now God be thanked!" cried the Earl. "And you too, Sir Roger — ay, and you, Jocelyn. Come, brim the wine. . . . Sir Roger, I pledge you! And now prithee tell of your stained glove — an' you will."

Sir Roger took up the gauntlet to eye it somewhat askance.

"Look you now," said he, shaking his head in self-reproach, "where were my eyes not to ha' noticed this until Sir Philip remarked it? Faugh!" he exclaimed, tossing the gauntlet upon the fire. "The blood of a traitor and renegade!"

"Renegade?" repeated the Earl in awed whisper. "Sir . . . you mean — ?"

"A would-be queen-slayer!" quoth Sir Roger. "Hearkee, my lord! Upon a time Philip of Spain paid a man, one Gerard, to murder the Prince of Orange, and, look you, the good Prince was duly killed. Of late, this same Philip sent forth three men, largely rewarded, to kill our Elizabeth and lo — she lives and shall live, pray God! For to-day the third and last of her would-be killers lieth dead in Sir Philip's closet."

"And 't was you . . ." gasped the Earl, "'t was you . . . ?"

"Killed him, my lord? Ay, marry, it was so! Our old *imbroccata* from low to high, Jocelyn."

"Nay — nay, but," quavered my lord, "Sir Philip tells you were with him in Shoreham the while — "

"So was I," nodded Sir Roger, "till came a certain burgess at my orders and carried Sir Philip away on business should keep him sufficient time for my purpose. Well, I ride a speedy horse, my lord! Reaching the manor unseen, by good hap, I confronted this Ringrose. We fought and I killed him sweetly and silently as I might and so back to Shoreham and Sir Philip, that we might ride and together find this villain's carcass, — the which we did. And thus, for the time being, the secret menace 'gainst the Queen, her life and the weal of England ends. God be thanked! Remaineth but to play my part as this murderous Ford, that is duly hanged ere now, I hope — secure your damning signature, my lord, and lay t' other plotters by the heels. To the which pretty purpose I would, by your leave, my lord, walk with my old comrade beneath the moon a while."

"Yet first," said Jocelyn, rising and once more glancing up at the great Red Hand conspicuous above the wide, low arch of the great fireplace, "yon hand, Richard! I've heard it called the Hand of Glory."

"'T is called as well the Hand of Salvation, Jocelyn."

"Salvation?" repeated the Captain, nodding. "Verily methinks this were the name most apt for 't, Dick. As now, by your grace, I 'll essay."

"Whatso you will," answered the Earl, glancing at Jocelyn's intent face with sudden interest.

Then coming to the fireplace the Captain reached up and laid his open hand upon this carved and painted hand of wood, pressing sudden and strong. Now as he did so, the ponderous graven pilaster to the right of the hearth turned with no sound of movement and swung smoothly outward, discovering a narrow passage beyond.

"How . . . how learned you of this?" cried my lord, all amazed.

"By inference, Richard. By the Red Hand shall be salvation. Doth it grieve or offend you that I — "

"Ah, never, Jocelyn! I 'd ha' no secrets from thee . . . indeed I would have shown thee the trick of this had I thought."

"There be others do know of this, I guess, Dick?"

"Ay, true, there is Ione."

"And . . . mayhap . . . thy Cousin Fane?"

"Nay, how should he? And yet, I am not sure."

"To know the trick on 't," nodded Sir Roger, peering into the dark passage, "may peradventure serve our turn at a pinch. But now come you, Jocelyn, and stare on the moon with thine old comrade a while."

## CHAPTER XXIII

SOMETHING flickered through the open casement, smote the heavy canopy of wrought velvet and dropped lightly upon the bed with small, soft sound, yet, almost in that moment, Captain Jocelyn was awake but, like veteran campaigner used to sudden perils, lay as if still asleep, though with every sense tingling and alert. For upon the silken coverlet above his breast lay a light-shafted, glossy-feathered arrow such as might be sped by the slim hand of Dian's very self; and then he saw this for a bird-bolt, since in place of cruel steel barb it was armed only with rounded knob. Now lapped about this shaft was a strip of paper tied there by dainty blue ribband. So Jocelyn took the arrow and loosing the paper, opened it and saw this:

*You shall*        *find me*
*in the*    *Home Woode*
*Bring you*    *this for its*

*resolving*

*Wait you patientlie*      *for what shall be.*

The words were written in bold yet delicate hand that he thought to recognize, therefore leaping from the sheets, he arrayed himself with soldierly speed, thrust the paper into his doublet, and catching up hat and cloak, paused, dubiously eyeing his heavy main gauche dagger where it lay; finally he set it in his girdle and went forth of his chamber very softly, along wide gallery and down the great stair.

Birds were piping in jubilant chorus near and far, the young sun had lit a myriad dewy gems that sparkled everywhere as the Captain, drawing his cloak of orange-tawny about him, went forth upon his way, viewing the fresh, green world glad-eyed, breathing deep of the sweet air, but with his mind full of wonder and no little amaze.

So came he to the coppice where ran that murmurous brook beyond which lay the denser green of those great woods that stretched away, mile on mile, to the distant, purple Downland. Now in the act of leaping this brook to reach this wilder forest land, he paused to look down into these rippling waters that dimpled so brightly in the sun's level beams and to hearken to its pretty babble that had never seemed so like the voice of a friend; then, moved by some impulse, he took off his cloak and spreading it beneath a tree, sat him down to wait, his ears and eyes expectant.

It was a very still morning with promise of heat to come, with no breath of air to stir the leafy wilderness around him and no sound to break the pervading quiet save the plashing murmur of the brook.

Now presently his wistful, roving gaze chanced upon a daisy that bloomed all solitary in the grass beside him and, acting once again on impulse, he stooped, plucked this daisy and thereby saved his life; for in that moment was faint musical twang like plucked harp-string, something whizzed past his ear, smiting the tree behind him and Jocelyn, guessing what this was, uttered a hoarse cry and swaying sideways, sank to the grass and lay there motionless, only his eyes, very fierce and bright, watched the dense woodland before him. And lying thus asprawl, he presently espied that he expected: From behind dense thicket a hairy head stole to view, peering very hideously, for the face was masked. A long moment the head remained thus motionless; only the peering eyes glittered as they surveyed him; then from the screening underbush stepped a man, a squat fellow whose powerful body was clad in the gaudy rags of a Gipsy or Zingari. Slowly, cautiously, the figure began to steal nearer, hideously masked face watchfully outthrust, broad shoulders bowed, in one hand a powerful crossbow, a long, narrow-bladed knife in the other. Yet Captain Jocelyn lay there utterly still, but with every nerve and sinew strung for swift and terrible action.

Suddenly upon the stilly air rose a sweet, rich voice singing a merry catch and the creeping figure halted, murderous knife poised but glancing instinctively towards this approaching singer — and in that instant Captain Jocelyn was afoot and had leapt the brook, whereat the gipsy uttered a gasping cry and, turning, fled, with the Captain pursuing, dagger in hand.

But the gipsy, for all his seeming clumsy build, ran very fleetly; moreover he seemed well acquainted with the leafy mazes and thorny tangles of the wood that grew ever denser and more wild; yet Jocelyn held after him fiercely resolute, well knowing the fellow would have no time to rewind his crossbow for another shot. So on he sped, following the sound of his quarry's flight until, bursting forth of the underwood, he came out into a glade, a place of smooth turf with a great jag of craggy rocks beyond, down whose mossy sides a limpid spring bubbled with tinkling plash; but save for this pretty babblement, other sound was there none, nor any sign of the gipsy fellow, search how he would. Wherefor the Captain, though scant of breath, cursed aloud very heartily and was yet questing to and fro like a baffled hound when was great stir and rustle of leaves, a voice cried his name and Ione came running.

"Oh, sweet Lady of Heaven!" she gasped, leaning against a tree to catch her breath. "What . . . what was it . . . a mercy's name?"

"A rogue, madam, a scurvy gipsy fellow."

"Nay, but . . . why such ferocity?" she questioned. "You showed so direly fierce I thought you would kill him!" And she pointed accusing finger at the dagger in his hand, whereupon he made haste to sheath it.

"Howbeit the fellow escaped me, madam."

"Why then, why must you give me such wild, strange look, prithee?"

"'T is strange, wild place this, my lady."

"'T is hateful abomination!" she exclaimed with sudden passion. "'T is an evil place, ah, it is accursed place; let us begone." And now he wondered to see her all trembling and very pale. "Come!" she whispered, glancing about them with eyes of terror. "It was here we found . . . my father twelve years agone . . . dead! Take me away. I feel as evil were all about us! Take me into the good sunshine." The question on his lips was forgotten quite, for her hand had slipped itself in his to nestle there with such warm, sweet intimacy that he could think of nothing in the world except this soft, clinging hand that seemed athrill with much warm, quick vitality.

So, thus handfast, they left this dismal place and, being come into the glad sunshine, Ione paused to look about her, eager-eyed; and as she stood thus in her simple tyre, for she wore no cumberous farthingale, Jocelyn bethought him of the Golden goddess Eos, opening with her rosy fingers the gates of Day and pouring dew upon the thirsty flowers.

"Oh, but 't is a lovely world!" she sighed in quick rapture and then, meeting his wistful gaze, flushed rosy as sweet Aurora's self or shy rustic maid, seeming so unwontedly abashed indeed that Jocelyn, for her relief, retorted with an airy extravagance:

"Indeed, 't is sweet world being new. For Nox and Somnus are but lately fled and Aurora, flinging wide the curtains of Night, cometh on the world gemmed and be-spangled like a bride."

"So — ho!" quoth my lady, nodding at him, "our so euphuistic soldier waxeth poetical! These flowery periods do tell me 't is sunny morning dewily damp. But a bride, quotha! Hum, sir, and ha! This doth mind me of Cousin Philippa, a wife fast wed and to thy comrade Master Florian, so Aunt telleth."

"Ay, to Florian, madam——"

"And this new day, sir, being so marvellous fair, you shall call me Joan and suffer that I share your cloak yonder awhile." So they came to the soft-chuckling brook; but here she paused and, though she knew its every stepping-stone and had crossed it, paddled through and leapt it many a time as child and long-legged girl, to-day she must needs view it askance and command his aid. Therefore Captain Jocelyn gave her his hand again, very solicitous lest she wet her dainty, rosetted shoes or splash those twin miracles, to wit, her Spanish knit stockings of silk; and she, simple gown drawn daintily high and very conscious of his watchful, earnest gaze, spoke him demurely sighful:

"Alas, Jocelyn! My feet are none so small nor so pretty as those of that lady o' your devotion——my aged aunt."

"You are shaped on nobler plan," he answered, in tone of such utter sincerity that she laughed, gleeful as any schoolgirl and, forgetting her wonted stateliness, bobbed him a curtsey from her perch on mossy stone and would have toppled into these laughing waters had he not caught and swung her lightly to the flowery bank beside him.

"Right featly done!" she laughed. "Considering the very 'noble' weight o' me. Come now, let us sit a while and enjoy this glad morning together." Thus saying, my lady sank gracefully upon Jocelyn's orange-tawny cloak, quite unaware of the grim thing whose murderous point was buried deep in the tree just above her head and, obeying her imperious gesture, he sat beside her and for awhile both of them very silent.

"Madam," said he, at last.

"Tush!" she exclaimed. "This morning I am Joan, Jocelyn."

"Why then, Joan I . . . I pray you," said he, his usual serenity a little troubled, his gaze on the green depth of the wood, "I would fain know wherefore you are abroad so early?"

"Alack now!" she mocked. "Methought from your air of so deep and ponderous gravity you would ask question of most vasty import. Know, then, it was this goodly sun, ay, 't was old Sol kissed me from slumber; he lured me to my lattice and showed me the world all fair and sweet and in the midst thereof — Dinwiddie! And . . . well . . . here am I to talk and be talked to, so talk, Jocelyn."

"Of Florian, his marriage — "

"Nay, you ha' sung his praises enough. Tell me of . . . of Joan, the how and why of her, according to Dinwiddie."

"With all my heart. Yet first this, — Florian wed your cousin, this great lady, believing her no more than she seemed — a very sweetly humble maid and niece to Dame Margery Bly — "

"So, 't was there she hid herself! Howbeit mine aunt voweth dire vengeance and I would fain aid them an' I might — "

"Why, this is well bethought, Joan, and — "

"But methinks, Jocelyn, they shall need little help of mine whiles they have friend so marvellous as — Dinwiddie. Thus since a tender Providence hath blessed them with such potency of friendship, let us leave them to Dinwiddie and talk of . . . ourselves."

"Of Joan?" he questioned, and thrust hand into his doublet where lay that small scroll of paper.

"Ay, tell me of Joan herself, whatso you deem you know of her, an' you dare!"

"Faith now," he answered, sombre gaze on the sparkling water, "I would dare much on such morning. First then — "

"Nay, wait!" she commanded. "On second thought, first must I tell you of . . . my Robin!" Now at this the Captain started and forgetting that paper in his bosom, glanced at her swiftly askance and found her regarding him, also askance, beneath drooping lashes and her vivid lips quivering to a smile.

"Pray, madam, what of this sweet gentleman?"

"Oh, verily sweet indeed!" she sighed. "For, Jocelyn, I do protest to you that each day I love him more — on paper! Oh, marry now, were his tongue the half so

eloquent as his pen, I vow I could love him even . . . perchance . . . to wedlock! But — " Here she paused to
steal another look at Jocelyn who stared hard at the brook
without glance or word; therefore she essayed him again:

"But alas!"

"Well, madam?"

"Alack, Jocelyn! 'Twould seem the poet that with
written word may throw us into a rapture and seems a very
demigod, oft proves merest ordinary creature and dumb as
any fish! For verily, since this new power of poesy took
him, and so strangely sudden, — Robin is become more
Robinish than ever. Do I but praise him he falls a-stam-
mering, he flusheth, droops his so honest eyes like guilty
wretch or talks in strange wild sort of hawks, dogs, horses
— anything but his poems. — Yesterday 't was of a new
breed of sheep. Now prithee, Jocelyn, why should this be,
think you?"

"Madam, the thing is simple. For, perceive you not
sweet Philomel is no more than a voice in dun feathers, e'en
as soaring lark and shy linnet? Also he that achieveth is
no chatterer. The great, good things be all simple and the
silent man oft thinketh the more, words are but a mask, a
cloak for — "

"Thus is Dinwiddie masked to the eyes and cloaked to
the heels, for here be words a-many. Pray you be dumb a
little, for here have I brought divers of Robin's newest
poems for your judgment."

"But your ladyship knows I have no gift o' poesy and
therefore can be no judge."

"Ay, true!" she nodded. "This we know. Therefore
you shall read them aloud and I will be judge." And from
her bosom she drew certain papers, one of which she
tendered to him, gently imperious.

So Jocelyn took the paper, warm and fragrant with the
sweetness of her, and bowing his head above it, began to
read. But he had scarcely voiced three words than she
stopped him:

"Nay, fie, 't is villainous!" she exclaimed. "''T is mere

soulless gabblement! Slower, prithee, slower!" Again he began and again she checked him. "Beseech you!" she sighed, "wherefore now so hoarsely harsh, Jocelyn? Pray you, speak me these sweet lines more tenderly, as yourself were yearning lover had writ each word from your very heart. Imagine yourself such and I will strive to so believe you." So saying, she leaned back against the tree, crossed her shapely legs, folded her slim hands and fixing Jocelyn with dreamful gaze, bade him proceed. Then the Captain, scowling down at these words he knew so well, forthwith read as follows:

> "Since tongue of mine is all too weak
> My love for thee to show or speak
> The birds my choristers shall be
> And all my yearning sing to thee — "

"And this," sighed Joan, "this as I do think is vastly pretty fancy."

"Nay, but — " he began and there she stopped him:

"Venture no judgment, I pray you; 't is matter above your wit, alas! Your part is merely to read. So Jocelyn — read!" The Captain humbly obeyed:

> "The lark at morn on dewy wings
> Shall wake thee with all lovely things
> Then shall on soaring pinions rise
> To praise thee to the very skies.
> And, poised thus high the world above,
> Tell forth the passion of my love
> Till other birds, both far and near,
> His sweet, melodious tale shall hear
> Then, blithely all, shall speed away
> To sing my love the live-long day."

"Heigho!" sighed Ione. "And last time my sweet Robin sat with me he talked of tups and tegs and ewes and how he hoped to make Downland sheep more famous. Then it was but yesterday that 'Robin', said I, 'in thy sweet verse breathes Poesy's very soul!' And he babbles o' sheep, forsooth, and so sits dumb!"

"Whereby you shall know him sincere!" retorted the Captain. "For Love soareth beyond puny speech."

"And you are seldom dumb!" she mocked. "Thus, being immune from love, you should read of love most eloquently. Come now, pray you speak me these last lines of Robin as Robin never may. These of all he hath writ me I do love best. Take and read me them as from your very heart, Jocelyn." So he took this second paper and, submissive ever, read this:

"Thou wert mine own since Time began
Thou my loved Woman, I, thy Man.
Full oft we've lived and loved and died
Since Love and Life alway abide.
Oft back through Death to Life came we
By Love to re-united be.
So, if to-day my love prove vain
Here is kind solace to my pain
Sometime — we needs must love again.
Since doomed to live and love are we
Through Death to all eternity.
For thou wert mine ere Life began
Thou my one Woman, I, thy Man."

The reading done, he folded the manuscript and gave it back, nor looked on her nor spoke; instead he leant to stare again into the hurrying waters of the brook, whose pretty babblement seemed louder than ever; and Joan, folding the paper with gentle fingers, viewed his down-bent face with a strange intentness and when she spoke it was in whispered yet eager question:

"Oh, surely no man could so think, so write, except he loved . . . very greatly? Is it not so . . . Jocelyn?"

"Ay, beyond all doubt!" he answered, nodding at the brook. "And 't is thus . . . Robin Netherby loveth you."

"Robin . . . Netherby?" she exclaimed: and then, in tender murmur: "Oh, 't is noble thought, Jocelyn, that life and love should prove stronger than death, nay — by death return to life through all the ages."

"This," he answered dreamily, "this hath been the dream of Wisdom, Joan, since ever man learned to think, — the immortality of all good things that by oft experience of life do grow to perfection at last."

"And, Jocelyn, do you so believe?"

"Ay, I do! Creation were a sorry scheme else, and this span of life, so pitiful short, no better than cruel jest."

"'Oft back through death to life came we!'" she quoted.

"'T is hard, to think our good, simple Robin could pen such line, — he that knoweth more of sheep and horses than the old philosophies — "

"'T is love hath inspired him, Joan; it hath wrought many a miracle ere now. . . . But, good lack!" he exclaimed, rising, "the sun climbs apace and we — "

"Nay, 't is early yet!" she retorted. "Be seated, for I 'm minded to hear somewhat of this creature you name Joan, so — " the words ended in a gasp, and looking down at her Jocelyn saw she was staring at the deadly missile that stood so deep-planted in the tree bole.

"A crossbow bolt!" she cried in voice of horror.

"Ay, 't is a quarrel," he answered, wondering at her look, "and this the reason for my pursuit of yon gipsy fellow."

"Then it . . . it was aimed — at you?"

"And so truly that my woes were ended all, but for an accident." Up sprang my lady, pale and trembling, staring upon this shaft with ever-growing dread.

"A crossbow . . . bolt!" she repeated, whispering. "Ah, 't was such as this . . . killed my father! Come, let us go — "

"Your father?" quoth Jocelyn amazed. "Killed — "

"Like King Rufus, as he rode a-hunting . . . I was a child then . . . but I saw! We found him . . . my nurse Robina and I . . . in the Home Wood yonder. . . . Oh, prithee — come away!"

So Jocelyn, catching up his cloak, followed whither she led.

# CHAPTER XXIV

## TELLS HOW JOCELYN GAVE A WARNING

LIKE one dumb-smitten she went beside him, swift and light of foot though he knew it was not the speed of their going that caused her breath to labour so; and more than once he caught her viewing him with glances swift and almost furtive, so that he knew a sudden yet indefinable unease.

She brought him into the rose garden and there seated in the vine-clad arbour, she began to question him suddenly, breathlessly, watching him the while with persistent but half-fearful intensity.

"What like was this . . . this villain would have shot you?"

"A gipsy-looking fellow. But you saw him —"

"Nay, I glimpsed but his back. Saw you his face — to know it?"

"No, he wore a mask. 'T is strange a gipsy that goeth masked —"

"But why should he shoot at you?"

"Perchance for that I was there for him to shoot."

"This is the second time your life hath been attempted here at Aldrington. Why, Jocelyn, why?"

"Doubtless there be those do think I were better dead. And verily dead I should be but for a daisy flower that showed so solitary I must needs stoop to pluck it, in which moment crossbow twanged, quarrel flew to wound the tree and I fell and lay for dead, to draw my murderer in reach, and then — singing, you dawned upon us like the very spirit of this radiant morning —"

"But, oh — why is your life in such jeopardy?"

"Some men, Joan, must needs go by perilous ways."

"And wherefore you, Jocelyn? Is there . . . aught

you have done . . . are doing . . . to bring your life in such danger?"

"Alack!" he answered lightly, "I am Dinwiddie, a man destined it seems to go scant o' friends but with foes a-many—"

"Ah, why will you put me off with mere words, empty words that tell me nought?" said she in quick reproach, wringing her hands with tremulous anxiety. "Who are these stealthy, murderous foes that menace your life, Jocelyn — who?"

"Well," he answered, drawing the scroll of paper from his bosom and smoothing it out pensively. "It was an enemy writ me this dainty lure; 'twas another, as I think, shot it into bed to me this morning, lapped about a pretty birding arrow, and yet another, belike, that lay hid i' the wood yonder, waiting for this same delicate lure to bring me where his bolt should smite sure and true—"

"Lure?" she repeated. "That paper? Show me!"

So he gave her the writing, he watched her lovely eyes scan it once and, opening wide, read it again, than flash on him amazement, anger and— terror.

"Oh, God — Jocelyn!" she gasped, "this is my monogram; I have a jewelled neckpiece so designed! These words are writ . . . much as I do write."

"Why, there is a likeness!" he nodded.

"And you imagined this hateful thing my doing!"

"I do confess it something befooled me at first or I should have gone better armed, pistols and—"

"Oh, shame now that you should think so basely of me. That you should dare imagine such dishonour upon me for a moment, for single instant! Ha, vile, vile and most detestable!" And she tore the paper across and across with passionate fingers.

"And yet," said he, watching her with his wistful, musing gaze, "it so befalls that I do know your handwriting passing well and—"

"Impossible! How should you?"

"Suffice it that I do," he answered gently. "And thus,

as I went to this false rendezvous, I began to doubt, insomuch that, 'stead of going on into the Home Wood where Murder waited, I sat where Murder must creep to me. Moreover, a kindly Providence set growing a lonely daisy for me to cull and lo — I am alive!"

"And . . . in your heart . . . no doubt . . . of me?" she whispered, her eyes widening on his.

"Joan, I had as lief doubt God His mercy!"

Now at this, she uttered a little cry, soft, inarticulate, and reached him her hand that nestled again in his firm clasp with that same sweet intimacy; yet when he looked up, he saw her still very pale and greatly troubled.

"Oh, Jocelyn," she whispered, glancing fearfully about them, " who is it that, wishful to kill you, knoweth so much — to feign my handwriting and draw you my monogram?"

"Would God I were — sure!" answered Jocelyn fervently; and now his look was troubled also. "Joan," said he, keeping his face averted from her, "will you tell me more of my lord your father his death; who rode with him to the hunt that day and — "

"Ah, no!" she sighed. "I mind little but the horror of it . . . his pale, dead face . . . the blood — Ah, no, a mercy's name, speak me no more of this! Let us rather strive to be merry. Win me to laughter — tell me of Ione Fane, the how and why of her, so much as you can. Let Dinwiddie in his wisdom judge me what I am. Resolve myself to me, Jocelyn, speak me something of my faults, if there any be, yet wax eloquent upon my so many sweet virtues since these be legion; in fine, be truthful as you may — and dare, Jocelyn."

"A friend that is friend assured might dare much," he answered very gravely. "Now is thy friendship truly mine, Joan?"

"Do you doubt it yet?"

"Why then, let us put it to the proof. For 't is thus I read you in so far as man may: Ione is noble lady very proud and stately. Joan is eager maid, very tender, quick with life, dreaming of future joys — "

"Pray you what joys?"

"A husband. A home. Children. And it was to such sweet purpose God formed her. And thus might she live in happy and ever-growing content but that my proud Lady Ione will not suffer it."

"And wherefore not?"

"Because my Lady Ione is for ever at odds with tender Joan. Is she not so?"

"Why," laughed Ione, "in some sort — belike she is. But why look you so sudden gloomy?"

"Because," he answered, very earnestly, "I begin to dread lest my Lady Ione, in her wilful pride, destroy this sweet Joan . . . ay, by God's light, I fear lest she bring her to swift and shameful death!"

"Death?" she repeated. "Nay, 'tis an ill jest to —"

"Here is no jest!" he answered. "This proud Ione, stubborn in her politics as religion, is deadly menace to Joan, her better, gentler self, — a menace that groweth ever more deadly."

"A menace?" she whispered. "Ah . . . you mean —"

Now, meeting his look, she recoiled slowly, lifting her hand as against some nameless evil and, even now, the sick terror in her eyes smote all his old doubts of her to instant wakefulness with a dreadful fear that held him dumb.

"Jocelyn?" she whispered. "Oh, what is it? Do you . . . threaten me — you?"

"God forbid!" he answered. "I am not your danger nor ever could be. But Joan . . . dear child . . . you walk perilous track, blind, as I do hope and think — ay, blind and all unaware." Ione shrank trembling like any frightened girl, closed her eyes as against some horror, opened them and, sitting up, became her own serene and stateliest self.

"Jocelyn," said she, regarding him with her clear level gaze, "you have said too much or not enough. So I bid you speak me plain — all that you know or suspect. Yet first I will tell you that twice of late I have been . . . warned against . . . Dinwiddie."

"The which surpriseth me no whit," he nodded, frowning. "Pray were these same warnings — letters, by chance, anonymous letters writ in a crooked, disguised hand?"

" 'T is no matter, sir, since, believing the testimony of mine own eyes and ears, I nothing heeded them, having faith in you."

"I pray God your faith endure, Joan."

"Then show me what is in your heart — speak!"

"Know then," he answered, looking deep into these eyes that met his keen scrutiny so steadfastly, "there is a plot against Queen Elizabeth her very life; she is to be murdered here at Aldrington —"

"No! Ah, no! . . . God forbid it!" gasped Ione, leaping afoot in swift horror.

"Amen!" said the Captain, bowing his head reverently. "Yet, Joan, beside this, is yet another plot touching only you and Richard, a scheme to so implicate you both that whether this vile business succeed or no, ye shall be known as prime movers therein —"

"Abominable!" she exclaimed fiercely. "Yet who shall dare think such baseness of an Aldrington?"

"Ay, who indeed?" sighed Jocelyn. "But there are those do so think, ay, and are scheming to draw you to their evil purposes and — your own dishonour and destruction —"

"But how know you all this, to seem so sure; how know you, I say?"

"Joan," he answered, leaning near to whisper, "dear, my lady, I hold such proofs of this as might bring you — ay, even you — to the horrors of prison and — ha, God forbid it — but in such fearsome times as these, to . . . a traitor's death —"

"A traitor? . . . I?"

"Hush!" he whispered. "Lo, here now — see!" And drawing wallet from the breast of his doublet, he took thence a folded paper. "This is but copy I made," he explained, unfolding the paper, "the original is writ in secret ink, as you shall see later and destroy. Read it, Joan, read and mark the deadly subtlety."

"No . . . no!" she whispered, shrinking back. "Do you read it to me, Jocelyn." So, bending near where she crouched so very still and great-eyed, he read this, whispering:

"'Ione, Lady Fane, thou art the chosen. For it is now certain the woman Elizabeth called Queen, shall come to Aldrington. Thus unto thee, noble lady and faithful daughter of Holy Church, is given the happiness to aid the Religion.

He that beareth this shall be thine instructor, to his guidance submit thyself and also to our good and trusty son, Philip Drayton of Shalmeston. To this holy work are pledged the noblest in England as: the earls of Arundel, Northumberland, Worcester, Cumberland, Viscount Montacute, Lords Dacres, Vaux and very many else. Be it also thy duty to add unto these proud names that of the noble youth the Earl of Aldrington, thy brother. Lift up thy heart, nothing fearing. Be thou faithful in this work of salvation to win England back in the loving arms of Holy Mother Church, so shall thine be the blessing of Heaven now and hereafter. Amen.'"

"But here is none mention of violence to Her Majesty," said Ione, studying each word of this missive for herself.

"And therein lieth the devilish cunning of it," he answered. "You, as Catholic devout, must yield yourself blindly obedient and all unsuspecting, to be led on deep and deeper, until you are involved beyond all hope, — you and Richard also! And thus much for this letter, Joan! But, more than this, you have been already denounced to Sir Francis Walsingham — "

"Denounced? I?" she gasped. "By whom?"

"Ah, would to God I knew — "

"And of what . . . am I accused?"

"Here is the catalogue as I mind it," he answered, glancing furtively about and speaking softer than ever. "That you have been heard to speak 'gainst the Queen's

Majesty, bitterly condemning her policy regarding Mary Stuart — "

"Why, so I did!" said Ione. "Ay, I did — yet only as any other might that loveth justice. And I say again that Her Majesty's treatment of Queen Mary is — "

"Hush thee, Joan — "

"And . . . oh, 't was you heard me!" she cried wildly in swift and bitter accusation. "It was yourself heard me . . . you and Robin only! Was it you denounced me therefore? Was it Robin — "

"Can you think it, Joan — ?"

"Yet none other heard me! Of what more am I accused?"

"That you frequent the company of Sir Philip Drayton of Shalmeston and other suspected traitors."

"Yes. And what beside?"

"That you hold secret Mass and practice to draw Richard from his allegiance. This is the list, Joan, as I remember it — "

"And it is . . . all true!" she whispered. "Yes, 't is all exactly true save this last item, for I seek only to keep Richard faithful to the Religion, no more than this. But who . . . ah, who can know all this of me? Who hath so denounced me?"

"Alas, this is yet to learn. For, Joan, I am persuaded there is some secret enemy doth haunt the place in familiar guise, plotting the destruction of you and Richard — "

"Ay, but who . . . who? And to what end?"

"It is this I live to discover, Joan," he answered grimly.

"A secret enemy! Are you assured of this?"

"I am so sure, Joan, that either he dies or I must — "

"You?" she exclaimed, viewing him with such dreadful look as troubled and perplexed him greatly; but when he would have spoken, she bid him be silent and clasping her hands, wrung them, swaying herself back and forth as one in an agony of fear and doubt that found vent at last in breathless rush of words:

"Oh, I'm all 'mazed! I cannot think! And yet my

thought is that you — you . . . of all men alive yourself alone could know and bear such deadly testimony against me . . . you . . . you!"

"Why so I do," he answered, with his sadly wistful smile. "I denounce my Lady Ione, her proud wilfulness, to the maid Joan, that is, I hope, my gentle friend. Ah, Joan, dear my lady, I do but warn you of lurking dangers, to beware of this secret enemy, to set a guard upon your words henceforth, your every look and gesture, lest they may be turned against you. Trust you no one and keep your faith in me — "

Now at this she laughed in strange, wild fashion and rose, but, even as she laughed thus, he saw her shiver violently and instinctively reached out his hands to her:

"Joan . . . my lady — what is it?"

"This . . . secret enemy!" she gasped. "Creeping . . . and watching me all unseen . . . unknown! Not to be sure . . . oh, 't is this so daunts me!"

"Courage, child!" he murmured. "For I am here and — "

"You?" said she again and with another pitiful laugh. "Ay — thus it is, — God is in Heaven to hear my prayers and on earth is Dinwiddie! And yet . . . women, more innocent than I, have bled . . . and died! Torture and the . . . axe!"

"Never think it!" he pleaded, trying to stay the tremor of her hands with his lips. "First will I die, Joan . . . oh, believe this — "

"God help me!" cried she. "Oh, God help me, for I know not how to believe . . . or what! The world methought so glorious is all dark and hateful . . . a place of creeping spies, horror and death! Come now, oh, prithee, come and show me this secret writing where it is that I may destroy this so damning evidence at the least, — come, show me!"

# CHAPTER XXV

THIS day was still young when, breakfast done, Jocelyn came wandering forlorn to lean and peer down idly into the fish pool, his mind lost in dark and troubled revery. But after some while he became aware of Master Rickaby, my lord's High Steward and Chamberlain and, without lifting bowed head, the Captain watched this imposing personage his stately approach with bright and calculating eye.

Reaching the fish pool, Master Rickaby halted and, with scant bow or grace of gesture, spake in his most official and impressive tones:

"I am desired, sir, by my Lady Ursula, Countess of Hartesmere, to command your instant attendance."

The Captain merely glanced up to beckon with sinewy finger; said he:

"Sweet Master Rickaby, you may approach. Lo, here — these pretty fishes! They are sleek, they are fat, they are something grown since you came first to Aldrington, I guess?"

"'T is like enough, sir," answered Master Rickaby, staring, "for I have office held at Aldrington these many years. But Madam the Countess — "

"And the carp is long-lived fish, I think. See how they fan their fins, flirt their tails and flaunt their golden armour, the pretty wantons! And, being long-lived, 't is reasonable to suppose they thus fanned and flirted ere you hither to — "

"'Sbud, sir! I know nought o' fish. And my lady the Countess doth command — "

"Ay, Master Rickaby, these pretty fish thus fanned them, flashed and flirted all unconcerned, good faith, — e'en when their master the great Earl lay gasping out his life upon a certain crossbow bolt—"

"God's life, sir! What—"

"Yet here at Aldrington would be mighty stir and to-do that fatal day, ha—good Master Rickaby?"

"I . . . sir, I cannot say . . . I know nought . . . myself was then Grand Steward to my Lord Riderwood at Hoove—"

"Nay, but, precious sir, it was at Hoove the Earl was killed, in the woods that do lie 'twixt Hoove village and Kingston Buci—"

"No, no!" cried Master Rickaby, forgetting his wonted stateliness. "It was here, sir; it was here at Aldrington they found my lord, here i' the Home Wood."

"Nay," retorted the Captain, "certainly you are wrong—"

"Certes I am right, sir! Verily I heard it of them that found the Earl his body—"

"Ha, but so did I, man!" nodded the Captain. "I was told by Dame Robina Shaw they call the witch—"

"Sir, this tragic corse was found by my Lord Riderwood and Mr. Fane here at Aldrington in the Home Wood. I heard them speak on 't that same night."

"Well, and what said they?"

"Sir, I heard my lord declare—" Master Rickaby stopped suddenly, coughed and went on in his usual stately fashion, "suffice it, sir, 't is beyond all doubt the tragical mischance befell here at Aldrington. But—"

"And these fishes, look you," sighed the Captain, "being merely fishes, fanned and flirted, all unmindful—"

"Captain Dinwiddie, my office comports not with such idlesome chatter! Sir, I warn you again that Madam the Countess commandeth your instant presence, and she is lady not to be lightly thwarted or—"

"Forbid it, heaven!" cried the Captain. "Therefore, sweet Master Rickaby, I pray you commend me unto her ladyship and say her devoted servant begs she will honour him with her gracious presence here to philosophise on fish."

The High Steward blinked and with scarce a bow and never a flourish, strode majestically away, while Jocelyn, chin in hands, stared down at the fish again in a revery less gloomy yet more profound than ever, nor stirred, nor raised his thoughtful eyes until the Countess was screeching at his elbow.

"Ten thousand devils!" she gasped, breathless with rage and speed, and so was dumb, whereupon the Captain bowed, plumed bonnet a-flourish:

"I pray you continue, madam!" he murmured, on which the aged lady, having recovered breath sufficient, instantly assailed him with such flood of curseful invective that she grew more breathless than ever; perceiving which, the Captain set long arm about this small fury and seated her gently upon the marble bench beside the fish pool and stood bareheaded, looking down on her with his wistful smile.

"A sweet morning to your ladyship!" sighed he.

"Tush and the devil!" she snarled. "So I must come a-seeking your High Insolence, must I? Ha, what the plague is this present creation coming to, this vile world and base mankind? Tell me that, thou oaf!"

"For the present, madam, we study these pretty fishes to envy their innocence and—"

"'Sblood! Are you mankind, creation and the world—ha?"

"Their very epitome, madam. To wit: A deathless soul in dying body pent, infinite in the finite, angel and devil to love and hate, work good and ill, in fine—a man!"

"Soho! Well, Man, what d' ye learn of these fishes?"

"That 't is better to be a fish and swim in shady pool than a great lord and die in a wood."

"Aha!" muttered the Countess, with flash of her bright, keen eyes. "You speak of my brother-in-law, poor Charles, I think? Sit you, Jocelyn man, here close beside me, now—in thine ear! There was, as I do think, something strange in his sudden end."

"The which groweth stranger, madam. For my lady Joan—"

" Her name's Ione, man!"

" But Joan is more heartily English, madam."

" Ay, so it is. Well?"

" She tells me it was herself with her nurse Dame Robina Shaw found the Earl dead."

" Well, and so it was."

" And yet here, madam, Master Rickaby averred, betwixt my fishy speeches, that the true finders were Lord Riderwood and Mr. Fane."

" How should he know this?"

" He was then in Lord Riderwood's service at Hoove and saith he heard talk of this the same night betwixt my lord and Mr. Fane."

" Then, i' the fiend's name, why should they have kept this a secret all these years?"

" And there's the strangeness on't, madam!"

" Ay, marry!" nodded the little Countess. " Well, what think you on't?"

" So much," answered Jocelyn, rising, "that I would fain have speech with Dame Robina Shaw —"

" What, the curst witch? Dame, forsooth! And you must name her 'mother!' Ha, and snatch her from the water with mighty flourish and heroical to-do —"

" And sundry shrewd bumps, my lady. But, for the nonce, by your leave I will go seek her —"

"'Mother', quoth he!" exclaimed the Countess, instantly pinning him by the girdle. " Old Robina! A black witch! And he must name her 'mother!' The sweetest word in all this world! This hag Robina! And she was twice a mother, whiles I . . . alas, the solitary one! Ha, by the devil his dam! Must I be forever alone? Bide, jolt-head, and sit ye down again! Canst not see I'm nigh to weeping for very loneliness, breaking my poor desolate heart? Mother, forsooth! Ha, Beelzebub! Why must ye be off hag-hunting for this Robina, fool?"

" Dear my lady," answered Jocelyn, seating himself beside his fierce, small companion again, " it was Robina first spake me warning —"

" Of what ? "

"Of impending evil, of lurking danger for these proud children of Aldrington."

" Children, ay ! The boy 's a fool and the girl scarce better — "

" Nay, madam, I — "

" Tush ! Richard was sickly child expected to die and dead he 'd be, but for Ione's care ; ay, 't was devoted sister I grant ye, yet nothing more. For when she 's reared him and he 's old enow — away he rides with Lord Riderwood this damned wild rogue to guzzle and gamble and play the fool. Whiles Ione, 'stead o' following, 'stead of taking her proper place i' the world, must bide a-moping here, — a swan amid country ducks, playing at piety with her secret Masses and Jesuit Fathers, plague on 'em — "

" Your ladyship is not of the Old Religion, then ? "

"A Papist ? I ? " screeched the Countess. " Never dare think it ! "

"Not for the world ! " he answered, kissing the small fist she had shaken at him.

"Well, what was you telling me of dangers and warnings, my man ? "

" It is rather what Dame Robina might tell us."

" And she shall so, good faith ! Bide ye still ! " And forthwith the Countess emitted one of her sudden, piercing screeches, whereupon, and very suddenly, appeared one of her ornate and stalwart retainers somewhat breathless yet instant to serve.

"Watkin," said she, " command to me instantly Dame Shaw — go ! "

" Ay, my lady," answered Watkin, rolling eyes distressfully ; " but an' your ladyship will tell me who and where — "

" The witch, dolt ! The black witch ; ye know the curst witch ! "

" Ay, for sure, m' gracious lady, for sure — who don't ? " So saying, Watkin bowed and sped away.

" And there 's for ye ! " mocked the Countess. " Dame

Shaw, says you!　Dame!　And 'mother', forsooth!　Dost mind thine own dear mother, boy?"

"No, madam."

"Ha!　And so must be for crying 'mother' on every old hag 'twixt here and London town —"

"One, madam.　And she very sorrowful and oppressed. They tormented her with the rack, damn them!"

"Ay, damn them with all my heart, Jocelyn.　But there be tortures o' the mind sharp as any rack, boy. . . . Hush!　There strikes the clock . . . ten!　In an hour we ride to confront Philippa and her villain . . . aha, her spouse — to hale him forthright to the dungeons in Lewes Castle, mayhap.　And how say ye to this, my bold Captain?"

"Not a word until his wife hath spoke, madam. . . . And yonder cometh old Robina!　But no need for your man to so hurry her —"

"Fiddle-faddle, man!　Her legs be sound enough, I 'll warrant 'em.　Sit ye still!"

But as she spoke, the Captain rose and my lady, watching 'neath bent brows, saw him meet the old creature, catching her hands to stay her eager curtseys and speaking her with such smile that old Robina's look of troublous apprehension vanished and into her great eyes came a light that was not of the sun.

"Hither, woman!" cried the Countess, with imperious gesture.

"At your ladyship's will!" answered Robina, bobbing humble curtsey.

"Sit, woman, ye may sit."

"Gracious madam, I had liefer stand."

"Then stand ye, with a murrain!　Wert ever plaguey contrary as young maid, I mind."

"And your leddyship was ever kinder than ye seemed."

"Nay, folks were afeard of me, Robina, even then?"

"Never such as kenned the heart o' you, my leddy!　You as so loved all little childer, ay, and every poor, ailing soul —"

"Robina Shaw, ha' done!   Lo, here stands this Captain fellow!   Ye told me you'd die for him and —"

"So will I, my leddy, God wot, an' need be!   For he was kind to me when all the world was cruel; he —"

"Ay, woman, and he named ye 'mother'—ye boasted to me o' this yestere'en.   Well, he now would question thee, and I bid thee answer him nothing fearful, for here be none but thy friends."

"Full and free I'll speak, my leddy . . . for I do be troubled.   There be evil all about us, — peril and death for some on us, belike, — "

"My stars!" exclaimed the Countess.   "Death, sayst thou?   Ha, what the plague dost mean, Robina?   Death — how, when, where — be plain with us."

"Lack-a-day, madam!   Nought be plain; I do but read such signs as I may.   Yet sure am I that Aldrington is threatened."

"Ay, but how, woman, how?"

"This, my lady, I will tell you anon," said the Captain, "but for the present, I pray you suffer me.   Robina, my Lady Ione tells me 't was you and she found her father's body the day my lord was killed."

"Dear my master, 't was a-laying there i' the Home Wood, nigh to the rocks where the cave is."

"A cave, sayst thou?   Hum!   Had my lord been killed by an arrow or crossbow bolt?"

"'T was bolt, sir, — short and thick and no feathers, and it had smit him through the back atwixt the shoulders."

"Was his horse there?"

"Nay, sir."

"Can you mind what gentlemen were at the hunt that day?"

"Alack no, my master; they was so many."

"They met here — at the Great House?"

"Indeed, sir, a great company and very merry."

"But you will remember some of their names?"

"Well . . . there was my Lord Braxted, Sir John Scrope, Mr. Weston, Sir Giles Standish — many o' these be dead since, Lord Riderwood, Lord Veryan, Mr. Denzil, Sir Thomas Vincent — he were very young — Master Hugh Morton and many other great gentry I ha' forgot."

" Was Mr. Roland Fane there? "

" I did na see him, sir."

" You were nurse to the Lady Ione? "

" Till I wed my John. But he sailed away wi' Captain Hawkins and was lost and I wi' my babes like to starve. I lived to Maidstone in Kent then. So being skilled in yarbs and simples I brewed elixirs and waters agin the axey and wrote out spells and charms . . . they called me a Wise Woman then."

" And when did they begin to call you ' witch '? "

" Not till I come back into Sussex, five year agone, young master."

" And who put it about that you were a witch? "

" Sir, I cannot tell."

" Who were your chief accusers before the justices? "

" Sir Thomas Vincent, Mr. Morton, Master Denzil and Mr. Fane."

" Now prithee, Robina, when you found the Earl lying dead — what did you? "

" Cried on the child, my Lady Ione, to run for aid. Then came I and knelt by my lord to lift his poor head and knew he was surely sped."

" Ay and then, — what did you then? "

" Grew sick and mortal afeard, my sweet master, and tried to pray for the passing soul of him, and then I saw how he clutched somewhat in 's right hand and this a strip o' velvet orange-tawney. So I bent to take it but heered a shout and saw my Lord Riderwood come a-galloping and with him Derek Crouch. So I cried on them that my lord was dead and they looking on me so fearsome I prayed God save me, for Derek had jumped from 's horse."

" Who is Derek Crouch? "

" Mr. Fane's huntsman. Then Lord Riderwood axed me what I 'd seen and I told him how I 'd found my lord there dead. Then a frowned on me a while and I all of a

trimble, whispering prayers to God. And presently my
Lord Riderwood bid me go fetch aid and away sped I. But
looking back, I saw my Lord Riderwood wi' the strip of
orange-tawney velvet in 's hand, showing it to Derek. But
Derek saw me watching and came after me running and a
knife in 's fist, yet my Lord Riderwood called him back and
I ran on — but not to the Great House, no, for I was
mighty afeard. I fled to Shoreham and that same week was
wed to my John, for . . . oh, gentle sir and lady, I guessed
then that my master, the great Earl, had surely been
murdered."

"Ha!" cried the Countess, raising small, clenched fist.
"And by one in cloak of orange-tawney velvet — eh,
Jocelyn?"

"Nay," he answered musingly, "the Earl was slain by
crossbow bolt, from a distance . . . a crossbow bolt —
hum!" quoth he, tugging moustachio and so silent and
thoughtful that the little Countess, gripping his sleeve,
shook him in her impatience.

"What meaneth your 'hum' man — what?" she demanded.

"I was but thinking, madam, how crossbow bolts do
sometimes miss their mark."

"Yet the Earl, my misfortunate brother-in-law, died
o' one."

"Alas, my lady, there was no daisy flower to woo his
fingers and save his life! And now, Robina, of this
cave — "

"Nenny!" cried the Countess. "First, sir, expound
me your riddle o' death and a daisy."

"Willingly, madam. Yet first, Robina, what o' this
cave you spoke on?"

"'T is hid within they rocks i' the wood, sweet master,
a great cavern hard to be seen by strange eyes. Folk do
tell 't is haunted . . . ghosts as do flit o' nights . . . devil
fires and jack-o-lanthorns. Years agone I heered as there
was secret way . . . a passage under ground to the Great
House — "

"Ha — bah!" exclaimed the Countess. "Talk rather o' this strip of orange-tawney velvet, — how it should come in a dead man's hand."

Answered Jocelyn:

"I will hazard guess, my lady, that the Earl seized on one that wore such cloak, whereupon ensued some little striving, since the cloak was torn . . . that the wearer thereof won free, after which, very suddenly, the Earl was shot down and, as I do think, by another hand."

"An orange-tawney cloak!" repeated the Countess. "Ha, good lack, there would be many cloaks o' such modish colour."

"There are, madam!" Jocelyn nodded. "Mine own is, the new cloak I bought me o' late. Faith, 't would seem this orange-tawney is fateful colour — for the Earl, for one of his slayers and for thee, Robina. For, good mother, I do think thy persecution for sorcery, the pain o' the rack and all the harms and dangers hast endured do spring from a strip of velvet — orange-tawney. . . . And my lady, hither comes one of your stout henchmen — "

"And yonder strikes the clock — eleven!" quoth the Countess, rising. "Ho, Watkin, is the machine to door — my carosch?"

"At your leddyship's service!" answered brawny Watkin, bowing.

"Why then, go warn 'em I come, and see my escort be mounted. Now, Jocelyn man — your hand here!"

"A moment, madam, I pray," he answered; and setting arm about old Robina's thin shoulders, "Good mother," said he gently, "if Death is to grow busy hereabouts, as I do think is very like, prithee wander not alone, more especially towards the Home Wood."

"God bless thee, my sweet master," she whispered, catching his hand to kiss it very suddenly. "I shall not die yet awhile, except I be willing . . . and to good purpose!"

# CHAPTER XXVI

### How Florian Came Near Death and Won Him a Friend

They found the great coach with its six plump horses and twelve heavily armoured outriders drawn up in the court-yard; into this vasty conveyance the small lady mounted forthwith, beckoning Jocelyn beside her. And presently, with rumble and jingle, clang and tramp, the ponderous vehicle rolled heavily away with mounted men-at-arms clattering before and behind.

And when the din of their stately progress was somewhat silenced by muffling dust, the Countess, drawing Jocelyn near, questioned him, thus:

" Well, my man, are ye vexing your male mind whether or no to trust a wordy old woman with your high state secrets? "

" State secrets? " he repeated, keen glance on the sharp eyes that gave him look for look. " Why, your ladyship may ask what you will and I shall answer as I best may."

" Which means you'll put me off wi' side answers whenso your Wisdom deemeth proper, ha? "

" Essay me, madam."

" Why then, Captain Dinwiddie, what ha' you learned o' late concerning this plot to murder the Queen? "

Now at this he turned to survey his questioner in such blank amazement that she chuckled, nodding at him like small, mocking elf.

" Madam, whence had you this? "

" Sir, from the Queen herself when she lay at my house in Hogsden, scarce a se'nnight agone."

" Are you then familiar with Her Majesty, madam? "

" Ay, marry, all her days! I mind her when she was

small, despised brat in Harry's Court at Greenwich; she
was called the little bastard in those days, her bluff, kingly
sire made it so the custom, and none dare anyways notice
the sorry, neglected imp save poor Ann Cleeves and myself.
Well, Ann is dead these many years but I yet live and —
Elizabeth never forgets. So now, wilt dare trust me,
Jocelyn?"

"Ay, with all my heart!" he answered fervently.

"Then first, what's your tale of crossbow bolt and daisy
flower?" So, while the great coach rumbled slowly
through the dust of shady ways, Jocelyn told how narrowly
Death had missed him this morning, what time the Countess
hearkened speechlessly until he was done, then smote small
fist upon the cushioned seat with fierce, great oath:

"'Sblood! And Ione must come in time to scare the
villain away! Ha, Beelzebub! Another minute and your
dagger had been through his weasand — and she must needs
come stalking on her long legs and mar it all! Ha, this
Papistical wench with her secret Masses, and speaking
'gainst the Queen, and consorting with suspected traitors,
and — ha, let her weep — "

"Madam . . . madam . . ." stammered Jocelyn, "in
God's name, how knew you all this?"

"Why, from Walsingham, from Frank. 'T is small wonder he shakes head and begins to eye Aldrington askance!"

"But, madam, indeed it is not like the secret Walsingham to babble such tales — even to you — "

"To me, sirrah, to me? Good lack, sir, I ha' known
him since he was lean-shanked lad. I have made myself his
go-between with Her Majesty many's the time when she
was in her tantrums and he out o' favour. . . . But as for
Ione — ha, you talked with her this morning, and of what,
Jocelyn, what?"

"I warned her, gently as I might, of these same base
accusations Walsingham holdeth against her."

The Countess shook her head dubiously; quoth she:

"Ione is not easily affrighted, nor weeps she lightly, yet
this morning I left her crouched afore her great crucifix,

whispering prayers and her eyes all blubbered, and when I questioned her a did but sob the more and — 'would I were dead!' says she."

"Now crass fool that I am!" exclaimed Jocelyn in fierce self-reproach. "I should not have told her — "

"Tush, man! 'T is not for this she so grieves, no — 't is her heart, man, her heart or I 'm a cabbage!"

"Her heart? How so? Wherefore? Madam, I beg — "

"How think you of these accusations, my man?"

"A most damned calumny! But what mean you by — "

"And yet, Jocelyn, she is as determined Catholic as her father afore her, alas!"

"Yet is she ever and always — herself, madam. But prithee — "

"Well, but who shall have laid these so vile accusations against her, think you, my captain?"

Now hereupon Jocelyn told all his dark and troublous perplexities and of the deadly scheming that was to drag Richard and Ione to their ruin.

"Soho, a secret enemy in familiar guise, sayst tha'?" nodded the Countess. "Here is some explication of Robina, her warnings. Well — whom dost suspect, — ha, Jocelyn?"

"My lady," he answered with troubled look, "I can as yet do no more than ask myself — who is there should anywise benefit by Richard's death?"

"Aha — *cui bono?*" whispered the Countess. "And by my soul, we know who this is — But 'swounds! Why are we stopping? Watkin!" screeched the Countess, thrusting apart the leather curtains, "Watkin, what 's to do?"

"Why, my lady," answered big Wat, riding up, "it do be no more than a man, my lady, a-laying i' the road, dead, as I think, your ladyship, and a bloody poll. No, he ain't dead, my lady, leastways the lads ha' got un to his legs — " As he spoke, came two of the escort and between them a man, hatless and dusty, who wiped blood from his eyes; in which same moment Jocelyn was out of the coach and had grasped this man by the shoulders.

"What, John?" said he, peering into the bloody face.
"Ha, John Bly, what 's amiss?"

"Oh, Cap'n, here 's luck! 'T is you I come a-seeking
. . . your friend, sir, Master Ferndale, be a-fighting . . .
two on 'em . . . hard beset he be, sir, and him wounded — "

Staying for no more, Jocelyn beckoned the nearest horseman to alight, swung himself to saddle, and not waiting to
find the stirrups, spurred the plump animal to unwonted
speed and galloped headlong down the dusty road.  Reaching the Peck of Malt tavern he dismounted and, drawing
his sword, stepped into the cool dimness of the great kitchen
where showed a strange disorder, for the heavy table had
been twisted askew, chairs and benches lay overturned, at
the stairfoot a man lay asprawl as though dead, but of
living presence sight or sound was there none; the place
seemed pervaded by an unnatural and ghastly stillness, an
ominous quietude that chilled him with sudden dread.

"Florian!" he cried.  "What, Florian!"  From somewhere overhead came faint answering cry with a muffled
knocking; so leaping over that stilly, sprawling shape, he
sped up the stair and, guided by these sounds, reached the
door of Florian's chamber, to hear Philippa sobbing
prayers and Dame Margery crying to be let out.

"Florian," he demanded.  "Where is Florian?"

"Oh, Jocelyn, is 't thou?  Thank God!" cried Philippa.

"Let us forth, sir — let us out!" pleaded the dame.

"Nay," he answered, "the key is gone.  Tell me where
is Florian?"

"Alas, good master, us dunnot know.  There came two
men that drank and would ha' plagued us, so master Florian
took sword, locked us here and went down to 'em — we
heard them fighting — "

"Oh, Jocelyn, save . . . save him!" sobbed Philippa.

The Captain was halfway down the stair when the
Countess' coach rumbled into the yard and a moment later
she was standing on the threshold.  She glanced from
Jocelyn to the sprawling figure, she stared round about at

the wild disorder of the place, then stabbed the air with small, pointing finger.

"See!" she whispered. "There, man! And there again! Blood!" It spattered the floor in wide circles, it zigzagged here and there . . . to the open door and out beyond into the sunny garden. Forth leapt Jocelyn but, seeing no one, checked and stood uncertain; then from behind tall, clipped hedge rose a breathless laughter and a gasping voice he recognized:

"Another veney . . . one more . . . the last, sir . . . death to one of us . . . or both — " Even with the words was ring and sudden clash of meeting steel in furious thrust and parry; now, coming in eyeshot, Jocelyn checked again and, crouched for swift leap, stood motionless, nor dared to move lest Florian, his attention thus momentarily distracted, should in that moment meet death, for his antagonist was pressing him with close assault, plying thrust on thrust; a tall, dark man, buffed and booted like an officer, who fought with rapier and dagger, his face showed blood-streaked, but his attack very strong and skilful; while young Florian, eyes ablaze in dead white face, leaned feebly against a tree, with no chance for counter or deadly riposte, also he had no dagger and his left hand and forearm showed hideously gashed.

So Jocelyn crouched, waiting for the breathing space that he knew must come. Suddenly Florian's long blade, sweeping in dangerously wide parade, seemed to falter in recovery and, gasping breathless oath, his antagonist drove in a full-armed thrust, but Florian, swaying sideways, beat down the deadly steel with naked, bleeding hand, his own blade flashed, darted . . . and loosing the weapon, he laughed fierce and shrill and reeled back to the tree and leaned there, staring down where lay his adversary, transfixed and glaring up at the bright sun with wide, unwinking eyes. Thus laughing, Florian sank to his knees, to his face and, caught up in strong arms, looked into the Captain's working features.

"Ha, Florian . . . damned lad . . . sweet fool — " the words ended in a choke.

"Art here then, *amigo?* . . . God love thee! . . . Two o' them . . . none so ill, comrade . . . considering . . . only my adored . . . Cecily . . . alas . . ."

"To me! Give him to me!" A flurry and rustle of silken draperies and the Countess, seated on the grass, had the swooning youth clasped to her bosom.

Thus presently, opening great eyes misted with pain, Florian gazed up at the old face bent above him and spoke in joyous whisper:

"Now if this . . . be death . . . oh, kind mother o' mercy . . . kiss me." So and very gently, the Countess stooped to this comely young face, now more beautiful than ever by the nearness of death, and kissed the smooth brow, the closing, dream-filled eyes and thereafter gazed down on him a while very still and mute.

"Madam . . . is he dead?" questioned the Captain.

"No!" she answered. "Not yet . . . pray God . . ." And then, as young Florian's head rolled weakly back, she glared up at the Captain through blinding tears. "Ha, fool!" she snarled. "Crass fool, ye told me he was no better than mere soldier o' fortune . . . hardened man o' blood as yourself . . . and he is but sweet boy to be mothered. Go, bid my fellows hither — go!" And, without other word, Captain Jocelyn went.

# CHAPTER XXVII

## Concerneth a Dead Man and a Letter

A LARK carolled joyfully high in the sunny air, a black-bird, perched on lofty twig, piped sadly melodious, and Jocelyn stood looking down upon the dead man whose sightless eyes stared wide on a cloudless heaven, glorious now with sunset. A tall man this had been, dark-haired and saturnine, and with one ear mutilated by an old sword cut.

"So!" murmured Jocelyn, nodding down gloomily on the dead. "'Tall, black-avised, lacketh half an ear, and called Vince!' So here, sir, lieth the poor, mere husk o' you, but yourself now wiser than the wisest! Well, may you sleep sound and wake anon, mayhap to better living. But for the nonce, needs must I make inquisition. Come, then!"

So saying, the Captain sank upon a knee and unfastening the dead man's leathern jerkin, drew from this still breast a heavy purse and small, jewelled crucifix which he returned, and a sealed letter which he smiled at very grimly, for in bold, scrawling characters it bore this superscription:

To Roland Fane, Esquire, of Kingston Buci these.
Post haste by the hand of Captain Gregory Vince.

Thrusting this letter into his bosom, he rose and turning towards the inn, saw John coming to meet him, his broken head swathed neatly in snowy clout and bearing in his fist a leather blackjack of ale topped by creamy foam, the which he tendered to Jocelyn, saying:

"Thinking as you might be needing a drop, sir."

So Jocelyn thanked him and blowing off the foam, drank deep, while honest John talked:

" Lord love us, Cap'n, these be the days! My lady, the Countess, be aloft wi' my dame and the young Vi-countess, and the yard arl a-clank and a-tramp wi' her men, as do be a-spurring and a-galloping every which way for chi- rurgeons, and 'pothecarys and leeches and I don't know what. And a dead man a-laying here in my orchard and another on 'em a-laying in my kitchen, arl blood and gore, and me wi' a cracked sconce — Lord love us, your honour, these be the days, ay — by the pyx! "

" Meanwhile, John," said the Captain, handing back the empty blackjack, " I 'm wanting a thin, flat-bladed knife."

" Ay, ay, sir; come your ways."

" And a room with a fire, John, where I can be private."

" This way, Cap'n."

Thus presently alone in small chamber, Jocelyn heated knife in fire and therewith unsealing the letter, opened it and read this:

FRIEND ROLAND : Here is Tom Vincent in mighty taking with tale of death and damnation, vowing our scheme blown upon and them- selves and plot undone and discovered, except I bring the where- withal to check young Richard's crowing and abate his new-found valour. But pray thee, my Roland, wherefore not deal with him forthright and be done. Like sire, like son, a bolt from the blue.

Howbeit I come presently to settle my score with this Dinwiddie, unless haply Captain Vince achieve this for me, though my arm is well and supple as ever. Look for me at Kingston Buci three nights hence at ten o' the clock and know me ever

thine assured friend
RIDERWOOD.

Having read and pondered this letter awhile, Jocelyn thrust it into his bosom and hastened forth, eager for news of Florian. Reaching the kitchen, he found it deserted yet orderly as ever, since all grim signs of the recent affray had vanished and with them the sprawling figure at the stairfoot. But overhead was vague stir, a softly per- sistent bustle, and guessing what this portended, his anx- iety and gnawing suspense grew ever more keen. Crossing aimlessly to the open casement, he leaned there, gazing vacantly on the pleasant garden, then turned swiftly as down the stair sped Dame Margery, carrying a basin and stained bandages and questioned her, low-voiced and eager:

"Will he live?"

But, intent on her business, she seemed not to hear and hastened away, unheeding his gesture of appeal. So came he to the great fireplace and leaned there, head on arm, staring blindly down upon the smouldering fire. And, after some while, again he started to the light, quick tread of feet and beheld Philippa, her lovely face pale and set, her eyes woefully inflamed.

"Oh, child," he whispered, "how is he?"

"God have mercy . . . on him . . . and me!" she sobbed and, weeping, was gone.

Then Jocelyn came to the wide settle in the ingle and there sat, chin on clenched fists, staring at the floor; and thus presently stolid John found him.

"John," said he, beckoning. "John man . . . how say they? What 's the word, John? What o' my lad Florian, is 't life or death?"

"'Las, master!" mumbled John. "My dame do rackon as he be sped, a-dying, sir, sure-ly! An' him so young! And scarce wed, do ee see! It be cruel 'ard. Will I draw ee summat, sir, — a drop o' comfort, Cap'n?"

"Thankee, no, John! I 'll out i' the air . . . I 'll walk in your garden, John. Do you learn of him and warn me how he doth . . . I 'll to the garden. And should you see the Countess, say I beg a word with her."

So forth again went Captain Jocelyn, head bowed and heavy of foot, roaming forlornly until in his so aimless wandering he chanced where lay the dead man.

"Ha, Captain Gregory Vince," quoth he, scowling into that ghastly face, "hast stolen sweet youth from joy o' life, it seems . . . hast robbed me of my friend. So could I now curse thee to deepest hell. . . . Yet 't was in fight. . . . And who am I to judge thee? Better to hope, an' he must die, that ye that each other killed and thus by death ennobled, shall some day grow in love to friendship . . .

some day . . . mayhap. But as for me . . . I am lonely! Well, when I die, may my passing be swift and merciful as thine, sir Captain." Then, hands clasped behind him, he went wandering on again, with head bowed in grievous meditation:

" Nigh forty years of life," he muttered, " and what have I achieved save wounds . . . loneliness . . . and loss of friends? "

Beneath the windows of Florian's chamber he halted to watch and listen and was turning away disconsolate when to him came honest John.

" Cap'n, sir," said he, jerking thumb over shoulder, " Countess be i' the kitchen, but Lord, sir, in sech taking I dassent speak her for my very life."

" John, is my lad dead? "

" Sir, I dunno. Only there be leeches and 'pothecarys and physicians along o' him now."

" John, there was a man lay asprawl at foot o' the stair."

" Ay, so there was, sir. I thought Master Florian had killed he sure-ly."

" Well, where is the fellow? "

" 'T is past me, Cap'n. Haply he weren't 's dead as he seemed."

" Then find him, man — yet no, let be! If the fellow is 'scaped, 't is no matter." So saying, he entered the kitchen softly as possible and there beheld the Countess whispering with Dame Margery, so he stood mute a while, scarce daring to frame the words; at last he spoke, whispering also:

" Madam, pray tell me . . . is Florian yet alive? Can he live? "

" Nay, man, ask this of God," she answered, " for only God knoweth. These damned chirurgeons do but shake their ears and prate Latinity with a curse! But, an' love and careful nursing may save him, live he shall or I 'll die for 't! "

" And so God bless your ladyship."

" Ha, man," she whispered, shaking fierce, reproachful

head at him, " how could ye so mislead me?   To suffer me think him a paltry rogue, a needy wretch, a tramping, scheming, villainous, out-at-elbows rascally soldier ruffian — this sweet lad! "

" Madam, I told you he was my honoured friend — "

" And how should this recommend him?   Ha, you sir, master Physician! " she cried suddenly, in tones of hushed command as a somewhat pompous personage descended the stair, " what of the young gentleman, your patient — well, man, well? "

" Alas, no, your ladyship, no! " answered the Man of Physic, bowing.   " The gentleman is beyond all arts chirurgical, nor Galen himself, nor the blessed Hippocrates — "

" Blessed horns o' Beelzebub! " cried the little Countess, suddenly ferocious.   " Stand aside!   Out o' my way, man! 'T is woman's motherwit and tender care now.   I 'll to him:   Margery woman, come ye! "

And presently, unremarked and all unheeded, Captain Jocelyn got him to horse and rode away.

# CHAPTER XXVIII

## Which Is Chapter of Plot and Counterplot

Vigilant by habit, Captain Jocelyn kept the middle of the road, and though his head was bowed in grievous reverie, his ears and eyes were alert and watchful as ever. Thus and very suddenly he had wheeled his spirited horse to front a leafy rustling and had cocked and levelled a pistol as out from the underwoods that bordered the way hereabouts rode young Robin Netherby.

" Ay — shoot man! " he cried, tossing wide his arms; " shoot me, Jocelyn, and dying I'll thank thee! Snatch me from this sickness called life and win my gratitude . . . this rat's nest of a world! "

" Hum! " quoth the Captain, ramming pistol back into holster. " Speak you from heart or stomach, Robin? "

" From bleeding heart, sir! " answered the young squire, his smooth cheek flushing painfully. " And 't is yourself hath ruined me! By your counsel I am undone, my soul withered, my dear hopes all blasted! Ione scorns me! My lady hateth me; so is life a curse, an emptiness — and all by reason o' you! "

" Why, here now is heavy news, Robin — "

" She hath discovered the cheat o' these verses we put off on her as mine . . . oh, death and damnation! I am but now from her presence and her words sting me yet! She named us cheats and liars . . ."

" You told her then how 't was I writ these rhymes? "

" Told her? Hell's furies, man, — she had it out o' me ere I knew! She so bemused me with her passion of questioning I was confessing the cursed imposture ere I knew."

" And what said she, Robin man, her very words? "

" Words, sir? Her words were legion and best forgot.

Yet I do mind this: 'Robin,' says she, her eyes like blue
flames, 'thou art no worse than mere fool to think I might
be won by such deceit, but he' — meaning you, Jocelyn —
'he is a liar, and a liar,' quo' she, 'I will nowise suffer. So
should you see him anon,' says she — meaning yourself,
sir — 'say I bid him not trouble my sight so long as he
chooseth to remain at Aldrington.'"

"And so much for me!" said the Captain, nodding a
little grimly. "But what now for you, friend Robin?"

"I'll to the Netherlands!" cried the young squire bitterly. "Ay, I'm for the wars, to get me honourably slain
so soon as maybe."

Then, with no touch of hand or word of farewell, this
woeful young gentleman spurred his mount to swift action
and galloped away, leaving the Captain to gaze after him
very wistfully.

At last, looking up at the glowing western sky and round
about upon the lengthening shadows, he urged his horse to
purposeful gait that brought him to a certain narrow bye-
road down which he turned, a lane this that dwindled to a
bridle path winding among thickets and trees that grew
ever denser to a leafy wilderness where ran a bubbling rill.
This murmurous streamlet he followed until it had guided
him through these leafy solitudes to a glade where stood
mighty tree beneath which, and puffing tobacco tranquilly
through small, clay pipe, sat Sir Roger Williams.

"Comrade," quoth he, jerking thumb towards the western glow, "art something late, look you."

"Man Roger, my lad is dead . . . or nigh to it."

"The lad, quotha? What, young Florian that ye saved
from Alva's bloody claws at Antwerp in '75?"

"Even he!" answered Jocelyn, dismounting to tether
his horse.

"Why, how befell this, Jocelyn?"

"In fight with Captain Vince, him you warned me of,
and another. Vince lieth dead; his fellow 'scaped wounded."

"Why then, Cot pless the lad!" cried Sir Roger, un-
covering his bullet head very reverently. "An' he die,

't will be in fashion soldierly, look you. And py Heavens, old comrade, he doeth thee vasty credit; 't was passing good swordsman to outfight yon Vince — "

"On whose body I found this letter, Roger. But first thy news, man? Hast heard from the Queen?"

"Ay, faith. She quitteth London to-morrow, comrade. She will lie three days at Guildford, a week at Godalming and ten days hence — on June the twenty-first, to wit, she cometh to my Lord Richard here at Aldrington."

"Ten days!" repeated Jocelyn, rubbing square chin a little dubiously. "Well, this should suffice us to do — what we must, eh, Roger?"

"Ay, troth, time and to spare for the likes o' you and me! We 'll achieve, I 'll warrant us!"

"We needs must, Roger. Saw you Captain Nicholas and his brother at Shoreham, to warn them of our plan?"

"Ay, I did. They be itching for 't, they and their tarry sailormen — "

"So shall these plotters be spirited away and none the wiser."

"Ay, there it is, Jocelyn, — none the wiser! And 't is thus I boggle at thy plan, lad. For look you, — here shall be for us no pretty swordploy, no imbruing of steel, no honest business o' cut and thrust — "

"Yet 't is sure, Roger man."

"Sure?" growled Sir Roger. "Ay, 't is sure that Her Majesty, all unknowing, and hither coming to find all quiet, cursedly safe and serene, shall incontinent laugh at our past warnings and mock us heartily for windy scare-mongers."

"Why, 't is very like she may, Roger."

"She will, man, beyond all peradventure she will. She 'll mock us, jibe and jeer us, — thee for watchdog that bays vainly at the moon, and myself, look you, for her Mad Welshman, — to be patted o' the poll, py heavens! "

"Howbeit, Roger man, her peril will be over. She and England shall rest safe a while."

"And ourselves laughingstock o' the court, py the

bones! Ha, could we but show her a fresh corpse or so, or e'en some little effusion o' traitrous blood, 't would serve us. But thy plan, Jocelyn, lacketh powels; 't is too guileful for our good; 't is, as I say — "

" Very sure and certain, Roger."

Sir Roger snorted fiercely and knocked the ashes from his little pipe very tenderly.

" Know ye the secret chamber in Aldrington great hall? " he enquired.

" I know of it and how to come to it, as you 'll mind, Roger."

" Ay, but 't were well ye should learn it, every nook and corner, comrade, for three nights hence there shall convene divers o' these treasonable gentry and with them — I, as John Ford."

" So will I explore it this very night! "

" And lookee, comrade," chuckled Sir Roger, " in all England is no rebel so bloodily minded as this same John Ford, — no, nor in Spain or Rome any hater of our Bess more wordily eager for her murder! Py heavens, when I hold forth, these plotting gentry o' Sussex do shake their ears and gloat! Only Sir Philip Drayton eyes me askance."

" Well, there is nobility in the man, Roger."

" Tush — tush, 't is cursed traitor! "

" Yet sincere Catholic — "

" Ay, that would kill our Bess! Aha, and py heavens, look you — there be other such sincere Catholics, Jocelyn — notably and to wit, — Ione, Lady Fane! "

" Well, Roger? "

" Ill, man — in that she is rarely beauteous creature, young and — above all, ha — a woman! Venus was no fairer, alack! But for her loyalty to the Queen, doth your faith yet hold, Jocelyn? "

" Ay, truly! "

" Even to the jeopardy o' that head o' thine? "

" Even so, Roger."

" Yet is she proud piece and of mortal bold spirit, as appeareth. A Catholic! And what is worse, a woman

— and therefore compact o' wiles and artifice beyond man's
knowing. Ha, Jocelyn man, I would to God wert older,
ay, and grizzled as myself and, like myself, with a natural
mislike and distrust for aught in petticoats — ay, I do,
py my soul!" Now at this, Jocelyn grasped his companion by the arm and drawing him close, spoke quick and
low-voiced:

"Lookee, Roger, heed me and perpend! Here at Aldrington is plot within plot, — murder attempted but this
morning and murder done ten years agone! Hearkee,
man!" And now, while Sir Roger hearkened very earnestly, the Captain recounted all that had befallen since he
and Florian had carried the young Earl home to Aldrington. Scarce had he ended than up started Sir Roger, so
suddenly as to trip over his own spur:

"'Sdeath, man, here's tale o' villainy!" he exclaimed.
"Devil's work as I'm a soul!"

"Yet never a tittle of proof, Roger."

"Proof, quotha? To the devil with 't, say I! Strike,
man, strike where suspicion pointeth and clap what proof
you may atop o' Master Villainy, his grave for tombstone.
I marvel young Richard hath been suffered life so long an'
your suspicions be anywise true."

"Why, his sister Ione hath been his good angel thus
far — "

"And she a Catholic, Jocelyn — "

"And right noble lady, Roger!"

"Have ye warned the lad?"

"Ay, of secret enemy in familiar guise, as I did his
sister — "

"And i' the fiend's name, why not speak plain?"

"Roger, I will asperse no man without evidence clear
and manifest."

"Pish! Thou'rt too nice, comrade, too high-
stomached! This calleth for mine own simpler method,
to wit: denounce the villain for 's villainy and should the
rogue deny, ram thy tuck through his midriff and so end
him and this danger neatly in a trice — "

" Thereby opening the door to other like dangers, Roger. No — villain must be villain proved — "

" And how if young Richard die meanwhile. A ' bolt from the blue ' — ha ! "

" Ay, there it is ! " sighed Jocelyn ruefully. " Until Her Majesty arrive, I 'm minded to set him safe aboard ship with Captain Nicholas."

" Would he go, think ye? 'T is proud and wilful younker."

" Hum ! " quoth Jocelyn and stared moodily into the rippling brook, while Sir Roger conned over Lord Riderwood's intercepted letter again, following each boldly scrawled word with blunt finger, then read aloud:

" ' At Kingston Buci three nights hence at ten o' the clock.' This should serve us very handsomely, eh, comrade? A matter of ambushment and sudden onfall, — a brace o' shot from the hedge, look you, then at 'em with our steel. My Lord Riderwood and whoso journeys with him shall gallop no more o' nights — and the world the sweeter for their sudden dying — "

" But I would ha' no killing, Roger man."

" No . . . killing, quotha? "

" Not at this time or in such fashion. I 've better plan as — "

" Nay, but 't is right roguish lord and consorteth with rogues and traitors damned — "

" So when he dieth, Roger, as I guess he will anon and suddenly, it shall be i' the light and face to face with me ! "

" But, Cot's body, man ! " cried Sir Roger, snorting indignantly, " this villain lord hath attempted thy murder, his money pays for thy Florian's killing, ay, marry ! And according to thy tale, he is an approved cheat — "

" And my scheme, Roger, is this — "

" Also I 've heard that, upon a time, the Lady Fane loved this accursed lord — "

" And Roger, as I say, my scheme is this — "

And when Sir Roger, plucking his beard impatiently, had pished and pshawed a while, he clapped sudden arm about his silent, wistful-eyed companion and, if his voice was something harsh, there was an infinite kindness and comfort in the grip of this sinewy arm:

"Say on, old wardog, mine ears attend thee. . . . And Jocelyn . . . ha, friend, mayhap thy lad, thy Florian . . . perchance old Death shall not snatch him from thee yet awhile. . . ."

# CHAPTER XXIX

## Which Is Chapter of Doubt and Disbelief

Clocks near and far had chimed midnight when Captain Jocelyn stepped softly from his bedchamber and stood motionless a while to listen.

The great house lay all hushed and dark about him, its many inmates deep-plunged, it seemed, in the quiet blessedness of slumber for, save his own breathing, no sound troubled the all-pervading silence.

An oriel window at one end of the long gallery flecked the dusk with shafts of faint radiance, for the young moon was up; and it was toward this pale light his gaze was directed as he stood hearkening so intently and thus wholly unaware of the eyes that watched him with such dreadful apprehension.

Presently, hearing no sound, he crept silently along this stately gallery into the gloom of wide stairway, down which he stole sure-footed and silent ever, all unwitting the shape that flitted after him as silently.

With unerring, stealthy tread, he crept by remembered ways, while silent and sure as his, other feet crept after; and so he came to the great hall, a place of glooming mystery with the vague glimmer of lancet windows high overhead. Crossing to the wide hearth, he pressed the Red Hand of the escutcheon, heard a faint creak of movement and, stepping into the secret passage, closed it behind him, struck flint and steel and lighted the lantern he had brought.

A narrow passage this, that turned sharply at right angle and so brought him to a door that yielding soundlessly beneath his touch, disclosed a roomy chamber furnished with a small bed, table and chairs; a second door faced him beyond the table and, crossing to this, he had reached hand to latch when the door behind him closed sharply; — out flashed his dagger and turning swiftly, he saw Ione leaning towards him over the table. Her head was bowed, also her breath seemed to labour, yet when she spoke her voice was soft and kind.

"Wouldst not stab me, Jocelyn!"

"God forbid!" he muttered, hiding the weapon behind him.

"Yet . . . oh, such stealth!" she murmured. "Creeping, Jocelyn, creeping hither . . . i' the dark like any thief!"

"Joan — "

"The secret of the Red Hand was thought to be well and truly kept . . . known to but very few, yet how should it stay hid from such omniscient demigod as — Dinwiddie? A demigod, and yet . . . so furtive! A demigod, forsooth, that must peep and pry — more like knavish spy — "

"My Lady Ione, an' you 'll suffer me to speak — "

"I will, Jocelyn. Oh, you shall! You may speak when I have spoke. Let us sit then and talk a while, thou and I, whiles all honest folk do sleep. Be seated, Jocelyn." And sinking into chair beside the table, she leaned back to smile up at him, but in her wide, bright eyes was that which gave the lie to her smiling lips.

Wondering, he seated himself opposite, as from the bosom of her loose and simple gown she drew a folded paper and the Captain, guessing what this might be, flushed a little guiltily and spoke:

"Is it . . . those poor verses . . . to reproach me — "

"Verses?" she repeated, laying the paper on the table before her. "Ah, you mean foolish Robin's poems to me that he never wrote? No, no, this is prose, Jocelyn, — but first a game of question and answer, as thus: I ask thee: Hast been a soldier all thy days, Jocelyn? And you answer now?"

"Since my youth, Joan."

"And fought often in battles?"

" Very often."

" And seen men die? "

" Too often."

" There was one, — a certain Sir William Travis, he died — very suddenly, Jocelyn."

" And 't was the best thing he ever did, Joan. But — "

" You killed him, Jocelyn."

The Captain started and turned on her a look wherein she thought to read sudden apprehension.

" Was it not yourself killed him? " she questioned.

" Ay, it was," he confessed. "But — "

" In an alehouse, Jocelyn? "

" We fought in a tavern at Bergen-op-zoom — "

" A drunken brawl, sir? "

" A prearranged meeting, madam."

" There was again a Captain Peter Shand, — him you also killed."

" Ay, I did. He had betrayed divers o' my comrades to an evil death and a town to fire and ravishment. He should ha' died sooner — "

" You were concerned in many other private killings."

" Since your ladyship tells me so, I 'll not deny it. Though how you should know thus much o' my — "

" You are in Sussex here, Jocelyn, as secret agent of — Sir Francis Walsingham."

" As servant of Her Majesty, Elizabeth. But pray, how know you all this? "

Instead of answering, she sat mute and rigid, staring into the lantern and when at last she looked at him, the flame seemed to have got into her eyes, for they flared with such bitter scorn and loathing that he recoiled instinctively.

" Why, Joan — Joan — my lady — " he stammered.

" Now, I pray God punish you! " said she in awful, whispering voice. " Oh, God, pity me! You are convicted out of your own mouth. A treacherous spy! There — read the vile thing I know you for at last! Let God forgive your hateful, cruel treachery an' He may, but I never will."

Then she was afoot, but Jocelyn, never even glancing at the

paper she had thrust before him, leapt to the door, and then she was struggling wildly in his arms.

"Joan!" he pleaded. "Oh, child . . . loved Joan, never doubt me! For God's sake, for thine own dear sake, stay and suffer me to speak — "

"Lies!" she gasped, spurning him with passionate hands, "more lies! And Dinwiddie hath . . . golden tongue . . . subtle . . . wicked! Let me go, or I'll scream my brothers' gentlemen upon you! Let me go — "

But as she uttered the threat a powerful hand was upon her throat, the arm about her tightened painfully and in the face so near her own she saw such sudden, dreadful change that pride and anger were lost in horrified amazement.

"Silence!" he commanded, in voice harsh and fiercely changed as his look. "Be silent and hear me, or now shall be an end, for better you die here upon my heart than 'neath the axe . . . this fair body hewn asunder by the executioner's knife . . . the vile death of a traitor. Ione Fane, here is no season for your fine-lady whimsies, no time to flaunt your folly o' pride, for God's my witness, death is all about us, treachery and murder, — whiles you, pitiful creature, would run blindfold on destruction! So now, will ye hear me? Yea or nay?"

For breathless moment she stared up into this face once so gentle and kindly familiar, but now so direly transfigured, so distorted out of all knowledge that it bred in her a sick dismay worse than fear. . . . Her breath caught and, with shuddering, inarticulate cry, she hid her face against him, her red-gold hair agleam upon his breast; and for a space they stood thus, speechless and very still.

Then she was snatched up, borne across the room and seated in a chair; and he, scowling down on her with the same grim, relentless look. And presently, though her eyes met his unquailing, she spoke him with meekness.

"Jocelyn, wouldst have choked me indeed?"

"There be worse deaths!" he answered, turning to frown at the lantern.

"Alas, my poor throat!" she sighed, dolefully touching that fair, unmarked column with cherishing fingers. "Is it much bruised, prithee?"

"Ha, folly!" he exclaimed. "Have done with these coquet airs, madam!" And he glanced at her with such very evident disdain that she flushed painfully, her eyes glittered and her new-found meekness was consumed in sudden flame of anger.

"Spy!" she retorted, matching his disdain with bitter scorn. "Oh, spy, now let me watch you read in that letter what I know you to be; read it aloud an' you dare!"

So Jocelyn took up the letter and, seating himself at the table, drew the lantern near and, while she watched him 'neath sullen brows, read forth these words:

"IONE, LADY FANE. Right noble lady, in God's name and for your own sake, beware of the man calling himself Dinwiddie; he is by trade a spy and hath been concerned in many secret killings, notably Sir William Travis and Captain Peter Shand, and hath also betrayed many others to the torture and death. . ."

"Now hold there!" she cried. "What say you to this?"

"Nought, madam. And more followeth, to wit:

"He is of late one of Walsingham's secret agents of destruction set to spy on you and my lord your dear brother, and shall turn your lightest words or acts to manifest treason and your certain destruction. Thus you, my lady, are already denounced to Walsingham for the following treasons, namely: That you have been heard vehemently to condemn Elizabeth, her policy touching Queen Mary of Scots. That you frequent the society of notorious recusants and suspected persons. That you hold secret Mass in defiance of the Edict. And that you practise to seduce the Earl your brother from his allegiance. . ."

"Stay!" she commanded, pointing accusing finger. "'T was thus you professed to warn me yesterday; these were your very words."

"No, madam! These were the words of your indict-

ment that I read on Walsingham's table, writ by your
nameless and unknown accuser. . . . But here is yet more
to read, as thus:

"Therefore, noble lady, for the life and honour of yourself and the
Earl your brother, take instant and any means to be rid of Dinwiddie this vile informer ere he outwit you and it be too late."

" And here endeth this screed anonymous, madam."

" Why then," said she, leaning towards him across the
table, " 't is now for Dinwiddie his subtle tongue to argue
it into nothingness. Well, sir? "

But he never so much as glanced towards her; instead
he conned the letter again and, tracing certain words with
his finger, read them aloud, musingly:

" ' Instant and any means.' Hum! "

" Come, sir, be eloquent to vindicate yourself," she urged,
her rich voice a little mocking but her eager eyes watching
his down-bent, pensive face with strange anxiety. " What
have you to say 'gainst the black accusations in yon letter
. . . to disprove them? "

" Never a word, madam."

" How then, will you not even attempt to justify yourself in some sort? "

" No," he answered, still intent upon the letter, " it were
but waste of time and breath, since your ladyship hath
judged and condemned me already. Wherefore I would
have you remark this, the advice of your anonymous friend
here, — to be rid o' me by ' instant and any means! ' By
the which means he means, I judge, such means as poison, a
stab i' the back, or e'en a crossbow bolt. Well, crossbow
hath been tried and failed — once! How say you, my Lady
Fane? "

" You think," she gasped, " oh, you dare to think I
would stoop to such infamy? "

" Lady, I said not so nor can I ever so believe. But he
that shot at me and missed may shoot again or attempt
my life by other method. The question is — how? For
I would not be quit o' life — yet awhile."

" Then begone! " she whispered. " Get you from Aldrington, steal away . . . to-night."

" And now, madam, let us consider the plight of your ladyship and young Richard — "

" No! " cried she. " No, you have warned enough. What of this letter its truth and your admissions? I would know of you! I would be assured what you truly are."

" I? " he answered ruefully. " I am, now as ever, the very Jade of Circumstance, stumbling 'neath burdens not mine own, a fool, God wot, in pain to serve others, wasting his strength on thankless tasks, scheming to the profit of any save himself! Well, so be it, an' the Queen's Majesty be saved alive and my Lord Richard snatched from this peril o' creeping murder — "

At the word she was afoot and had caught his arm, shaking it in passion of sudden dread:

" Mean you my brother? My Richard in peril! Ah, what new horror is this? "

" Madam, 't is horror ten years old that hath menaced him since the day my lord your father was murdered in the Home Wood — "

" Murdered? Ah, never! This . . . oh, this was but cruel mischance — "

" This was fell and wanton murder, madam! And since you so doubt me, question you your Aunt the Countess. I would God she were here! Howbeit, Richard's life is threatened and I go about doing what I may to keep him in life, therefore if you will not aid, do not hinder me — "

" Ah, no — no! " cried she breathlessly. " I will help you . . . with my very life. Teach me how . . . tell me more . . . everything. Confide . . . trust me."

" Not I," he answered, loosing her fingers from his sleeve. " No, my Lady Fane, you are too apt, like weathercock, to twirl with every wind. Your aunt, 't is steadfast soul, — she knoweth all. Ask of her an' you will."

" I can be steadfast also, Jocelyn."

" To others belike, madam, but as for me I prove you vastly otherwise."

"Oh?" cried she, in sudden gust of fury. "And is yourself so immaculate, sir, to sit in judgment on me thus?"

"Since you ask me, madam, I—"

"Be silent, sir! And is it so great wonder I should doubt your honesty and you so strangely mysterious, so full of guileful conceits and hidden purposes? Did you not come to my service like hireling bravo newly from prison? Ah, have you not deceived me from that first hour? Ay, and God forgive it you! Did you not make even my honest Robin a cheat and liar to cozen me with verses he never wrote, since they were made by you? Confess it!"

"I do admit this, madam, but—"

"Have you not tricked me with your hateful subtleties, bemused me by your countless duplicities, your craft, cunning, cheats and double-dealings? You have! So then— am I to blame that you forced me thus to doubt you? I am not! By my soul, I vow here is reason to doubt an Archangel from heaven, much less a mere human man, a soldier of fortune from God knoweth where! Yet speak, — justify yourself, win back my faith, and you shall find me steadfast, heart and soul — ay, to death and beyond—"

"Or until the wind o' your suspicions shift and change again, madam!" he retorted, folding up the letter and thrusting it into an inner pocket. "But the night wastes away and I have much to do. Come then and I will light you forth." So saying he arose, and taking up the lantern, opened the door and stood waiting, for Ione had not moved.

"So then," said she unsteadily and with face averted, "you refuse my . . . proffered aid and . . . friendship?"

"Child," sighed he wearily, "get you to bed, but ere you sleep, pray for yourself and loved brother . . . ay and for me also. For should I be suddenly dispatched, by some or any means, Aldrington shall see dire and vasty changes, which God forbid! So be you very eloquently prayerful on Dinwiddie his behalf, doubt him how you may."

Then he went forth of the chamber and she, silenced now, perforce followed whither he led.

# CHAPTER XXX

## Of an Encounter by Night and How They Took Oath

The flickering beam of his lantern showed a narrow, stone-flagged passage, between walls of solid masonry, with other passages here and there, leading away to right and left, but Captain Jocelyn, disregarding these, kept to that which seemed to follow the conformation of the great house, and thus, turning sudden angle, came to a flight of narrow steps that led down into an arched gallery wider than any other, very dry and airy, though he judged it must run beneath the very foundations. And this passage ran pretty straight, trending gently down to a second flight of steps that brought him again, as he surmised, to the ground level; a vaulted tunnel this, where breathed an air cool and sweet with the scent of dewy woods, and he hastened towards where this passage made a sudden bend; then he halted, as from the mysteries before him there came a vague flurry of sound, a soft yet horrible scuffling, a single, gasping outcry.

Instantly Jocelyn put out the light, set down the lantern, drew his dagger and with this grasped in his right hand, crept forward, his light shoes soundless on the stone flags, his left hand outstretched, groping in the dark before him. . . . And suddenly this hand touched an unseen, moving figure that instantly closed with him in fierce grapple, and mid the pitchy gloom of the secret passage began a strife silent yet very deadly. . . . Jocelyn's dagger hand was caught and muffled in the folds of a cloak, steel smote him gasping to the wall and a harsh voice panted:

" Ha, py Cot's body — another ! "

" Roger ! "

" Sancta Maria ! Oh, lad, have I harmed thee ? "

" No whit . . . save a bruise ! " panted Jocelyn.

" Then, i' the Fiend's name — why not ? " panted Sir Roger. " 'T was shrewd blow and this my dagger o' Toledo ! "

" I borrowed shirt o' mail from the armoury, Roger. But one groaned. . . ? "

" One did, comrade. Come ye into the cave . . . thy hand — so ! "

Turning the bend, Jocelyn beheld a soft radiance that lit yet other stairs leading down to a jumble of rocks, and amid these a path by which they came presently into a roomy cavern with narrow, jagged entry, beyond which opening the young moon rode high in a starless immensity.

" Lo, the groaner ! " quoth Sir Roger, halting to stir a dim-seen shape with his toe. " 'T is hangdog rogue I found crawling hereabouts, so rapped me the sconce of him with my dagger hilt. Know ye the knavish visage of him, comrade ? "

" No," answered Jocelyn, peering down at the inert body. " Have you killed him ? "

" Not yet," answered Sir Roger, unsheathing ready dagger.

" Nay, hold ! " said Jocelyn, interposing. " He shall prove more use to us alive, mayhap. Hum ! A serving man, by 's looks — "

" Yet rogue, I 'll be sworn, lad, and therefore, look you, better dead — "

" Nay, I 'd fain question him, for 't is in my mind — " Jocelyn paused and stole hand to his own dagger as from that dark woodland before them stole a soft, clear whistle, — three or four flutelike notes twice repeated, and then into the moonlit glade rode a horseman who, drawing rein, sat to look about him.

" Ha — Roland Fane, py heavens ! " whispered Sir Roger.

" Ay. But why here ? And at such ghostly hour ? "

" Villainy, I 'll warrant him — "

# An Encounter by Night

"Ay. But what?"

"This he shall instant declare or swallow steel. I 'l out to him and —"

"Softly, Roger man! Bide you still and watch."

"Nay, I 'm for action, instant and to the point, look you. Now shalt see my method the heartily downright. 'Sblood! Yon fine rogue shall die biting grass or I will. Mark now —"

"Nay, Roger — wait!" whispered the Captain, grasping his impetuous companion's arm. "He comes nearer! Is 't a rendezvous? And to what purpose? Let us see." Even as he spoke, Mr. Fane rode nearer, whistling again very melodiously, then checked as if hearkening for some expected answer. And now, before the Captain might prevent, forth of the cave strode Sir Roger, hat truculently acock, and swaggering ferocity in every line of him.

Mr. Fane raised hand as in salutation, rode nearer, halted, stared, then swept off his hat and laughed jovially.

"Why — 't is good Master Ford!" quoth he.

Sir Roger snorted.

"Mr. Fane," said he arrogantly, "I am bold to demand your business hereabouts."

"Worthy Master Ford," smiled Mr. Fane, "I am bold to answer that my business is verily my business."

SIR ROGER (*Legs straddled and arms akimbo*): Sir, I take liberty to say I like your answer no better than your air, your visage, your mien, manner, looks, habit — in fine, your very self, sir!

MR. FANE (*His joviality becoming slightly aggressive*): Good Master Ford, I grieve! Your mislike is affliction I shall doubtless weep for anon.

SIR ROGER (*Advancing a step*): Mr. Fane, 't is my joy to pronounce you thrice damned liar!

MR. FANE (*Bowing*): Sweet Master Ford, I am what I am and therewithal reasonably content —

SIR ROGER (*Laying hand to rapier*): Mr. Fane, joyfully and man to man, look you, I declare unto you and the world that yourself is smiling villain, six times accursed. And how now, sir?

Mr. Fane (*Flourishing*): Now, Master Ford, being what I am, I plead Fortune deal tenderly with you, what you are notwithstanding.

Sir Roger (*Snarling and flashing out rapier*): Then thirdly, sir, I scorn thee for prating poltroon, a base craven, a creeping, bloodily minded hypocrite ten thousand times condemned, and may the devil take thee! And what o' this, sir?

Mr. Fane (*Baring his curly head*): This, worthy Master Ford, bloweth past mine auricular like tender Zephyrus his caress. God and the saints bless you, sir, and a fair good night!

"Cot . . . Cot love my soul and pody!" gasped Sir Roger, rolling wild eyes in very ecstasy of amazed and baffled fury. "What thing art thou? No man o' plood and powels, I 'll vow!"

"What then, do I puzzle thy so deep intelligence?" laughed Mr. Fane.

"Sir, look you, I say and aver thou 'rt no man o' spirit, heart or — "

"Tush, sir!" quoth Mr. Fane lightly. "I count myself far better thing, to wit — a philosopher, ay and more, a king o' dreams that liveth in fair world few may enter — "

"A cur dog!" roared Sir Roger. "A vile cur that will eat dirt — "

"Even so — an' I gain my desire and triumphant win to my kingdom. And so, fair dreams to thee, sweet Master Ford, — fare ye well!" So saying, Mr. Fane laughed jovially as ever, flourished plumed hat graciously and, wheeling his horse, cantered into those leafy shadows and was gone, while Sir Roger, sword in hand, stared after him in a sort of rageful trance, nor moved he until Jocelyn touched him and spoke.

"Put up thy tuck, Roger man," said he, whereat the outraged knight, muttering oaths Dutch and Spanish, rammed his useless rapier into scabbard and fell to swearing heartily in English:

"Ha . . . 'sdeath and damme! The fellow is lewd, lilly-livered, chicken-hearted coistrel, a — "

"The man is crafty, Roger! And was here to some purpose that is now beyond our discovery!"

"The rogue's a dastard!"

"A man o' wit, Roger, and outmatched you with his tongue as you would him wi' your sword."

"The dastard's a chicken-livered nidget, with a plague! I say a coward, — with a wanion!"

"And, Roger, there is a nature of seeming cowardice more deadly than valour the most heroical. Well, thy downright method having failed, — to-morrow, God willing, shalt see mine."

"Thine — ha? As how, Jocelyn, how, i' the devil's name?"

"First, what bringeth thee here at such hour, Roger, and thus unexpected?"

"Why, Cot's my life, — what but to warn ye again, lad. To-night my Lord Riderwood came to Hoove, he and his following, lusty fellows all, and vowing death on thee, as I do hear — "

"Saw you him, Roger?"

"Not yet. I but heard of his sudden arrival from Sir Philip Drayton and the same marvellously angered against this lord for speaking lewdness o' the Lady Fane."

"Know you how and what, Roger?"

"It seems this pestilent fellow, by his own avowal, comes for two purposes, namely — to make bloody end o' Dinwiddie and wed this lady."

"Wed her?" repeated the Captain. "Hum!"

"Why 't is no so long since he was her most passionate suitor and she none so cold, as I do hear."

"And you hear a marvellous deal, Roger!"

"Ay, marry, I warrant me I do! I 've rambled roving hither and yon o' late, and I 've eyes, ears and a tongue, as you may remark."

" Will he come to Aldrington, think you? And soon, Roger man? "

" Doubtless, since there must he come for speech wi' this lady and blood o' thy life, — he and his friends, look you, to be your death one way or t' other, — a rogue's stab i' the back which you cannot foresee, or honest duello the which you cannot accept. For comrade, shouldst be anyways incapacitated, thy counterplot miscarries and our Bess shall hardly escape bloody death. So, Jocelyn lad, old comrade, take now oath on my sword here, vowing afore God to chance no risk in quarrel personal until this thy work be accompt."

" Roger, I swear! Though indeed our mission is and shall be first with me."

" Cot pless thee, comrade! " quoth Sir Roger heartily. " So 't is now mine intent to meet this Riderwood i' thy stead, pluck him simply by the beard or twist 's ears, in fashion downright, until he shows steel and thereupon shall I ram my tuck through 's vitals, look you, and so be done featly and with a sweet dispatch."

Now at this, clapping arm about Sir Roger's shoulders, Captain Jocelyn emitted one of his rare laughs.

" Aha, Roger man," said he, " thou mad and lovely Welshman, hearkee now! My plan is also thy plan — our plan, and we Her Majesty's plotters to watch over and serve her to our deaths. So, here now on my sword, swear me afore God to run no private risk until our mission be done, — swear, man, swear! "

" But, Jocelyn . . . old friend, look you now — "

" Roger — swear! "

" Why then, py Cot, I swear! But how an' this swashing lord seek thee out, — ha, Jocelyn? "

" He shall wait my time to kill me, — until when I must avoid him, match my wit 'gainst his, or suffer his affronts as best I may. Howbeit, our swords and lives are first for Elizabeth. And now let us to question the fellow you smote i' the cave."

But when they reached the cave Sir Roger swore fiercely

while Jocelyn gloomed dismally, for the man was gone. And Sir Roger, having cursed awhile, grew dismal also.

" Alack, Jocelyn! " sighed he reproachfully, " this cometh o' thy queasy-stomached mercy, — a wanion on 't! Better I had slit his rascal throat and made sure."

The Captain glanced towards the sinking moon and shivered.

" I smell the dawn," said he, " so let us to bed ere day-spring.   Where is your horse? "

" I' the thicket yonder by the rill."

" I 'll go with thee so far."

So they went together, silent and gloomy still, nor spoke they until Sir Roger was in the saddle; then quoth he:

" As for this Fane now, comrade, what 's your method for coming to terms downright with him, ha? "

" A snare, Roger, a gin I have baited with — myself. This should prove sufficient lure or I lose my guess . . . to be rid o' Dinwiddie — hum!   Well, to-morrow shall prove this, one way or t 'other.   At twelve noon, Roger man, be you at Aldrington village, the inn called the Aldrington Arms, to see what you shall see.   On the stroke o' noon!   And so Good night and God speed thee, comrade."

# CHAPTER XXXI

## How My Lord Riderwood Came to Aldrington

THE Queen was to visit her loyal county of Sussex, wherefore in town, village and hamlet, east, west and southward to the sea, Sussex rejoiced.

God bless Royal Elizabeth!

The Queen's Majesty was coming to Aldrington, to the Great House, and there would bide awhile, the guest of my Lord Richard the Earl; thus, and ever since couriers had ridden in this morning with the stirring news, the Great House had hummed with a fury of endeavour, its many inmates busied with to-do of mighty preparation, from Master Rickaby, loud-voiced and more important than ever, to sweating lackeys, chattering maids and giggling pages.

" Her Royal Majesty is coming! And so soon! And so much to be done! God bless her, of course — but bustle there, bustle! "

Aldrington village was athrong, more especially its cosy inn, besmocked peasant and sturdy yeoman, red-faced country squires and rustic gallants, gentle and simple jostled each other cheerily, for here was much quaffing of nappy ale, sack, and Rhenish, with three times three and hurrah for Queen Bess.

And amidst all this merry babblement and simple-hearted jubilation — only one gloomy face where, in corner remote from the throng, an untasted stoup of ale before him, sat Mr. Robin Netherby who, sighing oft and deep, surveyed his world and all therein with lack-lustre, jaundiced eye.

But presently as he sat thus, arms folded and chin on breast, the very picture of hopeless lover, to him tripped, and somewhat unsteadily, two sprightly young gallants befeathered, be-cloaked, booted and bibulous.

"What, Robin — ha, Rob!" cried one, clapping Sir Despondency on bowed shoulder. "Here's a rouse, man, here's Bess in a bumper, and confusion to Spain!" And he wafted slopping alejack in wide-armed flourish.

"And lo," answered Robin gloomily, having sipped his ale, "your toast is honoured, Sir Oliver."

"Sir Oliver, quoth a? Good lack, Rob, 't was Noll but yesterday! I was ever thy Noll at school and thou my Rob. And lookee, Rob, when the Queen cometh t' Aldrington, thou 'lt be there, thou 'rt great with th' Earl as I 'm great wi' thee, — so, Rob, d' thou speak for me to my lord that I come as his guest t' the Great House and kiss Her Majesty's royal fist, Rob man . . . I that was thy loved sc-schoolfellow and playmate, Robin, and do love thee, good faith, with ay, wi' all my heart . . . t' kiss the fist o' Majesty, Rob, the hand o' the peerless G-Gloriana . . . ay, th' inspiration of all true English hearts like me and this my friend Anthony Fearn — you ha' n't forgot Tony Fearn that 's ready to shed 's blood or drink himself blind for the glory o' Bess . . . of Eliz'beth, of Glori — " here Sir Oliver being cut short by a hiccough, Mr. Fearn spoke incontinent:

"Ay, and me, Netherby," he cried, reaching unsteadily to pat Robin's other shoulder, "thy Tony, sweet gossip. We 've drank together ere now, thou and I, hawked and hunted, so prithee, bring me likewise to my Lord Richard's notice — "

"'Sheart, Rob," cried Sir Oliver, slapping at Robin's broad back again but with so ill an aim that he missed and all but fell, "Rob lad, I love thee, plague on me but I do! I love thee dearly as — "

"Why then, Oliver, fare you well!" sighed Robin. "I 'm company for no man — "

"Nay now, Rob, why so? Wherefore that doleful visage and — at such time? Go to, Rob, go to! Laugh, man! Sing, drink, be merry — "

"Not I!" growled Robin, beginning to scowl.

"Why then, t' cure thy doleful dump . . . a cup o'

Rhenish, a pottle o' sherris sack, — cry a toast, be merry."

" I 've no mind for merriment — "

" No? Why then, sweet lad, here 's myself and Tony ready to weep wi' you for pure good fellowship; ay, we 'll mingle our t-tears wi' thine and all . . . all for love o' thee, Rob."

" Sir Oliver," quoth Youthful Despond haughtily, " be so good to leave me — "

" Nay why, Rob, oh, wherefore — "

" You 're vile drunk, sir! "

" D-drunk, sayst tha? 'Swounds! My fox here shall bite him, dare so 'sperse me, eh, Tony . . . what sayst thou, my Anthony? " Thus questioned, Mr. Fearn viewed the speaker from head to foot, first with eyes very wide, then with eyes half-shut and thereafter, staggering but solemn, pronounced verdict:

" Rob 's i' the right on 't, Oliver! Thou 'rt drunk as gaffer's sow! So 'm I! We 're both drunk 's loyal gentlemen should be, or p-pretty nigh. So what I say is . . . fill again and a cheer for Royal Bess — " But speaking, he reeled into and clutched at a small man who chanced nearby, a plump man, round of head, eye, and nose, and who, steadying Mr. Fearn very deftly, spoke in hoarse and cheery encouragement:

" Easy, my lad, easy it is, — haul about and lay to."

Now at this moment an open paper fluttered to Robin's feet and, picking it up, he saw, written in bold characters, these words:

At twelve noon, I shall trouble to hear you at the Aldrington Arms and pay according as your news shall serve me.

" By your leave, young sir, yon be my property."

Robin started, glanced into a pair of round, bright eyes and, flushing guiltily, muttered an apology.

" Meaning as you 've read same, sir? " enquired the round man, taking the paper.

" Indeed . . . before I knew — "

"Well, it don't signify.  But, since you ha' read it, could you recognize the writing o' t?"

"Yes, I think I can."

"You 'll not ha' seen me afore, eh, young sir?"

"No."

"Yet I 've seen you and in company wi' a great gentleman and soldier."

"Whom d' you mean, pray?"

"Captain Dinwiddie."

"Oh?    And why d' you call him ' great '?"

"Well, young sir, now who do ee think writ this here writing?"

"At a guess, I should say a Mr. Fane."

"Young sir, be you a friend o' Captain Dinwiddie?"

"I hope so."

"Then should you hap to drop 'longside him, you might mention this here — seeing as you chanced to read same." Then, touching his bonnet, he lurched away, rolling in his gait, and Robin was yet staring after him in no little wonderment when on the road before the inn was sudden hubbub, trampling hoofs, shouts, expostulations, and then, louder than all, a voice that roared:

"Room, there, room!  Make way for my lord and gentlemen!"

Scowling at this so dictatorial voice, Robin Netherby glanced towards the door and his frown grew blacker as in upon them all stepped one, — a tall man richly habited; jewels sparkled in his plumed hat, in his ears, upon his hands, his Spanish ruff was edged with lace, his velvet cloak of modish brevity and he bore himself with such assured air of lofty arrogance that humble folk uncapped to him instinctively and those of the better sort made way.  Even Sir Oliver and Mr. Fearn blinked, awed and half sobered by the mere look of him, as he stood sniffing delicately at the silver-gilt pomander he had raised to his arching nostrils:

"Casson," said he, with gesture of languid abhorrence, "bid mine host show me private chamber or make me in-

stant clearance here; the air is rank o' rusticity! And
Martin, demand me a chair with arms and cushions, —
dispatch! And if there be person o' quality here, I would
be informed the reason for this so unsavoury convention."
Forth stepped Sir Oliver, bowing, hat aflourish, though
somewhat unsteadily.

"Sir . . . my good lord," he answered. "Her Most
Glorious Majesty doth shortly honour us here at Aldrington Great House with her Royal Presence — "

"Ha," quoth my lord, nodding; "this much I 've
heard — "

"Ha!" mocked Robin, gloomily contemptuous. "Then
why ask?" My lord glanced at him, sniffed at his
pomander and answered:

"Because, sir, this clamourous ale-swilling offends me,
for one thing, and — "

"Then take your unwanted daintiness otherwhere!"
growled Mr. Netherby.

"Have a care, young sir," cried a stoutish, mottle-
faced gentleman; "you affront my Lord Riderwood, no
less — "

"So much the better!" retorted Mr. Netherby with
growing truculence. "For I know him and he me."

"Faith, now — do I?" quoth my lord, viewing the sullen
young face with contemptuous stare. "As I live — I do!
'T is the lad Netherby that, plaguing certain lady, dared
look and sigh where I wooed, wherefore scarce a year since
I threatened to horsewhip him — "

"But," cried Robin, glaring, "thereafter rode post for
London!"

"Well, I am back again, Master Robin, back to woo and
win, and doubtless we can find a horsewhip — "

Up sprang young Robin, and snatching alejack, hurled
it at the speaker but with so passionate and wild an aim
that it smote and showered the mottle-faced gentleman and
all was uproar. In the midst of which tumult, as Robin
stood tugging at his close-fitting doublet, came deft hands

to aid him and he beheld again the small, round man who spoke him cheerily:

"How now, young master? Your two consorts hang i' the wind! So here be one to second ee, even Captain Nicholas Fell and that's myself. How sayst tha?"

"Ay, with all my heart," answered Robin, frowning where Lord Riderwood suffered himself to be likewise stripped for the encounter.

"They do say he be dangerous, yon!" whispered Captain Nicholas; "so play cautious, young sir — "

"I know he is," answered Robin, "and so much the better!"

"Now, sirs," cried the mottle-faced gentleman, "if ye be ready, — come!"

"Belay!" roared the little sea captain. "Stand by, my masters all — I'll see your man's flesh first — no hidden shirt o' mail, no secret amulets nor spells for we. Show us your noble skin, my lord."

With disdainful gesture Lord Riderwood drew back the fine linen from throat and breast and, advancing a step, lifted his long rapier in flourishing salute. Scowling, young Robin did the same and then, watched by the silent, staring company, the antagonists approached each other, swords advanced, daggers clutched to their breasts, eyes glaring into eyes. The rapiers crossed and so remained a moment touching yet motionless, then they whirled glittering in sudden attack, — feint, thrust and parry. Awhile they circled each other with nimble volt and traverse, until hot young Robin, scornful of such cautious play, pressed in with desperate thrust that was turned by wrist of iron and reeled from my lord's counter-stroke, an ever-widening bloodstain on his shirt sleeve.

"And so enough, my masters, — avast!" roared the little Captain in his mighty sea voice, interposing the broad blade of his own sword, whereat my lord turned on him with laugh like a snarl and Robin, panting, bade him stand away.

"But you 'm wounded, young sir — "

"Naught . . . 't is naught!" gasped Robin. "Away . . . away! I 'll see his blood . . . or die for 't — " and in he leapt to attack again, scornful of risk and furious as ever.

So while the silent concourse held its breath to crane and peer, crouching against walls, staring from open door and lattice, these deadly blades whirled, flashed and darted, glittering daggers parried and feinted, these nimble feet leapt, shuffled and stamped in ceaseless effort — until my lord's breath came a little faster, while his keen eyes, half-closed, watched his antagonist's young face, the sweat that streaked it, the open mouth that gasped so painfully, the eyes that widened in a dreadful foreknowledge . . . then Lord Riderwood laughed fiercely, his rapier, wielded by powerful, skilled hand, beat the heavy weapon from Robin's failing grasp to fall clattering a yard away. Thus defenceless, Robin, gasping bitter curse, hurled way his dagger also, and spreading wide his arms, spoke in panting distress:

"Smite and . . . make an end!"

"Oh, never doubt it!" laughed my lord and, advancing on his defenceless antagonist, drove sword through him. Robin swayed, tried to laugh defiantly and, choking, fell back into the arms of Sir Oliver and Mr. Fearn.

Now from the crowd rose a murmur that swelled to an angry muttering, dominated by the hoarse roar of Captain Nicholas:

"And be damned to ye for murdersome swab!"

"Who dare say so?"

"I say so!" cried the little mariner, rolling forward, "I say devil seize ye for bloody-minded dog! And what then?" Riderwood raised his sword, then stood motionless, staring into the muzzle of a pistol Captain Nicholas had whipped from somewhere about his chubby person.

"One step, my lord, and 't will plunge ee into hell fire," he warned, "one step now — come!"

Smiling contemptuously, my lord turned his back.

"Casson," said he, beckoning one of his servants, "cleanse me this sword. As for you, Master Robin, you have but what you sought, enough to tame your heat awhile; such high-chest thrusts seldom prove dangerous. Be thankful I spared your foolish life. And so a fair good morrow! And now, Colonel and gentlemen, our private chamber should be ready — come!"

So saying, my Lord Riderwood passed through the muttering company, his friends chattering loudly about him, while Sir Oliver dabbed ineptly at young Robin's wound, stammering alternate oaths and prayers very distressfully, for Robin lay aswoon. . . . But to them now came the little sea captain, bearing napkins and basin of water and who, kneeling beside the stricken youth, viewed his hurt with the sage eye of much experience, bathed, staunched and bandaged with the quick, deft hands of a sailor, commenting meantime, on this wise:

"Bad enow, my masters, but I've seen worse at sea and in bloody Flanders, and many on 'em living yet, hale and hearty, as Captain Jocelyn, for one, as should be dead a score o' times. . . . And yon beastly lord — keelhaul him I would, ah — trice him up by 's thumbs, or let brother Nat gi'e him a Spanish touch or so. . . . A stout-hearted lad this, ay, faith, and friend to Captain Jocelyn. Now had but the Captain been here — ! Well, my masters, here's the best I can do for the lad. Handle him precious now . . . have him to bed and see no surgeon swab bloods him! . . . Why, Lord love me, it lacketh but scant ten minutes to noon! Off wi' him, sirs — steady, so, and easy it is! To bed and no bleeding, mind ye!"

The wounded young gentleman having been carried tenderly above stairs, Captain Nick called for ale, and seating himself beside the open lattice, drank at leisure and thoughtfully, his round eyes very alert and turned ever towards the road; suddenly he finished his ale at a gulp and rose as a horseman dismounted before the inn, tossed his reins to an ostler and stepped through the open doorway, glancing expectantly this way and that. To this gentleman went Captain Nick, hat in hand, accosting him with the air and voice of a simple countryman.

" Pray, sir, be your honour Mr. Fane? "

" Well, fellow, are you he hath information? "

" At your sarvice, master. Do ee step along o' I now, and mun 'll show ee arl as ee can want — "

" Out where, clown? "

" Along o' I, maister, wheer us may speak wi' none to pigs-ear on we. Lookee, sir — writin's! And I 've a mort to tell ee tu — outside."

So Mr. Fane followed whither he was led — to be seized by mighty arms, his indignant outcries choked by sinewy fingers, to be whirled up and borne away into the spicy gloom of stables. . . .

Thus the clocks were on the stroke of twelve when Sir Roger Williams, riding into the inn yard, beheld a small, plump man who stood in the doorway of one of these stables, his booted legs wide apart, hands tucked into broad belt, roundly innocent eyes upturned to the blue sky, chewing placidly on a straw.

" Ha, Nicholas! " quoth Sir Roger, drawing rein.

" Ay, sir, 't is myself a-waiting yourself, according to orders."

" Well, Nick, well? "

" Ay, ay, sir, all 's snug, — lookee, here! " And, stepping aside, he jerked thumb towards a long, shapeless bundle, swathed in canvas and lashed securely by cords, a bundle that despite its bonds so artfully knotted, yet stirred in fashion very singular and odd.

" Zounds! " exclaimed Sir Roger, eyeing this in no little wonder. " What a plague ha' you there, Captain Nick? "

" Dunnage, my master, for stowage. Aboard ship. And this writing was on same." Sir Roger took the proffered letter and unfolding it, saw this:

MR. ROLAND FANE. Sir. If you would know more of the man calls himself Dinwiddie, his secret mission and how he shall be taken and made an end on, come you to the Aldrington Arms to-morrow at twelve o'clock, noon.

"Oho!" quoth Sir Roger, leaning from saddle to peer again and closer at that strange, feebly writhing bundle. "Dunnage, d' ye say?"

"For stowage! Aboard ship!" nodded the little Captain, his round visage broadening to sly smile. "Also — Master Ford, I am bid tell ye as this be the method o' — you know who!"

Then Captain Nick signalled with plump hand, whereat was sudden stir and lo, — from the dim stable upstarted four lusty fellows who, stooping together with cheery yo-ho, swung their "dunnage" across a pack horse, covered it with a heavy tarpaulin and with this bundle in their midst, went rolling forth of the yard in the wake of their small captain.

"Zapperment!" exclaimed Sir Roger, smiting hand to thigh, then laughing loud but short, he turned his horse and galloped away.

# CHAPTER XXXII

## In Which My Lord Riderwood Becomes a Menace

My lord the Earl of Aldrington, notwithstanding press of business, despite certain cares and secret anxieties, was none the less in his glory. For since he was so soon to be honoured by England's great Queen and play host to Royal Elizabeth, all his world made breathless haste to honour and pay court to him. Hourly they came and from all directions, these gentlefolk old and young, male and female, to bend in homage before this so exalted and right potent nobleman (who was yet no more than slim, great-eyed, sensitive boy) — to sue the privilege of his patronage, the mere mention of their names in Royalty's ear.

Surrounded thus by such brilliant, albeit humble, suitors, hearkening to their oft-repeated flatteries and adulation, their diffident pleas and humble requests, it was small wonder my lord should grow a little more arrogant than usual or that this naturally simple-hearted, kindly boy should be lost in the proud earl.

Nevertheless, he found time to be himself now and then as, for instance, this afternoon, — for though the house, the park and gardens shewed gay with fluttering cloaks and begemmed farthingales, and though so many eager eyes sought him, my lord sat alone with Captain Jocelyn, shut in his sumptuous bedchamber; though, just now, the lordly visage wore sullen look and his tone was peevish.

" Nay, fie, Jocelyn! I 'll not suffer it! I say I 'll never permit that you leave me."

" Nor will I, Richard, until Her Majesty be come and safe returned to London."

" Well, but wherefore leave me then? "

" I 've work to do, lad."

" Then I shall ha' work found for you here, Jocelyn."

" God love thee, Dick! But alack, I 'm not sorted for silken ease! I 'm wanted yonder among the dykes, where a little, heroical people fights for very life — "

" Ay, you mean the Netherlands. Well, thither we 'll go, Jocelyn, aha — thou and I! Good faith, I 'll raise and equip a great and notable company of gentleman volunteers, — I 'll call it Aldrington's Regiment. I 'll have 'em in blue and gold, their armour black and a scarlet plume — "

" Best wait you a year or so, Dick — "

" And wherefore, man? I 'm nigh old as Florian and he fought out yonder."

" Ay — Florian! " sighed the Captain. " He 'll fight abroad no more — "

" Well, why must he be such fool to get married? Howbeit, 't is good to know he yet liveth and is like to do, as my lady aunt sendeth word."

" Ay, God be thanked! "

" But as to my Volunteers, — I 'll make thee my second in command, Jocelyn, captain-commander under me. I 'll speak o' this to the Queen so soon as I may — "

" And be suddenly out o' favour, Richard! For to openly aid the poor Dutch nowadays runneth counter to her new policy ; she bloweth mighty cold these times."

" No matter, Jocelyn! An' thou go, I go! Ay, I 'll wear my new armour, the Greenwich suit o' gilt you praised t' other day in the armoury."

" And what of your sister, ha? My Lady Joan? "

" Tush, man! She shall nowise let or stay me. War is matter but for us men and beyond woman's powers. And this doth mind me! Why is Ione so strange to thee o' late? "

" Is she, Dick? "

" Zounds, man! Where be your eyes? Ha' n't you noticed? "

" Well . . . nought to mention."

" Ay, but I have. At mere sight o' you she falleth suddenly dumb. If you come by one way, she goeth by t' other. And — she watches you, Jocelyn!"

"Doth she so?"

"Ay, with strange, great eyes till you chance to look on her, then instantly a frowns on whoso or what is nearest and sweepeth herself away with mighty play o' petticoats. Now wherefore?"

"Troth, Richard, thou 'rt mighty observant."

"I am, Jocelyn! Ay, faith, I am! A man must needs so be, in especial gentlemen o' such rank as mine. And so 't is I roundly questioned her concerning this strange treatment of thee, and thou honoured by my friendship!"

"And what said my lady?"

"Well . . . she made vilely personal answers that angered me, Jocelyn. Ha, these women, their whims and unreasons! Beyond the knowing of us men. To dare so affront thee, and thou my friend!"

"How so, prithee?"

"Why then, — let it not anger thee, Jocelyn — "

"Nay, on my life!"

"Well, for one thing, it seems she hath taken sudden unkindness for thy . . . the hair on thy lip."

"Zookers!" exclaimed the Captain, tugging the hair in question. "Sayst thou?"

"Nay, 't is she so saith."

"Faith then, here 's reason I should be shaven and go smock-faced — "

"It were but vain labour, Jocelyn, since she also mislikes thy nose, oh, bitterly — "

"Ha! Gave she any reason?"

"None — save only that — 't is set on thy face."

"Alack now! And I 've thought it well enough as noses go, and suits my poor visage — "

"Ay, but she dispraiseth thy visage most unkindly of all."

"Beseech thee, what said she on 't, Dick?"

"So much, Jocelyn, that I ha' forgot all save that 't was a wolfish jowl, — ay, a jowl and thou my loved and honoured friend, as I told her, whereat she abused thee so shamefully I vowed you should hear on 't. 'Why then, tell him!' cries she. 'I will!' says I. 'And this too!' cries she, and forthwith vowed thy face crafty as fox's, fierce as wild boar's, venomous as adder's, loathly as toad's — and so I left her, Jocelyn."

Now at this the face in question shewed by turns amazed, grim, wistful and then was transfigured by its slow, rare smile.

"A wolfish jowl!" sighed the Captain. "And alas, Dick, this poor face is my fortune, my *passe partout*, my open sesame, the key wherewith I would unlock the hearts of such as might love me — " At this moment was knock on the door and, receiving permission, one of my lord's gentlemen entered who, advancing with many bows and flourishes, tendered a letter.

"Put it down, sir," sighed my lord. "I shall read it anon."

"My lord, the gentleman himself is below e'en now and very instant to see your lordship."

"What gentleman, pray?"

"My lord, he would give no name." The young Earl frowned, sighed wearily and, condescending to glance at the superscription, started violently and waved the bearer to begone; scarcely were they alone than he turned on Jocelyn a face of horrified dismay.

"Riderwood! 'T is from Lord Riderwood!" he gasped. "How dare he show his face here! What . . . ha, Jocelyn, what shall he want with me, think'st thou?"

"Belike his letter shall tell you, Dick." So my lord broke the seal with shaking fingers and, having read, sank back in his chair, pale, trembling and dumb.

"Nay, lad," said the Captain, rising to clap him on the shoulder with comforting hand. "'T is but knavish lord and thou art — Aldrington!"

"Ay, so I am!" cried Richard, throwing up his young head. "But the fellow is here . . . hath dared . . . and this letter . . . ah, 't is threat 'gainst my life, except I

. . . Ione — Read it, Jocelyn, read and tell me what I must do."

So Captain Jocelyn took up the letter and saw this:

To MY LORD THE EARL OF ALDRINGTON, humbly these: Right noble lord, since all the world doth woo thee, needs must I come a-wooing also. Yet, being myself, and therefore exempt and individual, I woo like to none save myself. For I woo thee, Richard, that thou woo thy life of thy sister Ione, that my wooing of her may prevail. For she, when my wedded wife, shall woo of me thy life, that lieth inscribed on certain treasonable document treasured of me under bolt and bar, for thine and most beauteous sister's sakes. Ione, even she I have so long adored and that, so whispereth mine heart, upon a time returned my passion. Prithee tell her I come a-thirst for sight of those many beauties must soon be the joy, delight and solace of

their early possessor

RIDERWOOD.

"God . . . God aid me!" quavered the young Earl. "What must I do?" Jocelyn flicked the letter from him as it were something unclean.

"Did she . . . Joan . . . ever love this fellow?" he demanded.

"Belike . . . at one time . . . as I think. But what matter for this? He is here and I . . . what must I do?"

"Be yourself, Richard. Show him a bold face and arrogant if you will."

"Yet what shall I say, — how meet him?"

"Like the great Earl of Aldrington — "

"But he is — Riderwood! And threatens my very life! And the Queen here so soon!"

"And lookee, Richard! 'T is Her Majesty and your own sense of honour shall prove your salvation — "

"But you, Jocelyn, you! Now! What can you do?"

"Well, I shall endeavour my part, yet not now, — and there's the rub, I must needs wait!"

"What shall you do then?"

"Watch."

" How?   Must I meet him — alone? "

" Nay, Dick, let your gentlemen attend you.   Be gracious to your guests and seem to nowise heed or notice my Lord Riderwood.   Rather make him seek you out and when he doth, be your lordliest, suffer him no chance o' private speech — "

" Ay but . . . if he insist? "

" Order him forth."

" And if . . . if he threaten? "

" Command your people remove him."

" Why, so I would, but — oh, Jocelyn, the paper!   He hath that accursed paper I signed all unwitting . . . this deadly thing! "

" Leave this to me, lad, and believe it shall never come to Her Majesty except by your own hand, if need be with the truth of how you were cozened into its signing.   So get thee to thy guests and remember — thou art Aldrington and beyond reproach or fear."

" Have you ever been . . . greatly afeard, Jocelyn? "

" Often, Dick."

" Then what did you? "

" Made such vasty show of hardy valiance, lad, that craven Fear, being deceived thereby and very craven, fled clean away.   And sure am I there is no man but knoweth fear of some sort at some time; to outface it proveth the man.   So be comforted, Richard, for thus it is I do know that Aldrington shall be worthy his great name."

" Now God love thee, Jocelyn! " cried the Earl.   " I will — ay, I will! "   For a moment this fearful boy clung to the Captain, trembling; then he stood away, straightened his gorgeous apparel, settled his deep ruff, squared his shoulders and pale, yet very resolute, hurried away.

# CHAPTER XXXIII

## Telleth How Captain Jocelyn Ran Away

Now, being alone, Jocelyn came to a window and leaned there pensive awhile, his brow furrowed in anxious thought of his many cares and the vast responsibilities each hour brought nearer.

Thus as he stood gazing across wide park to the dark line of distant woods that stretched away across hill and dale, he sighed wearily and yearned to be riding those leafy alleys, quit forever of all these plots and counterplots, — or aboard ship sailing for the war-ravaged Netherlands to hazard life again for the hard-pressed Dutchmen and, in the hearty welcome of old comrades, the stress and turmoil of siege and desperate onfall, to forget these latter days and more especially The Woman and the hopeless folly of his desire, his futile dreaming; though he knew that, wheresoever Chance might take him henceforth, Ione's glowing beauty and staglike grace might no more be forgotten than the low, rich voice of her.

Up from the gardens below came stir of joyous life and, glancing thither, Jocelyn beheld a crowd, ladies and gentlemen, that bowed, flourished or courteseyed greeting to Richard the Earl who, followed by divers of his own suite, welcomed them graciously, though glancing about him now and then with look of furtive apprehension; therefore Jocelyn, knowing the reason for this, looked about also and presently espied Lord Riderwood advancing with three of his friends.

Lord Riderwood bowed gracefully; the young Earl bowed stiffly. Lord Riderwood spoke, gesturing; the Earl answered, shaking his head. Lord Riderwood spoke again, gesturing more vehemently; the young Earl turned his back and, followed by his chattering guests, stalked out of the Captain's sight. . . . For a moment Lord Riderwood stood like one amazed, then, beckoning his friends angrily, strode off in pursuit, leaving this part of the gardens vacant, save for one who stood, booted legs apart, staring at the great house, window by window, wherefore Jocelyn leaned forth, arm aflourish, for this solitary one was Sir Roger Williams. Moreover, Sir Roger was fanning weather-beaten visage with his hat, noting which signal Jocelyn called down to him:

"What, Master Ford! Bide you." At this, Sir Roger clapped on his bonnet and fell to pacing leisurely to and fro until the Captain joined him.

"What now, Roger man? Is aught amiss?"

"Nay, all's very well, lad, more especially — thy method, so far as it goes. For, look you, your man, being taken, is yet alive and thus may 'scape and come back to mar all, ha?"

"And yonder went my Lord Riderwood! So come away, Roger."

"Ay, I remarked him, a mighty arrogant gentle by's looks, yet a right sword master, as I hear, and hath killed divers at rapier play."

"'T is so reported. But what bringeth thee hither, old comrade?"

"Yesterday he came nigh to ending young Squire Netherby at the inn."

"Ah, did he so? Was the lad much hurt?"

"Bad enow, so Captain Nick affirmeth. It seems your fine gentleman, having disarmed the boy, ran him through at leisure."

"Hum!" quoth the Captain and tugged moustachio.

Being come to the sequestered rose garden, into that remote and bowery corner where stood the arbour, these comrades sat therein, talking together in cautious tones:

"Well, Roger?"

"Nay, but — is it, lad?" questioned Sir Roger, shaking his grim head. "This Lady Fane, now — this Ione!"

" What of her, man? "

" Walsingham's suspicions wax apace."

" How know you this? "

" To-day he came secretly to Shoreham and summoned me."

" Well, Roger? "

" Well, lad, he showed me yet another unsigned letter — "

" And this the last of them, I pray God, and so believe, Roger. What said this letter? "

" Charged her with conspiring here for the Queen's assassination, comrade."

" Ay, but — with whom doth she conspire? Named the letter no other? "

" None."

" Why then, is 't not manifest she alone is aimed at? "

" Ay — but with how much o' truth, lad? "

" No whit, Roger. I 'll be sworn! "

" Why, belike you will, comrade, for she is young and of a beauty delectable as Venus, look you — "

" Ha, folly, man, cursed folly! "

" Moreover she is woman, Jocelyn, and therefore creature o' guile, by nature full o' subtleties and — "

" What said Walsingham of her? "

" Much! Since he knoweth her for lady in her own right, having vast possessions — "

" True — alas! " sighed Jocelyn.

" And therefore a right potent lady and very proud, a stiff-necked Papist mighty determined and of high courage."

" Well, Roger? "

" No, — ill, comrade! For I too ha' met her and my eyes do tell me she is verily woman o' bold spirit and dauntless will, scornful o' danger, a creature Amazonian and therefore, plus her beauty, rarely dangerous — "

" Yet I tell thee, Roger, that 'neath all this show of arrogant pride there hideth a gentle maid, a terrified, trembling girl — "

" Nay, lad, thou 'rt sufficiently young and perceiving

this, 't is thus she puts thee off, cheats thee, playing on thy very manhood. A woman is by Nature many-faced, — ay, *multum in parvo* — "

" Then hearkee, Roger! I will prove her faith and loyalty to the Queen beyond all doubting."

" Well and good, comrade, but how? "

" As thus. To-night is — the night — ha, Roger? To-night our treasonable gentry do meet for the last time and our plotting shall end — "

" Ay, to-night we shall be done, one way or t' other. But — "

" Nay, hearken! To-night you, as John Ford, shall address this meeting — "

" Ay, lad, and speak right bloodily, I 'll warrant me! "

" Why then, in your speech you shall say thus, — nay, wait! Here now, I 'll jot down that you must say."

With this, out came Jocelyn's tablets, wherein he wrote hastily awhile, what time Sir Roger eyed him, his intent face, a little dubiously.

" There, man! " quoth the Captain, thrusting what he had written into his companion's hand. " Canst read it? Is 't plain? "

" Ay! " nodded Sir Roger, conning the scribbled words. " Yet how shall this prove her traitor or no? "

" Herself shall be there, hid where she may hear, all unknown to any save you and me."

" Aha! " exclaimed Sir Roger, clapping hand to thigh. " This should do 't! Ay, marry, this shall prove her! But — will she be there — in such place, at such ghostly hour? "

" She shall, Roger man! Ay, she shall hear thee, e'en though I needs must carry her . . . drag her."

" So be it then! " nodded Sir Roger, folding the paper and rising. " Now I 'm for cup o' my lord's wine ere I get me to horse; how sayst thou, lad? "

" Nay, I 'll lurk remote till Lord Riderwood be gone lest he fall foul o' me."

" And should he so, Jocelyn, hands off thy steel, no

private blood-letting until our Bess be put safe out o' danger!"

"You have my oath, Roger."

"And thou mine, Jocelyn. Well and good! So fare thee well, comrade and . . . to-night, at twelve!"

"God speed thee, Roger man! And us! At twelve to-night! I shall sleep sounder thereafter." So they gripped hands, nodded at each other a little grimly, and Sir Roger strode housewards, long rapier acock and spurs jingling.

Alone in the arbour Jocelyn sat some time, lost again in wistful revery when he was aroused by a man's mocking laughter and started afoot, since he knew instinctively this man could be none other than Lord Riderwood. Stepping from the arbour, he now heard approaching footsteps and then that one voice, so rich and sweetly mellow, that had for him a joy beyond all other earthly sounds.

"Why have you followed me?"

"Because 't is so my bliss to follow thee anywhere, my Ione, be it to Paradise or to Acheron's blackest deep."

"Then, since you are here, you shall know my thoughts of you."

"Beloved creature, Beauty's Quintessence, speak on ——"

"Be silent, then." So saying, Ione reached the arbour to find it quite deserted, but instead of entering she stood in the doorway, fronting the man whose hateful glance wandered over her young shapeliness from gleaming hair that showed rebellious beneath jewelled coif to slender shoe peeping below her wide-skirted, embroidered farthingale.

"Time agone, my lord," said she, "I wrote forbidding your presence here ——"

"And lo, Ione, I am here, braving e'en the peril o' thy displeasure for love o' thee, as 'fore God I'll brave all other perils, human or divine, for thy warm loveliness."

"You affront me, sir! Your words, your looks, yourself I find alike hateful."

"'T is no matter, dear Heart, since yours, being yours, are my delight. Yourself, my Ione, ay, all that's in and about you but lives, moves, breathes to be my rapture for, do what you will, mine are you henceforth. Wilt deny me, Sweet? I'll find an added transport in thy shame, thy tears, thy breathless supplications; striving shall but spice my raptures — "

" Villainy be hushed! " she commanded. " I am no coy timidity to be affrighted by such base thing as yourself, — stand from me! " And she reached for the jewelled chatelaine that hung from her girdle. " Off, I say, lest my penknife grow foul o' your blood! " And she showed him the little blade, gripped in dimpled yet very resolute fist. Lord Riderwood glanced from it to the fierce beauty of her face and smiling, shook his head.

" Fie, now, fie, my Ione! " he laughed. " Here shall be no such foolish striving as this; thy struggles shall begin but when these happy arms close on and round thee as my wife."

" Oh, verily, you are run mad! " she nodded. " Or else were sottish fool! Rather than wed with such or know the nameless evil of you . . . I would be mine own destruction."

" And, by the pyx," he answered, " knowing your desperate nature, I do believe you would, — but, knowing also your doating love for Richard, sure am I that you cannot, will not and never would destroy him also. And herein, Ione, lieth my assured hope and most sweet certainty of thy possession — "

" And now," said she, stepping from the arbour, " I'll be quit of you — "

" Not yet," he answered, barring the way, " for and 'spite the menace of your little, pretty knife, you shall stay and learn wherefore and why all that tempting loveliness calls itself Ione Fane must and shall bless my arms in despite of Ione Fane, — this, thou Lovely Disdain! I hold, secure and safely hid, that which at thy pleasure shall be destroyed or — send thy pampered pet, thy so loved Richard and lordly brother — to the scaffold."

" Liar! " said she, scornfully.

" Sweeting! " he retorted. " I tell thee, shall behold thy

so loved brother's young head grin down on thee from spike on London Bridge, an' you cross me! I have his name by himself inscribed and duly witnessed and attested, set to such treasonable matter as shall make him crow's meat within the month."

"Oh . . . liar!" she repeated, but in fearful whisper now.

"It is yet very truth, Ione. Ask of Richard himself. So the case betwixt thyself and myself standeth thus, — now, mark! Come you to these arms as my wife, no matter how shamefast and unwilling, and those pretty hands shall destroy this fatal, damning evidence. Refuse me and your brother — "

"My Richard! You dare!" she gasped and, with the cry sprang, lithe and fierce as any tigress, and with knife upraised; but her wrist was seized in iron fingers, a strong arm was fast about her struggling helplessness, and he was raining fierce kisses on her distorted face, her red-gold hair, her snowy throat and neck, and then my lord's hat was twitched lightly from his head and, loosing his struggling prey, he whirled about and stood dumb and amazed to behold Captain Jocelyn turning this resplendent bonnet on lean finger of his right hand. Thus, in a tense silence, they faced each other eye to eye, while Ione, leaning weakly in doorway of the arbour, glanced from Riderwood's scowling, livid ferocity to Jocelyn's serene face and, dropping her knife, clasped tremulous hands and waited dreadfully for what should be. . . . A long, breathless moment. . . . Then Lord Riderwood leapt to sudden action, his foot stamped, and deadly rapier flashed out — straight for the Captain's breast; but Jocelyn, timing this expected, murderous stroke, shifted his foot, swayed gently; down swept his hand, shielded in my lord's jewelled bonnet, to parry and grip the blade close to the counterguard, to wrench it violently from my lord's hold, in which same moment — upswung his knotted left fist 'neath daintily bearded chin and Lord Riderwood went down half-stunned.

"My lord," said the Captain gently.

Opening wild eyes, Lord Riderwood beheld the point of his own sword at his throat and, looking up the narrow blade, saw beyond a lean visage ferociously sardonic as merciless and utterly confident as his own was wont to be. The Captain spoke again, and though his tone was so gently passionless, the fallen man seemed shaken by some frightful spasm.

" Your lordship will notice I 've handled like rogues ere now, therefore, my lord, I 'll trouble your lordship for your lordship's dagger." Gasping yet speechless, Lord Riderwood hesitated . . . a speck of blood flecked his ruff and, wincing from the merciless steel, he hurled his dagger to the Captain's feet, who took and thrust it into his own girdle. Then Jocelyn set knee to the captured sword, snapped it asunder and tossed the pieces behind him.

Now at this, Lord Riderwood seemed possessed of a sudden frenzy, for he leapt afoot, quivering fists above his head.

" Wait . . . wait! " he stammered breathlessly. " Another sword . . . wait till I be armed . . . another sword! " And, stumbling in his haste, away he sped like a madman, while Captain Jocelyn gazed after him with his sadly wistful, gray eyes and my Lady Ione, her clasped hands outstretched towards him, gazed on Jocelyn in a kind of awed amazement.

" Jocelyn! " she whispered, and her voice at its softest, sweetest, tenderest note. She saw him start, glance towards her, glance away . . . and something in his attitude chilled her, his very aloofness shamed her bitterly, turning proffered kindness to quick rage; therefore these hands, that had implored, pounced fiercely to grasp his arm and shake it in sudden fury.

" Fool," she cried, " why must you let him go? He threatens my brother's life . . . he shamed me and — you suffered it! "

" Alas, madam — "

" Hush! " she cried. " He comes back . . . oh, listen! And with his friends! "

" I hear them, — "

" You might have killed . . . rid the world of him and you let him go! "

" Alas, madam, I am no murderer — "

" You had your sword to fight him."

" Alas, madam, I cannot fight him."

" But . . . ah, you must, you must.   He comes yonder with his friends . . . and you but one . . . he means your death!   Oh, pray God make you strong 'gainst them, for now . . . fight you must."

" Alas, madam, 't is impossible! " he sighed, looking deep into her wide, anxious eyes.

" Then what . . . what shall you do? "

" Run! " he answered; and to her speechless amazement he turned and sped away very fleetly.

## CHAPTER XXXIV

### Telleth How Jocelyn Climbed Through a Window

My Lady Ione stood before the Italian looking-glass in her spacious bedchamber, viewing her loveliness by light of great candles of perfumed wax, while two of her ladies made ready to undress and put her to bed.

"Anne," said she, glancing down at the crumpled ball had once been a letter, "did he — was it Captain Dinwiddie himself gave you this, Anne?"

"Indeed, my lady," answered demure Anne, gentle-voiced, "at foot o' the stair, very suddenly, as I was following your ladyship, and was very urgent I must give it into your ladyship's own hand."

"How, Isobel, dost giggle, my sweeting? I prithee wherefore?"

"Oh, madam," replied pert Isobel, "I do but as is the fashion, for my Lord Riderwood hath made the Captain a rare jest; some of the gentlemen were vastly merry at his cost."

"How so, pretty minion? How came this?"

"'T was this evening, madam, and the guests departing, when to them cometh my Lord Riderwood and there before all, did publicly make mock of him — "

"Of the Captain? How? Did you hear this?"

"La, madam, we all did, for Lord Riderwood was very loud and merry yet terribly fierce withal in his pronouncements."

"What said he?"

"Oh, madam, he named Captain Dinwiddie as craven rogue, a spiritless dastard, a cur dog to be whipped — and more beside."

"What more?"

"That he was but a thing to be . . . spit upon!"

" Heard my Lord Richard all this? "

" In some part, madam, and there before them all gave Lord Riderwood the lie and drew his sword, oh, sweetly gallant, my lady."

" Ah — and what said Riderwood? "

" Laughed, madam, he and his friends and galloped away."

My lady turned to scowl down on the crumpled letter more fiercely than before, yet, when she spoke, her voice was gentle, almost pleading:

" Tell me, my Isobel and you, my sweet Anne, having seen this Captain Dinwiddie so oft of late, how think ye of him? "

" A proper man and of gallant showing, my lady, though a beareth himself something too stately."

" And ah, my lady, such notable, good leg! " sighed demure Anne.

" And a visage comely, madam, yet something grim! "

" Yet such a tender sadness in his eyes, my lady! " murmured gentle Anne.

" Sweet souls," said my lady, reaching a hand to each, " think ye he would run from any man — even Lord Riderwood? "

" Indeed, madam, 't is hard to believe it — "

" I believe it not, nor ever will! " murmured Anne.

" Yet, my sweetings, I tell you — run he did and — shamefully fast! "

Four bright eyes opened very wide and two pretty mouths rounded upon two rosy O's.

" Oh, my lady! " sighed Anne. " Methought this so angry lord was indeed a very liar! Our Captain showed ever to me so gently valiant, so kindly heroical, so — "

" Oh, madam! " cried Isobel, " indeed none should ha' guessed him runaway craven by 's grimly visage! "

" Well, my dears, there is tale of ass in a lion's skin! " quoth Ione, frowning on the letter again.

" But, ah, sweet my lady," murmured Anne; " he hath a lion's eyes also! "

" And now will your ladyship be pleased to be un-dressed."

" No! " said Ione, with strange vehemence.   " You shall but doff my gown and then begone to bed."

So four deft, white hands rid their lady's shapeliness of that cumbrous discomfort called a farthingale, where-upon she kissed them good-night and away they tripped, chattering like two magpies.

When the heavy door had closed, my lady sat down and smoothing out that sadly crumpled letter, read it again very deliberately:

MADAM : At a quarter before midnight I shall be waiting you in the Tower Garden with intent to prove myself your very faithful friend and humble servant.

Therefore I beg you will not fail me, for indeed your future safety and welfare depend on this.   So meet me you must or I myself shall fetch you, even though it be through your chamber window to snatch you from bed in your night rail.   For thine own sake, Joan, fail not.

Having read this, every word, she looked in the mirror again, opening her beautiful eyes very wide and, since she was alone, spoke to her reflection:

" Here now is an audacious madman, a brutal soldier would shame me — an' he dare. . . .   And he will dare! " Rising hastily, she crossed to the open casement and leaned out to measure the distance with calculating eyes.

" Indeed it is none so far — for such a man.   A ladder might reach!   Or these thick ivy stems. . . .   Oh, Saint Michael defend me! "   So thinking, she closed her lattice and fastened the hasp.   Then back went she to the looking-glass to regard herself and the letter again.

" In my night rail! " she exclaimed.   " Oh, the shame-less wretch! "   Nevertheless, she proceeded with her dis-robing very serenely; then off came jewelled coif, laced cap and snood, and she loosed down the rippling splendour of her hair.

" To ' snatch me from my bed ', forsooth!   Indeed, —

and would he so? . . . Ay, on my life I do believe he would! . . . Nay, this he shall not do, though I sit up all night! . . . Well now, do I fear him? Yon hasp is but slender thing and soon broke! Well, do I fear him? Yes, I think I do . . . not!" Here my lady, free-limbed now as young dryad, came again to the casement and lifted the hasp. "So!" she murmured. "Now if he come, nay — when he cometh — he shall find no tremulous wretch shivering behind bolts and bars! I'll be scornfully defiant. So now, thou bold Iniquity, — come how you will and take me how you may, but — not in my night rail or snatched screaming from my bed!"

And now my lady, having covered her scant draperies with light cloak, reseated herself at the mirror, very resolute and calmly determined. Yet presently she was up again to consult the jewelled timepiece beside her vast, heavily curtained bed.

"Heigho, half an hour to wait!" she sighed and in this same instant started and, glancing in quick apprehension towards the unlatched window, caught the cloak about herself as two gaunt hands swung the lattice wide and into her vision rose a plumed bonnet, a small, plain ruff and between these Captain Jocelyn's lean and sober visage.

For a long moment they gazed on each other, mute and very still, then her lashes drooped and she turned away and sat posed with such gracious art that, although her face was screened in the silky curtain of her long hair, this perfidious cloak revealed the warm white bewitchment of snowy neck and throat, of gleaming, rounded shoulder and the sweeping line of waist and hip and limb; and having sat thus a breathing space, she spoke:

"You are earlier than . . . you threatened."

"You knew I should be here?"

"I remembered you are . . . Dinwiddie!"

Folding his arms upon the window ledge, he leaned into the room.

"Then why unbind the wonder of your hair?" he de-

manded. Now at this she started, clutching betraying
cloak more closely about her and, knitting haughty brows
at him, glared; and when she had swept him with what poor
Robin had called " the blue flame of her eyes ", she con-
descended speech:

" Sir, this is my bedchamber and should be sacred to
myself, exempt and immune from all save such brutally
shameless wretch! "

" And yonder is my letter! " he nodded. " A warning
to be ready, and here am I, no fool lad prying on your
secrecy, nor hot youth bold for amorous escapade, but
mere servant would lift you from peril o' death despite
yourself and wilful folly. So — wind up your tresses,
madam, and follow me."

My lady turned to the mirror and, taking up ivory
comb, began smoothing out her gleaming hair with slow,
graceful movements and thus busied, spoke in soft, cooing
tones:

" God hath made a fair world, — with rosy children and
sweet flowers and pretty fowls to sing His praise. And
yet in this same world hath set also such loathed, noxious
things as toads and rats and worms and snails and, amongst
these most loathsome, — Dinwiddie! "

With the word, away flew the comb and up she started,
graceful yet fierce as any goaded stag — and leapt to close
the lattice; but, lithe and swift as she, Captain Jocelyn
was through the casement and into the room. And now
she reached where stood the silver bell of service, but he
snatched it first, muffled it in his long scarf and dropped it
out of the window.

" And now," he began, " I am here, thus before my time,
since I — "

" You! " said she, between white teeth, " you that are
a reproach and a bye-word! You that men laugh at! A
craven published and proclaimed . . . a craven! "

" Why to be sure, I ran away! " he nodded.

" Ay — from a man and thus may dare a solitary

woman!" she retorted. "You that so vaunted Dinwiddie his heroical prowess and yet flees a man and so shamefully — fast!"

"Ay, I 'm nimble o' leg, madam."

"You, — to so dare me that fears no man! The so valiant Captain that my Lord Riderwood denounced as vile thing to be spit upon!"

"So Richard told me, madam, but with a generous shame and anger; yet now his gentle sister, this noble lady, must twit and taunt me with 't — "

"Well, why must you play the dastard?" she demanded, her angry gaze drooping beneath his serene, untroubled look; "why suffer yourself to be made a public shame, a thing of mockery and contempt? If Dinwiddie's guileful tongue can explain this . . . why then . . . oh, prithee — speak!"

"You shall know," he answered grimly, "but in mine own time. Now, hear this: To-night at Aldrington, ay, here in your brother's very house, do meet divers gentlemen, and some o' them your familiar friends, set on by Romish Spain, to discuss how best to here murder Her Majesty the Queen."

"No!" cried Ione, recoiling, "I 'll never believe it — "

"Lately, madam, to Walsingham went yet another anonymous letter, accusing you of being one of these murderous conspirators."

"Well, 't is shameful, wicked lie!"

"Verily, madam, yet how shall the authorities be well assured o' this — "

"Well, I am a Fane and defy Walsingham and all his creeping spies!"

"Ay, madam, and thus it is I am here and very patient, God wot, — to bear you up and beyond reach of all suspicion, or chance of it, henceforth. So come you; let us go."

"Whither would you take me?"

"Where you shall hear, most explicit, how and where the Queen must be murdered. Come then, — nay, first wind up your hair, cover it lest spiders chance to roost in 't.

Also you will give me your word to creep silently as I shall creep, to be dumb whatsoever you see or hear. Well, madam, is 't yea or nay? Will you walk free or must I carry you strangling in my cloak? Choose now!"

For a moment she stood hesitant, raging at his severe assurance and passionless determination, then — leapt for the open window to scream. But, in a stride, his arms were about her, his fingers on her throat, bruising the delicate flesh, cutting short her cry of quick terror, her very breath; she was dragged back, muffled in stifling cloak, hoisted to uprearing, powerful shoulder and borne helpless towards the door . . . then she wailed feebly:

"Jocelyn!"

The cruel grip relaxed, the cloak fell away and, seeing her piteous face, he loosed her, stepped back and she sank before him on her knees.

Now beholding her as she cowered thus, head aback, her pride all gone, her defiant spirit broken at last, no more now than weeping, terrified maid, he fell upon a knee to fold her close, hiding her tear-wet face upon his breast as he were comforting some frightened child.

"Ha, love o' God!" he exclaimed, in voice like a groan, "why must you defy me that will die in your service? Why strive to be dead . . . forcing me to save alive this sweet body in despite of you? Ah, Joan . . . my lady, I hold thy life dearer than my own honour or aught under heaven save thy . . . loved. . . ." His voice broke and in this moment she nestled to him, sighful and trembling as she had been child indeed . . . or very woman. And the Captain, looking down on this golden head so strangely, sweetly abased, was minded to kiss it, yet did not, lifted his hand to touch its rippling glory, clenched it to quivering fist instead and spoke, sudden and harsh:

"Will ye go, madam, on your own feet and — silently?"

"Yes!" she whispered. "Ah, yes . . . take me . . . where you will." So he raised her and they stole forth of the spacious chamber, hand in hand, foot and foot, along wide gallery and down the stair, swift and silent; nor did he speak until they had reached the echoing dimness of the great hall and then all he said, and in fierce whisper, was:

"To-morrow there'll be marks on that throat o' thine set there by my fingers yet wrought by thy own wilful folly!" Whereto she answered, whispering also and meekly as submissive child or very woman:

"My ruff shall hide it."

Groping in the dark, he found and pressed the Red Hand of Aldrington, guided Ione through the secret door and led her on, unhesitating in the pitchy gloom until before them showed thin line of radiance and they became aware of a vague stir, a shuffle of stealthy feet, the creak of chairs, hushed murmurs, and then the soft, modulated tones of Sir Philip Drayton:

"My lords and gentlemen, though I for one do abhor all thought of bloodshed, yet at such time as this, we must, alas, forget gentle pity and save Christian England from Black Heresy and further persecution as best we may. To the which purpose this house hath been chosen for a deed that shall in days to come make this Aldrington a place of holy pilgrimage, for here shall Heresy be ended, the Tyrant destroyed. But as to how this work shall be achieved, hear ye now Master John Ford, the secret legate. Speak, sir!"

The stamp of heavy foot, a jingle of spurs and thereafter the voice of Sir Roger Williams, something loud and harsher than usual:

"As thus, my masters, to wit! This Trouble o' the World we name Elizabeth must die! This bastard calling herself Queen must be made an end on! To rise 'gainst her in arms is no rebellion, since His Holiness o' Rome hath pronounced her no queen. To kill her shall be thrice blessed act, since she is declared excommunicate these many years and therefore meet for death and damned — "

"Nay, sir," cried Sir Philip, his voice much agitated, "no need is there for such — " But now this one voice was drowned by others, fierce, eager, yet cautiously lowered: "Silence! Order! Say on, Master Ford!" The stealthy clamour subsiding, Sir Roger continued, loud and fierce as ever:

"To this good end, my masters, I am here since here shall this accursed tyrant die. As thus! For, though my Lord of Aldrington prove broken reed, yet we hold him by written bond, — but sirs, his sister Ione, Lady Fane is, like her sire, of bolder spirit and fierce for the Faith — and mark now — 't is this same Lady Ione shall lure the woman Elizabeth to her death! On this wise: Myself and another, hid close in the arras, shall wait armed with crossbows, since 't is silent death; then to us presently my Lady Ione Fane shall bring Elizabeth, and knowing or unknowing, shall hold her in prattling discourse to the very instant of her death, ay, to that blessed moment when, smitten by our shafts, this tyrant Elizabeth shall foul the earth with her vile blood and Heresy be slain. . . ."

"Oh — Jocelyn. . . . Take me away . . ."

"Is it enough, Joan?"

"Yes! Oh, mercy of God! . . . That I should be chosen — to such dreadful purpose! Ah, take — take me hence ere I swoon."

Reaching the hall again, she felt her way to cushioned settle and sinking down there, rocked herself to and fro and he heard her breath come in deep, shuddering sighs.

"Oh, villains . . . murderers . . ." she gasped. "Oh, most detestable!" Then she was afoot, clinging to him, shaking him in a very passion of appeal.

"Jocelyn . . . we must stop them! We must save her . . . oh, Jocelyn, thou 'rt so strong . . . so wise, — ah, tell me what I must do . . . how save her?"

"The Queen lieth at Guildford, Joan, scarce three hours' ride."

"Then let us to her . . . now . . . this moment, thou and I."

"Nay, I must bide here."

"Then will I ride alone, so soon as I be habited! I 'll see Her Majesty this night or die for 't!"

"Now, God bless thee, Joan!" he whispered. "Go

then and prepare you. I 'll rouse Will Thurlow; 't is bold young giant and shall ride with thee."

" But . . . so dark! " she gasped. " Such long road and . . . so dark! "

" Nay, Joan, the moon is rising — see yonder! "

But, instead of looking, she clung to him only the faster and he heard her sob once; then she was away, speeding sure-footed through the gloom.

So Jocelyn went forth to the stables and there very speedily had big Will out of bed, listening and dressing both at once.

" I 'll tak' cousin Tom along, your honour," quoth he, tugging on spurred boots. " 'T is stout lad, do ee see — "

" You 'll take care of her, Will? "

" That us shall, sir, Tom and me! " So Tom was roused forthwith and presently down they went to saddle the horses.

" My lady 'll ride her mare Princess yonder, I guess, sir."

" Why then, I 'll saddle her. Are ye armed, lads? "

" I 've goodly sword here, your honour, and Tom hath his whinger."

" Have ye pistols? "

" No, sir, but — "

" Take these of mine! "

" Nay, sir, I should likely miss my man wi' a dag — "

" Not if you ram it under his belt ere you give fire."

" I 'd rayther ha' my bow, your honour."

" And lookee, Will, and you Tom, — your lives for her safety! "

" You may trust we, sir — "

" And hither she comes! " said Jocelyn, and was out of the stable to meet her.

" Art not afraid? "

" A little! " she answered, turning to look where the horses were led forth. " Where shall I find the Queen? "

" She lieth at Sir Robert Medwin's house and strictly guarded. Therefore you must ask for Captain Hope of the Yeomen and mention my name."

" You will not . . . go with me, then? "

" Would to God I might! " he answered and, sighing, beckoned to Will who came, cap in hand, with the horses.

Then Jocelyn lifted her to the saddle, settled her foot in the stirrup and stepping back, saw her face very pale in the light of uprising moon.

" Yonder 's fair lamp to light you, my lady," he murmured, " and God bring thee safe — " But as he spoke, she stooped to him very suddenly, he felt her gauntletted hand on his shoulder and, looking up into her eyes, saw them the brighter and more lovely for their brimming tears; and then she was whispering, softly tender, sweetly intimate:

" Jocelyn . . . oh, man . . . I have so doubted, so reviled and cruelly mocked thee that . . . if my throat be bruised, as indeed it is, Jocelyn, I shall be glad . . . oh, glad to bear thy mark on me! " So saying, she wheeled her eager mare and rode away with Tom and big Will clattering after.

And when all sounds of their going had died in the distance, Captain Jocelyn sighed and trudged off too, walking very slowly and his head bowed like one that is weary or oppressed by some grievous thought. And presently, lifting wistful, troubled eyes to the moon, he spoke his thought aloud:

" A penniless soldier . . . a very beggar . . . destitute now as ever! I must back to the wars . . . and suddenly! "

# CHAPTER XXXV

## OF CAPTAIN JOCELYN, HIS METHOD

THE moon had topped the trees when Jocelyn reached a certain glade and, here pausing, whistled softly, his keen eyes quick and watchful. And thus amid the jagged rocks hiding the cave that by common report was haunted, he saw a flash thrice repeated, and then a beam that danced to and fro; yet no corpse candle or will-o'-the-wisp this, but a lantern aswing in the fist of Captain Nick who, approaching softly, spoke low-voiced:

" Come your ways, Captain Jocelyn; we be standing by, your honour, at stations."

Reaching the cave, this flickering lantern showed dim shapes, yet no dismal ghosts or airy phantoms these that crouched, grasping bright steel so purposefully. . . . The light vanished to sudden darkness with a silence unbroken save for a little, fugitive night wind that sighed mournfully amid unseen leaves and was gone. . . . Silence. . . . A ghastly dimness. . . . An ominous, brooding hush that had in it something of dreadful menace. . . . A vague stir at last that grew louder. . . . A scuffle of feet, stealthy yet uncertain. . . . A murmur of muttering voices pierced suddenly by short, startled outcry:

" Ha, God . . . Betrayed!"

A pistol flashed and roared . . . a voice gasped, choking horribly, and in the cavern was sudden uproar quickly silenced. The lantern gleamed again to show seven men that writhed in bonds and one that lay face down and very still in a dark and ever-widening pool.

" Who is it? " panted Captain Jocelyn. " Who is it lies there? "

" Drayton! " answered Sir Roger Williams, wiping his dagger.

"Ay, 't is him sure-ly!" said the little Captain, rolling that inert shape face up to the lantern. "And dead as mutton, your honour."

"Then God rest him!" said Jocelyn, peering down into those pallid features.

"Why, look you now," quoth Sir Roger bitterly, "the villain meant death to the Queen, ay, and some of us."

"Yet 't was a goodly gentleman, Roger."

"Out on thee, Jocelyn! 'T was Papistical, murderous dog and traitor damned!" snarled Sir Roger. "Also my good dagger was quick and spared him worse death. Take up the carrion, some o' ye!"

And now from the dim woods horses were led, across which these helpless prisoners, bound and gagged, were securely lashed by quick, sailorly hands. This done, came the little Captain who, meeting Jocelyn's keen, questioning gaze, showed strange unease.

"So your honour's tactics was sound," quoth he, "all 's shipshape, sir, foul 's fair, the wind o' success sits abaft and all 's bomon. But now it is, my masters, as I must give ye tidings other . . ." Here Captain Nick took off his bonnet, put it on again, scowled on the moon and shifting from foot to foot, cleared his throat loudly and continued:

"Captain Jocelyn, that there Mr. Fane do ha' slipped his moorings."

"Escaped?" demanded Jocelyn sharply.

"No less, your honour. I had him clapped fast i' the lazarette wi' Joe and Tom Starky on ward. Well, Captain Jocelyn, I 'll be stove and sunk if yon fine gentleman did n't corrupt they curst lubberly rogues wi' his danged money and jewels, ay, he did so, and wins free, and Tom and Joe away likewise, rot 'em!"

"Ha, 'sdeath!" snarled Sir Roger. "Here 's what cometh by thy curst tender method, look you; by my will the villain should be safely dead. Yon other treasonable rogues now, 't were better we slit their throats and be done, look you — "

"Away with them, Captain Nick," said Jocelyn, turning his back on Sir Roger's raging ferocity; "they must be aboard ere dawn and — see you hold them secure — "

"My life on 't!" cried the little sea captain very fervently. "I 'll hold 'em, your honour, rot and sink me else. Hear ye this, messmates all, — my life lieth in pledge for their safe keeping. So, heave ahead, lads, and God save Queen Bess!"

Then the mariners, their helpless captives in their midst, marched away, a grim, silent company, melted into the leafy shadows and were gone, what time Sir Roger scowled up at the moon and Jocelyn watched him very wistfully. At last:

"What troubles thee now, Roger man?" he questioned.

Sir Roger snorted.

"Howbeit," sighed Jocelyn, "the Queen's Majesty is safe awhile, pray God, and our scheming and labours hereabouts be ended — "

"And over tenderly to my mind, look you."

"Sayst thou, Roger?"

"Ay, I do, and this moreover; you grow too queasy for comrade o' mine! 'Sblood! Do I pluck steel these days, your very bowels turn, — ha, what a plague ails ye?"

"The thought that I am not God to judge a man and snatch him out o' life for being Catholic and fighting for his creed — "

"Ha, these dogs would murder our Bess!"

"And what dogs shall murder their Queen Mary?"

"Zounds, man, I do believe thee very Papist in thy secret heart!"

"Nor Papist nor Protestant, Roger, yet perchance something o' both and therewith lover of my kind."

"Lover, quoth a? Ay, faith!" snarled Sir Roger. "Methinks this woman, this Ione Fane, hath bewitched and verily corrupted thee with her devilish — "

"And so — be done, Roger!"

"'Fore heaven, not I! 'Sblood! I protest this female with her beauty's arts hath spellbound thee — "

" Sir Roger, I beg your silence."

" *Mordieu,* sir, I say what I will, though the heavens fall, py heavens! And who shall let or stay me?"

" I shall, Roger."

They had reached the stately avenue of mighty trees that led from ancient, embattled gatehouse to the wide court-yard of the great mansion and here, as by mutual consent, they halted where a patch of moony radiance fell, and turned to front each other.

" Odso!" exclaimed Sir Roger, recoiling a step before the Captain's look. " What, are we for 't then, thou and I? Wilt invest upon me thy most especial passada, thy so famous charging blow? Well, my imbroccada shall match it, point contra point! Shall we tilt, ha?"

And stepping aside with practised fencer's lightness, he clapped hand to the hilt of his long Italian rapier. " Have at me then?" he challenged.

" God forbid, Roger."

" Why then, look you, an' you wag not steel, I wag my tongue as I will. And so I tell again how this lady — "

" Hold there, man! For whilst thy foolish tongue wag-geth to no purpose, this same valiant lady rides amain for Guildford to warn Her Majesty of this same Popish plot — "

" How? The Lady Fane, sayst thou?"

" Even she."

" Zapperment!" exclaimed Sir Roger, eyeing his com-panion's stern features very ruefully. " But she — a Papist!"

" Ay, Roger. But she is also Ione, Lady Fane!"

" Hum!" quoth Sir Roger. " Ha!" And walked him back and forth, scowling and yet more rueful than ever until, halting suddenly, he reached and gripped Jocelyn's hand.

" Wert right, old lad!" said he. " Wert very right and I most vastly wrong. I can say no more."

" Nor is there need, Roger man."

" Pray Cot she prove sufficient grateful to thee, lad!"

" ' Grateful ', quoth a ? "

" For thy so great faith in her, ay, to the peril o' that head o' thine.   And yet, py heavens, Jocelyn, we ha' found small gratitude hitherto, thou and I, ha ? "

" Well, I seek no gratitude, Roger, nor want it — from her."

" How, lad, not though it be her lovely head i' thy bosom, her white arms about thee — "

" No ! " said Jocelyn, averting his face.   " About me soon shall be buff and steel instead ; I 'm for the wars again."

" Why, so am I, comrade ; 't is my natural avocation. But thou ?   Hum !   Art young and a proper man, Jocelyn, wherefore not woo and wive thee and beget thyself a troop o' thine own, ha ? "

" A landless, penniless wight such as I, Roger ? "

" Nay, lad, were we but courtiers, thou and I, to know the trick on 't, we might contrive thee coat of arms and therewith goodly manor, a gift o' grateful Majesty ; mind you young Hatton's smock face that got him Ely ?   But alack, Majesty is seldom grateful and nothing generous to such as merit."

" Nor are we courtiers, Roger."

" Not we !   And beside, us ha' lately saved Bess for England and England for Bess, and so are like to get a flea i' the ear or rap o' the pate, as doth ever seem our fortune. Well, Prince Maurice shall rejoice to see us back among his dykes."

" True, Roger, there shall be honours for you and a command for me — "

" Together wi' wounds, Jocelyn, hardship and death, belike.   When shall we march, comrade ? "

" So soon as I have brought this Lord Riderwood to an account."

" 'T is good as done, lad, for there 's no man I hold thine equal at rapier play, saving only myself, look you.   And thus I — hearkee !   One rides at speed yonder . . . and this way.   Now who at such hour shall — "

"Come!" cried Jocelyn and began to run.

Thus it was they reached the stable yard in time to see big Will Thurlow ride in, — a bowed and swaying figure that clutched at horse's mane with bloody hands.

"What, Will, — Will lad, how now?"

"They waylaid us, sir . . . Lord Riderwood's fellows. I did my best . . . so did Tom! Woe's me, poor Tom's a-laying back there . . . on the road . . . and stone dead, I do think. . . ."

"And my Lady Fane?"

"They took her along."

"Know ye whither, lad?"

"Ay, sir, I . . . made shift to follow . . . and watch. . . . They have my lady to Lord Riderwood's house at Hoove."

"Aha!" cried Sir Roger, with chuckling snarl, "I'll go saddle our horses, Jocelyn, whiles you tend the lad."

"Art much hurt, Will?"

"I dunno, sir, — feels bad enow, it do, here i' th' arm and here again through my leg."

"Might be worse," pronounced the Captain, busied with his rough surgery. "I can check the bleeding but — "

"Never stay for me, Cap'n sir, and my lady there at Hoove . . . ha, though I did hear as Lord Riderwood be rid to Lewes wi' his friends for the night."

"Why then, the less need for haste, Will. . . . Thy finger on this knot — so!"

"Ay, but 't is a'most dawn, sir. And I can rouse my lads. And old Robina — she be wonderful skilled — "

"Ay, faith, and here's work for her. Ho, Roger, rouse the place and cry on Robina Shaw."

Very soon, awakened by Sir Roger's harsh roaring, grooms and stable boys came running, but though old Robina was sought high and low, it seemed she had vanished quite.

"Know you my Lord Riderwood's house, Roger?" enquired the Captain, as they prepared to mount.

"Ay, marry, that do I!" nodded Sir Roger cheerily.

"A desolate place beside the sea, very sweet to our occasions. "And look you, comrade, this falleth pat and very apt to fancy; ay, py heavens, 't is like answer to prayer, Jocelyn! Thereabouts shall be dead rogues asprawl to-morrow, or I 'm a bloody Spaniard, which God forbid — "

"And see, — yonder is the dayspring!" said Jocelyn, and pointed to the lightening East. "An hour's ride, eh, Roger?"

"Hardly so much."

"Hum! Then if Riderwood be from home, I must needs wait his return to settle our account."

"Why then, let us speed to be rid of his bravos and bullies first, a sudden onfall and surprisal, ha?"

"As you will, Roger man." So they swung to saddle, in went their spurs, hoofs clattered, sparks flew and they were away, galloping knee and knee.

And one was grave and silent and one laughed or hummed cheerily, yet each alike was terrible.

# CHAPTER XXXVI

### Chiefly Concerneth an Orange-tawney Cloak

It was that chill and deadly season just before dawn when the strongest seems weakest and the weakest die, that one came knocking at the Peck of Malt tavern, to knock and listen and knock again, until at last out from small lattice in the gable, John Bly thrust touzled head to demand hoarsely:

"Who knocks?"

"It be I, good master, Robina Shaw, to see my lady the Countess —"

"Away, woman, she sleepeth."

"Oh, master, good master, it do be matter o' life and death! Go tell my lady 't is for Captain Jocelyn's life — "

"Eh?" cried John, leaning from the casement perilously far in sudden eagerness. "Cap'n Jocelyn, says you? Why then, bide a bit, says I."

Thus, after some while, bolts squeaked, bars fell, a chain rattled and the stout indoor unclosed to show honest John half clad and a rushlight in his fist.

"Come your ways, dame," quoth he, "m' leddy 'll see ye." And, having barred, bolted, locked and chained the door again, he took up the rush, beckoned her to follow and whispered hoarsely:

"Come ye, mistus, but creep silent, for there be sickness aloft, Cap'n Jocelyn's comrade, mam." So, very hushed and quiet, they crept up the stair.

A cosy chamber lit by tall candles beside huge, four-post bedstead wherein sat a very small shape and bolt upright.

"Well, Robina woman, well? What's in your budget and what of our Jocelyn fellow, — more fighting?"

"No, my lady, murder!"

" Ha, sweet heaven — never tell me he 's dead ! "

" No, my lady, not yet, and yet like to be unless us do contrive somewhat."

" Somewhat ?   Ay, but what, woman, what ?   Plague on thy tongue, be plain !   Speak, Robina, speak me explicit, thy tale in a word, pronounce, creature ! "

" 'T is Derek, my lady."

" What, Roland Fane's huntsman — "

" And my Lord Riderwood, mam."

" Well, well, what o' these ? "

" Oh, madam, I ha' been watching o' late in lonely places by day and night, for 't is such times and places as Derek loveth best.   And yestere'en to Aldrington came my Lord Riderwood and there also was Derek lurking remote and — wi' his crossbow.   Now presently, my lady, being in the Home Wood, as I do know very well every path and thicket, mam, my lord he whistles and unto him creepeth Derek and after him creep I — "

" Aha, 't was bravely done, Robina, ay, marry !   And what didst hear, what ? "

" My lord showed mighty fierce, my lady, and Derek mighty sullen.   ' How 's this,' saith my lord ; ' the Captain yet lives, rogue.   Did not your master bid ye shoot the villain ? '   ' Ay, he did,' growls Derek.   ' And so I did, yonder by the brook, and 'stead of his mazzard hit me a tree ; my bolt stands there yet to witness.'   Then says my lord, ' Should ye know the fellow by day or night ? ' ' Ay, I do,' says Derek ; ' a weareth cloak of orange-tawney and red feather in 's bonnet.'   ' Well so,' saith my lord, ' 't is now I do command ye shoot this rogue, therefore look to 't and see your bolt miss not this second time, lest ye hang (oh, mark this, my lady !) for bolt that sped true — ten years agone ! '   ' Nay, my lord,' whispers Derek, ' hush thee and forbear ! '   ' Ten years ! ' nods my lord ; ' a fair shot clean betwixt Aldrington's shoulders, — ha, thou bloody murderer ? '   ' Why, I do but as I 'm bid ! ' says Derek.   ' Ay,' says my lord, ' and 't is thus your master must do my bidding ever since and shall do when he ruleth here, in place o' boy Dick.' Then says Derek, ' Prithee, sir, where is my good master?' 'How shall I know?' says my lord. 'Howbeit, when next you spy orange-tawney cloak — aim straight and true. Now begone!' So away creeps Derek and, when my lord is removed, away creep I."

" And when was this? "

" Last eventide, m'lady."

" Ha, fool, to wait so long."

" Alack, my lady, I needs must wait to come by — these." And from beneath her long mantle Robina produced a bundle and presently showed a close-brimmed hat adorned with scarlet feather and a horseman's cloak of that colour named orange-tawney.

" Why, God love us," exclaimed the little Countess, " these be Jocelyn's!' "

" Ay, verily, madam, and being here, they shall not betray him to Derek's arrow."

" Why, there's reason, woman, and yet himself may die unless he be aware. Didst warn him? "

" Alas, my lady, I found no chance; he hath kept him close o' late." Here the Countess, perched amid her pillows, chin on knees, became lost in a frowning revery and when at last she spoke, it was in shrill, fierce tone and with small fist upraised:

" Vengeance! . . . Aha, so the murder's out at last, the black mystery is resolved, and I'm for vengeance, justice, the very blood of atonement — "

" Ay, my lady . . . But what o' the Captain his peril? Oh, madam, I pray you — "

" Not me, — God, woman, God! And as for this Jocelyn fellow, send him hither to me; there none shall dare murder him in my presence. So speed you hence, Robina, find your Captain and command him instantly and incontinent hither to me. And tread softly as you go, lest you trouble my poor Florian's slumber."

" How doth the young gentleman, my lady? "

" So well, thank God, that I shall carry him to the

Queen's Grace for preferment when she cometh. I know Bess, ay, marry, and his faunlike beauty shall win upon her or I 'm a shotten herring! "

"Madam, what shall I with this hat and cloak? "

"Ay, this cloak of orange-tawney that seemeth colour mighty fateful — eh, eh, Robina? Well, I shall keep it; by perchance heaven or hell, my mother wit or remorseless Fate shall teach me what to do with 't. And now away, woman, thou wise creature and valiant soul . . . stay! This ring! 'T is thine."

"Dear, my lady, I seek none fee or — "

"Take it, I say! "

"Nay . . . oh, m'lady, I . . . I would die for him — "

"Ay, ay, I know — he kissed and called thee 'mother' — well, now, take my ring into the bargain and begone! "

So saying, the little Countess hurled it at Robina and with fierce imprecation vanished beneath the bedclothes. And presently old Robina took up the rich jewel and murmuring gratefully, curtseyed humbly and stole away.

# CHAPTER XXXVII

## How They Came to Hoove

MY LADY Ione Fane, locked secure in the great gallery of my Lord Riderwood's manor at Hoove, crouched in the window recess and watched for the dawn with haggard eyes, listening desperately for the sound of horse hoofs that should warn her the moment she so dreaded was upon her . . . at mere thought of which she burned with shame and shivered with sick terror, hating her body's very loveliness since this, as she knew, was the lure had brought her to this lawless house.

In this desolation of soul she fell upon her knees and with crucifix between hands clammy with fear, called piteously upon the holy saints, upon the gentle Mary Mother of Mercy for aid; upon Almighty God that he would snatch her hence, suffering her to die undefiled.

Now in this agony of prayer her wild gaze chanced upon that which brought from her quivering lips a cry of inarticulate joy, and leaping afoot, she crossed to table where, beside a whip, embroidered gauntlets and a pair of spurs, lay a silver-hilted hunting knife.

With this deadly thing clasped down between her resurgent breasts, she lifted radiant eyes to the radiant East where day was born, and whispered prayers of passionate gratitude; for now with this sharp steel clasped upon her heart, she watched and waited, trembling but resolute.

She heard a sleepy thrush pipe hoarsely, answered by husky note of slumberous blackbird . . . Up came the sun, at whose glorious advent thrush and blackbird, rousing, trilled in glad welcome, clearer, sweeter, louder, until all birds near and far, awaking too, joined in joyful universal chorus. . . . The sun rose higher; within the

house, around and above her was sound of life . . . feet,
heavy and light, went to and fro . . . a man laughed, a
maid tittered. . . . From below rose growing stir and
bustle, with rattle of pans and chink of pewter and crock-
ery. And so the house awoke. . . . The sun climbed
and Ione's haggard eyes watched the long avenue with an
ever increasing dread.

Loud voices in the courtyard and thither came four
swaggering, burly fellows, her captors, those same four
ruffians she had once seen attempt Jocelyn's life in the
orchard at Aldrington.

Oh, Jocelyn!

A key grated and the door opened to admit a round-eyed
serving maid bearing a tray. But the sight of food
nauseated her and, ere she might speak, a man's voice
called harshly, the door slammed, the key turned and she
was alone again.

From the courtyard presently came laughter, fierce oaths
and lurid curses where the four men sat dicing in the
pleasant sunshine. And then . . . the hands grasping
the bright steel that was to be her salvation clenched in
sudden spasm, for afar down the avenue two horsemen
approached riding leisurely . . . and one of these wore
neither hat nor cloak. Knee to knee they rode, these two,
at an easy trot, and this hatless man (oh, kind, merciful
God!) . . . even at this distance she knew that dark head
with its thick, close-cropped hair that yet strove so va-
liantly to curl. Now seeing this man so near, her eyes
were suddenly blind with tears of gratitude and a quick,
deep happiness that shook her from head to foot . . . the
hunting knife fell to lie unheeded and all unwanted now.
She dashed the tears away to look and look at this yearned-
for countenance, its lean, hawk look, the easy sway of that
supple body as he rode, the unconscious high nobility of his
every glance and gesture. . . .

But now the four men had seen these riders also and
stood, one and all, watching them uneasily; then cried one
suddenly:

"Look, ha, look — the hatless fellow — 't is Dinwiddie, by God!"

"Ay, so 't is, a pox on him!   Your pistols, Ben!   Dennis, d' you go fetch the calivers!   Try a shot now, Ben, — now — "   But in this moment the horsemen spurred to sudden gallop, out flickered two long swords and, stooping low in their saddles, they charged at full career. . . . A pistol cracked . . . heavy calivers roared . . . again, and yet again. . . .   Then the courtyard rang with the din of trampling hoofs, clashing steel and whirl of desperate combat. . . .   She saw Captain Jocelyn wheel his horse dexterously to ply his terrible sword right and left, with darting point and shearing edge . . . she saw a man go down, clutching the blade that transfixed him ere the deadly steel was wrenched free of the screaming wretch to smite down his fellow, headlong.   Then Jocelyn was out of the saddle and had vanished through the open doorway. She saw Sir Roger, there being none left to fight, set his foot upon a fallen antagonist and end his writhing misery with unerring, vicious thrust, then he too had leapt through the open doorway and the house was full of uproar and panic, — the wild patter of flying footsteps, screams, hoarse shouts, an echoing pistol shot.

Then spurred feet pounded swiftly up the stair, a key was thrust into lock, the door swung open and she saw Captain Jocelyn, rapier in hand, somewhat dishevelled and a little breathless.

Mutely they gazed on each other as in question and answer, then she ran to him, whereupon Captain Dinwiddie (the penniless soldier of Fortune, this poor Jade of Destiny) reached forth one hand to her; but she, not content with this, swayed within his rigid arm and thus, breast to breast, made as she would fall, — and so Jocelyn (the man) letting fall his sword, folded her close.   Yet even now, though she lay in his embrace her lovely head backthrown, her vivid lips so near his own, he looked aside and held her so awkwardly that she, with breathless, sobbing laugh, hid her face against him, murmuring:

" Art then afraid of me, Jocelyn? Do I affright thee so? Art not glad to find me again and unharmed? In my woeful terrors I prayed God for thee — oh, passionately, and lo, He hath sent thee to me! And shall I not welcome such Gift of God? Ah, sure this were irreverent. So . . . an' thou wilt not kiss me — then . . . needs must I kiss thee — " And she began to kiss him, his doublet, his ruff — all that her eager lips might reach.

" There child . . . there! " he gasped. " Thou 'rt all distraught . . . beyond thyself . . . lost in thy fears — "

" Nay, I am finding myself! " she murmured, and then — up swept her tender arms to clasp that sternly unbending head, to draw it down, and down until lips met lips; and, even as they kissed, she whispered: " Oh, Jocelyn . . . my gift of God, to-day hast saved my body, a while since didst save my soul from folly of wilful pride and a many other vanities; thus body and soul I am thine. So now I pray thee forget thy pride and take me lest I . . . break my poor heart. Wilt be so kind, prithee, Jocelyn? "

Now, striving for speech, he was dumb, but in this moment the icy bonds of his fierce self-repression melted and vanished clean away . . . she felt the quick, yearning clasp of his arms fold her nearer . . . upon her lips was the salt of his tears; and then he spoke whispering, brokenly:

" I have so loved thee! . . . So dreamed! Nor dared to hope. . . . Can such dream prove true . . . for such as I? "

" Oh," she murmured tenderly, " sure am I now that God but made me for — such as thou, Jocelyn — "

She gasped and snatched her hand to see these white fingers hideously smeared, but ere she could speak, he had cleansed these stained fingers on his sleeve:

" I was grazed by a caliver ball," he explained, smiling in gentle reassurance.

" But . . . thou 'rt bleeding — oh — "

" A little. 'T is scratch that Roger hath tended very fairly."

"Ay, but with what? How? I must see! Oh, it should be washed! Come, show me —"

"Nenny, sweet lady," quoth Sir Roger himself, bowing to her from the threshold, "I pronounce 't is very well and I am become an able leech by much experience in Flanders where your leeches and chirurgeons be hard to come by. Our Captain is very well; 't is lusty carcass his, or he were dead long since, look you."

"Why then, my good Sir Roger, dear sir, let us all away from this vile house. Come, let us go."

"Go?" repeated Sir Roger, fingering his beard. "Why, as to this, how sayeth our Jocelyn, ha?"

"That 't is excellent well bethought on, Roger. Here, my lady, is my good comrade shall bring you safe to Aldrington, — and so, for a while, farewell!"

"And prithee why 'farewell', my Jocelyn?" she questioned and with look so tenderly eloquent that Sir Roger blinked, pursed his lips as if to whistle and crossing silently to the deep window recess, stood there lost in profound contemplation of the world outside.

"Why, farewell now . . . or ever?" she murmured.

"Ah, Joan!" he sighed and would have drawn her nearer but she held him away, though very tenderly.

"Nay first, prithee answer me."

"I must remain here for word with my Lord Riderwood."

"Ah! You mean . . . to fight him!"

"Why, this is as my lord wills."

"But . . . wounded, Jocelyn! And — alone? Nay, this shall not be. I will not suffer it!"

Now at this, her gently imperious look, her tone of such sweetly intimate possession, his lean cheek flushed, his eye glowed, he was transfigured by that slow, gentle smile that could make his saturnine features so very nearly handsome; yet even now, he took up his fallen rapier, loosed off his girdle with its carriages and heavy dagger, and laid them upon the table with such evident purpose that she clutched his two hands.

" No! " she cried, and all heedless of Sir Roger in the window recess, " this shall not be. Thyself . . . this dear body is mine, all mine henceforth, nor shall I suffer thee to peril it for what ye foolish men call ' honour! ' I say you shall — not! "

" But, Joan — "

" What though you fled him in the garden? I know it was not for fear . . . I always knew. So now, let us haste to be gone."

" Nay, dear my lady," he answered gently, " there is, beside, another matter of far more import — "

" You mean the treasonable paper he holds 'gainst Richard? "

" So you see, Joan, I must needs see Lord Riderwood — for this same paper I will and must have — or see utterly destroyed."

" No! " she exclaimed. " Ah, no, the peril is too great. Riderwood hath killed a many valiant gentlemen . . . they say he is invincible — "

" And Richard is my friend! "

" Then for his sake, for my sake — come away."

" And the paper, Joan? This damning evidence against your — brother? "

" Let it go! We, Richard and I, will throw ourselves upon the Queen's mercy; we will tell her all."

" And yet, unless she see this paper, I fear Her Majesty shall doubt. For Joan, sweet soul, her life hath been so often attempted, her ears filled with such buzz of whispered lies, she is over apt to doubt Truth's very self, and small wonder. But if Richard shall set this paper in her hand or, better still, if it be utterly destroyed — "

" Aha! " exclaimed Sir Roger, beckoning, " 'bate now, abate further debate, sweet madam, for hither rides this lord himself, yonder cometh Riderwood. And wi' three friends, Jocelyn, making four swords, *vide licet* two for you and two for me — "

" Not so," said Jocelyn, stepping to the window, " you must away with my lady instantly."

" Oho! And what saith your ladyship? "

" No, sirs, a thousand times. We go all three or abide the issue."

" Cot's pody, madam Joan, now do I begin to love thee too, and despite thy subtle sex feminine, look you! "

" Ah, but dear Sir Roger, must he fight? "

" Fight? " cried Sir Roger joyously. " Py heavens, m' sweet soul, shalt presently see such fight — ay, to charm the very angels, in especial Saint Michael which by report is good swordsman, — and more especially if I myself wag steel! "

Through the open window came the tramp of horses, a murmur of talk . . . a sudden stillness. . . . Then a voice, loud and imperious called in quick alarm:

" Darby! Casson! What bloody villainy is here? What, Casson, I say! "

" Roar ye, my bully lord! " nodded Sir Roger. " Roar to crack your throat; your dead shall never wake! "

" Oh — dead? " whispered Ione.

" Sweetly and completely! " answered Sir Roger, drawing two long petronels from his girdle and cocking them. " Lo you, there's never a man in all this house but lieth supremely dead; I saw me to this, m' sweet soul; the rest being wise, fled all away — Sa ha, behind me, girl; here cometh my Lord Riderwood, intent on vengeance dire! Cot's pody, Jocelyn man, 't is like old times! "

# CHAPTER XXXVIII

## Telleth What Ione Saw

A FURIOUS trampling of feet upon the stair, a jangling of spurs, then the door burst open and in upon them strode Lord Riderwood, rapier drawn, only to recoil before the threatening muzzles of Sir Roger's long pistols who, beckoning herewith to the three gentlemen peering in the doorway, spake them very heartily:

"Be right welcome, my lord and gentlemen. You behold us, my friend Captain Dinwiddie and my humble self, much at your service. Ye are four and we two, but two yet shall accommodate ye very perfectly, I 'll warrant me. So let us incontinent strip and to 't, point contra point, sirs, — without further ratiocination let us forthright imbrue — "

Now, even as he spoke, Lord Riderwood turned very suddenly and putting by his friends, clapped to the door, locked it and tossed the key out through the open lattice. Then he laughed yet bowed to Ione very ceremoniously:

"My Lady Ione," said he with exaggeration of tender humility, "sweet soul of Loveliness, Beauty's Epitome, here ere I take thee to my arms, shalt see me prove my worthiness, perchance a little bloodily. I shall show thee how dread a thing is Death that, per contra, our Love shall seem the sweeter. Also, here upon my heart, lo, the Aldrington Amulet, the Pelican in Piety, that shall back to Aldrington when you are my wife. Now, gentlemen all, let us — "

"Not so, my lord," said Jocelyn, unbuttoning his close-fitting doublet. "The matter betwixt us — "

"Is quarrel to the death!" cried my lord, tossing aside his short cloak.

"And therefore, sir," continued Jocelyn, pulling off his doublet as he spoke, "toucheth none save us two, and no other lives shall be put to the hazard — "

"Nay, but," protested Sir Roger, "we be two to four, Jocelyn, very just and delectable odds for such as thou and I to deal withal."

"Verily!" answered Jocelyn, folding his doublet and laying it by, "but here to-day hath been over deal of killing, Roger. Therefore shalt second me but by thy presence, leaving his lordship and myself to settle our account solus and as best we may."

"Alack, now!" cried Sir Roger plaintively. "Wherefore deny thy old comrade thus miserably? Sure am I these valiant gentlemen — "

"Sirs," quoth Jocelyn, turning upon my lord's three friends who stood very solemn, a little anxious and extremely mute, "ye hear? So I ask — why peril your lives thus needlessly 'gainst one o' the deadliest swordsmen in Flanders, this my friend, Sir Roger Williams?" At this redoubtable name, the three gentlemen murmured faintly. "Well, sirs," demanded Jocelyn, "how say ye?" Here the three, glancing from the Captain's stern face to Sir Roger's eager ferocity, murmured again and drew back to the door as one man.

"Why, then," quoth the Captain, removing the body armour of fine link chain he had worn against unseen missiles, and baring throat and breast, "I am at your lordship's service. Let us to it without further parley, since the matter betwixt us goeth beyond words."

"Ay true, true!" murmured Lord Riderwood, standing languid yet very disdainful to be stripped for combat by his three friends. "I propose to give you bloody exodus, Sir Captain, and what place better suited than this my ravaged house?"

And now Ione sank weakly in a corner of the window seat, wringing her hands in very horror of dread, for Jocelyn had taken sword and dagger and now stood, head a little bowed, watching where Lord Riderwood prepared himself, and with his usual leisured assurance, for this encounter that could end only with death of one or other; while Sir Roger, pistol hands on hips, viewed all dispassionately, hissing a little tune between his teeth. Quoth he at last:

" Who and which is your second, my lord? "

" The Colonel here, Colonel Malone."

" Then pray, Sir Colonel, do we strike up their swords for a wound? "

" No! " answered my lord, testing his blade with expert hand. " Neither for one wound, two, or three. My Lady Fane saw me brutalized by a ruffian; she shall now, I dare promise, see that same ruffian die . . . by wounds . . . and slowly as may be."

Ione covered her face with shaking hands, — then she was afoot, all breathless, passionate appeal:

" Wounds? " she cried. " Oh, my lord, he is wounded already! Oh, Sir Roger . . . good gentlemen, the terms are not equal. . . . Captain Dinwiddie is hurt, see you his arm how it bleeds — "

" So-ho? " laughed my lord, viewing Ione's pale anxiety beneath lifted brows. " My proud lady showeth strangely humble at last and for — this fellow! She passions for her Captain! She pleads tenderly — "

" Ha, 's death! " exclaimed Sir Roger. " Enough, sir, we wait — "

" Verily! " answered my lord, his mocking gaze never leaving Ione's pale beauty. " You wait and shall, for 't is so my pleasure. But as for thee, my sweet Ione, doth this Captain his welfare so trouble thee? Hath he then so warmed the ice o' thee? Hath — "

" Ha, what a plague! " snarled Sir Roger. " Have at him, Jocelyn! Invest — invest! "

" Nay, Roger," answered the Captain, patient as ever; " here, I guess, croaketh a swan."

" Swan? " growled Sir Roger. " Aha, 't is fowl sings ever loudest at death, ha? "

" And therefore, my Ione," sighed his lordship, " an'

thy gentle heart be so in this business, — to maim your Captain, to kill him by small, tender strokes, inch by inch before those lovely eyes, hath now for me a double joy. Watch now, my Ione, — watch!" So saying, he bowed to her, kissing his rapier hilt, and fronted his patient antagonist at last.

Of the desperate and prolonged encounter that now ensued may be found mention in Sir Roger Williams his History, with much and very learned disquisition concerning *volta, traverso, passada* and *tempo*, wherein he proves most conclusively the dire futility of *rinverso* and *mandritto* against the deadly *punta*, swift *botta lunga* and dire *imbroccado* of your true sword-master. Whereby it is to be supposed that his expert eye took in every thrust, feint and parade and indeed (and in his own words) all the poetry of this deadly engagement.

But what Ione saw was this: Jocelyn's face, the brows a little frowning, lips a little smiling, but the eyes keenly, dreadfully intent; Lord Riderwood, fiercely disdainful, dark features arrogant as ever, and between these two faces the ceaseless flash and flicker of whirling, darting steel, while in her ears was the sound of their quick feet, now soft and nimble as a cat's, now stamping loud in fierce attack or swift recovery.

She heard Sir Roger, standing near by, begin to hiss his little tune again while those tireless bodies leapt and swayed with flash of sword and flicker of dagger.

There were long periods when she scarce breathed while these murderous blades leapt and circled, and once she moaned to see Jocelyn's wound was bleeding anew, until the hand that guarded his life shewed horribly red. . . . There were strange, sudden pauses when they stood foot to foot, eye to eye, while blade gripped and held blade in a dreadful silence, broken only by the sound of quick-drawn breath, the uneasy shuffle of three pairs of feet by the door and Sir Roger's hissing song.

It was during one of these sudden lulls that Captain Jocelyn spoke, breathing a little short:

" My lord, will ye . . . give up the paper young Richard
was foisted into signing, and the amulet, the Aldrington
Jewel, or must I . . . kill you for 't? "

" Damned braggart! " cried my lord, breathing even
shorter; then he laughed contemptuously and began such
furious assault that Ione scarce dared look, for Jocelyn
seemed to elude death by mere inches, — she saw his as-
sailant's darting point flash by his throat, his cheek, to
right and left . . . and then she moaned, for he was being
driven back, step by step, towards this window through
which the early sun shot a level beam to dazzle and blind
him. . . . Sweep of sword met and parried by sword,
leaping dagger caught and turned by dagger in the nick
of time. . . . Then her senses thrilled to see Riderwood's
shirt sleeve ripped from wrist to shoulder . . . and now he
was retreating . . . and his arm bloody also. . . . Sudden stillness again while sword held sword, dagger hands
ready for quick stab or instant parry. . . .

And now for the second time she heard Jocelyn's smooth,
patient voice:

" My lord, except I have . . . the paper, with the Jewel
I see your lordship wears, at our next veney I shall . . .
end you."

Lord Riderwood, striving to laugh, gasped but, gasping
leapt. . . . Thud of quick-stamping feet, fierce outcries,
clash of whirling, glittering steel in desperate onslaught.
. . . Ione was on her feet, arms wildly outflung:

" Jocelyn! " she gasped. " Oh . . . God . . ." For
the Captain's dagger was smitten from his grasp, his
supple body swayed suddenly, the long blades rang together
. . . strove entwined and Lord Riderwood's sword swung
loosely wide. . . . On the air was dreadfully muffled cry,
breathless, inarticulate, and suddenly choked.

" Habet! " quoth Sir Roger harshly and strode quickly
forward, as swaying oddly and with arms outspread, Lord
Riderwood dropped his weapons . . . sank to his knees
slowly and as if against his will; then his head bowed for-

ward and plunging to his face, he lay an awful, huddled thing. His three friends ran to lift him but, seeing his face, laid him down again and shrank away, while the Captain stood looking down on his handiwork beneath wrinkling brows. Then he stooped and from the dead man's neck took that strange amulet called the Aldrington Jewel.

"Dead as a herring!" said Sir Roger, covering that dreadful shape with a cloak. "Though, look you, Jocelyn, wert something longer o' the business than I had reckoned. And now what? The key o' the room lieth down i' the courtyard."

"Now, the paper!" said the Captain, and while Sir Roger stooped to search the so suddenly dead, Jocelyn felt through my lord's garments, every fold and inch of lining but without result. Therefore he turned to the three gentlemen who stood close together, eyeing him very much askance.

"Sirs," quoth he, "and in especial you, Colonel Malone, my lord held a document, as you know, bearing the Earl of Aldrington's signature and which document Lord Riderwood brought with him."

"Well, sir?" demanded the Colonel, eyes wide in the pallor of his large, flabby face.

"Where is this paper?"

"We cannot tell, sir, nor will be made accomplices in robbery —"

"Roger, be so good to cover me these gentry wi' your dags and fire an' I give word." Here was wild babel of protest from these gentlemen and, loudest of all, from the Colonel.

"Sir, what villainy . . . what outrage is this?"

"A persuasion to truth, Colonel Malone."

"Will ye murder us?"

"Instantly, an' I deem ye lying. So now — you know my lord bore hither this letter?"

"Ay, we do."

" He brought it into this house? Ye are sure o' this? "

" Beyond all doubt, sir. Lord Riderwood showed it unto me here last night."

" Saw you where he disposed it? "

" No, sir, but 't was in his hand when I left him for my bed."

" Then beyond all peradventure it is in this house? "

" We would swear to it, all three."

" Why then, Colonel, if one o' ye can contrive to recover the key, you are free to depart."

As one man the three came to the window and were deliberating the problem when their difficulty was resolved by the appearance below of a furtive, dishevelled being, at sight of whom the Colonel leaned forth of the lattice.

" What, Casson! " he shouted, whereat the man jumped violently but seeing who called, instantly made a leg and wailed:

" Oh, Colonel . . . oh, your worship, be they murderers gone? "

" Ay, ay, lad. Here 's none to hurt you. Lo, yonder — that key! No, no, fool — yonder. By poor Ben's head . . . ay, so! Now come you and unlock this door."

Very presently key grated, door opened and, without further word or look, the gentlemen turned to be gone, but the Captain's stern voice halted them:

" Sirs, take up my lord and bear him forth into the courtyard; do this last office for him that was your friend." For a moment they hesitated, then took up that muffled shape and bore it out and away.

" Oh . . . Jocelyn! "

She was kneeling in the window recess so pale and faint that he went to her and knelt also.

" Joan? " he murmured; shuddering violently, she swayed to him, hiding her face in his bosom.

Now, beholding the Captain's mute ecstasy, Sir Roger turned his back and went softly to and fro awhile, opening such coffers and drawers as he might, peering into every nook and cranny very pertinaciously.

"And thou 'rt nothing harmed, Jocelyn? No wound?"

"None," he answered and very humbly.

"Oh, 't is a miracle! Though I prayed for thee."

"God heard," he murmured, bowing his head before the glory in her eyes.

"Yet I doubted!" she sighed. "I thought thee slain and came nigh dying with thee. I could not live without thee now. Come, prithee, take me from this hateful place."

"Zounds!" exclaimed Sir Roger pettishly, as they rose. "We shall scarce discover yon paper in such house as this, lad."

"Nor need to, Roger."

"Eh, — no need? Then what shall ye do?"

"Destroy it."

"How mean ye, man?"

"Thus!" answered Jocelyn, and taking out battered tinder box he lit a candle that chanced near and therewith set the window curtains ablaze.

"Aha, fire, is 't?"

"None other, Roger man. Take ye other candle and help."

"Ay, and with all my heart."

Thus presently they went from the chamber of death, leaving an ever-creeping destruction behind.

And presently, being mounted all three, Ione must needs pause to look her last upon this house of dread and from this, silent and a little awed, to the man beside her, who seemed now so gently wistful yet could be so grimly terrible.

"Here 's brave bonfire, comrade!" quoth Sir Roger. "And perfect end to villainy, ha?"

"And what is better, Roger, to my Lord Richard's blighting dread."

Thus when they rode away, Ione very silent between them, she must needs steal her hand into the Captain's firm clasp to nestle it there, while Sir Roger, glancing back at that tall column of smoke and devastating flame, hissed gently to himself like one very well content.

# CHAPTER XXXIX

## CONCERNING A BREAKFAST

WITHIN a mile of Aldrington Great House they heard a cry and from thicket beside the way came old Robina in glad and eager haste.

"Oh, Captain Jocelyn!" she cried. "Good master, my lady the Countess begs ye 'll to her at the tavern."

"Begs she in sooth, good mother?" smiled Jocelyn, and then, suddenly anxious, leaned down from the saddle. "Tell me, is 't young Florian? Ah, Robina, doth the brave lad relapse — ?"

"No, no, dear sir, — and yet belike he may. Speed ye, sir — "

"That will I, mother — "

"And I with thee!" said Ione.

"Myself also!" quoth Sir Roger. So forthwith they wheeled their horses and spurred to a gallop, nor did they draw rein until they had reached the secluded, cosy tavern.

They beheld her ladyship in the act of quaffing ale, for she was at breakfast, whereto she instantly commanded them.

"Ad 's my life, this is well!" she exclaimed. "Come kiss me, child! Sit ye beside me, Jocelyn! And thou, Sir Roger, my sweet knight, come buss me roundly; 't is long since we met."

So down sat they all three to break their fast, and a cheery meal they made of it, though it was to be remarked that before her small, august, keen-visioned aunt, Ione's sweet eyes were demurely lowered, thus she seldom so much as glanced towards Jocelyn and very seldom spoke.

And indeed the little Countess seemed very much awake

this morning and now, her own hunger satisfied, she questioned (and as matter of course) Sir Roger and Jocelyn alternately, concerning their past cares and anxieties regarding the Queen's safety, and Ione thus heard so much of plot and counterplot, of lurking death and sudden dangers, that she forgot to eat. . . .

" You knew of all this, Aunt, — you? "

" Ay, marry did I, child, and thou something of it also, hadst been less sleepy numps, opened those eyes 'stead o' shutting 'em tight, in fashion so addlepatedly pig-headed and — "

" Your pardon, madam," said Jocelyn gently, " but — "

" And so enough, sir! " quoth the Countess, small finger upraised.   " Instead, tell me — and this so purblind Ione creature — what of our archvillain, the ' secret enemy in familiar guise ' you warned her against so vainly ; what of her dead sire's secret murderer and would-be slayer of her brother — "

" Aunt! " gasped Ione.   " Oh, Aunt Ursula, what monster is this?   Who is he — ? "

" Who? " repeated the Countess, with sharp snap of white teeth.   " Who but that same kindly, gentle, philosophic soul, that worthy, soft-smiling affability calling itself Roland Fane, — thy cousin, girl! "

" Roland? " cried Ione, hands clasped to her temples. " Cousin Roland?   No!   No!   I cannot believe it! "

" And indeed, madam," Jocelyn added, " all this is but mere suspicion unproven as yet."

" Nay, 't is fact, Jocelyn man! " cried the Countess in fierce triumph.   " It is very fact, whereto I ha' three witnesses, to wit, — Robina Shaw, Derek and Lord Riderwood — "

" Riderwood? " repeated Sir Roger.   " Aha! "

" And this bringeth me to other item, Jocelyn — mark now!   Thy life is in mortal peril! "

" Sweet saints forfend! " murmured Ione, fingering the ivory crucifix at her girdle.

" But m' sweet Countess,' quoth Sir Roger, " here 's no

news, since my comrade's life, like mine own, is passed in a peril perpetual, — and thus we live!"

"Ay, but, my gentle knight, our Captain is to be shot from ambush at Aldrington by an arbalester. Eh, Jocelyn, eh, — another bolt from the blue!"

"Why this we already know, madam — "

"Oh, God forbid it!" cried Ione, her anxious gaze on Jocelyn's tranquil face.

"Well, so say I, wench," snapped her aunt; "yet I don't devour the man wi' such wanton eyes! And Jocelyn, this murderous rogue must kill you or hang by order of Lord Riderwood."

"Zounds!" exclaimed Sir Roger. "'T is the more comfort to know the man is dead."

"Oh? Dead, sir? Riderwood dead? For this I 'll kiss thee!"

"With all my heart, madam. Yet buss thee my comrade Jocelyn first, for 't was he rid the world o' this singular plaguey rogue in fashion most apt and sweet to fancy."

"What, — a duel?"

"Even so, madam."

"Then, Jocelyn, my man, come buss me! Shalt kiss my lips — and mine, sir, not Ione's! See how the jade glares on me!"

"Indeed no, dear Aunt."

"Then wherefore not, Madam Hypocrisy? And you kissing him with your eyes so shamelessly this half hour, — and before my very face, with a wanion!"

"Did I so, Aunt?"

"Did you not, Niece?"

"Dear Aunt, I did. And love and thank thee for telling him so, lest he remarked it not, for men be sometimes slow to heed — "

"Heydey, mistress, what 's here?"

"Love, I thank God, sweet Aunt."

"Love, quoth a! Love for what, who, when, where, how, — ha, love?"

"Most truly, Aunt Ursula. For a man. Named Jocelyn. A love born ages agone. In Ultima Thule. From my heart and soul and body, all that is me. So here are thy questions answered all, and my Jocelyn waiting to kiss thee, — "

"Thy Jocelyn, forsooth! Thine? Ha, Beelzebub! Oh, monstrous impudicity! Such shameless vaunting avowal! And thou Ione! Thou that seemed cold Prudery's veriest icicle, mantled in prideful modesty! And now — a coal! A raging flame that glows 'neath my very nose and all — all for poverty-smitten soldier!"

"That waiteth to kiss thee, sweet Aunt. So kiss, lest I do it for thee — "

"Stint, girl! Abate thy so kissful madness! What, you are no country hoyden, no yeoman's wench or peasant's brat to wed as you list! You are Ione, Lady Fane, of estate too high to stoop to such as — this fellow."

"Nor shall I, Aunt. Rather shall I climb, and his strong hand lift me up to share the glory of him."

"'Sblood!" exclaimed Sir Roger heartily. "There spake great lady and, what's better, true woman, for though woman she — "

"Peace, knight — "

"'Sdeath, Countess! Jocelyn is my good comrade, and like me, gently born and, also like me, a lord o' the rapier and noble o' the gentle craft, with steel in 's blood, and therefore worthy mate for any woman, ay — were she Queen Bess, Gloriana's very self — "

"The Queen, — aha, hold there, Sir Roger! The Queen, sayst thou? Why then, hear this — "

"Nay first, dear Aunt, see you my Jocelyn waits — "

"Be dumb, thou bold-eyed Prudery! How an' I tell thee thou 'rt to be meat for his betters?"

"Then I 'd tell thee, Aunt, thy simile is basely coarse. Yet, meat or no, there is but one man shall eat of me and lo, Aunt, he waits thy kiss!"

"Ha!" cried the Countess, flourishing fierce little fist in Jocelyn's rueful face. "Off, thou doggish soldier; thou flesh-eating ogre away or — " she gasped in sheer amaze for, as he turned away somewhat discomfited, up started Ione, quick and light, to catch his hand, to kiss it ere he knew, and hold it prisoned on her heart. The Countess stared, and for once her quick tongue proving unready, Ione smiled down on her very kindly and spoke as to a fretful child:

" Oh, my dear, this man you see is yet no mere man, for here stands the very paragon of mankind — Dinwiddie, than whom there is not such another in all the world. And I doubted him, my dear, I mocked him — oh, me! Therefore that he should stoop to love this purblind me is Nature's wonder; except for this, we were made for each other ere time began."

The Countess rose, very small yet extremely dominating.

" Ione Fane," said she, " now must I tell you Her Majesty has already chosen a husband for you, a very noble gentleman that is your peer in fortune, rank and estate; so him you shall wed or lose the Royal favour — "

" Well, Aunt, I had rather hold the favour of Dinwiddie — "

" Oh, get thee hence! " cried the Countess as in sudden wrath. " Get thee to Florian and Cecily, — begone! "

With demure curtsey to her aunt and smile for Jocelyn and Sir Roger, my Lady Ione went, moving with that supple grace that was delight for the eyes — more especially two.

" So! " exclaimed the Countess, sinking back into her chair. " Here 's devilish coil, oh, a pretty pudder! And all by reason of beggarly soldier fellow — "

" Cot's pody! " snorted Sir Roger. " Py heavens, madam — "

" Knight, be silent! You, Sir Captain, what say you? Hast scarce spoke word so far; art dumb then? "

" Well nigh, madam . . . there be times when all words seem vain."

" Which means that you — love her? "

" Beyond the telling! " he sighed.

" Then tell her not, Jocelyn . . . she 's mad and knoweth not her own good. This marriage were wondrous match and the Queen hath set her heart on 't, mating rank with rank and welding two great powers, for Ione is great lady in her own right. And, ha, Jocelyn, the Queen's choice for her is one of the proudest, most potent lords in all England . . . the Earl of High Melton, no less. And what says you to this, my man? "

" That I am indeed beggarly soldier! "

" Ay, ay, but what 's in your mind, what purpose — ? "

The door swung open and there was Florian, very pale and thin, but his eyes quick with vitality and both hands outstretched.

" Jocelyn! " cried he.   " Now here 's joy! "

" And very miracle! " quoth the Captain, as they embraced.

" And lo, here the power that wrought it, *camarado!* " said the young invalid, snatching the Countess' two small hands to be kissed.   " She brought me up out o' death, Jocelyn!   She dragged me back to life — by the hair — with these! "

It was about now that landlord John, busied in the stables, was aware of a creeping shadow behind him and, glancing round, beheld a squat, bow-legged, very powerful-seeming fellow, whose broad, unlovely visage was half hidden in grizzled hair and whose sullen eyes yet held an expression of wistful sadness like the eyes of an oft-whipped dog.

" God den t' ye, neighbour John! " he growled.   " I be dry! "

" G' marning, Derek!   Bide ye here and I 'll bring ee ale. "

So Derek, seating himself in darkest corner, waited gloomily patient until John returned, bearing a foaming alejack.

" Wheer be from, Derek? "

" Hither and yon, " answered Derek, gulping thirstily. " I do be wearyin' for my good master, John. "

" What, Muster Fane?   Be his worship away, then? "

" Ar! This three days and more. You are n't see nowt of 'e nowheres, eh, John? "

" Nary blink, Derek."

" I be lonesome soul, John, — the women be fruttened o' me, the childer runs at sight o' me, but I are n't never done 'em no 'arm, nowhen."

" Why, ye see, Derek, it be your face, I rackon. And then ye beant nowise sociable-like, be ee? "

" Well, I mought ha been . . . once. But theer be never nobody but don't turn their backs on me . . . 'cept Muster Roland. Us was lads together, leastways 'e were a bit younger nor me. Muster Roland were kind to me then, 'e be kind to me now . . . sometimes . . . an' I don't cross 'e in nowt. . . . And I be wonderin' what should keep 'e away . . . lonesome I be, John . . . there beant nobody like Muster Roland, I rackon."

" You 'eered as the Queen be comin' t' Aldrington, Derek? "

" Ar. But don't mean nowt to I. Gimme my Muster Roland safe back and I don't ax nowt o' none. . . . John, ye don't think as he be — dead, do ee? Dead and a-layin' somewheres . . . i' the forest, say, and arl clobbered wi' . . . blood! On 's face, and wi' his arms . . . tossed wide and wi 's fingers . . . as claw and claw at the grass . . . eh, neighbour John? "

" Lord, no, Derek . . . why . . . what be t' matter wi' ee, man? " cried honest John in shocked amaze, for Derek's sullen eyes were wild and beneath matted hair his brow glistened with a dreadful moisture.

" Nowt, John, nowt it be. Summat ketches me time and again. . . . And you d' think as Muster Roland 'll come back to I . . . somewhen? Do ee? "

" Sure-ly, Derek! Muster Roland beant the sort as vanishes. And now I must indoors; we 've comp'ny and my dame can't nowise do wi'out me."

Left alone, Derek finished his ale and sighed dismally. Now as he sat thus, a butterfly lit upon his brawny leg, fanning its pretty wings in quivering ecstasy while sullen

Derek, the lonely one, watched it nor moved lest it fly
and leave him too soon; at last away it fluttered through the
sunny air, out from the stable yard and across white road
to the cool green of shady woods beyond, with Derek following heavy-footed until, coming to a certain tree, he
paused and from hidden cleft reached down a formidable
crossbow with quiver of bolts. Thus armed, he went by
solitary tracks, lonely as ever, unheeding now the butter-
flies that wheeled and hovered, the birds that chirped, or
aught under heaven save his one dark purpose.

# CHAPTER XL

## How the Queen Came to Aldrington

The young Earl, his slim person resplendent in satin and velvet, his deep ruff sparkling with diamonds, his doublet enriched with pearls, himself alternate flushed and pale, was busied on a thousand concerns; my Lady Ione, surrounded by her chattering ladies, was being inducted into jewelled stomacher and farthingale lined with steel and whalebone, with skirt and over-robe of silk and rich taffeta, and yet herself, despite all this, showing supremely happy. And Captain Jocelyn, spurred and booted as for a journey, having sought for hat and cloak and found them not, sat remote in the rose garden, tablets on knee, brows knit as in the throes of composition, and gaze upon the illimitable distance.

From these depths of thought jingling spurs roused him to espy Sir Roger approaching.

"Why so pensive, Jocelyn lad?"

"I would write message o' farewell, Roger."

"Of farewell? Hum! Make way there, suffer me beside thee, for I am pensive too."

"Thou, Roger man? And wherefore?"

"My beard! Plague on 't, my beard, lad! For, as beards go, 't is very well and hideth something o' my visage grim. But the Queen, ha — our Bess? And there 's the rub! Shall Gloriana know me in hair at first glance, thinks I? And, if she doth, shall this Spaniard-like beard offend or win of her those honours and golden bounty as never did my naked chops, God wot?"

Jocelyn laughed, though a little ruefully, and shook his head.

"Wilt mock my gravity?" he questioned.

" And therewithal, Jocelyn, would know thy reasons for any such message o' farewell."

" I 'm thinking o' the Netherlands, comrade, the poor Zeelanders' desperate need. . . . Also you 'll mind how Lord Willoughby promised me a command so soon as this murderous danger was averted? "

" Ay, 't is accompt, lad. So, except the Queen prove generous beyond all expectation, back should I ha' marched perforce, but now — ha! And as for thyself, Jocelyn — no! Hast won the love of great and right noble demoiselle, and this despite thy lean and hungry look, and here for thee in England shall be command sweeter methinks and better than any i' the world. Such love, Jocelyn, cometh not to every man."

" Verily and I know it, Roger, and 't is this same thought doth give me pause."

" How so, comrade? " enquired Sir Roger, taking out his little pipe to fill it.

" As thus: " sighed Jocelyn. " Whether it were nobler to make such love but a means of gratification, a stepping-stone to a leisured ease and such fortune as my mere wit or sword may never win; whether to clasp it to my heart to mine own supreme joy or, turning my back on 't, make it the pure inspiration to goodly deeds, but — myself go ever a solitary man? "

" Zounds! " exclaimed Sir Roger, " must you boggle because for once, *mirabile dictu*, Fortune smiles? Go to, lad, — and wait till I light my pipe! " This somewhat elaborate manoeuvre being duly performed (tinder box, flint, steel, etc.), Sir Roger, puffing joyously, continueth:

" Jocelyn, thou 'rt a luckless dog, e'en as I! Ay, faith, dogs twain we be, yet dogs that all do cry on at their need. Is trouble a-brewing, — they whistle us. Is there town hopelessly indefensible (say Sluys), we must defend it. Is it battle, — then, where blows be thickest and awards none, there are we. Destined by an unloving Fate to bleed for others their welfare, we ha' mourned our own ill fare until — to-day."

" To-day, Roger? How so? "

" To-day, lad, Gentle Love hath Dastard Fortune by
the throat on our behalf, look you, to squeeze nor loose,
till Fortune, perforce growing kind, shall endow us with
those benefits so long denied. Lo, thus Happiness shall
dandle us at last! "

" Happiness? " quoth the Captain wistfully.

" Wealth, lad! Power! A kindly ease! Jovial friends!
A hearth and home! For, look you, as I did share my ill
fortune with thee, thou shalt now share thy good fortune
with me, — ha? "

" Why, so I will! " said Jocelyn, laughing yet sad. " To
my last tester, or crust, or sup of water — out there in
the Netherlands, since I perceive we 're for the wars again."

" Jocelyn, thou 'rt vasty fool! "

" And thou, Roger, my trusty comrade to thus resolve
my difficulty, for 's life, Roger man, I 've been sorely
tempted! But yourself, ha, devil take us, but you could
no more exist on a pampering charity than I on my lady
Joan's bounty. . . . And so, comrade, such happiness
being not for me, I 'm done with the bewitching dream of 't.
'Stead of home and wife shall be field and sword. I 'm with
thee henceforth to the end, Roger."

" Ay, but," quoth the knight, scowling at his pipe, " here
is a prideful selflessness that, hurting thyself, shall yet
hurt one more tender. Ione wants thee, man, needs thee
and, py heaven, as I do think, will ha' thee yet — "

" Not an' I be aboard ship for the wars. . . . And the
Queen here bent on this great marriage . . . who shall
withstand Gloriana? "

" Art prodigious fool, Jocelyn, old comrade! "

" Well, better so with contented mind rather than wedded lover to exist like stalled ox — "

" But Jocelyn, you love her."

" Roger, I . . . worship her. And so it is I had rather
she remember me in honour and sigh awhile than have me
her doating slave till she sigh to have me man again, master
alike of her and my own fate."

" Jocelyn, is there ever a man of us master of his own fate, think ye? "

" Who shall say?   But, Roger, at the least I shall live and die a man and not a great and noble lady's mere husband. . . .   And so it is I must needs write me this letter o' farewell and thereafter — creep hence."

" A fool, thou 'rt a fool! " snorted Sir Roger.   " Yet fool am I also.   Thus here sit two fools that in their folly must needs love each other methinks and — la, what bedizened young springald hither comes to dazzle us with 's splendour? "   And he stabbed contemptuously with his pipe towards a youthful exquisite, a scintillant vision from curling feather to delicate shoe, a slender gentleman whose face, above snowy ruff, large-eyed, vivid of mouth, showed only the more beautiful for its extreme pallor.   Then Sir Roger gaped, for Jocelyn was up and out of the arbour, arms outstretched in glad welcome.

" So art here then, Florian! " he cried.   " And so glorious, that faith, I hardly knew thee! "

" Why, Jocelyn, all this is for the Queen.   My Cecily would ha' me so and thus . . . though, cock's body, man, I feel all a-flaunt like veriest parrot popinjay! "

" Nay, thou 'lt do, lad, thou 'lt do!   God send Her Majesty remark thee well; shalt be star yet to twinkle in Gloriana's Court — "

" Ay, but thou, Jocelyn?   Oh, dear my friend, what o' thyself? "

" As to this, lad, come you and hearken to Sir Roger."

But even as he spoke, the ambient air was riven by a familiar screech and, upstarting all three, they beheld the Countess speeding to them very nimbly despite stomacher, robes and enormous farthingale.

" Ha, Florian . . . oh, boy! " she cried breathlessly and clutching at Jocelyn's ready arm, " why a plague must you run away and the Queen within a mile?   I heard the crowds a-cheering but now!   Richard and his gentlemen be rid forth to meet her . . . and she must see thee, Florian; she must notice thee ere she light from saddle. . . .   And

you, sir knight . . . and thou Jocelyn. . . .   Ha, a pest
and plaguey murrain!  Why tarry ye here?  And Her
Majesty at hand!  Come ye . . . come away."

So saying, she hustled them before her, all three, swore
at Sir Roger's pipe until he tapped it out very tenderly
and put it away, anathametized Jocelyn's bare head and
cloakless shoulders, and so ushered them where stood the
Earl's great household richly habited, with Master Rickaby and his wand of office conspicuously posed; where Ione,
amidst her bower ladies, glanced about glad-eyed yet often-
est where stood Captain Jocelyn who, looking no other
where, spoke murmuring to Sir Roger:

"With their first shout when the Queen appears, let us
steal hence, comrade."

Distant cheering, a joyful clamour drawing nearer . . .
a vague stir growing louder . . . a roll of drums with
blithe fanfare of trumpets. . . .  And then through the
festooned arch of the ancient gatehouse England's great
Queen moved graciously into the base court, followed by a
brilliant company.  She rode a cream-coloured palfrey,
she blazed with jewels; beneath small, plumed hat showed
that strange, aquiline face, its pale austerity framed by reddish gem-spangled hair, yet no jewel so bright as the
wonder of her eyes.

But it was not the sight of Elizabeth that had halted
Jocelyn so suddenly; it was not this glorious Bess that
brought the strangled oath to Sir Roger's grim lips, but
one who rode at Majesty's left hand, dividing her attention with Richard the Earl, for there, bowing gracefully
to her smiling regard and within three yards of gloomy
Sir Francis Walsingham, bravely attired and smiling as
ever, was Mr. Roland Fane.

# CHAPTER XLI

## WHICH ENDETH THIS NARRATIVE

### *Morning*

SHE moved a little, tottering with small, mincing steps by reason of her narrow, high-heeled shoes and vasty farthingale, yet even so, contrived to be majestic; a slim, tallish creature with pale, oval face offset by frizz of reddish hair, spangled with gems, and small, lace coif; a dominating face lit by strange, greenish eyes, quick, vital and heavy-lidded, separated by thin, small arching nose with sensitive nostrils, — a mouth almost too thin yet very mobile; a face to be remembered, for pride was there, high courage and a mighty will; jewels sparkled everywhere, but brightest showed these keen, wonderful, ever-changing eyes.

So Elizabeth of England tottered to and fro within this sumptuous chamber, now frowning at the Orient carpets her small feet trampled, now at the small shrewd face of Ursula, Countess of Hartesmere.

"Sit you, madam!" said she suddenly. "Stand not to me, Ursula; let us forget State a while and be thou my faithful friend and loving gossip, wise in counsel and quick to cherish as in those evil days long past. Ha, to the fiend with cramping ceremony!" And with fierce kick left and right — off flew those little, jewelled shoes, and free-limbed, graceful as any martial youth, she strode up and down the splendid chamber.

"There be times, Ursula, when I would to God I 'd been a man — heaven save the mark!"

" 'Stead o' the which, Bess, God in His wisdom made thee one o' the greatest women, and for England's weal."

"Lord bless thee, dear Gossip!" cried Gloriana, and then stood sighful and pensive. "Indeed, my Ursula, 't is for England I have lived, striven, suffered, lied and — as dost know — denied myself that I have craved as women will. . . . For and despite my womanhood, I must be strong to pilot my England twixt the foul charybdis of France and the merciless rock — Spain . . . to seem hot and cold . . . to wait . . . and wait, alas — 'til Holland despairs and thinks me craven and all Protestant Europe cries out on me, — ay, even mine own hotheads! But France wonders and dare not move and Philip, little rat, is all unsure. Aha, 'spite their host o' spies, they cannot riddle me or fathom my policy! . . . Policy — " she repeated, and frowned. "Your niece's marriage is matter of policy, Ursula . . . this Ione, 't is a rebellious, a bold and stubborn wench!"

"Pig-headed!" nodded the Countess.

"She is a Romanist, Gossip, and of such great heritage I must have her wedded lord a Protestant, a man sufficiently powerful in the State and one I may trust implicitly in these evil times. Well, such is my Lord of High Melton, and by God, wed him she shall or forfeit to the State all she hath, every doit and acre!"

"Told you her so much, Bess?"

"Very plainly and, by heaven, the bold wretch dared to laugh and thank me!"

"'T would seem she doth not hanker for your earl, Eliza."

"What matter? Must our policy be thwarted by her whims? Never, I vow to heaven!"

"Why then, you'll beggar her?"

"By God's good light I will so, unless she wed the earl."

"Hum!" quoth the Countess. "The earl!"

"Indeed. Know you a better match, Gossip?"

"No, Bess, only a better man, for our England is rich in manhood, thank God."

"Well, who's your man?"

"A poor fellow yet veriest man, Bess; his rank humble,

his estate a sword, with nought to recommend him save his manhood. You call him your watchdog, or were wont to."

"How? Dinwiddie . . . Jocelyn? This man that crossed my friendly passages with Parma?"

"The very same, madam."

"You knew he made my secret overtures with Spain of none effect, and should have lost his head for 't, but that Leicester and Willoughby proved 't was done in his ignorance—know you this?"

"Indeed, your Majesty, 't was Willoughby told me on 't."

"The addlepate even slew my secret envoy!"

"He deemed the man traitor, madam, as verily he was, nor would believe your Majesty's policy could yield up a town to the brutal pillage and ravishment of Parma's fierce soldiery."

"Ursula, I vow to God I had Philip's sworn oath the place, once his, should be inviolate."

The Countess sniffed,—whereupon outraged Majesty swept down on her to seize this small, indomitable lady in slim, passionate hands, to lift and shake her with surprising strength, crying:

"Ha, woman, I know not how I suffer thee!"

"Because," answered the Countess, looking up serenely into the fierce bright eyes above her, "a great queen loveth me, knowing my heart surely as did a little, woeful child, in her shame and loneliness — "

"My Ursula!" The passionate hands became caressing, the fierce, wonderful eyes closed, to open glorified by tenderness of love. Then the Queen was walking again, pouring out her troubled thoughts as she so seldom did even to this, her life-long comforter and friend:

"To rule a people justly is a hard and woeful business, Ursula, a vile, heart-breaking labour. . . . Thus do I fawn upon Iniquity . . . truckle to villainy, yet only that I may smite them the harder, when I may. So needs must these valiant Hollanders suffer a while, the poor souls! 'Stead o' friend, I must seem their enemy . . . until my

England be ready. . . . Better some few o' these die, alas, than all Europe be ravaged by war . . . Spain ready to invade us and we so ill prepared. . . . Oh, who would be a queen and lonely . . . lonely? Hated, feared, lied to, tricked . . . and I alone to save our England how I may or . . . bring her to destruction. . . . And alone, Ursula! Forever and always . . . alone! The solitary child is become the most solitary queen that ever was."

"And I do think the greatest, Bess. For thou canst weep for thyself and yet be strong, sob thus upon my heart and yet save England and confound her enemies by thy mere womanhood, nay — perchance make this same England great and strong as thine own valiant heart."

"But . . . alone!" sobbed the Queen in small, wailing voice.

"'T is thy fate, Bess, now and ever, since truly, all great things must needs be lonely." And thus clasped fast in the comfort of these arms, that just so had often clasped and soothed her childish sorrows, great Elizabeth, this sorrowful Queen, wept a while, until — being indeed such very woman — she smiled anon, kissed and was kissed. Then rising, she dried her tears and, being Elizabeth of England, shut grief away.

"So you think well of this Jocelyn Dinwiddie?"

"I think him the only mate for Ione, madam."

"A mere commoner and soldier of fortune, Ursula?"

"Gloriana could yet make him great."

"Here be two men you 'd ha' me favour."

"For that they are men your Majesty may trust, ay, marry, even as myself, I 'll warrant!"

"Now of this other matter, Ursula. Your proofs, though hard to come by, are sufficient convincing?"

"Beyond all possibility of doubt, madam. Here am I with the woman Shaw, witnesses ready to be sworn."

"Why then, justice shall be done and speedily."

"Then, madam, since Cecil is here with Walsingham, I pray your Majesty — "

"We 'll none o' them, Gossip. . . . My gloomy Wal-

singham that seeth everywhere traitrous heads to be lopped!
And Cecil, creeping fearful where he should leap! No,
Ursula, thou and I, the evidence proved, shall handle this
matter as only women may. Sit you nearer and let us
scheme the how of it.". . .

Thus it befell some while later that Mr. Roland Fane,
seated in murmurous converse with Master Rickaby in the
chamber allotted for his comfort, became aware of voices
beyond the inner door of communication:

. . ." Ten years agone . . . a long time.". . . Master
Rickaby started violently; Mr. Fane leaned forward to
glance at that door with eyes widening to dreadful stare.

". . . and as they say, murder will out . . ."

" Who hath yon chamber, Rickaby? "

" Strangers, sir, — gentlemen of Sir Francis Walsingham — "

" 'Sdeath! " murmured Mr. Fane and rising, crept to
the door and stood there listening, though these voices were
terribly distinct:

". . . Derek, huntsman to his kinsman, Roland Fane
. . . ay, in the Home Wood . . . shot him dead with an
arbalest. 'T is all known at last . . .

" So, murdered him . . . and by command of his master,
this Roland Fane? "

" Even he. This knowing, Sir Francis holdeth him safe
here, and he all unsuspecting, till fitting time and season
. . . snatch him suddenly to judgment and death. . . ."

The High Steward was afoot, but upon his trembling
shoulders came two hands, fingers that twitched, but these
hands were compelling like these glaring eyes, this soft
whispering voice:

" Rickaby . . . must get me hence . . . now, this moment; dost hear, man, dost hear? "

" I would, sir, I would," whispered the Steward, wiping
sweat from haggard face, " but how, sir — how may I? "

" Essay, man, essay! Think . . . do somewhat, for
except I win hence, you shall verily hang — "

" Oh, Mr. Fane, for God's sake — "

"Tush! There is some secret way from the hall, I know — "

"Sir, the hall is athrong wi' company; the Queen goeth — "

"Why then, the old postern . . . the Tower Garden; 't is little used — nay, first to your own chamber awhile . . . they shall not look for me there. You shall lend me your cloak and hat, ay — your staff and chain of office belike. . . . Now, man, lead on . . . you first!"

"But . . . Derek, sir — "

"He shall never betray me, though they rack him in sunder. Up, I say — and go you first!"

Pale and shivering, my lord's High Steward crossed to the outer door and, opening it, peered forth into the wide gallery and, seeing it deserted, beckoned. Now in this gallery, together with other pieces of furniture, stood a great carven chest, whereon and carelessly disposed lay a red-plumed bonnet and cloak of the colour named orange-tawney; Mr. Fane uttered a stifled exclamation and, pushing Master Rickaby aside, reached out eager hands.

## Afternoon

Hot with anger from her recent interview with the Queen, Ione smiled and curtseyed her gracious way through the crowds of magnificence, male and female, thronging hall and antechamber, though her eyes showed brighter, her colour more vivid and herself more stately than usual, by reason of the furious indignation that raged within her.

Now on her way she chanced upon Sir Roger sitting remote and very gloomily drinking wine, to whom quoth she vindictively, white fists upraised and teeth agleam:

"Oh, this woman! This Elizabeth! This Protestant tyrant — "

"'Bate . . . abate thee!" gasped Sir Roger, upsetting his wine. "Cot's pody, child! Softly, softly, for thy life!"

"Queen or no, she shall never trample my heart 'neath her cruel feet! Where is Jocelyn?"

"He left me but now. And for thy life's good. I —"

"Pray you find him, bid him have horses ready and then to me in the small gallery."

Then away she sped like a whirlwind and, shut within her bedchamber, tossed aside her jewels, tore off her finery of robes and in their stead donned the very plainest and simplest of her tires and over these, a hooded riding cloak.

She found the Captain awaiting her but something in his air, the stern set of his lean features, chilled her; she paused, her words of eager welcome died unspoken and, being hurt, she grew angry.

"And have you no kind word for me?" she demanded. "No look of comfort? You know the Queen would bend me to her arrogant will like the red-haired shrew she is?"

"I know Her Majesty would have you wed a great and noble gentleman, child."

"Well, thus come I to Captain Jocelyn Dinwiddie. And what saith he?"

"But Joan . . . ah, my lady, the Queen —"

"Is a woman and I have defied this same woman because you are yourself and I am Ione Fane. And what say you to this?"

But instead of answering he bowed his head, fumbled with sword and dagger hilts, glanced hither and yon, the very picture of ineptitude, insomuch that her anger flamed anew; quoth Ione:

"I flouted the tyrant to her painted, bedizened face . . . how do I shock you?"

"Joan, she is England's great Queen and assured hope; she is my —"

"Yet have I defied her, sir, and to such purpose that I bring you only myself, without rank or lands or wealth to fright your prideful poverty and set it in arms betwixt us."

"Mean you that she . . . that Her Majesty hath . . . disinherited you, my lady?"

"Yea, verily, she hath made me destitute, and for this I vow to God I do almost love her. And what saith Din-widdie in his pride now, Jocelyn? Will he take this poor maid to share his poor fortunes?"

"Nay, but whither, Joan, whither?" he cried, a little wildly. "To the misery of camp and bivouac, child, the instant peril o' war, the hardship and jeopard of belea-guered town? I am but a soldier and such my life — "

"These hardships will I share gladly, Jocelyn."

"Never!" he cried, turning from the calm serenity of her eyes. "Must I watch thy beauty fade, thy valiant spirit faint and languish, that sweet body put to the vile hazard of sack and rapine? Rather will I die!"

"Then let us bide safe in England; how, do you not want me? Is your love so poor a thing it dare not the fu-ture?"

"Oh, my lady . . . Joan, tempt me no more — "

"My very heart is at thy feet; wilt not take it up?"

"No!" he cried, like one fierce with pain. "I may not . . . I dare not!"

"Dare not, Jocelyn? And the sweet verses you wrote me — I know them every line, the words of love you spake me — I can hear them yet, — what o' these?"

"A memory, child."

"Can it be that you fear the Queen, her disfavour?"

"Yes . . . yes!"

"Oh, liar!" she cried, in sudden fury. "I know Jocelyn Dinwiddie fears only himself. Oh, fool, to suffer wicked pride to ruin your life and mine! Now could I hate you most bitterly but that I love you so truly. Yet do I despise this loathed Dinwiddie! Oh, Jocelyn, thou poor soul to look on me with such eyes of yearning love, yet suffer Din-widdie his cruel pride to come betwixt us. . . . Now go, leave me that I may scheme how to woo Jocelyn to wed me in despite of Dinwiddie. . . . Yet heed this, sir; seek not to steal cowardly hence from Aldrington yet a while or, by mine honour, I 'll to the Queen, your hateful Protestant, Lutherean Elizabeth, and so defy and set her by the ears she shall prison me for rebel or Papist or what she will, — so beware! Now go!'"

Thus presently Sir Roger, musing over his wine, beheld Captain Jocelyn, a gloomy soul, and beckoned cheerily:

"Man Jocelyn," quoth he, "we are bid to private audience with Her Majesty after supper — aha! God send our Gloriana deal with us kindly at last, look you, e'en though it prove no more than harness and equipments."

"Meantime," sighed Jocelyn, "I'll out and walk."

"Then I'll with thee, lad, and speculate with thee on our fortunes good or ill, of Gloriana her purse strings, and the future."

So thus it befell that Ione, alternately sighing distressfully and frowning angrily as she walked haphazard beside the brook, suddenly espied a red-plumed bonnet and orange-tawney cloak and, halting as suddenly, was deliberating whether to meet their wearer sighful and tender, or frowning and aloof, when upon the air was whirring twang, a terrible and very ghastly choking cry. . . . She saw that plumed bonnet jerk back in strange, awful manner . . . two clutching hands that plucked and plucked at the murderous thing transfixing his throat . . . spurting blood — and he was down. . . . Then she was crying his name, gasping frantic prayers, running like a mad creature, until she tripped blindly and fell, to lie breathless and half aswoon, her face hidden in the cool grass, against that writhing horror. . . .

"Merciful God, save him yet . . . thy gift to me . . . my Jocelyn! Oh, sweet Mother of Heaven, let him not die . . . my beloved . . . ah, Jocelyn. . . ."

Strong hands that lifted her, gentle arms that cradled her, a voice that spoke blessed comfort, and Jocelyn's own face bent over her.

"Ah, but I saw . . . your hat and cloak . . . who?"

"Roland Fane."

"And . . . is he dead . . . shot?"

"Yes, Joan. A . . . crossbow bolt."

"Roland?  Why then . . ."

"He died of an orange-tawney cloak."

"Ah, yet thou 'rt alive, my Jocelyn, and I upon thy dear heart . . . thank God!  Now take me away, yet first . . . ere you loose me, prithee say ' beloved ' — once, and because I 'm so nigh to swooning — kiss me, Jocelyn."

"Oh, best and ever beloved!  Thou sweet and valiant soul!  Thou very woman!" he murmured and kissed her until she sighed at last and hid her face against him.  Then he bore her away.

Thus she saw not how Sir Roger, dagger in fist, dragged from the underwood a reeling, bloody wretch that, beholding the dead, howled like beast in pain:

"Oh, Master Roland . . . have I killed ee!  Yet I did . . . but as . . . bidden . . . Master Roland — "

The strange, animal heart seemed to break, for, with cry of ineffable woe, Derek the huntsman sank down beside his slain master, nor moved he again.

### Evening

They were in the orchard, a place remote and so far from the Great House that the music — flutes and viols, harp and recorder — stole faint with distance like sweet music of a half-remembered dream.

They sat beneath a tree and very silent for the most part, because great happiness is far above speech, and though the sunset made a glory all about them, their eyes saw only each other, and thus they were quite unconscious of the one who watched them beneath frowning brows and with such passion of envy.

"And she hath red hair, my Jocelyn, so very red!  Nay, do not retort on mine, for I vow my hair showeth no red except the sun shine on 't!"

"As now!" he murmured and, smiling, kissed a tress.

"And she would not see thee, Jocelyn!  Oh, alas, why should the Queen refuse thee audience?"

"To see me anon, mayhap."

" Yet she gave audience to Sir Roger."

" And, God bless her, hath proved generous beyond expectation! "

" Oh, Jocelyn, I 'm all afeard lest she hate thee and for my sake, lest my love, 'stead of blessing, prove thy curse and peril. For I have made thee rebel to her queenly will and she is so harsh, so arrogant — with her red hair! Dear Mother of God . . . if she should banish thee! Or a prison! Or the scaffold — oh, my Jocelyn! "

" Now comfort thee, dear Heart, 't is a great Queen and greatly just, and, 'neath all her cold statecraft is, I dare to think, a very woman tender and compassionate."

" Yet with cold eyes, Jocelyn, a hooky nose . . . and terrible in her anger . . . and now — God forgive me . . . mine is a love perilous to thee . . . thy life, this dear head, this so loved face — "

" Nay, Joan," he smiled, folding her close within the comfort of his arm, " prithee what now of this poor visage, this wolfish jowl that is yet like loathed load, like venomous asp, like brutish boar — " But here she kissed him, murmuring between laughter and tears:

" And shall I not miscall mine own? This thy face is mine; mine art thou the all of thee and always was, — though I had forgot a while . . . until we met. For Jocelyn dear

" Thou were mine own since Time began
I thine own woman, thou my man."

So even should the Queen frown on our love, part us, or what she will, yet shall I be thine own to death and beyond. . . . But, oh, to live that I might serve thy dear will in all things, — Jocelyn, let us flee away, hide we where the Queen shall never find us."

" Not so, my Joan; let us rather have faith in Her Majesty, trusting to the compassionate woman of her."

" Then we 'll to her now, this moment — nay, I will. And I 'll be humble for thy dear sake, to sue and plead and supplicate, I 'll sob and weep — "

" Crocodile tears ! "

Ione gasped, glanced up and, starting to her knees, crouched there to gaze dumbly into the pale face above her and fall a-trembling, for in these eyes, this aquiline nose with its cruel lift of nostril, these thin, down-trending lips, she thought to read a menace very deadly and thus, being greatly afraid for him, reached out blindly to clasp and hold Jocelyn's hand.

" Stand you up, Ione Fane ! "

Dumbly she arose and Jocelyn with her, and yet though she trembled, her eyes met these other eyes unflinching.

" So, madam," said the Queen, frowning, " with pride and rebellion hid in your heart, you would put on face o' meekness to cozen me to your whim ! "

" Your Majesty I . . . ay, verily, I will dare anything to win my love and yet save him from your Royal anger."

" And you, Captain Dinwiddie, I find you consorting with this rebellious termagant shrew — with her red head ! "

" Madam, I love her."

" Out on 't ! 'T is gaoler she needs. A strong man, her equal in rank, a man of potent will to command and be obeyed, a man I can trust, a man all do speak well on, a valiant man honest to his own despite and therefore, in worldly wisdom, something of a fool, a man that giving — fears to take and therefore much of a fool, a man that doeth, yet asketh in requital — nothing. Know you such a man ? "

Jocelyn, murmuring, shook his head.

" Then needs must I make me one. Bring me your sword." With fumbling hands, Jocelyn drew the long weapon and falling to a knee, proffered it to his Queen.

" Why, 't is heavy, sir," said she, wielding it in practised hand, " yea, and something longer than my edict alloweth. Yet, alas, our England shall need such swords anon, peradventure. . . . Both knees, sir." So Jocelyn knelt, bowing his head, felt the blade tap his shoulder and heard a voice grown suddenly kind and intimate:

" My watchdog that hath bayed death from me shall

be my watchdog yet, to sniff the wind o' danger and bare his fangs for England and me. Henceforth thou art Warden of this South Country and coast defences, to marshall and lead our forces 'gainst the Spaniard when he shall attempt us, — up, Sir Jocelyn."

"Your Majesty," said he, rising but with head downbent, " my gracious lady, deeds can but tell my gratitude . . . and love."

" And I like well a man can weep, Jocelyn, at times apt and proper. So do I think thy tears do thee as much honour as this thy sword won thee in Flanders, — here, take the thing; would to God there were none such in all this troublous world."

Then Jocelyn took back his sword and therewith her hand to kiss and kiss it, until she, looking askance at Ione, giggled like any schoolgirl.

" Come, thou red-head! " she cried. " Call off thy man, ere he devour me." Up started Ione, dignity, state and fear alike forgotten, to run with flutter of petticoats and sink upon her knees, tearful eyes upraised to the face above her, for now in these strange eyes, this aquiline nose with its sensitive nostrils, these thin lips quivering to weary smile, she read that which, seen through glad tears, awed her with joyous wonder.

" Your Majesty . . . oh, dear lady, now that I know the wonder of thee, I do perceive why they name thee Gloriana. So, dear madam, great Majesty, suffer I too may love thee — " And she reached up her hands, to have them clasped, to be lifted up, kissed and clapped on the cheek.

" Take your knight, girl, and, since he 's very man, feed him full, kiss him oft and see you contrive well together for the future of my England . . . as fair as thyself, as grimly masculine as thy lord — for the England that must and shall be greater than the England that is, or I have lived and grieved and wrought in vain, and your mating of none avail. . . . For ye — love . . . children, I pray; but for me . . . what? "

Then she turned and went from them through the evening glow, seeming not so much a great queen as weary, grieving woman.

And when she was gone, Ione turned to clasp her man, pillowing her head upon his breast.

"Thither goeth great soul, dear Jocelyn," she sighed; "but ah, thank God I am no mighty queen, but only — thy woman, for there went — solitude."

"Ay, truly, dear Heart," he answered, kissing her, "yet one to live and die for, my Joan, for yonder goeth — England!"

**THE END**